HADLEY BENTON

Agent Clark

Fourth edition

This book was professionally typeset on Reedsy.
Find out more at reedsy.com

This book is dedicated to the memory of
Scott Lewis Benton.

For Abigayle, Claire Hadley, Lindy, and Karen.

Contents

Acknowledgement

Thank you papa for sharing your life with us and especially for recording the tapes that spurred this book.

A special thanks to my cousins Virginia Meadors Barrett and Julian Harbour Clark III, for their invaluable writing and editing advice, their great ideas, and for their encouragement.

Heartfelt thanks to my mother Linda Clark Benton, Aunt Jeannine Clark Dunlap, Aunt Dawn Clark Hubbell, Uncle Jim Hubbell, Uncle Julian Clark II, sister Ashley Jeannine Benton, cousin Kirsten Clark McIntyre, and Rowan McIntyre for their words of advice, patience, and encouragement.

Jerry Todd for the design of my book cover and for putting up with all of my "suggestions," and thanks to my editor John Paine.

I am deeply thankful for the countless people that offered advice and encouragement throughout this project — Llew Haden, Marilyn Staats, Ethan L. Staats, Ed Martin, Jeff Herbert, Bryan Pope, Scott Mayfield, Lewis Jones, Jimmie Killingsworth, Rodes and Lindy Fishburne, Torch and Nicole Robinson, Captain Judy Helmey, Gretchen Hirsch, Chris Hart, Ira Pearl, Steve Barnhart, Jim Choate, Mark Dawson, Charlie Fiveash, Parker Hudson, Buddy Parker, John Kiedrowski, Ren Stanley, Charlie Gerakitis, Tom Boller, Dick Lea, Blain Allen, the Gentlemen of Ansley Golf Club, Arash Azizi, and Kerry Brown for keeping me caffeinated all of those early mornings at The Men's Grill.

Thank you Harold Martin for *This Happy Isle*, John Heitmann & Rebecca Morales for *Stealing Cars*, The Prohibition Museum of Savannah, Georgia; Ken Burns for his excellent documentary on Prohibition, Daniel Okrent for *Last Call*, and the Flagler Museum in Palm Beach, Florida.

A special thanks to Nancy Bell who helped me discover my love of reading in 1991 when she handed me an old paperback of Stuart Woods's *White Cargo* while living in her beach house in Ponte Vedra, Florida.

I

Part One

Prohibition will work great injury to the cause of Temperance. It is a species of intemperance within itself, for it goes beyond the bounds of reason in that it attempts to control a man's appetite by legislation and makes a crime out of things that are not crimes. A prohibition law strikes a blow at the very principles upon which government was found.
—Abraham Lincoln, 1840

Chapter 1

I woke up with the unmistakable metallic taste of blood in my mouth. My head was pounding, and I could feel the searing heat of the sun on my face. I had no idea where I was, and even after I slowly opened one eye, and then the other, I didn't recognize my surroundings. It was hard to focus at first; everything blurred just enough to be unrecognizable. After a few minutes the incessant thrumming in my ears became clear—grasshoppers. It's amazing how loud they can be when thousands of them are stridulating in unison. Then the heavy smell of pine brought the events of the morning flooding back into my mind like a tidal wave.

"Julian, Julian, Julian. When are you gonna learn to keep your nose out of other people's business?"

The slow southern cadence of Harold's voice hit me like a hammer, which was not unlike his fist, as I had learned earlier. He was sitting on the front bumper of a big tobacco truck I had been sent out into the Hammock to find. It was full of cigarettes when it left North Carolina—thirteen hundred cartons, to be exact. Now it sat here deep in the palmetto brush and pine of a remote Florida forest, completely empty. Not a bad haul for a two-bit thug like Harold Hunt. If not for a tip from one of my buddies back in Jacksonville, this would become its rusty grave in a matter of months. Not to mention that I wouldn't be here.

"Are you hearing me, son?" asked Harold. "How did you even find me out here?"

All I could muster was a slight groan as I tried to sit up, before realizing

3

my hands were tied behind my back with a piece of rope. The cobwebs in my head were slowly starting to clear, but not nearly fast enough. I tried to speak, but my mouth and throat were too dry to form words, and I could feel the dried blood and mucus from my nose and lip cracking around my mouth and chin.

"Julian, what do you say we cut through the bull? I'm running out of time, and I can't have you talking about what you found out here, and I sure as heck can't afford to have the owner of that tobacco truck find out who took it. You know how Hugh and Riley can be."

Harold was a talker, and I needed to stall long enough to come up with some kind of plan. He wasn't a cold-blooded killer, but I knew he would have no problem leaving me out here. He was a bare-knuckle boxer and plenty tough, and with my hands tied up, I didn't have much chance of getting away. If he left me out here without water in this heat and in this condition, I wouldn't last long, that's for sure.

Gulf Hammock was twenty-five thousand acres of pine forest and cypress swamps about forty miles southwest of Gainesville, almost to Cedar Key. There was no reason for anyone to come out here unless they were hunting white-tailed deer, hogs, or turkeys. If there ever was a place in Florida where you could get lost and never be seen again, besides the Glades, this was it. Most of the logging roads were grown over and there weren't any signs. There was not even a marked entrance or exit. The only reason I found it is because Sheriff Karel's clerk Delores over in Bronson told me how to find it. The sheriff was supposed to come out here with me.

"Do you have any idea how pissed off my brother was when you and that Detective Jones fella uncovered all that rum we brought up from Bimini in the back of those stolen cars?" Harold said as he paced around in circles behind the truck.

"Honestly, though, what are you doin' out here?"

"I could ask you the same, Harold."

"Well, seeing as this is probably the last day of your sorry existence, I'll tell ya. Riley got wind of this here shipment of tobacco coming down from North Carolina, and we decided to commandeer it for ourselves. We needed a little help stealing the truck—"

"I can only imagine who you went to for help," I interrupted.

"Shut up, Julian, you don't know shit. We had the tobacco sold before we even stole it. That was the easy part. Riley told me about this place, so I brought the truck out here to dump it."

Partially obstructed by the truck, I could see the remains of a small campfire in a little area he had cleared free of brush. I could also see the corner of a tarp tied to a tree he was probably using for shade and a couple pots and pans alongside a few pieces of clothing he had hung up to dry.

Still trying to keep him talking while I worked on loosening my hands, I said, "From the looks of this place, you've been out here a few days."

Harold looked at me suspiciously. "I needed to lay low for a few days until the heat settled. I been camping out here waiting for Riley to send word it's okay to come out."

Harold disappeared around the side of the truck. I could hear him messing around in some stuff when a subtle movement in the brush caught my attention. I kicked a stick to see if whatever I heard would move again. Sure enough, it did. The snake's camouflage blended in perfectly with the brush, so it was practically invisible. I needed to move – fast. Still disoriented, I slowly made my way to a standing position, using a small pine for balance. Harold came back carrying some rope before finally saying, "Sorry, Julian, but I warned you before to stay out of our business. Now I'm going have to leave you out here for the buzzards."

"Harold, you can't just leave me out here in the middle of this godforsaken forest," I said. He hadn't noticed I wasn't sitting in the brush anymore. I slowly started trying to move away from the snake, while also adding a little distance between the two of us, when I had an idea.

"Says who?" Harold said. "Are you that shit-off stupid you can't see what's going on here? You know, if Riley were here, you'd already be dead. Julian, you should have stuck to finding stolen Studebakers. I have no idea how you ended up out here, but boy, I'll bet you wish you never heard of Gulf Hammock about right now."

While Harold was running his mouth, I was slowly moving to my left. By the time Harold started toward me with the rope, the snake was in between us. Before he made it half the distance, it moved in the brush beneath him. The sound of a rattle told us both what it was. Florida was well known for big diamondback rattlesnakes, and the Hammock was no exception. Before I could yell freeze, Harold stumbled forward and that rattler shot up from the brush and hit him right on the inside of his upper thigh. It must have gotten its fangs hung up in his pants or else in his leg because it remained hanging there, whipping its tail around, trying to get free.

His reaction was to grab the snake and pull it off. He screamed as the snake's fangs came free from his pants and curled up toward his hands and tried to bite him again. Just as he was about to fling it away, that rattlesnake bit him a second time on the wrist and then fell to the ground with a heavy thud. As the snake slithered off into the brush, Harold started yelling.

"He got me! Julian, he got me! That damn rattlesnake bit me right in the crotch!"

Grabbing his inner thigh, Harold fell back on his backside all the while screaming, "He got me!" over and over. I noticed a dark stain growing on his pants as he rolled around in the dirt before I realized that snake probably got his femoral artery. Not good. I'm not even sure he realized it bit him on the wrist too, but that was probably just a dry bite.

I said, "You better cut that screaming out and calm down. The more you thrash around like a two-year-old, the faster that rattlesnake venom is going to circulate."

Harold clearly wasn't listening and kept thrashing around. I took a step closer when he cried, "Don't come near me, Julian. I swear I'll kill you!"

"Harold, listen to me," I began. "Diamondback venom works in two ways. The hemotoxin causes tissue damage and it affects your circulatory system by destroying blood cells, which leads to internal bleeding. That's the good part. It also has a neurotoxin in it."

"What the hell is that?" he yelled.

"That's the part that paralyzes your nervous system," I replied.

"You mean, I'm not going to be able to walk again?" he asked.

"No, I mean it's going to get harder and harder to breathe until you suffocate. That's if you don't bleed to death first. It looks like he got that big artery in your leg. If you don't stop that bleeding, the rattlesnake venom is the least of your problems."

"Julian, you son of a bitch! You get over here and help me or I swear, you are a dead man!" he yelled.

The sobering realization that we were miles from any civilization, not to mention a doctor, reminded me that I wasn't even sure where my automobile was. Even if I could stop the bleeding, how in the heck were we going to get out of those woods? Harold couldn't walk and there was no way I could carry him.

Harold finally stopped thrashing around and lay still. He was sweating profusely and his legs were covered in blood. His breathing was irregular, and I could tell he was taking big gulps and probably hyperventilating. I told him to calm down and try to relax, but he didn't say anything. As he lay there on his side, I went back to work on my knots. I tried using a small pine for friction to rub through the rope, but it was no use. I finally figured out how to lie on the ground and stretch my hands down the back of my legs and around my feet so that I could get my hands in front of me. Then all I had to do was use my teeth to work on the knots. After about five minutes my hands were free.

I sat there massaging my wrists as the blood began to flow back in them. After a few minutes I could feel the tips of my fingers again. Then I took out my handkerchief and tried wiping the dried blood off my face. I could tell the swelling was pretty bad, and my right eye was almost completely closed. My wife Frances was going to be really impressed.

"Harold. Harold," I said, trying to get his attention. "Harold!"

Harold didn't budge, so I got to my feet, trying not to lose my balance. I eased over toward Harold, but stayed ready in case he came at me. Once I realized that he was unconscious, I couldn't help but think about one of the last things he asked me. "Julian, what in the hell are you doin' out here?"

* * *

7

The previous night I received a call from a buddy named Harry Mega. Harry owned a used auto lot in Jacksonville, and he knew everybody in the business. He'd helped us recover more than a few stolen automobiles over the years.

"Julian, I assume your office heard about the tobacco truck that was stolen up in North Carolina not long ago?" Harry asked.

"As a matter of fact, Tomlinson and Jones were here just the other day asking about that truck. Sounds like one of our local auto thieves may have bitten off a little more than he could chew."

"Well I don't doubt that," Harry replied. "Tell the cops they'll never see those cigarettes again. But if you're interested in that truck, there are some rumors going around that it made its way down here last week."

"Is that so?" I asked. "And where might a truck that size end up without somebody seeing it and reporting it?"

"You didn't hear this from me, but if I were you, I'd be looking out in the Hammock."

"Well, I'll be," I said.

"A lot of things disappear out there, Julian, even a few people. You watch yourself if you go out there looking for that truck. Take the sheriff with you."

Something in his voice made me sit up. "Thanks for the tip, Harry, I'll be careful."

After I hung up, I sat there a few minutes thinking about what Harry said when Frances walked in.

"Who was that?" she asked. "I know that look on your face. What is it this time?"

"Harry Mega. Just a rumor, that's all," I said.

"Julian, the last time Harry called about a rumor, you almost got shot, and Mr. Coonts just about fired you."

"It's probably nothing, but I need to go over to Bronson tomorrow and see Sheriff Karel. I should only be gone for the day. If I leave early in the morning, I can probably be back by suppertime."

"Well, don't make promises you can't keep," she replied as she walked out.

After I was sure Frances was out of earshot, I called our office clerk,

Gwyneth Lovewell, to ask her for a favor. Gwyneth ran the office, and nothing happened without her knowing about it. She also handled all of our travel plans. If you planned to be out of the office, you better let her know. Technically, she was Director Coonts's secretary and sat right outside his office, but when he wasn't in, we basically reported to Gwyneth.

When she answered, I said, "Gwyneth, it's Julian. Sorry to bother you at home this late, but I need a favor."

"Well, thanks for asking, Julian. I'm just fine, and how are you?"

"Sorry, Gwyneth, it's just that I—"

She interrupted, "Oh, it's fine, Julian, I just like giving you a hard time. Now, what's on your mind, sweetie?"

"I need to go over to Bronson first thing in the morning and check out a lead. Would you please call Sheriff Karel's office first thing, and tell him to expect me by eight-thirty? He's usually there before eight o'clock anyway."

Gwyneth asked, "What's this about?"

"Tell him I got a lead on a stolen Autotruck tobacco truck, and I need his help to identify it. I'll fill him once I get there."

"Okay, I'll let him know. You stay out of trouble, Julian," she said.

"Don't worry about me, Gwyneth. I'll be just fine."

* * *

The next morning, I walked into the Levy County Sheriff's Department at eight-thirty to find Sheriff Karel and a few of his deputies sitting around, having coffee. The sheriff and his boys had helped us locate a few stolen automobiles in addition to breaking up a few theft rings. He was a good man and he ran a solid operation.

"Mornin', Sheriff," I said. "How are you doing?"

"Something tells me I was going be fine until you showed up. Ms. Lovewell didn't tell me much about your visit. What can we do for you, Julian? I haven't heard about any stolen autos around here lately."

"Not an automobile, Sheriff, a truck. A tobacco truck, to be specific. Rumor is, it's out in the Hammock."

9

As soon as I mentioned the Hammock, all three deputies put down their coffee cups and started for the door, all grumbling about things they had to do or investigate.

"What's with them?" I asked.

"Julian, I shouldn't have to remind you that the last time you came in here on a hunch, those three ended up dragging a dead cow a half mile down an old dirt road."

"You know that wasn't my fault. Besides, we recovered three stolen vehicles out there—not to mention all of that red liquor. Anyway, this is not a hunch. I have a reliable source that thinks that truck is out there in the Hammock, and this is more than just a case of a stolen truck—it was full of cigarettes. It looks like some of the regulars are trying to grow their business. Just a few weeks ago we found a bunch of liquor in the trunks of several stolen autos we connected to the Hunts."

"That's great, Julian, but you're on your own this time. I'm up to my eyeballs in alligators today, and I don't have time to go traipsing around in those woods. Have fun."

"Wait, I don't even know how to get out there."

On his way out the door, Sheriff Karel yelled back, "Ask Delores. She'll be here any minute and she can tell you. Hell, if you're nice, she might even go with you!"

Very funny. This was definitely not part of the plan. The smart move would be to get in my vehicle and go back to Jacksonville. I could always go out with another agent later.

* * *

I couldn't just leave Harold to bleed to death out there, so I took the rope he tied my hands with, and I wrapped it twice around his thigh just above the bite and tied it just tight enough to stem the flow of blood. I seriously doubted it would do any good, but it was better than nothing.

I found a couple of jugs of water in the front seat of the truck, and I left one next to Harold just in case he regained consciousness before I returned.

Upon seeing the keys dangling from the ignition, I figured I might as well give it a turn. He must have disabled it because when I turned the key, I got nothing. Not even a click. I pulled the hood release and walked around the front to take a look. Harold had pulled all of the spark plug wires out. That truck wasn't going anywhere, and I was running out of time.

After drinking about half of my water, I decided to take a look in the back to see if there was anything else I could use before hiking out to the main road. When I yanked the tarp covering the bed of the truck back, I came face to face with another man, only this one was already dead. The pallor of his skin was a dead giveaway, and his eyes were bugged out like somebody had stepped on him and everything inside had tried to squeeze out through his face. He had striations around his neck. What in the heck had Harold gotten himself into?

I headed out by following the same tracks that I used to find this place. The weight of the truck had left ruts in the sandy earth as well as crushed palmettos and small pines in its wake. Its trail should get me back to the main road, where I left my automobile. Hopefully, it was still there.

After at least an hour of staggering through thick brush, I was drenched in sweat and dead tired. My water was gone, and I could see out of only one eye due to all the swelling. I saw at least a half dozen more rattlesnakes, and probably as many bees stung me. As I stumbled on, looking for the main road, I thought about how foolish I had been to come out here alone.

* * *

Earlier that morning, after I left the sheriff's office, I got in my Chevrolet and drove about thirty minutes over to the Hammock. Delores's directions took me to an old barn on the edge of the property where she said I would find a dirt road about a hundred yards back in the woods that served as an old entrance to a network of logging roads. There were other entry points to Gulf Hammock, but most of them required crossing private property, so this was the most likely if you were coming from Jacksonville. At that point it was up to me to find my way. It didn't take long to find the tracks of the big truck. A recent rain had left enough mud for me to find where Harold drove it off the dirt road into the woods. I parked my Chevrolet and started out on foot.

I wasn't expecting anyone to be out there in these woods, so I was completely off guard when Harold Hunt jumped me from behind and whacked me across the back with an old fence board. When I turned around to see who was there, I caught two quick jabs to the gut and then a barrage of fists to my face. I ducked and covered as fast as I could, but not before he had connected with a solid right to my left eye and a few more glancing blows to my nose and face. The last thing I remember before I blacked out was seeing that big Autotruck in the distance.

* * *

Still following the tracks left by the truck, I recognized the clearing I was in and realized I was pretty close to the road. About five more minutes of fighting through the brush, I found it. It had been at least an hour since I left Harold with the truck, so I needed to get help fast, but when I stepped out into the road the sight of my vehicle told me that wasn't going to happen. It had four flat tires. I didn't even bother to stop when I got to it but just kept walking down that road, trying to find the barn. After a few minutes I saw a vehicle coming toward me at pretty good clip, leaving a wake of dust behind it. As it got closer, I realized it was Sheriff Karel. Thank God.

When the sheriff pulled up next to me, he rolled down the window and hesitated as he tried to take in what he was seeing. It took a few seconds before he recognized me, and when he started to say something, I just put up my hand and said, "We need help. Harold's rattlesnake bit and he's out there in the woods."

"Don't worry about it," the Sheriff replied. "Eddie's right behind me. What in the hell happened to you? Harold who?"

"Listen to me, Sheriff," I started when a deputy pulled up next to us. Deputy Eddie Linchcomb was driving, and he had two others with him.

I explained the situation to the three men and told them where they could find Harold Hunt. Sheriff Karel told me to jump in the vehicle with him while he radioed for an ambulance and a tow truck.

As we turned around and headed out, Sheriff Karel turned to me and said, "Harold Hunt the boxer?" he said. "Oh, good Lord, Julian, I should have known better than to let you go out there by yourself. Only you could have gone out into the Hammock and gotten tangled up with one of the Hunts.

"He's a bare-knuckle street fighter—not exactly a boxer—but yes, that's the one. He's also a thief just like the rest of 'em. The apple doesn't fall far from the tree.

"Are you okay? You look like hell. Why did you let him use your face like a punching bag? Let's go back to the office and get you cleaned up," said the sheriff. "I can't send you back to Jacksonville looking like this. Frances will have my hide."

Chapter 2

B y the time I got back to Jacksonville, it was Thursday afternoon, which was a good thing because Director Coonts was not in on Friday, and it gave my face three days to heal. The black and blue had turned to mostly yellow, and the swelling was almost gone. Unfortunately, Frances was home and none too pleased to see me when I got there.

"Dear God in heaven, look at your face."

"What?"

"Julian, do you realize you've been gone for three days? When you walked out that door, you promised to be home for dinner. Three days! When the sheriff called, I was sure you were dead. Why do you put me through this, Julian? You know I love you, but for the life of me, I can't understand why we decided to—"

"Baby I'm fine. It was sheer coincidence that I ran into Harold Hunt out in those woods."

"Where was the sheriff?"

"Baby, I—"

"Julian, you said you wouldn't be reckless about this job. You shouldn't have been out there alone."

"I know, baby, but everyone was busy and I was already there. It was supposed to be a simple investigation."

"Julian Clark, let me remind you how risky I thought this move to Jacksonville was."

"I know, Frances, you don't have to keep saying it. I'll be more careful

14

next time. I promise, but right now I've got to go to the office and brief Coonts and write all of this up."

"Fine," she said, turning and leaving the room.

After the sheriff drove me out of the woods, they towed my Chevrolet back to Bronson and helped me get four new tires. They also towed that tobacco truck back to the Sheriff's Department, where we were able to identify it using the confidential numbers stamped on the frame. The numbers on the block had been changed and it sure looked like a Hunt job. The truck had been stolen in Jacksonville, probably by Truby Hunt, but it would be tough to link him to it now. It had been loaded in Winston-Salem, North Carolina, and was bound for delivery somewhere in Florida—maybe Miami. They were still trying to identify the body I saw in the back, but they suspected it was one of the guards that disappeared in Jacksonville. Tobacco trucks were usually guarded and tough to steal. The automobile-theft gangs were definitely getting more brazen. Adding murder to auto theft would get you the death penalty.

As for Harold, he didn't make it. Rattlesnake bites were rarely fatal—as long as you got to a doctor within a reasonable amount of time for some anti-venom. Had he lived, we'd have prosecuted him there in Bronson for stealing the truck—unless he ratted out his brother or maybe one of the Gants. Of course, that didn't consider the body in the back. Auto theft would have been the least of Harold's problems.

When I showed up at the office Friday morning, everyone was anxious to hear what happened. It wasn't every day that we nearly got killed on the job, but it wasn't uncommon.

Gwyneth looked up when I walked in the office and said, "My heavens. Oh Julian, you poor thing. What happened to that sweet face?"

She was halfway across the floor when I became aware that everyone had stopped what they were doing, and they were staring at us. Gwyneth reached toward my cheek with her hand but stopped just short, as if she knew if would be painful to the touch—and maybe because she too was now aware everyone was staring. After a brief, uncomfortable silence she took a step back and reverted back to the office manager we all had come to love.

"Well, at least you didn't end up in the morgue like the other guy," she said.

Everyone came around to take a closer look and congratulate me on another recovery. Once I had made the rounds, Gwyneth pointed upstairs and said that Tomlinson and Jones wanted to talk to me. They were the two senior detectives in the Jacksonville police department. Since the National Auto Theft Bureau, or NATB, not only shared resources with local law enforcement but also set up investigative units in their departments, in certain cities the local police department also housed the offices of the NATB.

Jacksonville had one of the larger police precincts in Florida, and J. Edgar Hoover helped us set up the largest NATB office in Florida. We had most of the second floor in addition to part of the third. Rick Tomlinson and Bart Jones's offices were on the second floor too.

When I walked in their office, both agents looked up and whistled at the same time.

Jones said, "Julian, I can't believe you made it out of those woods alive. Harold Hunt? What the heck were you doing out there alone anyway? The sheriff made it sound like you are lucky to be here."

"Aw, it wasn't that bad. He exaggerates—you guys know that."

Tomlinson jumped in, "Tell us what happened, and then let's try to figure out what Harold Hunt was doing with those cigarettes. Something's not right. And since when did the Hunts start stealing cigarettes and whiskey?"

"Exactly," I said. "This whole thing stinks to high heaven, and we need to figure out what's going on. Although I'm not that surprised about the cigarettes. Prohibition has made cigarettes everybody's new *legal* vice, but I am surprised about the Hunt-Gant gang's involvement."

I spent the next thirty minutes telling them the whole story, starting with Harry Mega's call the week before. Tomlinson and Jones were two of the best detectives in the state of Florida, and if anybody could add something to this investigation, it was them.

Jones interjected, "Ever since we ratcheted up the pressure on Riley Gant, we heard Alva Hunt pretty much runs things down there in Bushnell. The Hunts still have their old man's Ford dealership, which we know is a hotbed of stolen vehicle activity. We just don't have any proof—yet. The word on the street is Riley's brother Hugh is running the fencing operation out of Webster. He's a real character, but again, we don't have anything we can pin on him either."

"Harold admitted he and Riley pulled off the robbery, so we know he was there. You can start trying to pin that on him. He never mentioned Hugh, but I seriously doubt Riley would have been there without him," I said.

"Let's hope they don't know about your scrape with Harold yet. If they think you had anything to do with his death, I wouldn't put it past them to come after you," said Jones.

"The last thing you want is Hugh Gant looking to get even," said Tomlinson. "He is suspected of a few suspicious disappearances already, according to one of our guys down in Fort Myers."

"The thing I can't figure out is why a bunch of automobile thieves would be interested in cigarettes," I said.

"Well, there's something else you should know. We found a stolen Ford not far from where Harold, or somebody, clipped that tobacco truck over in Turtle Creek on the north side of Jacksonville. The numbers looked like one of Truby's jobs. The thing is, the trunk was full of rum," said Tomlinson.

"Rum?" asked Julian. "That's the second time we found liquor with a Hunt job. What in the heck was he doing with a trunk full of rum?"

Tomlinson added, "I don't know, but it looks an awful lot like our boys from Bushnell have started to branch out. Maybe they're running liquor for somebody? Could be Red Overton out of Palm Beach County. It's possible he needed couriers and hooked up with the Hunt-Gant gang. I've got a buddy that's a revenue agent down there—name's Grady Emory. Maybe he knows something."

Julian said, "It's definitely worth looking into. You never know what might turn up. We should also consider the Ashley gang."

"Interesting thought," said Jones. "There's an awful lot of red liquor coming up here from the Bahamas. Sheriff Baker down in Palm Beach says John Ashley's brothers, Ed and Frank, have been using Jupiter inlet and some areas around Stuart to bring it in from Bimini. I can't see them hooking up with the Hunt-Gant gang, but it's still worth checking out."

"I thought the Ashley brothers made most of their own liquor down in the Glades. It's an easy place to hide a moonshine operation down there, and with all that sugarcane, it's the perfect setup," I said.

Tomlinson said, "Well, I would suggest you start by trying to connect that stolen Ford to Truby Hunt. It was parked pretty close to where that truck was stolen. Harold probably drove it there with the intent to pick it up later or have Truby come back and get it after they grabbed the truck. Better work fast too. Once word gets out that Harold died in the Hammock, things are going heat up fast. If the Hunt-Gant crew is connected, Riley Gant will be looking to get rid of his liabilities, not to mention Alva Hunt."

"Get me a look at it, and I'll tell you who stole it."

"We've got to go back to Turtle Creek anyway as part of our investigation. We'll get it towed back here," said Tomlinson.

"Well, there's something else I haven't mentioned yet," I added.

"What's that?" Jones asked.

"I found a body in the back of that tobacco truck."

They looked at each other with eyebrows raised. It was obvious my comment had struck a chord with both of them.

Tomlinson spoke first. "The reason we were called to Turtle Creek in the first place was to investigate a missing person or possible murder in conjunction with the theft of that tobacco truck. After they're loaded, those trucks are guarded pretty well. The guard for that particular truck hasn't been seen since that night. We found some blood in the lot where it was parked, but that's it."

"Sounds like your missing guard is the guy in Sheriff Karel's morgue. Bald guy—he had a spot of blood on the side of his head. Looked like they probably hit him with something heavy and then strangled him."

Jones added, "That's gotta be our guy. I'll call the sheriff and let him know who he's got in the cooler and make a positive ID. Then we can notify his employer and the family."

"Well, now it's even more important than ever to connect the Hunts to that stolen Ford in Turtle Creek, Julian. There's no way that jughead Harold

Hunt was alone in this. And now that he's dead, we can't ask him. I suspect the Hunt-Gant gang was behind the murder of that guard, but it won't be easy to prove," Jones said.

Tomlinson said, "Those boys have gone from stealing cars to booze and now murder? Doesn't make sense."

"Desperate times make men do some crazy things," exclaimed Jones.

I really needed to get going—Coonts was expecting me. "Thanks for helping me work through this one, guys. I can always use it. I'll do what I can with that Ford you found, but Coonts is getting pressure from Atlanta to figure out where Goldberg is getting all those cars, so he's not going to be too interested in the Hunts' involvement with that cigarette truck. We'll see."

As I headed out the door, Tomlinson called out, "Hey, Julian, when are we going fishing?"

"Let me see what Frances has planned. Maybe we can get out on Sunday," I replied. "I'll let you know."

"Sounds good," he said.

* * *

Eugene Coonts had been the director of the NATB in Jacksonville for five years. He had years of experience in law enforcement and was a great detective, but more important, he was a good man to work for. He was also a lot of fun to work with, which was great with as much time as we spent traveling around the Southeast together. Fun or not, as I made my way to his office, I couldn't help but expect to be reprimanded.

"Julian, I'm sure I don't have to remind you that several of us put our necks on the line to bring you down here," Coonts said. At sixty-five, he had gray hair cropped high and tight. He was a loud talker and not because of his huge stature. He was losing his hearing, so when he talked, he was practically yelling at you.

"Yes, sir. I know the situation sounds—"

"Save it, Julian," he interrupted. "You have a knack for detective work, and we are still confident that you are going to make a fine agent. Just try to stay out of trouble for a little while, okay? Durden chewed my ass over your little mess in Bronson the other day, and frankly, I'm getting tired of it."

"Yes, sir," I replied sheepishly.

"Now that we understand each other, what's going on with Goldberg?"

He started fumbling with his pipe, which was always a sign he was ready to move on to something else. Good.

The Goldberg case had the potential to be one of the biggest theft rings we ever busted in the Southeast. We had been trying to build a case against Asa Goldberg for weeks, but we still needed more evidence. It all started when a young man walked into a local dealer here in Jacksonville and tried to sell a late-model Hupmobile. The Hupmobile is pretty popular, so it's not uncommon that someone would be trying to sell a relatively new one, but this particular automobile happened to be registered out of state, which was a red flag. Besides, the young man was as nervous as a prostitute in church, which prompted the dealer to call us.

We got calls like this all the time and most of them turned out to be nothing, but something just didn't seem right, so Coonts sent Bart Jones and me to investigate. We rushed over there so this fella couldn't leave, and while Detective Jones questioned him, I went outside and examined the vehicle.

Before long we discovered that both the serial and motor numbers had been stamped over. It was clearly stolen, so now we had a choice to make. We could arrest him for transporting a stolen automobile across state lines—a Federal crime—or we could try to get information out of him under the threat of sending him to the Federal pen. Jones wanted to take him downtown, but something told me there was a bigger fish to fry.

Since then we had identified two other automobiles, both late-model Fords, which were registered in Georgia and brought down here to sell in Jacksonville. All three had been traced back to the Goldberg Motor Company in Savannah. Now, it was entirely possible that three different cars, all of which originated in the same place, legitimately ended up in Jacksonville, Florida, for sale as used vehicles. However, it was highly unlikely.

"Well, right now we still just have the three stolen autos," I replied. "The thief did a pretty shoddy job disguising the numbers, so it was easy to trace them back to Savannah, and Goldberg's. He owns several dealerships, but all three automobiles were registered to the one on Waters Street and all three were new."

"So no sale paperwork yet?" asked Mr. Coonts.

"Right. They were supposedly stolen off the lot," I said. "They were reported to the insurance company by a Mr. Ben Bloomberg, who has since filed a claim."

"What about the kid that tried to sell it?" asked Coonts.

"Cleve Parnell. He wouldn't talk so we put him on ice for a night. The next morning he made up a story about a buddy that asked him to bring that Hupmobile down here and sell it because he needed the money fast. The kid says he didn't know it was stolen. He wouldn't tell us anything about his 'buddy' either except that if he talked, he would get a visit from the knife. Whatever that means."

Coonts asked, "What did you do with him?"

"We let him walk," I replied. "Jones was pissed about it when he found out, but I know there's more to this than just a stolen Hupmobile."

"Sounds to me like it's time to go to Savannah and do some poking around," offered Coonts. "Start with Captain McCarthy. He'll know if there's been any suspicious activity up there related to Goldberg. Regardless, the Bureau of Investigation should have assigned somebody to the case also. I'll call Atlanta and find out whom. We need boots on the ground Julian. Get up there and find out what's going on."

As I headed out of the office Coonts hollered, "Remember, Julian—don't get distracted from the job at hand. We need a win and this Goldberg case will make us all look good."

* * *

The drive to Savannah was about one hundred fifty miles on Highway Seventeen. Most of it was paved, but the weather was nice, so I didn't have

21

to worry about the road conditions in the areas that had not. Unpaved roads could be a minefield of mud filled potholes and slippery shoulders that drop off without warning after only a brief rain shower. It was rare to find a decent stretch of flat dirt road that was not pocked with craters and mounds that rattled your teeth and jarred every joint of your automobile.

The dust made a relentless assault on your air cleaner as well as your eyes and nose if you kept the windows down. I always drove with the windows down—especially here. It was the only way to take in the symphony of sights, sounds, and smells of the coastal plain of my childhood. A place that lets the mind wander like the coastal rivers that meander through its landscape.

The Depression was building and weighed on everyone like a wet coat heavy with financial collapse. Driving helped me forget and gave me a hypersensitive focus necessary for good detective work. I am in my element here, driving while working on a puzzle of sorts.

The low country holds a vast maze of creeks and tributaries as well as a seemingly endless sea of marshland. It's a place where fresh meets salt to create a briny, brackish, brown roux of wildlife. It changes as much as the tide, but at the same time, it's a beautifully serene place.

As I wound my way through the Nassau River basin, low tide revealed the heavy smell of salt air and pluff mud and took me back to the many days I spent fishing in these creeks with my grandfather. The Nassau carved its way through the backcountry of a vast marshland before gently cleansing Amelia Island and then rushing into the Atlantic on either side. When I crossed the old bridge over the St. Mary's, leaving Florida for the Georgia coastal region, I could almost hear the clicking of white shrimp flicking their way through the marsh grass and fiddler crabs as they crossed the tidal mud flats in droves.

My grandfather loved bringing me to these isles to fish, but mostly to get away. Although we never discussed it, deep down I knew we shared the same lust for the tranquility of the water and peace that exists in this special place. Fishing provided him with the respite from daily life that I found undeniable as a teen. His wanderlust for the water was planted deep in my soul, and those roots gave birth to my own craving to be near the sea.

Ever since those days as a young boy, fishing had been my escape. These coastal waters were teaming with shrimp, and we caught them by the pound. Easily one of my favorite pastimes was eating boiled shrimp with my grandmother and grandfather at the old picnic table on their back deck.

The Satilla River finally gave way to the Jekyll Island Sound and then St. Simons and Sea Island beyond. The Highway 17 bridge crossed the river at a very wide section with a slow bend. There was a huge mud flat on the sea side of the bridge, and I could only imagine how the reds might pile up on that flat when the tide was just right.

With only eighty miles left until I reached Savannah, I started planning out the next several moves in my mind to hopefully get closer to solving the Goldberg case. By the time I crossed the Altamaha River and the magnificent Butler Plantation, I knew one thing for certain. Regardless of how this case played out, my encounter with Harold Hunt was only a precursor to a much bigger clash with two families that wanted me dead.

The black waters of the Ogeechee River gave way to the outskirts of Savannah, and I knew it was time to focus on the job at hand.

Chapter 3

Nearly getting myself killed in the Gulf Hammock after less than a year as an agent for the National Auto Theft Bureau wasn't exactly what Frances and I had in mind when we decided to move to Jacksonville. Dad always wanted me to go to college, but I knew it would be a big financial burden, so I got a job right out of high school as a file clerk.

I had been clerking for the NATB for a few years before being promoted several times up to Chief Clerk of the Atlanta office. It was a decent job, but the lure of being out on the road as a Special Agent was something I couldn't resist.

The Atlanta office was one of the largest in our organization, so I had plenty of opportunities for ride-a-longs with other agents in our office. I loved helping out with investigations and had gotten pretty good at detective work and tracing stolen autos, so when Mr. Asbury had a stroke, I was the natural choice to fill in—at least until he could come back to work.

I was only nineteen when Asbury stroked out, which made me the youngest man in the office, and also the youngest to ever lead an investigation. Technically, I wasn't an agent yet, but that was my opportunity to prove myself. When it became clear Mr. Asbury wasn't going to recover enough to return, I went to Director Durden to ask for a permanent assignment.

Asbury was one of our most respected agents and one of my mentors. He had recovered more stolen automobiles than all the other agents in the Atlanta office combined, and as a result, he always had his pick of cases. I suspected they would offer me a permanent job somewhere else, but I never expected to move to Florida.

After a lot of discussion, we decided it was the best move for my career, and Frances's manager at the Bell telephone company said they could transfer her to Jacksonville with no problem. We found a great apartment right on St. John's Avenue about a block off the water. After a couple of years, we decided to move to the beach.

The National Auto Theft Bureau was still in its infancy when Congress passed the National Vehicle Theft Act, or the Dyer Act, as it was more commonly known. The Dyer Act proved to be the key to federal policing of auto theft. We worked closely with J. Edgar Hoover to establish the punishments outlined in the law, and in return, Hoover made sure we had the resources to effectively deal with auto theft and prosecute the criminals.

Basically, our job was enforcing the law, but we couldn't do it without the help of local law enforcement. The NATB trained policed departments all over the country on how to investigate auto theft and bring the perpetrators to justice. We also supported the property insurers.

I couldn't help but think about how lucky I was to have this job when so many people were losing theirs.

* * *

Captain McCarthy was expecting me but not at the police department. The clerk at the front told me I could find him at "The Embassy" and gave me the address. Prohibition created some interesting dynamics between law enforcement and the law. It basically turned a country of law-abiding citizens into lawbreakers, and the cops were no exception. Why anyone expected the 18th Amendment to deter people from drinking is beyond comprehension, not to mention an Irish cop. Here we were almost ten years later, and there was more alcohol consumed than before the law banning its sale.

As I walked down the cobblestone streets of Savannah, I couldn't help but think of General Oglethorpe and the colonists that arrived here in 1733. I was also reminded of Captain Flint and all of the rabble-rousers that drank with abandon here.

Many of the establishments along the waterfront had rum cellars with secret passages to the river originally used for smuggling men and treasure to and from schooners at port. Now they were used for storing and smuggling illegal whiskey and some had been converted to speakeasies. It was even rumored to be a tunnel from under the old Pirates House on Broad Street to the river through which many an unconscious man was carried to a waiting ship in the harbor.

I expected the Embassy, or whatever it was called, to be well hidden, but after turning off Barnard Street and continuing a short distance into what was really just an alley, I found a short staircase in the back that led down to a small wooden door with a rusty sign nailed to it. The sign read, "Erin go Bragh!" with the year 1812 underneath. Ireland forever.

When I entered the bar, the miasma of last night's goings-on still hung in the air. I had never met Captain James McCarthy in person, but he wasn't hard to spot. He was sitting at a table with two other men whose chairs made a loud scraping noise as they got up from the table when they saw me approach.

"We'll talk later Joe," one of them said as they walked out.

McCarthy stood and offered a massive, fleshy paw. Shaking his hand was like trying to grip a ham. His nose was almost as big as my fist, and his ruddy complexion and gin blossoms made me feel like I was looking at a giant ribeye. "Captain McCarthy," he offered. "Good to meet you, Agent Clark. So what brings you to my town?" in a baritone that reverberated off the walls.

My town. There it was—that figurative line in the sand that many cops feel the need to lay down. Like a dog marking it's territory. This is my turf—enter at your own risk. For most, it was a sign of insecurity, but for some, it was a simple warning. In Captain McCarthy's case, it was the latter.

"Pleasure to meet you Captain. Director Coonts said you offered to help us out with an investigation. We really appreciate your cooperation."

"Well, I'll do what I can, although I'm not sure I'll be much help," he said.

"It sounds like you and Coonts go back a ways," I said.

"You could say that. He's a good man whom I trust. Your agency helped us out of a 'situation' a few years back that had the potential to get ugly, and Eugene Coonts was instrumental in making sure it didn't. Have a seat and let's talk about your case, and I'll let you know what I can."

McCarthy gave a subtle nod to the barkeep and just as we sat down he approached the table with two glasses of whiskey. Clearly James McCarthy was the unofficial ambassador from Ireland and this was his embassy. "My private stash," he said and then raised his glass. "Water of life," he bellowed.

It was more like water of fire and tasted like kerosene going down. It took a good minute for the burn to subside and I could finally speak again.

"It all started when we picked up this kid trying to sell a stolen Hupmobile in Jacksonville. He made up a story about a pal of his that needed money fast and asked him to bring the automobile down there and sell it. He said he didn't know it was stolen. A few days later, we recovered a couple of late-model Fords, which were also stolen."

"What's the connection?" McCarthy asked.

"We traced all three back to a dealer here in town—Goldberg's. It's clear that they were originally titled here in Savannah, and then they were reported stolen from Goldberg's dealership. A Ben Bloomberg filed a claim with their insurance company.

As I recounted the details of our investigation, McCarthy took it all in. An occasional nod or raised eyebrow was the only indication he gave that he either knew something helpful or the whiskey had set fire to something inside of him. He'd ordered another before I was finished.

As I sat there quietly sipping my whiskey, the captain stared across that old mahogany table as if in deep thought before he finally said, "Did the kid give you a name?"

"What kid? Parnell?"

"The one that was trying to sell the Hupmobile."

"Cleve Parnell—no, he didn't. He wouldn't talk, but he did say something interesting."

"What was that?"

"He said if this got back to Savannah, he would get a visit from the knife."

More silence, and then, "Neinstein, probably," McCarthy said.

"Excuse me?" I asked.

"I said Neinstein probably. His name is Al Neinstein. He's a piece of work this Neinstein lad. Goldberg's nephew I believe. We brought him in a few times—drunk and disorderly—stuff like that. But he's got a mean streak in him. He beat a man nearly to death one night for hitting on a girl he was sweet on. He's a loose cannon that one. Runs the used auto lot for Goldberg's. Seems like he's always got a lot full of practically new cars, and if he doesn't have what you're looking for, he can usually get it. Some around here call him 'the knife.' It's not what your probably thinking."

"What do you mean?" I asked.

"He looks like one. His head is so narrow his features are sharp—like a knife. Look at him straight on and you can hardly see the man's face."

"Sounds like maybe we should have a talk with him."

"I wouldn't go poking around Neinstein's yet until you have some proof that he's your man. You mentioned Ben Bloomberg. He runs the dealership for Asa Goldberg, and I've never had any complaints about the business. Seems like they run a pretty tight ship over there on Waters. I tell you what, why don't you stop by the precinct house tomorrow morning? I've got someone you should meet," Captain McCarthy said.

"Okay, captain. I'll see you tomorrow. In the meantime, I think I'll head over to Goldberg's and see about maybe buying a new automobile. Just kick a few tires if you know what I mean."

* * *

The Goldberg Ford Dealership was easy to find over on Waters Avenue. It looked like most Ford dealers, but the used automobile lot across the street was larger than most, and had a lot of late-model Fords on it. I parked out front, thinking I would go in and ask to see the owner, but before I could get out of my Chevrolet, an automobile salesman was standing at my door.

"Welcome to Goldberg's, Mr. …" he said, standing there with his hand out.

28

"It's Clark. Julian Clark."

He backed up enough to allow the door to open and then pumped my hand up and down too many times.

"Well Mr. Clark, I'm glad you stopped in. This could be your lucky day. That is a fine-looking suit you have on. You look like a man with a keen eye for quality. What do you say we go take a look at one of our fine automobiles?"

"Is the owner here?" I interrupted.

"Oh, you mean Mr. Goldberg? No, he's not here today, but I promise to introduce you to him when we have a chance."

Actually, I was glad the owner wasn't around so I could do a little snooping without raising any suspicion. As my overzealous salesman ran his mouth about this vehicle and that vehicle, I was eyeing several new Model A's parked out front.

"That's a fine-looking Chevrolet you're driving, Mr. Clark. What brought you in here today?"

The bureau provides us with automobiles, which was one of the perks of the job—especially in this economy. They were usually Fords, but oftentimes we had our pick, depending on what was in the pool. Sometimes the stolen automobiles we recovered couldn't be returned to the owner or maybe it had been used during the commission of a crime, so we kept them.

"I'm looking for a new ride for my wife, and I'm really interested in one of those new Fords over there. Do you mind if I take one for a spin?"

"Outstanding! Yes of course, we can arrange for you to take a test drive. You go ahead and get in and get a feel for the quality of this fine automobile while I go inside and get the keys. I'll be right back."

As I got in the Ford, I counted four more Model A's just like it sitting in a row. When the young man came back out, he approached the driver's side as I lowered the window, and he handed me the keys. "I'll just jump in the passenger seat, and we'll get going."

"I tell you what, young man, I would really like to take it for a spin on my own first so I get a good feel for it without any distractions. Then I'll come back and let you tell me all about it. How's that? I'll even leave you the keys to my Chevrolet."

Somewhat defeated, he said, "Well, I guess that would be okay. It's a little irregular and all, but I understand you want to really get a feel for the vehicle first."

As I pulled out of the lot in that new Ford, I could see the dejected look on the salesman's face in the rearview mirror. He probably felt like his sale was driving away too. Little did he know.

As I got around the block, I pulled over to the side of the road and released the hood. Before long I determined the numbers on the block were not original Ford identification numbers and had clearly been changed. This was a stolen automobile for sure. I doubted the salesman had any idea, and it was likely that only Mr. Goldberg was privy to that information.

When I got back to the dealership, the salesman was still waiting for me anxiously. I immediately got out and told him it wasn't quite what I was looking for, but I would keep them in mind if anything changed. He came at me like a dog in heat but hardly had a chance to give me his business card before I hopped in my Chevrolet and took off.

* * *

That afternoon at the Olde Savannah Inn, I decided to check in with Coonts and let him know what I had learned that day.

"Gwyneth."

"Well, hey love, where are you?" she asked.

"Savannah."

"How's your eye? Gwyneth said. "And the rest of your face?"

"It's fine. I've had worse."

"I don't know how that's possible. Did you find McCarthy?"

"Sure did," I said.

"He's a real piece of work, isn't he?" she said.

"No kidding."

"Well, hang on. I know you didn't call to chat with me. Coonts is anxious to talk to you."

"Gwyneth, you know how much I look forward to our little chats. Seriously, though, thanks for being concerned about me."

"Hold on," she said.

"Julian. How are you? Please tell me you found something up there. Did you meet McCarthy?" asked Coonts.

"Your pal Joe is a real character, that's for sure. I definitely wouldn't want to get on the wrong side of the law around here. He was holding court in that bar of his. Seems like he spends more time there than the precinct."

"He's a good man and trustworthy too. He's exactly the kind of man you want to have your back if you get in trouble. Keep that in mind. Now what did you learn so far?" asked Coonts.

"He said Goldberg's clean. At least he hasn't had any trouble with him. Apparently, he's got a nephew, though, that might be a different story. Name's Al Neinstein. Sounds like the local ruffian. He's been in trouble a few times but nothing major. Runs the used auto lot for Goldberg. He's got a reputation around town. I haven't had a chance to check him out, but the captain warned me about getting too close without any evidence, so I decided to go pay Goldberg a visit. It's a classy Ford dealership. He had several new Fords out front, so I took one for a test drive and spent a little time under the hood. Stolen."

"You don't say?" remarked Coonts.

"Yep. We've got enough to get a warrant, but I think it's a little premature. Give me a little more time to check out a couple more leads. I need to know more about his nephew, and Captain McCarthy asked me to meet him in the morning because he wants me to talk to one of his detectives."

"Okay, I'll give you another couple of days, but keep me posted. By the way, did Aubrey Warren get in touch with you?"

"No, why?" I asked.

"I'm not exactly sure, but it has something to do with a case in Waycross. Listen Julian; you don't have time to be messing around in Waycross. Stick to the Goldberg case. I don't need any more trouble like what happened over there in Gulf Hammock."

"I hear you, boss. I'll just call him in the morning and let him know I'm

31

tied up over here in Savannah."

"Julian—" I heard him start to say as I hung up.

* * *

The next morning, I met Captain McCarthy at the Savannah Police Department. It wasn't like most of the other police stations I had been in. The lobby was more like a hotel with massive wood beams that supported a coffered ceiling. Elaborate wainscoting adorned the framework that supported huge pieces of beveled glass separating visitors that came in the front from the clerk and the rest of the department. Once you entered and the huge front door closed behind you, you couldn't get out of the large vestibule without being buzzed in—or out.

The clerk behind the glass stood up and approached the window. "May I help you?"

"I'm here to see Captain McCarthy. My name's Julian Clark."

"Yes, Agent Clark. They're expecting you. Meet me down at that door to your right and I'll show you back."

There was an audible buzzing sound as I approached the door and the lock released.

The captain acknowledged me with a nod when I entered his office and in that big baritone said, "Agent Clark, this is Detective Thomas Byrne. I asked him to help you with your investigation—you'll understand why in a minute. Why don't you give him the short version of why you came up here?"

I shook his hand and said, "Nice to meet you, Detective Byrne."

Byrne was a handsome young man—almost too handsome for a policeman. He was short but had an athletic build like a wrestler. You could see the muscles in his neck and shoulders even under his uniform. He had sandy brown hair, a pale complexion like he never spent much time in the sun and deep green eyes. His handshake was like gripping steel. He was clearly a man who could take care of himself, but he had a very buttoned-up look about him. His uniform was impeccably clean and free of wrinkles, and his stance was very proper—chin up, shoulders back, hat properly positioned under his left arm and his right hand at his side.

After a few minutes giving him a rundown of the Goldberg case, I explained what I had found the previous afternoon on my fishing expedition to the dealership. "The numbers had been changed on that Model A. It was actually a pretty shoddy job—probably done in a hurry. Without the original numbers, it's impossible to determine where it was stolen, but it was hot, just as sure as I'm standing here."

"Son of gun," the detective said. "I should have known something wasn't right."

"What are you referring to, Thomas?" I asked.

"I just bought a Chrysler from Goldberg's used automobile lot a few weeks ago, and I got a hell of a deal. I figured they felt they were just buying some influence by giving a cop a bargain, but now I've got a bad feeling about it. I guess technically I got it from Al's, but everyone around here just refers to both of them as Goldberg's. Let's go out to my place and check it out."

This could be exactly the kind of break we needed. I just hated to get it at the expense of the detective. Captain McCarthy saw us out and asked us to keep him posted on what we learned. He reminded us not to do anything stupid, and to make sure we had rock-solid proof that Goldberg or any of his family was dirty.

On the way out, Detective Byrne turned to the captain and said, "Hey Joe, how did you know to bring me in here this morning?"

He replied, "Call it a hunch. As soon as Julian mentioned Goldberg and some stolen vehicles, I immediately thought of you and that automobile you bought recently. Sorry, Thomas, maybe it's straight."

* * *

As Hugh Gant picked up the phone he wasn't sure how much he was going to say or even what he was going to say. He knew Alva was upset, but this was a call that had to be made. Hugh's brother Riley said so, and what Riley said, Hugh did. He sat there for a few minutes thinking about his friend

Harold Hunt—Alva's little brother. Thinking about all the good times they had together. The Hunt and Gant families had been close for as long as he could remember. Not just friends, they were more like brothers. After all, Hugh and Riley's sister Katherine was married to Alva Hunt. They had all been running together since they were kids.

When Hugh and Riley got out of the army, they moved back to Bushnell and started working at the Ford dealership Mayor Hunt had opened when he moved down from Jersey with his four sons. Good with their hands, the Gants learned most of what they knew about engines in the army, so it was a natural fit to go work at the dealership as mechanics. They loved cutting up with the Hunt boys—Alva, Truby, Enos, and Harold, and that dealership not only provided a job, but also hours of fun and camaraderie.

Mayor Hunt wasn't much of a father, and before long his boys started getting into trouble. Harold was a fighter and wherever he went, trouble always followed. He was always getting his brothers into scrapes. Harold always dreamed of being a prize fighter, and he probably would have been pretty good had he not been influenced so much by the others. Instead he turned out to be one of the best bare-knuckle street fighters in the state. They were all well known by law enforcement.

Hugh put the phone down. Patience had never been his strong suit, which was ironic considering that was his mother's name. She died giving birth to him, and his step mom was a tough old bird. She made Hugh and Riley tough the way she disciplined them. Hugh was prone to violence and had a short fuse. He was lean and mean, and he had these forearms with muscles like rope. He was covered in thick black hair and looked like a black bear without his shirt on.

"Alva. It's Hugh," he said. "I'm real sorry about Harold. You know how much we loved him. It's not going to be the same around here without him."

"Yep," was all that Alva could muster.

"We need to talk. Not here. Not on the phone."

"Yep."

"Why don't you and Truby meet me over at the garage?" Hugh said.

"Give me an hour. I need to find him first, but we'll be there," Alva managed.

* * *

Alva looked like he hadn't slept in a while. He had dark bags under his eyes and he smelled like whiskey. His shoulders were hunched over, and he had a couple of days worth of stubble on his face. He looked haggard. Truby didn't look much better. Clearly, the entire situation had taken a toll on the two brothers.

"Listen, guys," Hugh started. "Again, I'm real sorry about what happened out there in the Hammock—"

Alva interrupted, "What happened, Hugh? Does anyone even know?"

Truby said, "I heard he bled to death, but nobody knows what from. He was alone, though, right? So it must have been some kind of accident."

Hugh shot a look at Truby.

"Why was he out there alone?" asked Alva.

"That was always the plan," said Hugh. "After Truby and I stole the truck, we drove it to Gainesville to unload all that tobacco. The other guys loaded it onto several smaller trucks. A couple headed to Tampa, while the others drove to Ybor City. Then we drove the tobacco truck out to the Hammock to dump it. We couldn't just leave it there in Gainesville. It would have attracted too much attention, and besides, the big boss said not to. Riley was supposed to go get Harold once things cooled down."

Truby had been sitting there listening when he finally said, "He wasn't exactly alone." He was staring daggers at Hugh.

"What are you talking about, Truby?" asked Alva.

"He wasn't alone. I heard from one of the sheriff's deputies that there was somebody else out there in the Hammock with him—two people, to be exact. Isn't that right, Hugh?"

"Uh, I don't know anything about two people. But, uh, I do know there was at least one other. Sort of," Hugh added. "I assumed Riley had already filled you in, Alva."

"What in the hell is he talking about, Truby?" asked Alva. "What are you two not telling me?"

Truby said, "Hugh, why don't you go ahead and tell Alva what else happened and then I'll fill in the blanks?"

"Well, like I said, we stole the truck up in Jacksonville while it was laid over from Winston-Salem. It was pretty heavily guarded, so we had to take care of the night watch or we never would have made it out," sighed Hugh.

"What exactly do you mean by 'take care of' the night watch?" asked Alva.

"Oh, come on. Don't act like you didn't know the risks when we got involved in this shit. He's not going to talk, if that's what you're worried about. Riley and I did what had to be done. What's done is done. We got paid and that's that, so don't give me that look like we screwed up," Hugh said.

The look on Alva's face was more than just disappointment. They could see the despair in his eyes with the sobering realization that there was no turning back now. Alva was the one who questioned getting into the liquor business—especially for a big-time Chicago crime boss. Now his worst fear had been realized, and he was just as guilty as the rest of them. It felt like someone had sucked all the air out of the garage. Nobody breathed or said a word while Alva sat there stewing.

Truby finally broke the silence. "According to our informant over in Bronson, another person was out there with Harold. Does the name Julian Clark ring a bell?" asked Truby.

"Agent Clark with the NATB? Son of a bitch. Seriously?" asked Hugh. "Damn, that detective doesn't know when to give up."

"You've got to be kidding me. That's impossible. Truby, how would he even know you were out there? Gulf Hammock is in the middle of nowhere. It's got to be a hundred miles from Jacksonville if it's a mile. And since when did auto theft agents care about tobacco?" No sooner had the words come out of Alva's mouth than he realized it had nothing to do with tobacco. "Shit," he said with the realization that Agent Clark was looking for a stolen truck.

Hugh said, "I can't figure any way that damn agent knew we stole that truck or that Harold drove it out to the Hammock to get rid of it. Nobody outside this room except for Harold and Riley even knew we went to Jacksonville. Well, except for that guard. But he sure as hell didn't tell anyone. The only possible snitch is one of those goddamned wops from Chicago. I knew we shouldn't have trusted those scumbags."

"Hugh, are you telling us that Julian Clark murdered our brother over a stolen tobacco truck?" Alva asked.

Truby answered instead. "Hold your horses, you two. All our guy said was that Julian Clark was picked up near the woods where they found Harold and the truck. He hasn't seen the coroner's report yet, so he didn't even know how he died exactly. One of the other deputies said he bled to death. I find it hard to believe that Agent Clark would have murdered Harold for stealing a goddamned truck."

A big vein in Alva's forehead was bulging as he said, "I will kill that sorry Agent Clark myself if he's responsible for Harold's death."

Alva wasn't nearly as prone to violence as Hugh, but right now it seemed like he was angrier than he had ever been in his life. Maybe it was the realization that they had all crossed a line that never should have been crossed. Maybe it was because Harold was dead and Alva was feeling guilty. Regardless, it wasn't like Hugh to be the voice of reason. Perhaps he realized somebody had to keep things under control, or they could all end up in prison. Riley had warned him about Alva's reaction, and since Riley couldn't be there, Hugh would have to step up and show some leadership. Hugh was in uncharted territory.

"Don't worry, Alva, we'll find out what happened soon enough," Hugh said. "Truby, is this the same Agent Clark that arrested you for stealing that Chevrolet over in Lakeland, Florida?"

"That's the one," Truby replied. "He and that Deputy Clifton surprised us at that motel we used to stay at over near Lakeland."

"What do you mean, he surprised *us*?" asked Hugh.

Truby replied, "Me and some girl I was with."

"Anyway, let's not go off half cocked," Hugh said. "Once the cause of death is official, Riley and I will find out from our guy over in Bronson what happened, and then we can decide what to do. In the meantime, stay out of trouble until this situation works itself out. We don't need any extra attention right now."

"We've got runs to make, Hugh," Truby added. "I don't think *you-know-who* is going to give a damn about our problems."

Alva said, "Truby's right, Hugh. They're supposed to let us know today where to pick up the next load."

"I'm not suggesting we stop doing business. I'm just saying we need to be careful until this thing blows over. Don't go running your mouth about Agent Clark, Truby," Hugh said.

"I'll be in touch once I know where the next load is coming in," said Alva. "You boys be ready."

They all got up and left …

* * *

We took my Chevrolet Series AD Universal over to Detective Byrne's. As we pulled away from the curb in front of the police department, Thomas said, "So what have you got under the hood, Agent Clark?"

"It sounds like you may know a thing or two about automobiles, Detective Byrne," I said. "Tell me what you hear."

"Well, judging by the sound of it, I'd say you did something to the exhaust. And, it feels a little too strong to be the original Chevy six they put in the Universal. How many horses you getting out of her?"

"Not bad, Detective. As a matter of fact, we did make a few tweaks—including the exhaust."

"Who's we?" Byrne asked.

"Me and my buddy Torch. Actually, mostly just Torch. He's the one with the shop. He did all the work while I mostly watched. It's not the original Chevy motor, though."

"I didn't think so. What is it?"

"It's a Series 50 motor. I got it out of a stolen Buick we recovered down in Florida after a thief totaled it. The motor was about the only thing that survived. Torch shaved the heads and put a dual carb on it. "

"Hell of a company vehicle!" he said.

"It helps catch the bad guys," I replied with a laugh.

"Turn here," he said. "It's up here on the right."

Detective Byrne lived in a flat not far from the river in an area called Yamacraw Village, where the Creeks had settled two hundred years before.

"So what county is your family from?" I asked.

"Wexford." He looked at me with raised eyebrows.

The street was lined on both sides with identical flats that all had steps leading up to the first-floor entrance.

"Now turn into that little alley. The garage is in back."

I imagined most of his neighbors were immigrant families whose ancestors had come here many years before fleeing the Great Famine. Maybe they were part of the merchant class looking for work. The descendants of those original Irish settlers were hardworking, and the boom of canal building provided a lot of jobs for those willing to take on the hard labor.

He had a single auto garage under his flat with one of those horizontal swinging doors that lifted from the bottom. The entire door would swing out and up in one piece and then slide back along the ceiling above the vehicle. Two large eyebolts had been set in concrete at the bottom, and a metal ring had been affixed to both sides of the door by way of a metal plate that bolted on. A large padlock secured each side of the door, from the ring on the door to the eyebolt in the concrete. The door was also metal.

"Damn, Thomas, what the heck are you keeping in here—stolen automobiles?" I said.

I could tell by his silence my joke fell flat. He pulled a key ring off his belt and proceeded to find the two keys that opened the large padlocks. The door was spring loaded, so he had to be careful when he lifted it or the damn thing would take his shins and his chin off as it swung out first and then up into the ceiling.

Detective Byrne's Chrysler Series 75 Roadster was backed in and looked like it just had been polished. I could see my reflection in the immaculate black paint. It was lacking the gimcrackery of other makes or any of the extras Chrysler was known for slapping on, like side mounts with mirrors, extra head lamps, color accents, or whitewalls with chromed wire wheels. This one was unique because it was plain and its sleek look made it appear fast. Simple and refined—it was truly a beautiful automobile.

The garage was narrow, not leaving a lot of room, but as I tried to get around to the passenger side, I noticed the garage was actually much deeper than the automobile. It must have run the width of the building, and I bet he could fit at least two vehicles, maybe three, single file.

Byrne flipped on the lights, revealing one of the neatest garages I had ever seen. He had all sorts of mechanic's tools, oil cans, gardening implements, pieces of wood of different varieties, woodworking tools, paint cans, and even canned goods along the walls on both sides. The shelves were all neatly organized, and everything was stacked perfectly with its label facing out.

A workbench had a vise mounted to it and what looked like ammunition reloading equipment. His oil rags were neatly folded on the bench. I could practically eat off the floor, it was so clean, and he even had a small desk on one side with a reading lamp and shelves full of books on the wall above it. The books were neatly organized, so all the spines lined up perfectly by height.

A small set of steps led up to a door in the back right corner, which I assumed was the entrance to the flat, and a black curtain hung from the ceiling to the floor across the back wall.

I turned my attention back to the Chrysler and whistled before saying, "Twenty-nine?"

"Yup," Byrne replied.

"I got to admit, it's beautiful. Why don't you pull it out and drive it back in forwards so we'll have plenty of light over the motor? We need to get a look inside to figure out if the numbers are original."

Before getting his keys out to move it, Detective Byrne walked to the back of the garage and turned on a large oscillating fan. Then he produced the keys and got in to move it. When he cranked it up, it purred just as pretty as the day it was made, and he quickly pulled out of the garage and into the alley. The fan kept the exhaust from building up in the garage and kept the air moving so it was comfortable inside. He turned the vehicle around expertly and headed it back in. He pulled the hood release, and then he got out and closed the garage door.

I looked questioningly at him, but all he said was, "What? I don't want the neighbors walking by and getting a look in here."

"Get me a flashlight, Thomas," I said as I raised the hood. While he went to get a light, I walked around and climbed in the front seat. When Thomas came back, he handed me the light and I shined it on the instrument panel. "You see that little plate?"

"Yeah, what is it? The serial number?"

"It's a FEDCO identification plate. Depending on the year, make, and model, the plate was either mounted on the right front door pillar, or somewhere on or over the instrument panel. Chrysler started using them a few years ago to make their cars harder to steal."

"Well, that's good right? Maybe mine's clean, after all," he said with a little excitement.

"Not exactly. If memory serves me, a Chrysler 75 FEDCO plate should start with a C. Yours starts with an L. We don't see as many stolen Chryslers, so maybe I'm wrong, but I was expecting to see something like a CY and then three numbers and then another letter. Go get the little black book in my coat pocket over there. I hung it on the back of the door while you were turning it around."

While Detective Byrne went to get my serial number guide, I got out and walked back around to the front of the automobile. When he came back, I was shining the light down inside the engine compartment, looking for the numbers stamped into the block. On this vehicle they should be on the left side of the block just above the water jacket cover. There weren't any.

"You see that?" I asked, pointing.

"No. I don't see anything—except a few scratches."

"Exactly. That's because somebody ground the serial numbers off. If you look from the side like this, you can see the marks where they polished it smooth," I said, leaning to the side for a better angle.

Byrne looked like he was going to be sick. "Well, maybe they stamped them somewhere else on this model. You said yourself you don't see many

Chryslers."

"I've seen enough to know where the engine stamp should be. However, you are actually right. They do stamp them in other places. The trouble is, we can't get to them without getting underneath or raising the frame. Hand me that book." Flipping to the pages with the Chrysler guide, I found what I was looking for.

"The FEDCO plate is basically a code. Your plate says L-S-4-9-5-P. The code is derived from Chrysler's name—Walter P. Chrysler or W-P-C-H-R-Y-S-L-E-D.

"That's not how you spell Chrysler."

"Thanks. The R was already taken. They used it to denote the six-cylinder motor—don't ask me why. Each letter corresponds to a number 0 – 9. The L equals 7, the S equals 6, and the P equals 1. So your code translates to 7-6-4-9-5-1. The serial number is in the code and should be stamped on the engine block. Since the plate seems to be a mismatch, we need to get the engine block number and work backward. The number on the block should start with an R."

"I thought you said it started with a C?"

"No, I said the plate on the instrument panel should start with a C. All Chrysler 75's have a straight-six motor, and the designation for the six-cylinder motor is R."

Detective Byrne leaned against the wall and stared up at the ceiling with his hands over his face, totally dejected. "This is all too confusing."

"Wait right here." I needed something from my automobile.

I lifted the garage door just enough to duck under. As I headed out to my Chevrolet, I considered the alteration of the plate as opposed to the stamp on the block. It took a pro to change the plate. FEDCO plates were made of three layers of white metal oxide over copper and were affixed to the instrument panel with two rivets. If anyone pried off the original, the two rivets would mutilate the face because they left large holes in it. They were practically impossible to alter because of the multiple layers of embossing.

In spite of the difficulty, we had seen our share of fakes. Either somebody had figured out how to make the plates, or maybe they were just stealing them from the source.

Regardless, what I didn't understand was: why go through all of the trouble to counterfeit the serial plate and then just simply grind off the engine stamp? The automobile had obviously been tampered with, as anyone that knew anything about stolen vehicles would realize—especially a dealer.

After retrieving my bag from the back seat of my automobile, I returned to the garage to find Detective Byrne slumped in a chair, staring at his Roadster. As I pulled the door back down, he asked, "Now what are you doing?"

Pulling a small jar of liquid out of my bag, I said, "This will show us what was stamped on the block originally. When they strike the cast iron block with a die, it leaves a deep impression. You can file off the surface so you can't make out the numbers with the naked eye, but the impression is still there—it's just too deep to see. This little mixture of acid and copper chloride will help bring it back. Here, hold the light for me."

While Byrne held the light, I removed a small hunk of modeling clay from my bag and carefully molded it around the edges of where the numbers should be. I made a small frame around the numbers so I could pour the etching solution into it without it all running off on the floor. I carefully poured a small amount of the liquid onto the surface. "You don't want to get any of this on your hands, or it will burn the hell out of them."

"Why, what is it?"

"Basically, it's hydrochloric acid." It bubbled and fizzed before I used a swab to rub the surface of the metal. "Hand me that mirror." I positioned the mirror at just the right angle so I could see the numbers as they started to appear. "Do you have a pencil?"

Thomas hurried over to the desk and grabbed a piece of paper and a pencil. "Let's have it."

"R – 2 – 5 – 7 – 9 – 5 – 7. No, wait, that last number is a 1. I think."

Byrne did some figuring before he finally said, "So according to your code, the plate should say CY-795-P. Damn."

"Sounds about right. And look here," I said as I opened up my little black book. "That's exactly what a Chrysler 75 Roadster FEDCO plate should say. I hate to be the bearer of bad news, Detective, but this automobile is as hot as a whorehouse on dollar night."

I sat at Detective Byrne's desk to think about the case and our next move while he cleaned up and put everything back in its original place. Clearly, Goldberg, or somebody that worked for him, was crooked, and they were using his dealership and his used automobile lot to move stolen cars through Savannah.

As I looked around the garage, I couldn't help but wonder what Thomas was hiding behind that black curtain. While he had his back to me, I grabbed it and threw it aside. The sound of the rings sliding along the bar near the ceiling caught his attention, and he whipped around to see what I was doing. What should have been a wall behind the curtain was actually a recessed area in the wall, and stacked neatly in the recessed area were a bunch of boxes—whiskey boxes. Byrne had enough Irish whiskey in his garage to stock every speak in Savannah for a month. After I surveyed the contents, I turned to look at him for an explanation, but all he said was, "Don't ask."

"This seems like a fine time for a drink if you ask me," I suggested.

Byrne pulled out another chair, sat down at the bench, and said, "I think you might be right, Agent Clark." He opened a cabinet under the bench and took out a bottle and two paper cups. He poured us each a shot of whiskey and then slumped back in his chair with a big sigh. "I used my entire savings to buy that automobile," he said, looking at the Chrysler. "What are the chances I get any of it back?" he asked.

"Honestly? Slim and none. It's possible, but by the time we wrap up the investigation and run old Goldberg, or whoever is behind this, into court, the money will have dried up and the dealership will probably be broke. We'll find out who actually owned the vehicle and possibly have to return it to them or at a minimum to the insurance company."

As I drove back to the DeSoto Hotel, I couldn't help but feel sorry for Detective Byrne. One thing was for sure; I needed to help him channel all that anger he was harboring for Goldberg and his nephew toward my investigation. Byrne had skin in the game now, and that was a good thing.

* * *

44

The next morning I had a meeting with Vernon Chris of the Bureau of Investigation. He was stationed in Savannah but reported to Atlanta. Coonts had asked our Atlanta office for Federal support because transporting stolen automobiles across state lines was a federal crime and required federal prosecution.

Vernon was well aware of the Goldberg case, but had only had a cursory briefing up until now. He would be instrumental in helping us make an arrest and wanted to review the case file before committing Bureau resources to an investigation or to an arrest.

Agent Chris was already sitting at a corner table facing the entrance when I walked into the little diner on Broughton Street. He waved me over as a waitress hollered from behind the counter, "Mornin'! Can I get you some coffee?"

"Black, please," I replied. "Vernon, how are you?" extending my hand.

"Good to see you, Julian. How's Frances?" he asked.

"She's great. Thanks for asking. She's working for Bell, and still worried to death about me."

"It comes with the territory, Julian. It gets easier, but let's be honest, this can be dangerous work, and not knowing where you are for days at a time is not easy to handle. There's always a level of anxiety that never goes away."

"You've been in law enforcement for a long time. How does your wife handle it?" I asked.

"Not very well," replied Vernon. "Like I said, it's not easy. Delphine knows there's always a chance I won't come home tonight. But it's the life we chose. Or maybe I should say, I chose. She stays busy when I'm out of town or working on a case. She has lots of friends here in Savannah and is very active in the garden club. I think staying busy is the distraction she needs to not focus too much on what I'm doing. We feel lucky, though—this financial situation is tightening its grip on everyone, and having the security of a government job can't be overlooked. Anyway, let's talk about this Goldberg case. Director Durden gave me the highlights of your investigation, but why don't you bring me up to speed with the particulars?"

For the next half hour I recounted the details of the case over breakfast,

45

occasionally looking at my file to verify something that Agent Chris thought was important. I started with the three stolen cars in Jacksonville and the young man, Cleve Parnell, that we picked up trying to sell one. We discussed tracing them back to Savannah and the Goldberg Company, his nephew Neinstein, the stolen Ford I took for a test drive, and of course, Detective Byrne's Chrysler. I also mentioned the insurance claim filed by Ben Bloomberg.

I asked, "Well, what do you think? Do you know Goldberg or any of his associates? Ever cross paths with him?"

"Everybody knows Asa Goldberg. Savannah's not that big a town, and he's got the biggest Ford dealership for a hundred miles. He's involved with the community, a member of the local rotary club, and active in a couple of local charities. Supposedly, he's a real family man too. He's got three or four daughters that are also well liked around town. The Bureau has purchased a lot of vehicles from him, and we've never had any reason to suspect his business dealings aren't on the up and up. I don't know anything about Bloomberg, but this Neinstein man is a different story. He's slick like you would expect a used-auto salesman to be. I understand he's been in some trouble. Nothing too serious, but apparently he's a hothead and prone to pop off without much reason. From what I've learned, he's a better suspect than Goldberg. However, you and I both know there are plenty of good men that have gotten on the wrong side of the law."

"Goldberg sounds like a pillar of society," I said with a smirk. "And by the way, he's got five daughters. McCarthy said he was clean too, but he doesn't trust the nephew at all. Says he just about beat a man to death over a girl."

"Yeah, I heard that story too. What did you say his nickname was?"

"They call him the Knife." I said.

Upon hearing his nickname, Vernon had a look on his face like something smelled bad. "Well, I'll ask around. It's possible somebody will recognize that name and connect it to criminal activity. What else can I do for you?"

"Not much that I can think of until we need a warrant. I have a feeling that if we tried to serve them now, they would produce enough legitimate paperwork to make us all look like fools."

"You're probably right. Have you thought about chasing down the insurance side of this?"

"Insurance fraud is hard to prove here, but it's definitely worth following up on. I actually know the president of the insurance company that paid the claim. He and my grandfather were friends. He's also one of the founders of the original NATB."

Agent Chris added, "There's a gang in Maryland that has been under investigation for some time by our organized crime office in DC. Durden said the NATB in Maryland has also had their eye on them."

I asked, "Are you referring to the Coll gang?"

"Might be worth a trip to Baltimore. Talk to Agent Strong—our Bureau man up there—as well as your lead investigator at NATB."

"I appreciate the help. Hopefully, I'll be in touch soon to request that warrant," I said as I stood up to leave.

"Anytime, Julian. Let me know what you find out."

After shaking hands, I headed for the door, but then I heard Vernon call out, "Hey, Julian?" As I looked back, he said, "Be careful."

Chapter 4

Two days later I was sitting in Bob Brook's office in Baltimore Maryland. Bob was the president of the National Mutual Insurance Company— one of the original companies that formed the NATB. Before the National Vehicle Theft Act was passed, it was actually the insurance industry that took the first steps toward curtailing automobile theft. In 1912 the biggest insurers got together and formed the original National Auto Theft Bureau. However, it wasn't until J. Edgar Hoover came along that the NATB became part of the law enforcement structure in the U.S. The Dyer Act became the leverage we needed to prosecute.

"Julian, it's good to see you. Or should I say Agent Clark? Congratulations, by the way. When your grandfather told me Durden was going to make you an agent, I wasn't surprised one bit. I always felt you would make a great detective."

"Thank you, sir. I really appreciate that. Frances and I weren't so sure about the move to Jacksonville, but we've settled in and she's made a lot of good friends through work and the community. I have to admit, being near the water is something I'm really getting used to."

"Glad to hear it. Once you get used to being near the water, you'll never want to go—"

Bob was interrupted by a knock at the door. It was already open, and a gentleman was standing there, waiting for Bob to invite him in.

Bob said, "Hagood, I was just catching up with Julian from your Jacksonville office. Julian, this is Agent Pierce, Baltimore NATB. I'm sure you guys know some of the same people, or maybe you've met before."

Agent Pierce extended his hand and said, "Agent Clark, you work for Coonts, right?"

"That's right. Nice to meet you," I said, shaking hands with the man.

"Our directors are friends, and I had the opportunity to meet him during a conference last year hosted by the Atlanta office and Director Durden."

I replied, "Oh yeah, I remember it well. I wasn't officially on the force yet, but I was there. You probably don't remember me—there must have been a least a hundred other men there, including the police and sheriff's departments. I taught the session on identifying original serial numbers."

"Now I remember. Great job, by the way. You've got quite a reputation around here," said Pierce. "So what brings you to Baltimore? Bob says you guys are working a case that involves the Coll gang."

"Well, we're not sure, but the stolen vehicles started showing up in Jacksonville, and then we traced them back up here. The trail originally led us to Savannah and a dealer named Goldberg, but the manufacturer's statement of origin led us to Baltimore. Agent Vernon Chris with the Bureau in Savannah said they had been investigating the Coll gang and suggested their possible involvement. What can you tell me about them?"

"The Coll gang is into bootlegging mostly, but stealing autos is a close second. They run a numbers racket too, but it wouldn't be a stretch for them to be behind your stolen vehicles. The Bureau can tell you a lot more than I can, but I'll tell you what little I know," added Pierce.

Bob Brooks spoke up, "By the way, Raymond Strong from the Bureau of Investigation will be here soon, but go ahead and we'll let Ray fill in any gaps."

"Okay, swell. In the meantime, here's some of what I know. Vincent Coll is an Irish mobster from New York. He's a close associate of Dutch Schultz—I think he's Dutch's security man. Basically, he's a hit man, but he has a big family and they are all involved in organized crime. Schultz and his boys run a bunch of speakeasies in New York City and a very big beer bootlegging business. I think Coll's men run the trucks. Anyway, a few of them made their way down here because our port doesn't get nearly as much attention as New York's. A couple of Coll's relatives set up shop and made Baltimore a permanent home. There have been a few sightings of Vincent down here, but no serious trouble out of him that I'm aware of. Although I heard he and his boys had tax problems recently and that George Remus helped make those problems go away. You know who Remus is, right?"

"The big-time lawyer from Cincy—and an even bigger bootlegger."

"That's the one," replied Pierce.

About that time a tall gentleman dressed in a black suit, black tie, and black fedora, stuck his head in the door and tipped his hat towards Bob Brooks. Brooks jumped up, "Ray, come on in! How the hell are you? Thanks for coming down. This is Hagood Pierce with the NATB here in Baltimore, and that's Julian Clark with the NATB in Jacksonville. Gentlemen, this is Raymond Strong with the DC Bureau of Investigation."

Agent Strong removed his hat and shook our hands. He was an imposing man well over six feet tall, and he had intense dark brown eyes, almost black, and silver stubble on his head that was buzzed military style. He had an athletic build, but I could tell he was much older than his body and condition let on.

"Jacksonville? What brings you all the way up here, Agent Clark? It must be something good," Agent Strong asked.

"Probably not nearly as exciting as the stuff you see in DC."

"Well, I don't know about that. Tell me what's going on and we'll see if the Bureau can help," he replied.

Agent Pierce jumped in, "I was just telling him about the Coll gang. There may be a link between some stolen cars down in Jacksonville and the gang here in Baltimore."

"That wouldn't surprise me one bit."

After I filled Agent Strong in on what we found down in Jacksonville, and the trail of evidence that led to Baltimore, Strong gave us some additional background on the gang. "Peter Coll is one of Vincent's brothers that moved down here. He lives in a small Irish enclave near the harbor, with a bunch of their relatives and friends. Crime runs rampant down there, but the Colls seem to stick mostly to bootlegging—and women. They have a few fast boats down at the harbor, but we've never been able to catch them with anything. They have camps all up and down the Chesapeake, which they can use for hideouts, and there's just too much water and shoreline for us to police. If they don't bring it into the harbor, we aren't going to catch them. I suspect many of the trucks they use for delivery are stolen and probably a lot of the automobiles they drive. Vinny is ruthless and so is that Dutch Schultz character—fortunately, they spend most of their time in New York. The rest of the clan down here is pretty rough. The Coll brothers are all crazy as hell and wouldn't hesitate to kill anyone that got in their way. As a result, the local police mostly leave them alone. If they stick to bootlegging, they won't have much of a problem with the law. I know it sounds crazy, but the police and the revenue agents just don't have the resources to stop every suspicious truck that comes through."

Bob Brooks spoke up. "Ray, I can't afford to keep insuring the autos, trucks, and boats these men are stealing, not to mention the property they have damaged or destroyed. You gotta do better than that."

Ray looked at me. "Agent Clark, how confident are you the evidence you have will hold up?"

Before I could answer, Agent Pierce said, "They're good. We haven't been able to pin any auto thefts on the Colls—only a few of their gang. They have a very good numbers man, and the paperwork is as good as we've seen."

"I inspected a Chrysler a few days ago with a fake FEDCO plate on the dash. Those are hard to come by. The interesting thing I found, though, is that the serial number on the motor had only been ground off. If they have such a good numbers guy, why do such a sloppy job on that vehicle?"

Agent Pierce's expression told us he didn't have any idea.

"We only have a handful of stolen autos in Jacksonville that we traced back up here—so far. However, I just saw a half-dozen new Fords on the Goldberg lot, and although I was only able to inspect one of them, I'll bet money they are all stolen. Based on the volume of business Goldberg does, there would have to be dozens, maybe well over a hundred stolen automobiles running through his dealerships or used lots. How would these boys move that many vehicles that far? Automobile thieves usually only cross one state line—not five. We're talking about well over six hundred miles," I exclaimed.

Pierce replied, "That's a lot of driving. Maybe they're not as established as you think."

"The Clyde," said Agent Strong slowly, like he had just had an epiphany.

"Who?" I asked.

Strong replied, "It's a boat."

"They have their own ferry?"

"The Clyde line is a shipping company. They have steamers all up and down the East Coast, from New York to Florida. They even go to Cuba. There's a ship that stops here a couple of times a week at least—on it's way to Savannah, Jacksonville, Palm Beach—name your port. That would be the most efficient way to transport multiple vehicles at a time."

"Makes sense," said Brooks. "Mix the stolen autos in with all the legit ones being shipped south. There could be dozens of legit autos on any given shipment, though—how would you pick out the stolen ones? You can't possibly inspect every automobile on board."

"True. But if we knew ahead of time which ones were suspicious, we could narrow the list down considerably," said Agent Strong.

Hagood and I were looking at each other grinning because we were both thinking the same thing.

"We already know which ones are suspicious," I said. "We have a list of them."

Every week the NATB was responsible for publishing a bulletin of all the stolen cars from the previous week. These bulletins, or hot sheets, listed each vehicle by make and model and included the identification numbers and tags. Weekly bulletins were usually mailed on Friday to every police and sheriff departments as well as every Bureau of Investigation office. Our region included nine states, and the mailings numbered about two thousand a week. Friday afternoons were "all hands on deck" as the staff sat around conference tables, folding and stuffing envelopes.

"You have a list?" Strong asked, looking at Agent Pierce.

"Sure do," Hagood said.

"Outstanding. Why don't you get your list while I call down to the docks and find out when the next Clyde will be there?" offered Strong. "Care to take a steamer back to Savannah, Agent Clark?"

* * *

"Julian, let me walk you out," Brooks said. "I want to introduce you to my son Joe before you leave. He's headed to the Georgia coast this weekend."

"You don't say?" I asked.

Bob led me down the hall to another office and stuck his head in to ask his son if he had a few minutes. I heard him say, "Sure thing, Dad. What's up?"

"This here is Julian Clark from Jacksonville. His daddy and I go way back. He's investigating a possible automobile theft ring down in Savannah—it's actually one of our customers."

"Really?" Joe asked. "Which one?"

"Goldberg. Remember those three stolen cars in Savannah that we paid a claim on recently?" said Brooks.

Joe replied, "Oh, yeah. I talked to Mr. Bloomberg about it not too long ago. What's the story?"

I decided to jump in. Shaking Joe's hand, I added, "We think Goldberg, or somebody associated with his dealership, is moving stolen cars through Savannah. By the way, nice to meet you."

"So what brings you up here?"

"Well, so far we traced the stolen autos back to Baltimore, and a couple of detective buddies down yonder suggested talking to your dad as well as a Bureau contact up here."

Bob Brooks added, "I just introduced him to Ray Strong and Hagood Pierce."

"Ray and I are headed down to the port to check out the inventory on a steamer headed south," I said. "It stops in Savannah. It's a long shot, but I figured it's worth a try at least before I head back to Jacksonville."

"Say, Julian, you should come over to Sea Island this weekend. There's a big party on Saturday night. You go through Brunswick on your way home, right?" asked Joe.

"Your grandfather used to spend a lot of time out there fishing, if memory serves me," said Bob.

"Wait, you fish, Julian?" asked Joe.

"You better believe it. Especially saltwater."

"I have a better idea," Joe said. "Why don't we meet early Saturday morning and I'll take you out fishing? I keep a little boat down there on Sapelo. We'll be done with plenty of time to get cleaned up for dinner at the Cloister."

Sapelo Island. The Cloister. I knew Frances was expecting me home this weekend, but I would have to be a fool to not take him up on this offer. While I stood there mulling it over, Joe added, "Goldberg will be there."

"I'm in."

* * *

By that afternoon I was standing on the starboard side of one of the Clyde Line's steamers, watching the dock disappear in the distance, wondering how I ended up here. What would Frances think if she knew where I was at this moment?

Agent Strong had a source down at the dock that told us when the next ship was due. He was able to get my Chevrolet on board just in time—compliments of the Bureau. He was also able to find out that there were twenty-six new and used automobiles on board from five different manufacturers. We really needed to see the paperwork on all of them, but we decided not to take a chance that the Coll gang had a guy at the dock or on the inside at the Clyde that could twist us up. We were hoping to get lucky and find at least one match on board.

The autos were located on a lower deck. It was just above the water so they could easily drive the vehicles down a ramp into the ship. Regardless of the tide, it was easy to get them on or off. It also probably helped stabilize the ship by putting all of that weight closer to the water to lower the ship's center of gravity.

The hold could probably carry as many as fifty automobiles, but on this trip it had a variety of what looked like heavy marine equipment and shipping crates of different sizes filling up the space not occupied by autos, which were parked mostly in the front of the hold. The lighting wasn't bad, but I was definitely going to need a flashlight to see under the hood. Luckily, I found one mounted on a bracket next to a fire hose and case with an ax in it. The flashlight was a heavy industrial model painted with the same gray marine paint as everything else in the hold.

A shipping clerk sat in a small office with a large glass window in the rear corner. The clerk was responsible for checking cargo in and out and keeping an eye on everything in general. Somehow I needed to get a look at the manifest in that office, but first I had to determine if any of these automobiles were suspicious.

I had a list of seven in my pocket that Hagood had pulled from the office bulletin. It had been a busy week for thieves in Baltimore. My list had four Fords, two Chryslers, and a Nash on it so at least I could narrow it down. I decided to check the Chryslers first and see if their FEDCO plates had been tampered with and then confirm that the numbers at least matched up with the year, make, and model. Once I ruled those out, I could start checking the Fords. I'd have to get under the hoods to check those.

Checking the vehicles turned out to be a lot easier than I originally anticipated. The people on board were all above deck, so my only real concern about getting caught was the shipping clerk in the little office. Fortunately, several large crates and most of the automobiles blocked his view from where he was sitting at the desk. A steel support beam just outside the office provided additional cover.

I found the first Chrysler immediately because it was white and easy to spot. The FEDCO plate matched the make and model, and it appeared to be a straight automobile, so I started looking for the next one. I couldn't find the second one so I started looking for the Fords, keeping my head down while sneaking from vehicle to vehicle as quietly as possible. Locating the first one, I carefully opened the door to release the hood, trying not to make too much noise. The sound of the steam engine gave me plenty of cover, but I couldn't be too careful. The first two Fords were straight, so I started looking for number three. I found it closer to the middle of the hold.

Before long I determined this one had been tampered with. The numbers on the block had been filed off without much concern for concealing the job. While I was leaning down inside the engine compartment, I accidentally dropped the big flashlight, which clanked a few times on its way down past the motor before it landed on the deck with a loud thud. I froze to listen for any sign the clerk heard the noise. I waited a full minute before I recovered the light and gently closed the hood. I decided to hide behind a large crate for several minutes just to be sure.

The next automobile on my list was harder to find, but I finally located it near the far side of the hold, farthest from the office. It was a red Nash four-dour sedan. I wasn't exactly sure where to find the serial number on this model, so even after checking my notes, it still took me several minutes to locate it—or at least the spot where it should have been. While I was still leaning over the sill, I noticed a shadow of something, or someone, being thrown across the engine compartment. Somebody was standing behind me.

Before I even had time to turn around, the hood was coming down on my back. I arched up to prevent it from closing any farther while whoever was behind me was trying to force my head down. With the flashlight in my hand, I was able to get it up and positioned between the hood and the frame, so there was no way the person trying to crush me underneath could close it any further. The weight of the giant hood still had me pinned underneath, and that's when I caught the first punch to my kidney. My side was totally exposed, and unless I figured something out fast, my assailant had a clear shot to use my kidney like a punching bag. The pain was excruciating.

Sensing the position of my attacker just to my left and slightly behind me, I had to come up with some offense fast. It was a desperate move that required some luck. Before he could get in another punch, I used my left leg to kick with all I could muster toward what I hoped would be a kneecap. I was slightly off, connecting with his leg just below his knee, but the angle was good. I felt his lower leg give, and then a primal scream came from behind as he went down. I forced the hood back up with my back and grabbed the flashlight before letting the hood slam back down.

My attacker was writing in pain on the floor. As I turned to face the clerk that had been sitting in the office, he started rolling under a piece of equipment parked in the opposite aisle. The way they had stacked the cargo, there wasn't enough room for me to squeeze through to the other side without going to the end of the row and around. So I had to scramble all the way down one side and around the last crate to come back up the other aisle.

By the time I got to the other side, the clerk was nowhere to be seen. Just as I started to get down on all fours to do a quick search from deck level, I heard a grunt behind me. As I turned, he was coming at me while clearly favoring his left leg, which made him slower and put him off balance. He was wielding an iron bar or tool of some kind and had it cocked back like he was going to crush my skull with it. He was swinging for the fences, so I used the flashlight to deflect the bar and simultaneously ducked. As the bar barely cleared my forehead, I gave him a jab to the midsection with my right fist first and then another quick jab with the flashlight in my left that made solid contact to his right abdominal oblique.

It felt crunchy—maybe I got a rib. Regardless, I could tell he was in serious pain from the guttural sound that left his mouth, but not enough to give up. His swing had his torso wound up tight, so he released all of that energy with a back hand swing towards my head. I was ready for it. I ducked under the iron bar again, and its weight forced him to over rotate in the other direction, but this time I lunged into his midsection, jolting him up against the wooden shipping crate behind him, forcing the air out of his lungs. But not before he brought the heavy bar down on my back.

As he started to slump toward the floor, I used the heavy flashlight to jam him in the gut, making sure he didn't get a breath, and then I brought it straight up under his chin, connecting solidly and snapping his head back against the crate. The sickening thud was followed by his total collapse onto the floor in a heap at my feet.

I heard footsteps coming from the other end of the aisle, but as I turned to run the other direction, I heard a voice say, "Clark!" I turned to find Raymond Strong coming toward me with his gun at his side. My attacker was out cold, and when Agent Strong strode up, he said, "I guess you don't need my help, after all."

"What in the hell are you doing here?" I asked.

"Mr. Brooks suggested I tag along and keep an eye on you. We were both suspicious that the guys at the dock were working for Coll, so we figured they probably had connections with the shipping company. What happened?"

"I was checking under the hood of one of those automobiles when this guy sneaks up behind me and slams the hood on my back. He tried to crush me with it before coming at me with that piece of pipe."

Ray bent down to check for a pulse before saying, "I'm willing to bet this guy is being paid by the Coll gang. Why else would he jump you like that without even asking you what you were doing under the hood of that Ford?"

"Is he okay?" I asked.

"He's still breathing. What'd you hit him with?" Strong asked.

I raised up my flashlight.

Strong said, "Nice."

"At least now we can take a look at that manifest in his office without having to ask," I added with a grin.

"Did you find anything under that hood?" he asked.

"It's what I didn't find that matters—no serial numbers. At least two of these automobiles appear to be stolen. Let's go take a look at the paperwork and find out where they are headed."

Ray and I dragged the unconscious clerk back to his office and laid him carefully on the floor next to his desk. While Agent Strong checked his pockets for identification, I found the manifest on his desk and started comparing it to my list. The two suspicious vehicles were being shipped to a dealer named Savannah Motors. I seriously doubted it was a coincidence.

Strong looked up. "What did you learn?"

"Well, they are definitely headed to Savannah. Some dealer called Savannah Motors."

"Are you familiar with them?" he asked.

"Never heard of them," I replied. "Probably owned by Goldberg." I tore the page out of the manifest, folded it up, and put it in my pocket.

"Let's get out of here before somebody comes looking for this creep," said Strong.

"What do we do with him?"

"Just leave him. What's he going to say? 'I found somebody looking under the hood of one of those automobiles, so I tried to kill him without asking any questions?'"

"Let me go finish checking that Nash, and then I'll meet you back up on deck." I grimaced as I noticed how painful by back and side felt. I reached back with my hand where one of the hinges on that hood had jabbed me and felt a wet spot.

Strong noticed what I was doing and said, "It's only a flesh wound, Julian. I think you'll live."

Chapter 5

With my Chevrolet safely parked on solid ground and my body a little worse for the wear, I was glad to be back in Savannah. I was sore, to say the least. I had a couple of huge bruises on my back and a cut where the hood hit me. My side ached from the kidney punch I took, and I moved a little slower because of the pain.

The Western Union office was on Bay Street, not far from the port and on my way to the police department anyway, so I decided to go let Frances know where I was and where I had been. I also needed to let Gwyneth know I was back in Savannah and check and see if Coonts had left any instructions.

The clerk saw me come in the door, and she immediately stood up and walked over to a file of telegrams on the front desk.

"Hello, Agent Clark, welcome back to Savannah," she said with a smile.

NATB agents traveled all of the time, and we used Western Union for a variety of services. Western Union had phones, but telegrams were the cheapest way to send word. The NATB had an account with Western Union, so we could charge our calls or telegrams directly to our account, and we could also use them to get cash for our travel expenses.

I had been in this office two days earlier, and I never forget a face—especially one like hers. I'm sure we hadn't met before.

Peering over the counter to read her name tag, I said, "Thank you—Rachel."

Before I could ask if they had any messages for me, she produced two envelopes and said, "You received two telegrams while you were away. I printed them both myself as soon as they came in, and I put them aside for you. Here you go."

"That was mighty kind of you, Rachel. Thank you," I replied.

There was a brief moment of awkwardness as she stood there expectantly smiling at me before saying; "They both require a response, so I'll be happy to prepare your reply when you're ready."

"Okay, I'll be right over there until I'm ready," I said pointing to the high-top table across the room where they kept all of the writing supplies and blank paper. "Thanks. Say, I, uh, didn't get your last name."

She smiled and said, "McCarthy."

"What a coincidence," I said more to myself than to her.

"Excuse me?"

"Oh, nothing," as I took my telegrams and headed across the room.

The first telegram was from Aubrey Warren in Atlanta.

JULIAN, I'VE BEEN WORKING ON A CASE IN WAYCROSS FOR SEVERAL MONTHS. MOE STEVENS. COONTS TOLD ME YOU WERE IN SAVANNAH.WOULD LOVE SOME COMPANY. IT'S ON YOUR WAY. LET ME KNOW. AUBREY

The second telegram was from Gwyneth.

JULIAN. AUBREY WARREN CALLED LOOKING FOR YOU. HE HAS A CASE TO WRAP UP, PROBABLY WITH AN ARREST, IN WAYCROSS. SOUNDS DANGEROUS. GENE SAID TO REMIND YOU, DO NOT GO TO WAYCROSS. BE CAREFUL. G

Gwyneth knew me all too well. So did Director Coonts, for that matter. After reading them both twice, I pulled out a blank telegram form to write a reply. I included a telegram to Frances to let her know I was fine and still in Savannah. When I was done, I took it over to Rachel to charge our account and send. Then I made plans to drive to Waycross—that's where the action was.

As I left the Western Union office, I glanced back over my shoulder to get one last look at Rachel before rounding the corner of the building. She was watching me leave with that big smile, only now she was holding the telephone up to her ear.

* * *

When I arrived at the police department, the clerk at the front desk had a note for me. It was from Detective Byrne. He wanted to see me before I left town—something about Neinstein. I asked the clerk where I could find Byrne, and he told me to check his office first and if he wasn't there, try the break room. "He's usually making coffee this time of day."

"Are you sure it's okay?" I asked. Normally, cops didn't like outsiders walking around their offices without an escort.

"Don't worry about it, Julian. Almost everyone knows who you are. If anyone says anything, just tell them I said it was okay."

"If you say so. Thanks."

As I rounded the corner and stepped into the inner sanctum of the Savannah PD, several heads turned to check me out. After a cursory glance, everyone went back to his phone calls or reports or whatever they were doing, so I headed back to Byrne's office. When I got there, it was empty, but I lingered long enough to draw the attention of another officer whose desk was across from Byrne's. Byrne's office was spotless and the organization was impressive.

"Can I help you?" asked the young man across the hall.

"Oh. Hey. No. I'm just looking for Thomas Byrne. The clerk up front told me to come on back here or try the break room."

"I just saw him head that way."

"Thanks."

The Savannah PD was like every other police department I'd been inside, including Jacksonville, where the NATB office was located. Lots of cheap office furniture was crammed in too small a space, which made for a cluttered and chaotic workspace. The air smelled like coffee and cigarettes, and paper—lots of paper. Stacks of case files were piled on just about every desk, and the sound of chatter and phone conversations created a buzz that reminded me of our office. Amid so much activity hardly anyone noticed I was there.

I found the break room and sure enough, Thomas was waiting on the coffee maker. The obligatory box of donuts on one of the tables looked inviting, so I walked over and flipped the lid back. Byrne heard me and turned around.

"Agent Clark. Glad to see you made it back from Baltimore. Sounds like you found a little excitement up there," said Bryne.

"Not much gets by you people, does it?" I replied.

"What'd ya mean?"

"You can't break wind in this town without somebody in McCarthy's office knowing about it," I said as I sank my teeth into a glazed donut.

"Help yourself to the donuts, Clark. Want some coffee? It's fresh."

"Don't mind if I do. So what's this business you and I have?"

"Actually, it's your business. You aren't leaving until the morning right?"

"That was my plan. Is there some reason I should change it?"

"Nope. That's perfect for what I have in mind. We're going to take a closer look at Al Neinstein's Cadillac."

"Wait a minute. Captain McCarthy told me not to go anywhere near that guy."

"Let me worry about the captain. Besides, Neinstein won't be there. Actually, your pal Agent Vernon Chris is the one you need to thank. He's been keeping a close eye on our boy Neinstein, waiting for him to step in dog shit. He runs a pretty clean operation, but Vernon found out he and Goldberg are headed to Brunswick today, so nobody's going to be there."

"Are you talking about the used-auto lot?"

"Hell, no. That Caddy should be in the garage out back of his house."

"You're going to break into his garage—without a warrant?" I asked.

"Nope. You are. I'll keep lookout while you check the Caddy to see if it's stolen."

"And what if it is?"

"We'll cross that bridge when we get there. Let's find out if it's hot first, and then we can decide what to do."

"What if he comes home while I'm in his garage?"

"Don't worry about it, Julian. Agent Chris followed them down to Brunswick. He'll let us know if they leave before dark. If not, we'll have plenty of time to get over there, get you a look at that Cadillac, and get out long before they get back to town. Besides, you'd much rather run into Al than that gal he's been dating. She's got a mean streak the likes of which you've never seen, and she gets nasty when she's been drinking. I've never seen her sober."

"Sounds like fun. What time?" I asked.

"I'll pick you up at the hotel at dark."

"See you then," I said as I headed for the door. "By the way, thanks for the donuts."

* * *

Detective Byrne was right on time. He pulled up in front of the DeSoto just after dark in his Chrysler Roadster. At least the top was up. I hopped in, and he didn't waste any time pulling away from the curb as we sped off.

"We're riding in style tonight. Just like a couple of swells heading to the club."

"More like a couple of gangsters," Byrne said.

"I take it we're clear?" I asked.

"For at least two hours," Byrne replied.

"Let's do this."

Detective Byrne drove with a purpose. He had the respect for the road that a lawman should demonstrate, but he was pushing the limits of that Chrysler every chance he got, and we made quick time getting to Neinstein's. I think he was still torqued up about the provenance of his automobile, and the opportunity for retribution was burning inside him. When we got to Neinstein's neighborhood, he slowed almost to a stop and crept along the curb until he felt like we were safely out of view.

The Chrysler was parked in the shadows away from any lights, in front of a wooded lot. The nearest house was on the other side of the street, a good twenty-five yards behind us. The street reached a T-fork in front of us. Neinstein's was to the right, one house down on the left, Byrne had explained.

"Are you armed?" he asked.

"Yeah, but I thought you said—"

He interrupted, "You never know. And believe me when I say that his moll is a real Irish hothead."

"Got it. What's the plan?"

"Once you get across the street, I'll come over and hide in the lot next door behind that fence and keep lookout. The Cadillac is parked right next to the fence, so if I see anything or anybody, I'll give you a signal like this."

Byrne had a metal clicker in his pocket that he pulled out. When he pressed on the center of the thin-bowed piece, it made a loud click, and when he released it, it made another loud click as it went back to its original shape. He pressed and released quickly to make two loud click-click sounds.

He said, "If you hear this, take cover and hold," and he made it click-click. "If you hear the same sound again, that means all clear and get back to it, but if you hear a double click get out as fast as you can."

I said, "One click-click, take cover and two click-clicks, get out."

"Right. If I tell you to take cover, just wait for another click-click for the all clear. How much time do you need to check the numbers?"

"Once I'm under the hood, I only need about two minutes." This model should have a serial number plate mounted to the firewall inside the engine compartment opposite the driver. It should also have matching numbers on the engine block and frame rail. The engine block number was located on the crankcase on the right-hand side. Unfortunately, to do a thorough job, I needed to get a look under both cowlings, but I should be able to see the serial number plate from the right side, so I'd start there in case I didn't get time to get under the left one.

Byrne said, "Okay, good. Let's do this."

I got out and closed the door as quietly as possible and started walking toward the house. It was totally dark, with no sign of anyone at home, so I headed up the drive around the back. I looked back and saw Bryne crossing the street to enter the driveway next door on the other side of the fences.

Neinstein's Caddy was parked right where Byrne said it would be. Fortunately, he had backed it into the spot immediately behind the house, so the right side of the vehicle was away from the back door. I carefully opened the right side engine cowling and propped it open.

I had a small penlight that I used to locate the engine block numbers, and they appeared to be clean. Six digits. No evidence of tampering. I memorized the numbers to write down later. As I leaned across the motor to locate the serial number plate, I heard a door shut out front. I froze to listen for signs of someone approaching and heard a woman's voice and then laughter. It was more like a cackle— a lot like a drunk Irish lady. I found the plate right where it should be—the numbers matched. So far so good. Then somebody switched on the lights inside.

Click-click! Shit.

I eased back out from under the hood and froze waiting for another signal. None came, but I could hear voices inside. The woman definitely sounded drunk. The other voice belonged to a man. Criminy. I was slowly backing up to close the hood when I accidentally bumped into a trashcan. The lid fell off and rattled around on the ground before it finally came to rest. I immediately hit the ground behind the Caddy. The portico light flicked on above me.

Click-click. Click-click.

I was pinned down. If I got up, they would surely see me. I could hear the woman yelling something inside, but I couldn't make it out. Then the back door opened and she stuck her head out. "I'll cut yer balls off if'n I catch ya!" she yelled.

"Baby, come back inside. It's just a raccoon or something trying to get in the garbage," said the man's voice.

"Why doncha go check it out then, Mr. big shot," she slurred.

"Baby, it's nothing. Listen, they're already gone."

"Some man you are. Scared of a raccoon. Stay out of my garbage," she yelled out the door and then started giggling.

The door slammed shut, and I could hear more laughing inside.

Click-click. Click-click.

Really, Detective Byrne? You think I don't know I need to get out of here?

The light went dark, so I took off and didn't bother with the other side. I had seen enough to know the Cadillac was straight. Too bad. By the time I got to the bottom of the driveway, Thomas was coming out of the drive next door and practically ran into me.

"What happened?" he asked. "Did you get a look inside?"

"What happened was, they came home."

"Who was it?"

"That crazy Irish woman you warned me about, and I assume Al Neinstein."

Thomas was trying to stifle a laugh as we crossed the street. "Impossible," he said. "There's no way he could have made it back that fast, and besides, I heard his voice. That definitely wasn't Al Neinstein."

We had barely made it across the street when we heard the front door open. We both looked back to see a drunk lady stumble out on the front lawn before screaming, "I see you sons a bitches! I told you I was gonna cut yer balls off if I caught ya." She tried to give chase but took two steps and fell flat on her face. By the time we got back to Byrne's vehicle, she had gotten back up and was screaming again, only we couldn't understand a word she said. We heard two loud bangs as he started that Chrysler.

"What the hell?" said Byrne. "She's shooting at us. I outta go arrest her drunk ass."

"Boy, you weren't kidding. She's nuts!" I said. We both sat there for a few seconds in silence before we both broke out laughing. "Let's get out of here. We got what we came for." Detective Byrne began backing up until he had enough room to turn around so we could head out the way we came.

* * *

The next morning as I was checking out of the hotel, I heard a familiar voice behind me. "Julian?"

"Vernon? What are you doing?"

"I'm staying here," he replied. "I wish I had known you were here before now."

"Oh, and why is that?"

"Well, I could have bought you dinner last night, and besides, I could use a few minutes of your time to get an update on that case you're working on."

At least he was careful enough not to mention Goldberg's name in the lobby of the DeSoto Hotel. No telling how many people in here knew the man and his business. I looked around for some privacy and said, "Sure thing, Vernon. How about joining me for a quick cup of coffee over there at that table?"

"I'm right behind you," Vernon said.

I set my suitcase down next to the table and pulled out a chair while Vernon grabbed a cup of coffee. When he finally sat down, I briefed him on my trip to Baltimore. I told him about my conversation with Bob Brooks and Vernon's counterpart in Maryland, Ray Strong. He asked a lot of good questions about the case, particularly about the Coll gang and possible insurance fraud by Bloomberg. He got a real kick out of my scrum on the Clyde but seemed genuinely concerned about my well-being. It was obvious I wasn't one hundred percent. I also told Vernon about my opportunity to go to Sea Island with Joe Brooks.

"Sounds like it was well worth the trip to Maryland and back. Thanks for the debrief. We'll keep an eye on Goldberg while you and Coonts continue building your case. If you need anything from the Bureau, don't hesitate to ask."

"Thanks, Vernon. We appreciate the help. Now I need to get moving."

* * *

The drive to Brunswick was about eighty miles and then it was about another sixty miles west to Waycross. The road to Waycross seemed much longer because it was mostly macadam and in some places it was more like driving on crushed oysters. Waycross was about a third of the way to Atlanta from

Jacksonville, so I'd spent a fare amount of time there, and I always stayed at the Ware Hotel on Elizabeth Street. There was a Western Union next door, and the clerk's name was Roberta Ward.

Her face lit up when I walked in the door. "Hi, Agent Clark. It's so good to see you again. How are things down in Jacksonville? How's Frances?"

"Thanks for asking, Roberta, it's great to see you too. Things are just fine. We love it in Florida—so far."

She replied, "Well, I'm glad to hear it. You must be back in town on business. I've got a package here for you that was delivered this morning from the office in Atlanta." She handed over what felt like a thick file or stack of papers wrapped in brown paper and taped up on the sides. Written across the top in big letters it read, "Confidential," and underneath was "Agent Clark, NATB."

As I started to tear the paper off, Roberta looked around to make sure nobody was paying attention to us and then leaned in. "Julian, I know what this is all about. You be careful. That's a sorry bunch out there, and everybody knows they're dangerous."

"Thanks for the warning, Roberta," I said. "I'll be careful, and don't worry, I'm not going out there alone. I'll be over at the Ware if anything comes through for me."

"I know where to find you," she said as I headed for the door. "Agent Warren will meet you over there."

I was almost through the door when she asked, "Agent Clark, do you want me to let Mr. Coonts know you're here?"

"Um, I don't think so." I replied. "Thanks."

* * *

While I sat in the lobby of the Ware Hotel waiting for Aubrey Warren to arrive, I read through the case file that had been delivered that morning. Warren was leading the investigation from our Atlanta office, but he was semi-retired and getting up there in years. He couldn't get around like he used to.

He was a great agent and his notes were very thorough and easy to follow. Most of the evidence had been gleaned from an informant named Jimmy Walker. Apparently, Jimmy had been paling around with Moe Stevens's youngest son Will for some time and had seen a lot of things that his momma and daddy had told him he needed to tell the sheriff. Eventually, Aubrey had been able to set up a meeting with the Walker kid, and based on one of his tips, they located the first stolen auto. It was amazing how often a thief's undoing was a simple tip from an innocent witness that saw something that didn't look right.

So this family that everyone in Waycross was scared of had this big farm out in the country. It had several outbuildings, including a couple of huge barns in addition to the main house, which looked like a plantation mansion. The farm spanned several hundred acres, and the house was set way back in the woods so you could barely see it from the road. Agent Warren had a rough sketch of the property included in the file along with several grainy photographs taken surreptitiously from the road.

Mr. Stevens's wife had died a long time ago, and he lived out there with his three sons, Bobby, Amos, and Will. Apparently, a couple of high yellow women lived with him too. Aubrey suspected that Will was probably the son of one of those women. He was at least ten years younger than Amos, and looked nothing like his daddy.

The farm had a big pond, and Will fished in it during the spring and summer. Jimmy said they also played in the barns and in the haylofts. The barns were always full of hay, but he never saw any livestock or farm animals, so he never could figure out what they needed all that hay for.

Jimmy said one day they were playing out in the barn when he noticed an automobile buried under the hay. On another occasion, this young man noticed several late-model Fords hidden in the other barn and a huge stack of hay bales piled in front of the doors.

As I finished reading the case file, the dapper old Aubrey Warren himself came walking into the lobby of the Ware.

"Well, look what the cat dragged in," I said.

"Very funny. Having fun down there in Jacksonville? At least you haven't lost your sense of humor yet—*Agent* Clark." He enunciated the word *agent* with an air of haughtiness as if the moniker had been mistakenly given to me.

"As a matter of fact, I am."

"So what do you think?" he asked, sitting down.

"I think it's clear that getting older is easier than getting wiser," I replied.

"About the case file, wise guy, did you read it?"

"Oh, that. Interesting. It's very thorough. Written like a real detective. Who'd you get to write it? Flannigan?"

Flannigan was a junior clerk in the Atlanta office.

"You're hilarious."

"What do you need me for?" I asked.

"I need someone to hold my colostomy bag while I arrest this character. Think you can handle that, young man?"

"As long as you don't mistake me for somebody else and shoot me."

Aubrey Warren was at least sixty years old, and one of the best agents in the Bureau. He still had a head full of jet-black hair, a thin dark mustache, and wore a pair of thick, black, square-framed glasses. He was stocky with broad shoulders, and he always wore the same black felt fedora, dark suit, black oxford corfams, and black tie. His white shirts were crisply starched, and his shoes were like mirrors he polished them so much. He looked like Clark Gable—except for the glasses—and to most in the detective world he was a super man.

Aubrey was a retired Atlanta police detective that needed something to keep him busy. His wife had been murdered five years earlier by a member of the Chicago Outfit, and he didn't have any kids. It was a senseless act of vengeance.

Aubrey had been investigating a bank robbery and finally caught up with one of the robbers coming out of a speak in Atlanta. The crook jumped in his automobile and tried to run Aubrey down on his way out of the lot. Aubrey fired a single shot right through the windshield and into the face of Slim Serrano. What he didn't know was that he had a young lady in the front that unfortunately was the paramour of one Anthony Carfano—Slim's boss. Slim died instantly and the vehicle, completely out of control, ran through the intersection and got T-boned by a milk truck. The truck hit the passenger door, killing the young lady on impact. Carfano put a hit out on Aubrey's wife to get even. The irony was, the milk truck was hauling illegal booze, which was Carfano's line of business.

Aubrey was a real character, and he had taught me most of what I know about detective work. He also taught me how to fight with my hands and defend myself in close quarters. He was a state folkstyle wrestling champion in both middle and high school, and he learned judo after high school. Both disciplines required strength, alertness, resiliency, and, above all, agility and quickness. They also demanded mental focus.

He coached high school wrestling up until a few years ago, and we spent a lot of time in the gym together, so I developed very quick hands, great core strength, balance, and especially agility. Aubrey proclaimed my hand-to-hand wrestling skills as good as anyone he had trained. I doubted that, but I could hold my own. Unlike Aubrey, I was a notoriously bad shot, so I had to learn self-defense.

He was a gem and working with him was an honor. That fact that he wanted me out there in Waycross meant a lot, and there was no way I would have passed up this chance. Besides, if he got in trouble or got killed, I would never forgive myself.

"Coonts know you're here?" he asked.

"Nope," I replied.

"Are you sure you want to do this?"

"I wouldn't be here if I didn't. Don't worry about Coonts—he'll be fine."

* * *

When we pulled up to the house in my Bureau Chevrolet, a late-model Ford was parked right out front. A beautiful black on black Model A coupe with black wheels. It had an Alabama plate.

The house was pretty impressive with six huge white columns along the front, but it was in dire need of paint and it didn't look like anyone had taken care of the place in years. Two massive live oaks on either side provided shade for the entire house, and the yard was basically dirt and weeds. The first two feet of brick all across the front looked like someone had painted it a rust color. With nothing covering the red clay around the foundation, the rain had pelted it so frequently it had splashed up and stained the bottom of the house. Gaps dotted the railing along the front porch where balusters were broken or missing altogether.

A nice little side yard had a picket fence around it, but it was in need of paint too, and the gate hung from its hinges at an angle that made it drag on the ground. There was a semicircle of worn grass and dirt where it swung open, carving a place in the dirt if it wasn't lifted. There were several tombstones in the little yard behind the fence, and an old swing hung from one of the oak's massive limbs. The seat looked rotten and probably couldn't support any weight.

The file on Moe said he was seventy-one years old, and an older gentleman was sitting in a big rocker on the front porch. As soon as we pulled up, he got up out of his chair and walked over to the top of the steps as if he were going to greet us when we got out. He might be seventy-one, but he looked to be well over six feet tall and carried himself like he was still in pretty good physical shape. He had a thin, wispy, dark brown comb-over and several days of grayish stubble on his face. He was wearing dark blue coveralls like a mechanic and had an unlit cigar hanging out of the corner of his mouth. He fit the description Jimmy Walker had given Aubrey.

Aubrey and I got out of the vehicle, and while I walked around to the passenger side to join Aubrey, the old man stood there watching us. Aubrey finally commented, "That sure is a fine-looking automobile you got there. Looks brand-new. Does it belong to you?"

"Who's asking?" the old man replied. The cigar in his mouth wagged up and down when he spoke.

Aubrey let the question hang out there for a few seconds before I finally asked, "Say, are you Mr. Stevens? We were told a Moe Stevens lived here and owns this here farm."

Before he could answer, a man that looked to be in his late twenties came from around the side of the house. He walked over and sat down on the fender of that Model A, pulled a knife out of a sheath on his belt, and started cleaning his fingernails with it. He was wearing denim coveralls with no shirt on underneath, and he had a dust-covered hat on that was pulled down low so you could barely see his face. He had a big barrel chest, wide shoulders, and thick biceps sculpted by years of manual labor. The young man must have been two inches taller than his daddy and had distinct tan lines on his arms and neck so I could tell he normally wore a T-shirt under his overalls. The tan on his face and forearms was so dark, it made me wonder if there wasn't a little something else in the woodpile. I assumed it was Moe's oldest son, Bobby.

The old man chewed the end of his cigar and then spit on the ground before saying, "I don't know who that Ford belongs to. Got up this morning and it was just sittin' there. Got no idea where it came from."

"Is that so?" said Aubrey. "In that case I guess you won't mind if we take a look at it. By the way, I'm Aubrey Warren, and this here is Agent Clark from the National Auto Theft Bureau." Aubrey never introduced himself as Agent Warren.

I was already walking around the vehicle to the driver's side, but I made sure to give the kid on the fender a wide berth. I didn't expect him to try anything dumb, but I wasn't about to give him the opportunity. As I got around the other side, I could see a package sitting on the back seat, so I opened the door and picked it up. The label said it was some kind of mule medicine, but the interesting part was it had Moe Stevens's name on it and the address of the farm. I held it up and said, "This yours?"

I could tell by the look on his face, old Moe realized he didn't have much wiggle room left. I decided it was time to double down, so I leaned in the driver's side and popped the hood. The sound of the hood release startled the young man sitting on the fender because he almost fell off trying to get back. As I walked around to the front of the automobile, he started backing toward the old man on the steps.

With as much trouble as Stevens had been in over his life, I'm sure he was smart enough to know we didn't have the authority to arrest him, and without a warrant, we couldn't search the place either. The NATB didn't have the authority to serve warrants or make arrests. We were going to need the sheriff or a marshal for that. But old Moe made a mistake when he didn't object to Aubrey asking him if we could take a look at that automobile.

As I raised the hood, I noticed movement in one of the windows of the house. Somebody was watching us from upstairs. A few seconds later another young man stumbled out the front door. He was tall like his brother but lean and lanky. At first I thought he might be afflicted with something, but then I realized he was half drunk. He tried to stand next to his daddy, but he was swaying so much he had to grab hold of the railing to steady himself. This had to be Amos, the middle son.

Moe finally decided he'd had enough. "Boys, this is private property. Unless you have a search warrant, you best get back in your vehicle and get out of here. We don't want any trouble, but me and my boys here don't have any problem with it if comes to that."

I hadn't had nearly enough time to determine if this automobile had been stolen, but he didn't know that, so I decided to push our luck a little. Besides, with all of the evidence we had learned from our informant, we had probable cause enough to search this place. I leaned out from around the hood so Aubrey could see me, and I gave him a subtle nod.

"So what's it going to be, boys?" Moe said while working that cigar around in his mouth.

The drunken kid slurred, "Yeah, what's it going to be? You got no business harassing us like this. We ain't done nothing wrong."

Agent Warren had been leaning up against my vehicle with his arms crossed nonchalantly during the entire exchange, but he was keeping an eye on Bobby, as well as looking for trouble in the windows of the house.

I slammed the hood of that Ford, which startled the whole bunch because their focus had been on Aubrey. I headed over to stand next to him, but this time I walked along the passenger side between the Ford and the front steps. The big kid had backed up to the bottom of the steps, so he was a good ten feet away.

"What do say you let us take a look in the big barn out back?" Aubrey

75

asked.

"I'm not sure you heard me. You're not searching shit, and you need to get in that vehicle and get off my property," Moe said.

Aubrey stood up straight and gave me a slight wink, then reached back and gave the back passenger door a couple of knocks. The door opened slowly as a mountain of a man climbed out and stood next to us. As he slowly put his hat on and straightened his uniform, he looked quite impressive with his right hand resting on the butt of his service weapon. In his left he held a piece of paper.

With a nod all he said was, "Gentlemen."

"This is Luther Rickman," Aubrey said. "U.S. Marshal."

The look on Moe Stevens's face said it all. His cigar just hung limp and the blank look belied the truth behind his scowl. He knew he was cooked. The paper in Luther's hand was a search warrant issued by a judge that morning, and Luther was the reinforcement Aubrey had been referring to after breakfast. Marshal Rickman was six and half feet tall with shoulders as wide as the rumble seat on that Ford. He looked like he'd been chiseled out of stone.

"This is bullshit!" cried Amos as he stumbled across the drive toward the Ford. Luther was walking toward Moe to hand him the warrant while Aubrey and I flanked him on either side. It didn't really occur to me what Amos was doing to my left until it was too late. He was already behind the wheel when I turned to check on him, so I turned and started running toward my automobile.

Rounding the back of my Chevrolet, I heard Aubrey yell, "Julian, get down!"

Instinctively I ducked as the first shot took a swatch of paint off the roof. It was followed by a second boom as the bark on the tree next to me exploded and bits of pine and chunks of bark rained down. Marshal Rickman already had his gun out and trained on Moe, but it was a woman on the porch that was holding the double-barrel shotgun.

By the time I got in my vehicle, gravel was already flying as Amos drove out of there in that stolen Ford like a scalded dog. Once I had the big V8 in my Chevrolet in gear and was throwing gravel of my own, I gave chase and headed down the drive, but he already had a good head start, and he didn't slow down to make the turn on the road.

The dirt road in front of the Stephens' place ran parallel to train tracks, and a train was coming by at the same time I peeled out of the drive. I looked up the road to locate Amos, but all I could see was a cloud of dust. The road dropped off steeply into a ditch on the right and was confined by the railroad tracks on the left. There wouldn't be an opportunity for Amos to turn until he got to the next intersection, probably a mile up, and that would take him over the train tracks.

The big locomotive was creating its own wake of dust and steam. It looked like a huge iron beast churning its way toward Atlanta. We were getting on pretty good when apparently the train engineer noticed the chase. He started blowing the giant whistle on top of the locomotive, which added to the excitement.

My Chevrolet roared as I gave it gas, and I knew I wouldn't have any trouble catching that drunken fool in front of me. My concern was Amos making the first sharp turn up ahead as the road veered away from the tracks around a swampy area before it came back out of the woods to join the tracks again. I was gaining on him fast, but I eased off a bit so as not to push him too hard around that turn. Amos was sideways by the time he got to the apex but somehow kept it under control. He made the second turn just as smoothly as the first and hit the straightaway joining the tracks with almost as much speed as when he entered the woods.

My Chevrolet was heavy and a little sluggish around the turns, but I jumped on the accelerator as I came out of those woods and controlled the under steer as I pushed it hard into the straightaway. The train was parallel to us now, and I was only about fifty yards behind Amos. It was clear he was trying to beat that train to the next intersection, still about a half-mile away. The race was on.

The Bureau knew about the headers and the special exhaust I had on my automobile, but they didn't know about the other modifications I had made. That engine was far from stock, and it had been tuned to precision by one of the best rodders in Atlanta. This was one of those times when I was glad to have the extra power. The big engine was responsive, and with every little bit of gas I gave her she gave me a little more speed. The automobile wasn't overpowered to the point I was out of control, but it was close. The undulations in the road made it more challenging because at the peak of each rise the vehicle became so light it went skyward.

Amos was doing pretty good keeping his car on the road, but he wasn't putting much distance between himself and that train. The tracks were elevated above the level of the road by a foot or two, and as we neared the intersection, the engineer was looking down on Amos and blowing the whistle.

Amos was pushing that Ford as hard as he could, trying to make that turn. By the time he got there, he didn't have enough room, and he had to brake hard to make the left-hand turn. I was sure he was going to get crushed, and I eased off the gas because I knew there was no way I could cross. As he came out of a skid, he punched the gas and shot forward up the little incline before the tracks and went airborne across the path of that train about a second before the train crossed the road. I couldn't believe he made it. It was unbelievably stupid, but at the same time I had to give the kid credit for such a daring escape.

I hit the brakes to wait for the train to pass as the giant cloud of dust that had been chasing me overtook my automobile and then got sucked into the vacuum the train created as it parted the air around it. Fortunately, it wasn't a long one, but it still took about a minute to clear the intersection. I had stopped only a few feet from the tracks, so when it finally passed I could feel the suction as the caboose sailed by.

I figured Amos was long gone, but I wasn't giving up. As I crossed the tracks, I assumed he had to go right because the road to the left would take him out of town while the road to the right headed into the little town of Waycross, which offered lots of places to hide.

As I wound up the big V8 to resume the chase, I noticed a cloud of dust up ahead on the right and what looked like that Ford parked on the side of the road. I couldn't believe my luck. Either he had crashed it into the ditch or broken something when he made the landing on the other side of the tracks, but either way, he was stopped dead.

As I neared the Ford, I could see Amos over in the tall grass, staggering around with something, but I couldn't tell what it was until I got up close. I couldn't believe he made it this far, as drunk as he was. As I pulled up behind the Ford, it was clear that something had broken like maybe a right front ball joint or maybe he had a flat tire and broken the wheel. The automobile was hunched over on its right front side like someone had removed the wheel altogether.

As I got out, Amos fell over in the grass, and I could hear him laughing and carrying on. While walking toward Amos, the strong smell of moonshine liquor hit me, and that's when I noticed all the jugs in the grass.

"Crazy bastard! You almost got yourself killed back there," I said.

He came at me swinging, but I sidestepped him and he fell over in the brush again. I could see the anger in his eyes and knew he was going to try something, so I pulled my gun on him. Seeing it, he finally settled down. I hauled him up and shoved him in the passenger seat of my Chevrolet and took him back to the farm.

By the time we got back to the Stevens' place, Aubrey and Luther had assembled some additional reinforcements to search the property. Earlier that morning after breakfast, we had called Sheriff Jim Spivey over in Valdosta to tell him what was going on, and he brought Deputy Sheriff Joe Campbell with him. In addition to the sheriff's department, Luther had four men from the U.S. Marshal service come out to help. Moe Stevens and his son Bobby were sitting in the back of the sheriff's automobile, and one of the women was sitting on the porch with Will, talking to the sheriff's deputy. I assume the one that tried to blow my head off was being detained in one of the other cars.

We found seventeen automobiles stashed in those barns, some completely buried in hay. Later, we recovered another ten automobiles from various garages and barns around town, including one from a deputy sheriff who claimed he bought it straight but couldn't remember from whom. We raised the body off that Model A in which Amos tried to escape and made a positive

ID after locating the confidential numbers. Like most of them, it had been stolen in Alabama.

It turns out one of those buildings on the farm was full of liquor. We confiscated a few cases of moonshine, but most of it was rum they were bringing up from Florida. It was pretty common to steal a few cars and use them for running red liquor up from Palm Beach, Miami, or just about anywhere along the coast. The rumrunners were bringing the liquor up from the Bahamas and Cuba on fast boats and then dropping it at different points along the coast.

Moe was going to be tried in federal court and most likely sent to federal prison in spite of his age. He was dangerous and with all those stolen cars and that liquor, he was going to do some hard time. Bobby and Amos would probably cut a deal to stay out of prison, and the judge would go easy on Will too. Even that lady with the shotgun would probably get off easy. She claimed that if she had wanted to kill me, she would have. She was just trying to slow me down so Amos could get away.

We paid the young informant who tipped us the information a twenty-five-dollar reward for each automobile we recovered.

* * *

Back at the Ware Hotel that night, I called Frances to let her know what happened that day, our successful bust of a sizeable theft operation in Waycross. I didn't tell her about getting shot at. Intuitively, she knew this was a dangerous job, but she didn't need to know all the details—at least not until I could talk to her face-to-face and explain the whole situation. She was just glad to hear we were all okay and that we had made some arrests. She asked about Roberta and told me to tell her hello.

I also told her about my impromptu trip on the Clyde steamer and our search for stolen cars on their way to Savannah. I left out the part about the guy that tried to kill me. Again, that would have to wait until I was back home.

"Baby, I have a favor to ask. I need you to call Bill McCoy for me and ask him to get my name on the guest list for the party at The Cloister Saturday night."

She replied, "How do you know Bill is going to be there Saturday night?"

"I don't. But it doesn't matter if he is or isn't. He can still get me on that list."

"I suppose you're right." Then after a brief pause, "So whom should I tell him you're going with?"

"Well, I'm sure I can scare up a date by then. Just tell him—"

"Julian Clark, you wouldn't dare!"

"Aw, Frances, you know I'm just kidding. Just make sure I'm on that list."

"I suppose you're going to find a way to squeeze in some fishing too?"

"You know me too well, baby. Joe Brooks and I are going after some redfish Saturday morning. It should be good fishing."

"You just make sure those reds are all you go fishing for on Saturday," she added.

"Thanks, baby. I got to go. I love you."

After talking to Frances, I finally worked up the courage to call Mr. Coonts and fill him in. He was irate and didn't stop yelling at me for several minutes. I had to hold the phone away from my ear while he blasted me about disobeying orders and wasting Bureau resources. If I had been in the office, I think he would have ripped me in half. I knew he was going to be angry but nothing like this. When he finally ran out of things to say, I apologized for ignoring his orders to stay away from Waycross and Agent Warren. He finally calmed down enough to ask me if Aubrey was okay.

"So what happened out there, Julian?"

I proceeded to tell him the whole story of the confrontation with the Stevens family, and of course getting shot at by that woman on the front porch. I think he was a little jealous when I told him about the chase.

Coonts didn't let up with his admonitions and reminded me he expected a full report when I got back to the office. He was still noticeably hot under the collar, but I think he felt some guilt over how hard he came down on me and tried to change the subject as a diversion. I felt terrible I put him in that position.

"Julian, what are you doing next on the Goldberg case?" he asked. "You need to get your butt back to Jacksonville and follow up on some leads unless you need to go back to Savannah."

I replied, "The other day when I was in Baltimore, I met with Bob Brooks to discuss the Goldberg vehicles, and he introduced me to his son Joe. It turns out Joe spends a lot of time down in this area and has gotten to know a few folks. You see, Joe likes to fish, and apparently he has quite a reputation for knowing where to find them. The swells started hiring him to take them fishing."

"Julian, what does this have to do with the Goldberg case?" he interrupted. Clearly, he was still on edge.

My voice cracked. "I'm getting to that part." I hesitated, wondering if I should even finish what I was about to say. "Joe invited me over to Sea Island this weekend for some fishing. He said there's going to be a shindig on Saturday night and all the swells will be there—including Asa Goldberg. I think this is a great opportunity to meet Goldberg and maybe subtly put him on notice."

"You can spend your weekend any way you want, but I'm only picking up the hotel and gas since this boondoggle is only loosely related to our work. Your meals are on you. We still have a budget to mind."

I said, "Sounds fair, Gene. I'm going over to Brunswick in the morning and stop by the sheriff's. I'm meeting Joe Brooks early Saturday morning in Brunswick and follow him over to the launch."

"How are *you* going to get into the party?" he asked. He said "you" as if somebody like me wouldn't be invited to a fancy party over on Sea Island.

I responded, "You know me better than that, Gene."

"Yeah, I guess I do. Stay out of trouble, Julian, and be sure you tell Frances where you are. I'll see you back in the office next week. And by the way, this Moe Stevens thing—it's not over. We'll discuss the repercussions when you get back."

Chapter 6

I met Joe the following morning at a little diner in Brunswick. When his dad first introduced us back in Baltimore, he was sitting behind a desk, so I didn't notice how tall he was. He was ruggedly handsome with broad shoulders and the build of an athlete. He shook my hand with an iron grip and said, "It's great to see you, Julian. I'm really glad you could make it."

"Thanks for the invitation. Your dad knows how much I love to fish. What a great coincidence that you were headed down to Sea Island anyway."

Joe said, "I'm always looking for an excuse to get out of the office. Did you catch your automobile thief? Dad and I were talking about it after you left the other day. Although we would hate to find out it's Goldberg or his man Ben Bloomberg behind it all, we'll do whatever we can to help you figure it out—customer or not."

"Thanks. We're still working on it, but I expect them to be on the island this weekend. Maybe you can introduce us," I said.

"I think I'll stick to selling insurance—and fishing. Let's go wet a hook."

I followed Joe over the recently constructed F. J. Torras Causeway to St. Simons Island. For years the only way to get over there was on one of two ferries—the *Emmeline* or the *Hessie*—that took at least an hour.

My grandfather first met Howard Coffin while attending the races up in Chatham County. After the Vanderbilt Cup on Long Island lost its luster, Coffin and his contemporaries started coming down here for the Savannah Road Race to test their automobiles in the tough conditions it presented.

Most people around here don't know Howard Coffin built his fortune in the automotive business. His early success in automotive manufacturing allowed him to invest heavily in real estate, and he started buying up land in Georgia. He bought Sapelo first and then later bought Sea Island in 1926.

Coffin's considerable wealth allowed him to contribute heavily to the Great War effort giving money, manufacturing, engineering, and other resources to the Allied Powers. Even the design of the famed Liberty aircraft engine was largely credited to Howard Coffin.

My grandfather said he said he was one of the nicest men you'd ever meet—generous to a fault and genuinely concerned with making things better for his fellow man.

After crossing the marsh and Frederica River, we drove across St. Simons to a road headed north. The sandy tracks were covered with crushed shells, and it bisected the island in two. About a half mile north we came to a gate with a small clearing. Joe waved me over and told me to park, since there was no reason for us both to slog through the backcountry of St. Simons. While I parked my Chevrolet out of the way, Joe went back and closed the gate and waited for me to get in with him.

"This is part of Hamilton Plantation. I've got permission to access the river from here, so we don't have to worry about trespassing. Eugene Lewis owns almost everything from here all the way to Hampton Point on the Altamaha River. The fishing is great all around this island, but I have something else in mind today. Mr. Lewis has a little runabout he said we could use to take over to Sapelo. That's where I keep my boat. We are picking up a friend on Sapelo before we head into the Altamaha Delta backcountry. Don't worry, you're going to love it, and I guarantee you that you will catch fish."

"Whatever you say, Joe. You're the expert here. I assume you know what you're doing."

"I think expert might be a little much, but this isn't my first adventure back here, so we'll be fine. Besides, Dembow will be with us, and he knows these waters like the back of his hand."

"Where exactly do you keep your boat?" I asked.

"Mr. Coffin has a boathouse on the south end of the island. He lets me store my little skiff there and in return, I take him fishing," replied Joe.

84

"Who's Denbow?" I asked.

"It's Dem, D-E-M. Dem-Bo. He lives on Skidaway Island, just north of Sapelo. His daddy was Mr. Coffin's chauffeur and guide when he first started coming down here. Ebo Jo is his name, but everybody just calls him Jo. He's got a little fish camp over on Skidaway. Mr. Coffin has kept him busy over the years. He and his friends love to fish, and old Jo knows how to take care of them. His wife Mamadoe cooks for everyone, and Jo and Dembow take them fishing. They're Gullahs, and their ancestors were slaves—worked the plantations down here. They're simple people, and loyal as the day is long. Most people can't understand a word they say, but once you've been around them a while, they start to make sense. Bo's different—he grew up around whites, so he sounds more like you and me. Mr. Coffin makes sure they are taken care of and in return, they watch out for him and his property."

The drive through the live oak forest of Hamilton Plantation was one of the most beautiful stretches of road I'd ever seen. Trees and plants on Georgia's barrier islands had to adapt to the harsh conditions. The quick drainage of the soil, balmy humidity, and high salt content allowed only the heartiest flora and fauna to thrive. The Hamilton property was no exception. The scaly bark of the red cedar stood out against the live oak and the southern magnolia with its huge and fragrant white flowers. The spiny saw palmetto grew low while the resurrection fern hung from the lowest branches of the oaks. Cabbage palm was a staple of these islands as was the Spanish bayonet.

Although we bounced around a fair amount, the road was well maintained, in spite of the fact it wasn't paved. The sand was firm and the tracks were packed with crushed shell and stone, and it had good drainage on either side. The road was lined with giant live oaks dripping with Spanish moss. These trees had to be a hundred years old. The distinctive smell of the islands comes from a combination of the salt air and the strong wood smell of the Spanish moss.

Joe was a good driver, and he handled the road with ease. After a half mile, we turned right and headed due east toward the Atlantic. This road wasn't used nearly as much and was barely wide enough for one vehicle, but was still well maintained.

When we reached the Hampton River, there was a little dock next to a clearing and a small shed for keeping boat gear. The tide was running pretty good, and the water looked like coffee. The current swept sea grass along in bunches mixed with foam as the occasional mullet jumped clear of the water in rapid succession. A little whaler was tied to the dock, and I could see by the stain of the waterline on the side it didn't get much use. The inside was spotless, though, and I could tell it was well taken care of. Joe invited me to climb in while he undid the padlock on the little shed and went inside to fetch a couple of life jackets. The outboard cranked on the first try and purred quietly while we untied the lines holding it to the dock. As soon as we were clear, the boat started drifting quickly downriver, evidence of how fast the tide was moving.

We headed out toward the mouth of the river, and once we rounded the southern point off Little St. Simons Island, Joe opened it up and the boat got up on plane. The sun was still low on the horizon, and a soft, hazy layer of mist was coming off the backwater of the Altamaha. As we motored past Wolf Island, a pod of dolphin joined us in Doboy Sound and followed us over to Sapelo, occasionally rising for air and then closing in tight near the bow as they rode the fat hump of water the hull plowed up for them.

As we were pulling up to the little dock on the south end of the island I asked, "So, Joe, how well do you know Mr. Coffin and Sapelo Island?"

Over the din of the motor he said, "Coffin? Great guy—what I know of him. He and Dad are good friends, but I've only met him a few times. This island of his is incredible. He's got a big house over on the Atlantic side and a hell of a yacht moored over on the Frederica. Called it the *Zapala*, which is the original Indian name for the island. Imported all sorts of exotic plants and animals. Filled these rivers with oysters. Even has a cannery over on the other side of the island. Spent a fortune on the place, I'm sure."

"It's amazing everything he's done for the area," I replied.

"It is, but this is his private getaway. The hotel and cottages he's built over on Long Island aren't too shabby either, and we all get to enjoy those," said

Joe.

"You mean Sea Island?" I asked.

Joe said, "Whatever they're calling it now. Dad always called it Long Island, but I guess you're right."

"The Brunswick papers have been referring to it as Glynn Isle," I added. "Probably just wishful thinking."

"Julian, whatever it's called, if you haven't spent any time over there, you need to. It's truly an incredible place. Tonight should be quite a party. Saturday nights at The Cloister have become legendary lately."

"Yeah, I've heard. I've also been fortunate enough to spend some time over there already."

We were approaching another small dock attached to a long catwalk that went back into the marsh grass and up to the shore. Right about then a young black man stepped out from the woods and came running down to the dock to help us tie up. Joe waved and yelled something that may have been hello.

"Dembow, meet Julian Clark," Joe said. "Julian, this here young man has forgotten more about these waters than almost anybody else in Glynn County will ever know, including his daddy, who has a fish camp over on Skidaway Island. Isn't that right, Dembow?"

"I 'spect you be tellin' the truth, missuh Brooks," Dembow replied in what sounded sort of like a southern accent mixed with creole.

"Dembow and his kin are part of the old Gullah Indians that once inhabited these islands. He may be hard to understand sometimes, but by the end of the day, you won't care because you'll be catching so many fish," Joe chuckled as he got out and gave Dembow a big hug. "We're taking my boat out today. Give me a hand, will you?"

Joe opened the door to the boathouse, which left me in awe. One wall was covered with mounts—redfish, trout, snook, and one of the biggest marlin I had ever seen. There was even a couple of large blackfin tuna. There must have been twenty fishing rods of various sizes and lengths, neatly organized in rod holders and several shelves of reels. Next to the rods was a small workbench with an assortment of tools and lubricants for maintaining the gear.

There was a small kitchen area for cooking and one of the most beautiful tables I had ever seen. It was a piece of a live oak probably eight feet across and eight inches thick that Joe said had been hand hewn right there on the island. It had eight rustic chairs, also handmade from local wood, and I could only imagine the stories that had been told around that table. A huge coat of arms on the wall opposite the kitchenette had been made out of another giant cross section of a tree—probably locally cut too.

Three small skiffs and a canoe were lined up neatly in the middle of the boathouse, and a rack, which wasn't much more than a sawhorse, held three small outboard motors. Dembow was already positioning a dolly under one of the boats to help us wheel it out to the water. The skiff was about eighteen feet in length and had an unusually flat bottom but still a relatively soft chine. The transom was fairly shallow, but the sternpost was much deeper and had a slight rake aft. It was pale blue inside, except all of the thwarts and cross members had been left the natural color of the wood. It also had oarlocks on it and a short rail around the bow that only extended about three feet down either side of the gunwales.

"What is it?" I asked.

Dembow replied, "Missuh Brooks's pride and joy."

"Mr. Brooks? He built it," Joe said, pointing at Dembow.

"Missuh Brooks like to say it mine, but he told me everything to do."

"What's it made of, Joe?" I asked.

"Mostly white oak. The carvel-style bottom, the sides and the seats are at least. Pretty much everything else is fir—the transom, thwarts, gunwales, and keel. I wanted it to be flat for stability, so we could stand in it and fish, but it also needed to get in skinny water. This baby only draws about twelve inches. We can motor for distance and then use the oars for stealth. That rail up front is for leaning on when you're fighting a fish or casting. It's nice to have a handhold in rough water too. Check this out."

Joe grabbed a short section of rail off a shelf and brought it over to the boat. There were four holes drilled through the forward thwart or seat, and the legs of the rail fit perfectly through the holes. The base of each leg seated nicely in the bottom of the boat in a thicker fir cross member than the rest.

"What's it for?" I asked.

"It's for stability. I'm already pretty tall, but that front seat is made to stand on, and I can lean my butt against the rail for balance. I get an extra two feet of height standing on that bench, which gives me a lot more visibility for sight casting. You'll see why later," Joe added.

He was just starting to build a reputation as a guide in the world of fishing, but not until that moment did I realize he was much more than a guide. This young man was a pioneer. He was literally taking the sport to a new level. I couldn't wait to get on the water with him to see how he used the long bamboo fly rods he had brought with him.

Once Joe was ready to leave, he cranked the little twenty-five horsepower Mercury motor and pulled away from the dock. Joe was clearly an expert at handling his little boat. We used Wolf Island as a buffer from the rougher water off shore and cut through Little Mud River before heading west on the Altamaha. The little boat made cracking sounds as the bow slapped the water.

"She's terrible in rough water, but we aren't going far. Today's supposed to be pretty calm, or else we probably would have used Mr. Lewis's boat."

* * *

The warehouse in Brunswick was used for lots of things, including storing red liquor and stolen automobiles. It was originally a chop shop, but Prohibition changed that. It was a lot more profitable to deal in liquor than stolen automobile parts. Prohibition helped shape the economies of coastal towns like Brunswick, Georgia, all up and down the East Coast.

The revenue agents had gotten wise to the coastal supply chain and knew most of the serious players. In the early days they could bring the liquor right into port and offload it into one of a thousand warehouses just like this one. Now it was too easy to bust the runners right at the dock, and the liquor never made it into the port. The runners stopped using the same ports and varied their drop points all along the coast as well as their schedules.

Oftentimes, the runners would hide the liquor at different drops, and then a distributor would pick it up once they knew it wasn't being watched. These deals were made weeks in advance, and in many cases, the cash had already changed hands. Now it was just a matter of getting the liquor into the warehouse and then moving it inland.

Stolen autos and trucks were widespread in the trade because they could be abandoned at any time. They could also be modified to change their identity as well as hopped up for speed. A good source for stolen automobiles was almost as important as the liquor. They couldn't make as much profit if they had to buy a fleet of automobiles to move their product. The medium-sized players were good at using somebody else's labor and delivery vehicles.

Another popular method of getting the liquor on shore was to simply go get it. Large boats and ships dotted the East Coast outside the three-mile limit of international waters, carrying booze from all over. They were so prolific off the East Coast, especially Florida and New Jersey, everyone called it "Rum Row." At night it looked like a city of lights gently bobbing up and down. A fast boat, a few good deck hands, and a shoebox full of cash was all that was needed to make a run—that is, until they extended the limit to twelve miles after 1924.

The Sicilian was standing next to a table looking out the window in the back of the warehouse, smoking a cigar. His silhouette was unmistakable. He was corpulent but only in the middle and always wore suspenders to hold up his huge pants. He had a typical olive Italian complexion, pockmarked cheeks, and an almost bald pate that he usually covered with a hat. He always had a fat Cuban cigar in his mouth, and he loved sweet iced tea.

His name was Vincenzo Genna, but he was known only as Jim in the Florida and Georgia circles in which he worked. He lived in Ybor City—a small Cuban enclave just outside of Tampa where he ran a few restaurants and a nightclub.

There were lots of rumors about Genna. Some said he was part of a big Italian crime family, and others said he was a rumrunner from Cuba. People likened him to Al Capone and suggested he was a gangster, thief, bank robber, and bootlegger. The swells around the golden isles of Georgia loved saying they knew someone like Vincenzo Genna. It was scandalous and made for good fodder at dinner parties. Besides, everyone liked to drink, and if men like Genna made it possible—what was wrong with that? The Eighteenth Amendment was a travesty anyway.

Wilbur Moore knew the real Jim Genna, which meant he also knew he was not to be crossed. He was a trustworthy businessman, and his word was gold, and if he said he was going to kill you—he meant it.

"Mr. Moore, thank you for coming. Please, have a seat. Would you like a cigar? Iced tea?" He was always a gracious host. "Forgive me for asking you to meet me here, but it was the best I could do on short notice. Besides, we shouldn't be seen together. Not up here."

"No, it's fine. Thanks. I'm fine. Um. I mean—I don't need anything," Moore said. He wasn't used to meeting directly with Genna. It was stupid. Genna needed him—not the other way around. Wilbur Moore had carved out a nice business, bringing in rum from the Bahamas, and he was one of Genna's main suppliers. He had good product and he was reliable. *This overweight wop should be so lucky to have a supplier like me. Shouldn't be seen together? What the hell does that mean?*

"I trust we don't have any problems with supply?" said Genna.

"No. We're good. Four thousand gallons is a big order, though. You have to understand the challenge of getting that much rum on shore. We'll have to use two boats, and I'll need a few extra hands for the exchange. We need some extra muscle to keep watch while we offload all of that booze. There are risks," added Moore.

"If you can't do it, just say so, Mr. Moore. I can find another source," Genna said.

"No, no, that won't be necessary," said Moore, dreading what he was about to say next. "However, there's the matter of the price. The Coast Guard has stepped up its surveillance, and the government has doubled the number of revenue agents around the Palm Beach area. We have a new drop point picked out already, but it means we have to run farther. One boat can only carry two thousand gallons max. And then there's the extra manpower, and the—"

"How much?" Genna said.

"Fifteen thousand dollars—per boat."

After a brief pause, "Done. I'll pay you half today and the rest on delivery. If all goes well, expect the same next month, and every month thereafter, unless you hear different from me," he said.

"Outstanding," said Moore as he tried to do the math on that much liquor.

"Tell me," said Genna. "I'm just curious. How does one go about getting that much rum on shore?"

"You let me worry about that, Mr. Genna. That's what you're paying for, after all. My expertise." *Wouldn't you like to know, you fat fuck, thought Moore while smiling. I'll just tell you all my secrets so you can slit my throat and take over my business. No, thanks.*

"Very well, then. I look forward to my next shipment. My men will get you your money and show you out. Be sure and let them know where the new pickup location is. If you need any help finding some reliable muscle, just ask." They shook hands.

As Moore got up and headed for the door, his thoughts were on the logistics of making this work. He had two custom boats designed specifically to carry thousands of gallons of rum. Each boat had dual two-thousand-gallon fuel tanks—one for diesel and one for rum. A special fuel delivery system allowed them to mix the contents of the two tanks with the flip of a switch. If they got caught, the diesel and alcohol mixed together, and it was impossible to tell they had been using one of the tanks for smuggling booze.

The powerful boats were light and fast, with twin Liberty aircraft engines to propel them at speeds of fifty knots in calm seas. In rough water they could still do thirty knots. The trip from Bimini took about two and a half hours at that speed. Two thousand gallons of rum cost Moore about twenty-five hundred dollars in the Bahamas. Genna was paying him fifteen thousand per load, but he was probably selling it for close to forty-five thousand. The business of Prohibition could be very lucrative indeed.

* * *

Wilbur Moore should have been as concerned as Jim Genna about being seen together in Brunswick because unbeknownst to him, Ed Lawrence of the Bureau of Investigation had been watching his every move. Ed was assigned to Palm Beach, a hotbed of rum-running activity, automobile theft, and other related crimes. The money flowing in and around the Palm Beach area was immense, and it had attracted a darker element to the county. They even had a few bank robberies, and a revenue agent had been shot and killed recently while executing a search warrant. Wilbur Moore, one of the wealthy residents of Palm Beach County, was a suspect in an auto theft ring and the murder of the revenue agent. He was also loosely connected to a well-known rumrunner named Red Overton.

Ed Lawrence had tailed Moore to the warehouse, but lost him once he went inside. He parked his automobile a few blocks away and was able to gain access to the empty building next door to the warehouse Moore had entered. Not knowing who or what was inside, Ed decided to play it safe and keep a good distance, for there was a lot of activity around the warehouse, particularly on the waterfront side. Eventually, he found a window that had a direct view into another window on the side of the warehouse. The glass on both was covered in crud, but he could easily make out Moore talking to a larger gentleman before shaking hands and leaving.

From inside the building, Ed watched Moore get in his automobile and leave before sneaking out the side and going back to his own vehicle. He had no idea who Moore had been meeting with, but he had a pretty good idea who would. As he pulled away he considered where he might find Agent Vernon Chris.

* * *

"You know everyone that works fo dem two calls dem Big boss and Lil boss," said Dembo.

As we rounded a bend in the river, a loud screech startled us all.

"What was that?" I asked.

"Chachalaca," replied Joe.

"Haints," said Dembow.

"What are haints?" I asked, looking back at Dembow.

"Here we go," Joe said. "You never should have asked."

"Haints be dem spirits," replied Dembow. He was looking around at the banks like he expected something to be there.

I chuckled, "Oh, you mean haunts. Like ghosts, huh?"

"You poke fun. You'll see what happen," Dembow said.

"The Gullah are very superstitious, Julian. You remember those houses we saw with the underside of the porch roofs painted that pale blue?" Joe asked.

"Now that you mention it, I was wondering why they all had the same color blue on the porch ceilings."

"That's haint blue. It's supposed to keep the spirits away. It's the same color as the inside of this boat," Joe said as he maneuvered us around a fallen tree that stuck out in the river.

Playing along, I said, "Well, that's a relief. I guess there's nothing for us to worry about as long as we're in this boat."

Joe started laughing.

Dembow acted offended. "You'll see. One of deez days you'll be sorry. Don't say I didn't warn you."

The chachalaca started wailing again, and this time Dembow jumped.

"It's a bird, Julian. They came from Guatemala. Actually, Mr. Coffin had them brought here. They're supposed to be good for hunting, but Dembow thinks they showed up for a reason. Slave spirits that need to be set free or something like that. Isn't that right, Dembow?"

I looked back at him, but it was as if Dembow were looking right through me. He was squinting at something up ahead. Without a word Joe cut the motor, and the little boat drifted silently in the current. With the motor noise suddenly gone, it was if somebody flipped a switch and turned on the sounds of nature. The river opened up into a wide area, more like an inland bay, and the expanse of water was cut in two by an island of marsh grass. At least a hundred yards of shallow mud flats led to the marshy island, with several oyster bars exposed by the dropping tide.

Joe finally said, "There must be hundreds."

Dembow corrected him, "Thousands."

As I concentrated on the shallow water in front of us, I finally noticed what looked like small pieces of brown marsh grass waving in the water. "Thousands of...?" I started to ask but cut myself off when I realized they were tails. A giant school of reds was feeding in the mud—noses down, tails up.

Dembow secured the oars in their locks without a sound and gently pushed us toward the waiting school. As we got closer I could see little puffs of mud bloom on the bottom each time a fish poked his nose down in it.

Joe said, "Julian, get a shrimp out of that bucket and rig it like we showed you back at the dock. I want you to cast up above the fish and let the current take your shrimp across the flat, but don't cast until I say so. Whatever you do, don't be short and don't cast into the school or you'll spook them."

As Dembow rowed us into position, I heard Joe quietly say, "Now, Julian."

My shrimp landed with a plunk in the deeper channel above the flat, and just as Joe said, the current slowly washed it into the shallow water.

"Take up the slack and be ready to reel down on him," said Joe.

A big tail turned toward my bait, and a huge boil of water was followed by my line growing tight. Keeping my tip down, I started reeling and that's when he started to run. The fish took off across the flat, sending the others into a frenzy. My drag was singing as the fish peeled off line, so I used my palm to add more drag and slow the big fish down. Just when I thought it would spool me, I got him turned back toward the channel. After a good ten minutes of give and take, the fish finally tired and Dembow scooped it up in the net.

"Nice fish!" Joe said. "Get a fresh shrimp and do it again."

Dembow had already taken the fish off and was putting a live shrimp on my hook when I noticed Joe getting his fly rod ready. Before I could get my bait back in the water, he was standing on the bow seat, false casting over our heads with an elegant grace that made me stop and simply watch in wonder. He deftly landed the fly right on the nose of a large red that instinctively sucked it under, and immediately the fight was on.

An hour later, we had seven more fish in the boat. I got tired after three and convinced Dembow to start fishing. We finally decided to take a break for lunch and eat some sandwiches Joe brought along.

"Joe, I have to admit, I think you might be in the wrong business. Your true calling is right here on the water."

"Funny you say that. I've been second-guessing my decision to work for Dad for a while now. I just felt like it was more important to take a more traditional route. Besides, I grew up with the insurance business. My grandfather started the company, and my dad built it into the success that it is today. Maybe it was more about not disappointing Dad."

Staring out over the water, Joe added, "You know the Baltimore Orioles drafted me right out of school? Who knows? I might be pitching in the big leagues if I hadn't gone into insurance."

"So when did you get interested in fishing?" I asked.

"My grandfather started taking me fishing on the Susquehanna River when I was only about ten years old, but only in the last few years have I developed a passion for fly fishing. We caught lots of stripers on that river, using big bucktail flies. What's really exciting is sight casting to big stripers on the grassy flats of the Chesapeake Bay. It's not unlike what we're doing today. Most of us cut our teeth in fresh water, catching trout. The satisfaction an angler derives from fooling a distrustful trout is one of the things that make fly fishing so enticing. But I think salt water has so much more to offer. There are so many species that I want to catch on a fly, and they're so much bigger. You saw all those fish on the wall back at Sapelo? It takes being in first-class physical condition to battle such monsters with light gear, and the odds are far greater for losing the fish than for landing him, but the battle is worth it."

Joe's passion for fishing was infectious.

He went on. "The greatest enjoyment derived from the use of the fly rod is not necessarily the fish caught—although it is my contention that, given reasonably good fly fishing conditions, the fly rod will out-fish any other rod—the greatest satisfaction lies, rather, in the performance of the cast, the dexterous use of the entire equipment, rod, line, leader, and fly. The fly rod

96

offers other inducement than merely winning the physical fight with some hard-hitting denizen of the seas."[1]

"Damn, Joe, maybe your true calling is writing about fishing. What you just described is exactly what I witnessed today, only I could never explain it as eloquently as you."

Dembow looked at the two of us with wonderment as he finished his sandwich. "Well, we gonna fish or we gonna just sit here and talk about it?"

We fished for a few more hours, but mostly I watched the two of them. The way Joe enticed those fish to the surface was truly a thing of beauty. I doubt he would have caught half as many fish without Dembow, though. His eyesight was amazing. Picking up the slightest movement or shadow below the surface, he spotted fish a hundred feet away and then eased the boat into position so Joe could make the perfect cast. They were perfectly in sync—almost as if they could read each other's thoughts. Joe wielded his bamboo rod with strength but at the same time with finesse and grace. The fly obeyed his will until it landed on the water like a piece of down. Dembow wielded the little skiff with the same strength and finesse and grace. They clearly needed each other.

It was a fantastic day.

Chapter 7

Here care ebbs out with every tide
And peace comes in upon the flood
—Carlyle McKinley, Confederate soldier[2]

When I pulled up to the motor lobby on a Saturday night, I knew I was in for something special. The hotel greeted me with an understated elegance with its Spanish facade, red tile roof, and awning that hung unobtrusively over the main entrance. It was a beautiful hotel, but not ostentatious or overdone. The landscaping and grounds were immaculate, but still not grown in, as most everything was new.

Half a dozen cars were waiting in line—a Duisenberg at the front. The two cars immediately in front of me were both Cadillacs, and I noticed a Pierce-Arrow and Peerless in my rearview mirror. A stylish young lady got out of the Duisenberg and was immediately whisked inside by the hotel manager laughing hysterically, arms intertwined and carrying on as if they had known each other forever. I grabbed my tuxedo jacket off the passenger seat as the valet took my automobile and asked, "Will you be staying the night with us, Mr. . . . ?" He hesitated, waiting for me to fill in the blank.

"Clark," I added. "No, not tonight."

"Very well then, Mr. Clark. Enjoy your evening. Please see Mr. Baker, the hotel manager, when you get inside, and he'll help you find your table."

I took my time putting on my jacket and admiring the front of the hotel before I started toward the door. The couple in the Pierce-Arrow behind me had already gotten out and were headed through the doors when the face of the driver in the next automobile—a big fancy Cadillac—caught my attention. I looked away before he caught me staring, but I'm sure it was none other than Al Neinstein, and he was dropping off a gentleman I didn't recognize—probably his uncle, Asa Goldberg. Another gentleman I didn't recognize got out of the back seat and joined him. As Neinstein pulled through the drop-off area, I stalled just long enough to let the two men get ahead of me.

As we entered the lobby, the man I had seen escort the young lady inside sauntered over and said, "Mr. Goldberg. I'm Roy Baker, the hotel manager. So glad you could join us this weekend. No Mrs. Goldberg this trip?"

"Not this time, Roy. I'm looking for a little more, *action* tonight. If you know what I mean?" he added with a slight wink.

"Indeed I do, old boy," Roy said as he guided Goldberg and his friend toward the Spanish lounge. After he turned away, Roy rolled his eyes before turning my way. It was clear he didn't have a clue who I was. "Sir, could you please step over this way and see our hostess? She can help you find your table."

Hoping Frances and Bill McCoy had worked their magic, I wasn't sure if I was going to make it past the foyer.

"Good evening, sir. May I have your name, please?" she asked.

"Clark. Julian Clark," I answered.

"Ah yes, Mr. Clark. Here it is. Table thirteen. I see you are dining alone," she said while giving me a sideways look.

Not taking the bait, I simply replied, "That's right."

"Yes, well," looking down at her list. "There are some lovely people at table thirteen. Feel free to stop in the lounge before you go out to the south patio, where you'll find most of the guests, until dinner is served in the main dining hall. Our maître d', Harry Welch, will take care of you during dinner, and we hope to see you at the casino afterward for some dancing. If you need anything, Mr. Clark, it would be my pleasure to help."

I really wasn't surprised that Bill had gotten me on the guest list, but I never knew how something like this was going to turn out until it happened. Bill McCoy cast a long shadow up and down the East Coast.

* * *

As I walked through the Spanish lounge, I felt a hand grab my bicep. I turned to see Vernon Chris as he started sweeping me toward the door. Before I could say anything, he said, "Julian! How are you these days? It's been too long. May I have a word with you?" He whispered, "Whatever you do, don't call me Vernon. Just keep walking and pretend like we're old pals. By the way, the name's Walt Johnson."

Once we were outside and away from anyone else, I said, "So, Walt, what brings you to Sea Island?"

He looked around to make sure nobody was close enough to hear our conversation, but just as he started to explain, a waitress walked up with a tray of hors d'oeuvres. We each took a couple of wild-caught Georgia shrimp before she walked away.

"I'm undercover tonight," he started.

"Really? For a minute I thought you just liked to sneak around fancy parties and call yourself Walt. Why are you undercover?"

"After our conversation the other day, we did some checking around. The other guy that came in with Asa Goldberg is Ben Bloomberg. He's a former city councilman in Savannah and the current president of Goldberg Motor Company. They are both dirty. We can probably nail Bloomberg for insurance fraud, not to mention embezzling city funds and racketeering. Based on what you told me about Goldberg, he's probably going to the pen for auto theft, although most of our case depends on you," he said with a chuckle. "The office asked me to come down here and keep an eye on those two—it's likely they are here to do business."

"What kind of business?" I asked.

Vernon replied, "I'm not sure, but there's more to this story. You see that big fella over there talking to Howard Coffin? That's Jim Genna. He owns a couple of clubs near Tampa and is rumored to be mob. Apparently he's moving a lot of liquor through the area."

"Show me a club owner that isn't moving a lot of liquor," I said. "He won't be a club owner for long."

"Do you remember one of our Bureau guys down in Palm Beach named Ed Lawrence?" Chris asked.

"Sure, I know Agent Lawrence. He helped us make a couple of arrests down there. Why?"

"He followed a man named Wilbur Moore up here. He murdered a revenue agent down in Palm Beach County, but he's got a fancy lawyer and the judge thinks he'll walk. They found a stolen automobile at his house too. He's into liquor, cars, cigarettes—no telling what else. More important, Moore met with Jim Genna this afternoon in a warehouse down by the river."

"What's any of this got to do with me?"

"Not much other than it's probably more than a coincidence that Goldberg and Bloomberg are both here at the same time as Jim Genna. Just be careful, Julian. It doesn't take a genius to figure out why the NATB is here. You've got some serious balls coming out here."

"Wait, did you say cigarettes?"

"Yeah, why?"

"Nothing. It's a long story. Anyway, I'll be careful."

"And don't forget—my name's Walt," he reminded me as he walked away.

* * *

I was glad to be free of Vernon. I was really interested in talking to Coffin and meeting this Jim Genna character, and they were standing together on the south patio with a couple of other gentlemen that looked familiar. As I approached the group of men, I noticed they were giving me the once-over with a few quick glances and then some whispering probably about who I was. Hopefully, Coffin wouldn't give me up—yet.

Extending my hand to him, I said, "Mr. Coffin, I'm Julian Clark. It's a pleasure to see you again. Thanks for having me. Wow, things have really come along since the last time I was here. Especially that bridge."

Coffin replied, still holding my hand with the other on my elbow, "Beats waiting on the *Emmeline* and *Hessie*, doesn't it? Welcome back, Julian. We are glad to have you. Let me introduce you to Carl Fisher from Miami. And this is my good friend Jim Compton—he's one of my financial advisors. And that's Jim Genna. This is his first visit to Sea Island. He owns a club down in Tampa."

Shaking hands as he introduced each one, I said, "Nice to meet all of you." Then looking back to Carl Fisher, I asked, "*The* Carl Fisher?"

"I guess that depends, Julian," he responded.

Everyone was probably thinking I knew him from being one of the biggest developers and financiers in Miami. He and Coffin also co-developed a hotel on Star Island in Montauk. But that's not how I knew him. "Carl Fisher of Prestolite, glad to meet you."

Mr. Genna said, "Damn, Carl, you've been holding out on me. You started Prestolite?"

I said, "Just about every automobile in America has a lamp on it made by Prestolite."

Fisher said, "Well, maybe half of them."

"You can bet every Hudson got a Prestolite," Coffin chimed in. "I didn't care much for Carl, but I needed those lights." Everyone chuckled.

"Well it's quite an honor to be talking with such automotive engineering royalty," I said with a smile. "I never know who I'm going to meet when I come up here."

Genna replied, "Julian, you really seem to know your automotive history. Where are you from and what do you do?"

"My wife and I recently moved to Jacksonville, Florida, from Atlanta. I'm in the automotive insurance business."

"Really? You'll have to bring your wife over to Ybor City sometime and have dinner. What brings you to Sea Island?"

Mr. Coffin jumped in, "Julian was up here doing some fishing. Isn't that right, Julian?"

If he was trying to provide cover for me, he did a darn good job by changing the subject. I didn't know how well Coffin knew Genna, but the less Jim knew about my real occupation the better. The insurance business wasn't a far cry from the NATB anyway, so it wasn't a total fabrication.

"Yes sir, that's right. Joe Brooks took me out today. We fished the delta behind Sapelo. Beautiful stretch of water back there—and Sapelo, what an incredible place. I've never seen so many fish. We finally got tired of catching them."

"Dembo go with you?" Coffin asked.

"Oh yeah. He's quite a character."

"You know, his daddy Jo and I go way back. Talk about salt of the earth. He used to guide us around when we first started coming down here for the Savannah Road race. Hell of a fisherman. But that Joe Brooks—it's like he's got a spiritual connection to the fish that nobody else understands."

"I know exactly what you mean. He saw things on the water even Dembow didn't notice, and watching him cast that bamboo fly rod was a real thing of beauty. The entire day was really something special."

Coffin asked, "Did you take Gene Lewis's boat, or did Joe show you that skiff of his?"

"Both actually. We took Mr. Lewis's boat over to your boathouse on the south end of Sapelo, and then we took Joe's skiff out to fish in. His boat design was perfect for the shallow water where we spent most of the day," I said as I noticed the presence of someone coming up behind me. Everyone's eyes clearly trained on this person of considerable stature.

"Did I hear someone talking about building boats?" a huge voice behind me bellowed. I knew who it was before I even turned around.

Howard Coffin said, "Captain McCoy, glad you could make it."

William "Bill" McCoy was one of the most famous seamen and yacht builders on the East Coast. He looked quite handsome in his tuxedo, but it was the first time I had seen him without his signature straw fedora, white cotton shirt, and khaki pants. He was a big strapping man, and he was quite popular with the ladies. He looked a bit out of place tonight in black tie.

Bill built yachts for the rich and famous, including the likes of Andrew Carnegie, J. P. Morgan, the Vanderbilts, and he even built one for a Rockefeller. He also built one for Howard Coffin, who was a huge boating enthusiast. *Zapala* was his pride and joy. It was a hundred and twenty-four feet long and one of McCoy's favorites. Apparently, Coffin still let him use it when he was visiting the island, and oftentimes he still slept on it.

Bill was actually more famous, though, for being one of the biggest rumrunners on the Eastern Seaboard. Back in the early days of Prohibition, Bill and his brother fell on hard times so the two of them bought a schooner in Gloucester, Massachusetts, called the *Henry L. Marshall*. After a few successful runs to Bimini and Nassau in the Bahamas, they made enough money to buy several more schooners and become one of the biggest suppliers on rum row. Bill registered his boats in Great Britain and stayed in international waters as much as possible to avoid apprehension by the Coast Guard. He learned early on he could make a lot more money hauling rye, Irish, and Canadian whisky, and he became known for having the best product.

Proud to have never paid a dime to organized crime or law enforcement, Bill became the enemy of both. His luck finally ran out in 1923, when he got caught by a Coast Guard cutter while aboard one of his schooners. Even though he was outside the three-mile limit, they boarded his boat anyway, and when he tried to run, they started shelling him. Bill had to surrender or they would have sunk his boat, likely killing him and his men. McCoy spent nine months in prison before returning to Florida, where he invested his considerable wealth in real estate and started building boats again.

Stories of his escapades of running from the government and other rumrunners, and especially the story of his eventual capture, had been told and retold so many times, Captain McCoy was a living legend. The women at the Cloister were especially keen for his attention.

"Well, I was in the area, if you know what I mean. I couldn't possibly miss out on a Saturday night at The Cloister if I was going to be in the area, now could I?" Bill said as he shook everyone's hand and was introduced. "How's my boat?" he asked Coffin.

"*Zapala*? That ole thing hardly makes it out of the marina these days. She's probably full of cobwebs by now. I doubt she'll even crank."

"Blasphemy, you old dog. That's the finest yacht this side of Jersey, and she better look just like the day I left her."

"McCoy, you know Matilda says I take better care of *Zapala* than I do of her. You keep your girlfriends off my boat if that's where you plan to sleep tonight," Coffin said.

I chimed in, "Bill, you've come a long way since the days when we used to sleep on the *Amphitrite*."

"Watch it, Julian, don't be disrespecting that old warship," Bill said. "That iron hull saw a lot of action before she was decommissioned and refurbished into a floating hotel."

"More like a floating bug motel. I guess it wasn't so bad once you got used to the smell of diesel and the sound of rats chewing through the walls," I said.

"You know, Julian, a lot of people loved sleeping on the *Amphitrite*," said Coffin.

I replied, "I didn't see too many people sleeping on it after you opened those cottages and the hotel."

McCoy added, "Do you realize that ship fought in the Spanish-American War and in World War I?"

Just then we all heard the dinner bell ring.

"Well, let's catch up for a drink after dinner. See you guys over at the casino later?" asked Coffin.

Everyone agreed to meet up later at the casino. In the meantime, Bill McCoy and I headed to our table together.

"Bill, I can't tell you how much I appreciate you getting me on the guest list tonight."

"Julian, you know I'd do anything for Frances, but you could have called yourself."

"I know, but I was in Savannah, and Coonts was already getting impatient with me. I honestly didn't have time, and I knew you'd get a kick out of talking to her. So, how do you know Genna?"

"I just met him."

"Sure you did. I saw the look he gave you. Customer?" I asked.

"No comment. Come on, Julian. Let's go eat. The food here is incredible—all eleven courses."

As we made our way to the dining room, an orchestra started playing and the crowd started to find their tables. The dining room was as elegant as the ladies in their long dresses.

* * *

We got to our table just as Roy Baker quieted the crowd to give his Gaelic blessing. Bill McCoy and I sat next to each other. Arthur Wilson, the Swede who ran all of Coffin's construction, sat next to Bill. Arthur was even bigger than Bill and the two of them looked like Greek gods sitting next to each other. Joe Brook's date for the evening, Virginia Taylor, sat next to me, and on the other side of Joe sat Baron Collier and his wife. The Colliers were from south Florida and owned the Rod & Gun Club in Everglades City. Ms. Taylor was a local that Bill and Kit Jones had introduced Joe to. Her great-grandfather once owned a lot of land around here, and way back before anyone had settled on Sea Island, it was simply a place for the Taylor's cows, hogs, and goats to graze.

"Hey, Julian." Bill elbowed me to get my attention. "You see the head table over there where the Coffins and Joneses are seated? That's Delores Floyd and Miesse Baumgardner. Everybody calls him Bummy. He's the landscape architect for the company. Nothing gets planted here without his say-so. I'm sure you noticed how meticulously landscaped this place is. Mrs. Floyd—she's from Savannah. Howard said she named all the streets on the island after Indians, Spaniards, Frenchmen, pirates, colonists, and Revolutionary heroes. She wanted people to be curious about the names and learn their origin. Anyone who bothers to learn the history of the name will understand a lot about the history of these islands."

"Over there, that's Gertrude Redfern. She was married to Paul Redfern."

"The pilot?" I asked.

"The same."

"I've got to meet her. He's a real legend—disappeared down in South America, right?"

"Yup. Tried to fly that plane of his from here to Rio. Never made it. He was good for business back in the day. He helped get rid of the competition."

"What do you mean?" I asked.

"He used to fly low over the Georgia swamps and spot moonshiners for the government. Then they would go in and root them out. He used to take off and land right out there on the beach."

On the other side of Bill sat Arthur Wilson. He knew everything about the recent history of development on these golden isles, since he had helped supervise the construction of all of Howard Coffin's projects.

"Hey, Arthur?" I asked. "What can you tell me about that coat of arms out in the foyer when you first come in the hotel? I feel like I've seen it before."

He said, "Julian, the only way you could have seen it before is if you had been out on Sapelo in Mr. Coffin's boathouse."

"That's exactly where I saw it," I replied. "I was out there this morning."

"Coffin wanted something unique out front. He wanted something that captured the surroundings and the spirit of this place as well as the wildlife. His friends suggested the Spanish dancers, the golfer, and the young lady in the bathing suit, and Howard added the leaping fish, the running deer, and the flying ducks. I fashioned the first one out of a big piece of cypress. That's the one you saw on Sapelo. Coffin didn't like it—it wasn't big enough and he wanted it to look more like an old map on a piece of fabric or parchment. He found some artist to make the one out front, so I hung the original out on Sapelo."

"Did you build that boathouse too? I could live out there without a care in the world."

"You aren't the first visitor to Sapelo to say that. It's a fabulous getaway. That little fish camp and boathouse are the perfect place to recharge a man's batteries," said Arthur.

"Those trees out front are magnificent. I could spend hours in one of those hammocks," I said.

"Howard calls them the Three Wise Men. Those oaks are one hundred and fifty years old at least. He pointed out one day that they look robed in Spanish moss like three old men with long beards. Those three have seen a lot in their lifetime," Arthur said.

"Virginia, I understand from Joe that your family has been coming out here for quite some time?" I asked.

"Oh yes, Julian. Before my father, and his father before him, started using this island as a grazing area for their livestock, they used to come out in boats for marooning parties."

"What's a marooning party?" Joe asked.

Blushing, Virginia said, "Aw, Joe. Young couples would meet out here to carry on. They built bonfires and had parties—and necked." She elbowed him as she said it.

As an orchestra from New York played for a host of singers and dancers, the crowd started to get quite loud. It was obvious the champagne was gaining speed. Baron Collier had to practically yell across the table, "So, Bill, when are you coming back to Everglades City? We have another cast and blast coming up for prospective members. I'd love to put you on the list."

"You're killing me, Baron. You know how much I love it down there. I just don't think I'll have much opportunity to spend enough time there to make it worthwhile, and I don't want to be one of those absentee members," Bill said.

"A man in your line of work could really use it as a way to drum up business. We've got some well-heeled members, and those yacht parties out back have become quite the norm," Baron added.

"I'll think about it. You make a good point. I've got a delivery in Naples coming up, so it would be easy enough to at least stop by for a night," Bill said. "Say, have you had a chance to go to Cabin Bluff?"

"Best turkey hunting I've ever done—quail too," said Baron.

"What's Cabin Bluff?" asked Joe.

I said, "Another one of Howard Coffin's retreats. It's basically sixty thousand acres of the finest hunting you'll find, just south of here on the Cumberland River. The fishing is first-rate too."

Joe said, "Is there anything he doesn't own?"

Everyone looked at Arthur, who just shrugged.

"Bill, what do you make of table ten over there?" I asked, trying to keep my voice down so as not to be heard by the rest of the table. Everyone had started talking amongst themselves anyway. "The man holding court is Ben Bloomberg, president of Goldberg Motor Company. The other guy across

108

from him is Asa Goldberg."

Bill said, "Looks like they're with a couple of bangtails I've seen around here before. I'm sure the Mrs. Bergs would love to know about *them*."

"And what's your friend Jim Genna doing with them?" I asked.

"He's not my friend, but I can tell you he's bad news, so I would assume if he's hanging out with the Bergs, they probably are too," said Bill. "What are you not telling me, Julian, and why are you really here? Joe may be the best damn guide this side of the Mississippi, but something's up."

I replied, "Those two are running a large automobile-theft ring Coonts and I have been investigating. We're close to bringing them in, but when I heard they were going to be here this weekend, I figured it was a good excuse to combine a little business with pleasure. I just met Jim Genna, so I have no idea how he plays into this whole thing."

"I noticed one of your Bureau buddies snooping around. Is he here for the same reason?"

"Maybe. And how did you notice him? He's undercover," I said, smiling.

"Seriously? He's the only guy here not wearing a tuxedo. By the way, there goes your man." Asa Goldberg walked by our table headed for the lounge. I excused myself and headed after him.

* * *

"What's your poison Mr., uh . . . ?" asked Goldberg.

"Clark," I said.

"They have some mighty fine whisky here," he said with a thick tongue.

"None for me but thank you. I've got to drive back to Jacksonville early in the morning."

"So what brings you to Sea Island?" he asked.

"Call it a fishing trip," I said.

"Isn't everyone? I know I am."

"You know, I was in your dealership the other day doing a little *fishing*."

"Really? Did you find anything interesting?" he said.

"I drove one of those new Model A's you had sitting out front. Fine automobile. Turned out to be exactly what I was looking for."

"Oh, that's great, so you bought it? I didn't realize we sold one last week."

"Well not exactly. But I will definitely be back."

"Wait, aren't you from Jacksonville?" he asked.

"That's right," I said as Goldberg stared at me suspiciously.

"What business did you say you were in again?"

"Insurance. Automobile insurance. Now if you'll excuse me, I don't want to miss dessert. Will we see you over at the casino?"

"Absolutely, Julian. I'll see you later," he added.

As I started to walk away, Mr. Goldberg called out, "Hey, Julian, by the way, where did you find that Joe Brooks character? My partner and I might like to do some fishing, and everyone says he's the best."

"Baltimore, Maryland, of all places. He's actually in the automotive insurance business too. His father introduced us when I was up there early last week."

"Baltimore, huh? He's a long way from home. Well, thanks anyway," he said as I walked off.

* * *

Hopefully he'd tell his partner Ben about our little exchange, and the two of them would connect the dots. We'd see. In the meantime, I might as well go have some dessert.

Later that evening, we were all enjoying ourselves across the street at the beach casino. It was a relatively plain wooden structure, but it had a beautiful pool and boardwalk across the front and up the beach for a hundred yards. Most of the guests were dancing inside, and the others were either standing out by the pool, walking the boardwalk, or taking a romantic stroll on the beach. There was a brass band playing inside, but the lights and the music were spilling out of the large open doors and windows along the front of the casino.

I decided a walk on the beach might do me some good and give me time to think. The salty air was warm, but fortunately, it wasn't too humid or my tuxedo would have been glued to my skin. I took off my jacket anyway and hung it over the railing. It felt good to be out in the ocean air.

* * *

At the end of the boardwalk I took the steps down to the beach and decided to walk south toward the end of the island. After about fifty feet, the soft glow of the casino lights ran out and it became almost pitch black. Before my eyes could adjust to the darkness, I sensed someone coming toward me. I could just barely see a shadow of a figure coming up the beach. Assuming it was probably a drunk partygoer who had been out on the beach getting sick, I moved to my right to give him plenty of space to stumble by, but my eyes had adjusted to the darkness, and I could clearly make out the tall, slender silhouette of a man in a hat. My primal brain went on full alert, and I could feel adrenaline spike in my system.

The man's movements were clearly not those of a drunk. They had purpose and confrontation. The glint of something metallic caught stray light from the casino just in time for me to notice. The man made a sudden move in my direction, but I had already started to sidestep as he swiped the air with whatever he was holding. As the momentum of his swing turned his body to my right, I stepped in closer and planted a fist as near his right kidney as I could determine in the dark.

The grunt that came next told me I had connected solidly, but he didn't go down, so I must have been a little off target. He turned quickly enough to swing the blade he was holding back to his right. I tried to spin out of his reach, but I felt the blade catch the fabric of my shirt on the back of my right bicep.

I spun to square up with him again. The man was quick and now that he had his balance back, he came at me with a vengeance. The darkness made it difficult to time his movements, and he caught me in the midsection and took me down to the ground. I reacted by tightening my core and preventing our combined weight from forcing the air out of my lungs when we impacted the sand. One of the easiest ways to put your opponent on defense or even out of commission is to knock the wind out of them, but years of pushups and sit-ups had made my core hard as a rock.

He put the knife across my throat and leaned down in my face. I could smell the stench of cigarettes on his nasty breath as he leaned in and whispered, "I know who you are, Clark. Stay the hell away from Goldberg's, or next time I'll carve you up like a Thanksgiving turkey."

"Is that so?" I said. The blank look on his face told me he wasn't there to kill me, and the fact that I wasn't scared had him rattled. I reached up and grabbed both sides of his head and pulled violently down while raising my own head up. My forehead caught him squarely on the bridge of his nose, and I could feel the cartilage give way underneath. He immediately rolled off me, screaming in pain. Although I couldn't see his face in the dark, I was quite sure blood was starting to pour from his broken nose. I got up ready for whatever fight he had left in him. He came at me with a vengeance.

Even as dark as it was, I could see him coming with the knife, so I formed a quick cross with my wrists and easily stopped the downward stabbing motion he attempted. From that position it was easy to rotate my hands to the right while turning my right hand over his right wrist and lock onto it. I continued forcing the knife away from me and drove him downward while bringing my right knee up into his right side. He dropped the knife and grunted in pain, but quickly threw his elbow back to his right making solid contact with my forehead.

I stumbled back several feet, but fortunately the blow to my forehead didn't hurt nearly as bad had he connected with any part of my face. He must have thought his elbow had done a lot more damage because his stance was wide open like he thought it was over. I moved in low and fast; planted my shoulder in the center of his chest and drove forward while I grabbed the backs of his legs and pulled. He went down easily and when he hit the sand I kept driving downward into his chest to try and force the wind out of him. I jumped up and backed off when a hulk of a man appeared out of the dark and said, "Julian?" My attacker was back on his knees and looking like he was ready for more until he looked up and saw Captain McCoy standing over him.

"Watch out, Bill, he had a knife," I warned. The man started to back up, and I could see that he no longer had the knife in his hand. "Grab that son of bitch!" I said to Bill just as the man turned and started to run. Bill grabbed at him, but it was too late. The smaller man was more agile and much faster than big Bill, and he took off down the beach.

"Friend of yours?" Bill asked. "What happened to his face?"

"I think he broke his nose on my forehead, and no, he's not."

"Not what?"

"A friend of mine," I replied. "But I'm pretty sure I know who he is."

"Let me guess, one of the Goldblooms, or whatever their names are."

"Close. I'm pretty sure that was Goldberg's nephew, Al Neinstein. I saw him drop Goldberg off when I came in tonight. He runs part of the family business," I said.

"Looks like they made you," Bill said while I brushed the surface of the sand with my foot. "What are you doing?"

Just as I was about to answer, I kicked something in the sand. I bent over and brushed more sand aside until I found it. "Looking for this," I said and held up a switchblade. I closed the blade and slid the knife into my pocket.

"I guess it's a good thing I came by when I did," Bill said.

"I can take care of myself," I said. "But thanks anyway."

"I wasn't worried about you," he said with a chuckle.

We walked back to the boardwalk, where I grabbed my coat off the railing and put it back on. As we headed back inside the casino, Joe and Virginia came walking out looking for a little fresh air.

Extending my hand, I said, "Joe, thanks again for the fishing. I had a great time out there. Hopefully, we can do it again sometime soon. Tell your dad hello."

Joe replied, "Anytime, Julian. Are you leaving already? The party's just getting started."

"I think I've had enough action for one day. Besides, I've got to get an early start in the morning and drive back to Jacksonville."

"Well, in that case, here, take this. I was going to give this to you later, but since you're leaving early . . ."

"What is it?" I asked.

"A letter I received when I got back to my room. It included a list—actually, two. The first one was a list of every automobile stolen in the Baltimore area over the last twelve months. There are almost two hundred. Dad and I had Josephine pull it together from all of the weekly bulletins. The second is from Agent Strong. He's got a confidential informant down at the docks. After a little intimidation—don't ask what kind—his CI ratted out that goon that jumped you on the ship. He works for Coll. Strong paid the owners of the Clyde a visit and got a list of every automobile that was put on board in the port of Baltimore, regardless of its destination. There are over a thousand autos on this. You'll have to do some cross checking, but these should help."

"Thanks, Joe," I said.

"Safe travels, Julian, and let me know if Dad and I can do anything else to help your investigation," said Joe.

"It was lovely meeting you, Julian," said Virginia.

Bill and Joe shook hands and said goodbye as I headed back inside. I saw Ben Bloomberg and Asa Goldberg sitting at a table together with a couple of ladies I hadn't seen yet. I headed straight for them.

As soon as the two of them saw me approaching, they both straightened up and Goldberg put his hand under his coat. I'm sure he was carrying a pistol, but doubted he would be stupid enough to pull it out in here. When I got to the table, they were both staring at me with blood in their eyes.

Bloomberg started to get up, but Bill McCoy stepped up beside me and said, "Don't bother getting up, gentlemen." Bloomberg eased back down in his seat.

"What do you want, Clark?" asked Goldberg.

I pulled the switchblade out of my pocket and dropped it in his glass. As it clinked down in the glass of ice and whisky, a few people nearby heard it and stopped their conversations to look our way. "I think you know who that belongs to," I said. They just sat there with a blank look on their faces. "I'll be seeing you, Mr. Goldberg. I'm still thinking about one of those new Fords I saw the other day. Have a good evening." I looked at the two women and nodded. "Ladies," I said and walked away.

Out front, Bill McCoy and I shook hands. "Thanks again for the invitation and for having my back," I said.

"Sure thing, Julian. Next time I'll think twice about it, since it almost got you killed this time. Why does trouble seem to follow you around?"

"See you in Jacksonville, Bill," I said and walked out.

II

Part Two

Prohibition only drives drunkenness behind doors and into dark places and does not cure it or even diminish it.
—Mark Twain, 1867

Chapter 8

The Jacksonville branch of the Bureau of Investigation was only a field office, but it was the largest one in the state and was part of the Miami Division. It was located in the St. James building on Duval Street—a massive four-story stone and marble building with a stately presence. Everyone referred to it as Cohen's because the entire first floor was occupied by Cohen's department store. Originally, it had been the St. James Hotel, but the great fire of 1901 pretty much burned everything in downtown Jacksonville—including the St. James. The Cohen brothers bought the property and opened a department store in the newly constructed building and then rented out the rest of the space.

The Bureau only had about two dozen employees in Jacksonville, including a handful of agents, so they only occupied about a quarter of the top floor. There was a laundry in the back and a barber on one side. It also had an excellent restaurant, a few lawyers and land men, and conveniently—a telegraph office. There were also several reading rooms and some nice meeting space.

It was decided that we would all meet at the Bureau office because they had a larger meeting room than the Jacksonville PD building that we shared, and it was a lot quieter. Coonts and I drove over together in his NATB–issued automobile, and detectives Tomlinson and Jones met us there.

I wasn't sure what to expect when I climbed in the passenger seat. This was the first time we had seen each other since my indiscretion in Waycross, Georgia.

"Julian, I've had a lot of time to think about this, and as much as I hate to do it, you need to learn to follow orders. You're back on the desk until further notice."

I didn't know what to say. I knew I deserved it.

"I'm also docking you a week's pay."

I could feel him looking at me. I was seething inside, but I wasn't about to show it. I just stared straight ahead as he drove.

"Do we understand each other?"

"Yes sir," was all I could say.

We entered the building together through the rear so we didn't have to cut through the department store. There was a passenger elevator that people working on the upper floors could access without having to go through Cohen's. Vernon Chris had come down from Savannah for the meeting and was staying next door at the Windsor Hotel, so all he had to do was walk next door. Ed Lawrence had come up from Palm Beach, and he was also staying at the Windsor.

It was convenient for the Bureau with the hotel next door because agents were coming and going all the time. Normally, it would have been too expensive, but they had a special government rate.

A nice young lady greeted us at the front desk and showed us to the conference room. "Help yourself to coffee. Agent Ersley will be with you in a few minutes."

Thaye Ersley was the senior agent in Jacksonville and had lived there all of his life. He was tall but rangy and always somewhat disheveled in his appearance. Thaye talked too fast and acted all jittery like he drank a lot of coffee, but the thing was, he never did.

He was smart as a whip and absolutely loved his job. He had a law degree from the University of Florida but never practiced. As a youngster he always wanted to be a detective, and he spent years working for the Jacksonville PD, but when J. Edgar Hoover came knocking in 1924, he was the first one tapped to become a "special agent." Thaye was probably the most dedicated agent Hoover had and was respected as one of the best investigators in the state.

Vernon Chris was also a very good investigator, but he was more of a character than most of the Bureau's special agents, and most people thought the only reason he got the job was because of his daddy. The Savannah field office was part of the Atlanta Division, which was run by Earl Black. Earl and Vernon's daddy were really tight, and both had been fat cat lawyers in Atlanta. Vernon couldn't hack it in law school, so he dropped out and went to work for the police department. He drank too much, and he was a bit of a pussy hound but still a very competent agent.

We stood around exchanging pleasantries after helping ourselves to some coffee and waited for Thaye, who finally came rushing into the room like a whirlwind. He made his way around the table shaking hands, and I noticed he had already spilled something that looked like grape jelly down the front of his shirt. His hair was unkempt, and he stuttered a bit when he thanked us all for coming and asked us to please sit down.

Recognizing that this wasn't Thaye's strong suit, Coonts took over and started the meeting. "Gentlemen, we really appreciate everyone being here and helping us wrap up a few loose ends on the Goldberg case. However, it sounds like we may have a lot more to discuss than just those stolen automobiles. Maybe between the seven of us, we can connect a few dots and solve another case at the same time. Julian, why don't you bring us up to speed on Goldberg?"

"Sure, Gene," I said. "We really made a lot of headway the last couple of weeks. We think we have evidence of at least a hundred automobiles that Goldberg and his associates have moved through Savannah and Jacksonville, and when it's all over, I wouldn't be surprised if it's twice that many."

Vernon whistled. "Nice work. Sounds like you guys are getting ready to plug an awfully big hole in the market. I still have a hard time believing it was Goldberg. I would bet just about anything it was that nephew of his. Especially after all the shit we dug up on that character."

"Well, it's clear to us that Neinstein is also involved, and we'll probably get Bloomberg on insurance fraud too," I added.

"Tell us about the evidence, Julian," Agent Ersley said.

"I will but first, Vernon, do you want to tell us what you learned about Neinstein? It may help us fill in a few gaps."

"Well, he likes fast automobiles and fast women, which I can't say I blame him much for that. Seems like he drives a different automobile every week, but that's not unusual—he runs a used-auto business. He's only got one vehicle registered in his name, and it's a beauty—a 1929 Cadillac Roadster. I was able to get Julian an opportunity to take a peek under the hood and it's straight. He tries to maintain a clean image, but he's far from it. He's been arrested a few times for being drunk or fighting but nothing serious. And, he has quite a reputation with the ladies. Nice cars, fancy clothes, dinners and nightclubs. Word is, he gets rough with 'em. Several of his molls have been seen around town with black eyes and bruises, and one ended up in the hospital—her faced carved up with a knife."

"Talk to any them?" asked Agent Lawrence.

"We tried. None said a word. They're all scared he'd find out. We rousted a few of our informants around town for information. Most of 'em didn't react to the name Neinstein, but we got all sorts of reactions to 'The Knife.' Liquor. Guns. Automobiles. Gambling. Girls. Pick your poison—he can probably get it for you."

Thaye Ersley spoke up. "Julian, tell us about Goldberg."

"Our first break was the Hupmobile. Detective Jones and I got called over to Harry Mega's because this kid Cleve Parnell was trying to sell a used Hupmobile that was registered in Georgia. He was cagey as all get out, and he wanted to make a quick cash deal and get out of town. I suspected there was more to the story, so I let him walk." I said this as I glanced over at Jones and winked.

"For once your instinct was right," Detective Jones said as everyone chuckled.

"Anyway," I continued. "The kid made an interesting comment when we tried to press him about that Hupmobile. When I told him we knew it was stolen in Savannah, he finally let on that it belonged to a buddy back home and he thought he could get more for it down here in Jacksonville. More important, he wouldn't tell us his buddy's name, and he said something about the knife. He was clearly referring to Neinstein, although we didn't know it at the time."

"Will he testify?" asked Agent Ersley.

"He hasn't been seen since," Vernon said. "Actually, we can't even find a Cleve Parnell in Savannah, so I'm not convinced that was even his real name."

"Regardless, it doesn't really matter," I said. "He led us to Neinstein, and we have enough other evidence to convict *him*."

"For automobile theft but nothing else. Right? What if he's guilty of murder?" asked Ersley. Nobody said anything.

"So the Hupmobile was the last of three stolen autos we found here and traced back to Goldberg's?" asked Ersley.

"Right, the first two were actually reported stolen by the dealership because they were stolen off the lot," Tomlinson said. "They filed insurance claims on them."

"But can we prove they had something to do with it?" asked Ersley.

"Probably—but we may not have to. Once I nail the numbers guy, we'll be able to connect him to those automobiles," I said.

"How?" Agent Lawrence asked.

"Because the same guy changed them all. He's either working for Neinstein or Goldberg, but one of them hired him to help cover their tracks. It's actually more likely a guy in Maryland," I said.

"Why do you say that?" asked Ersley.

"Because most of the vehicles are being stolen in Maryland and then sold to Goldberg," I said.

"You can tell they were all changed by the same person?" asked Agent Lawrence.

"All of these guys have a signature. It's really a lot like a fingerprint. They tend to stick to certain conventions when doctoring the serial numbers, and if you know what you're looking for, you can trace them back to the individual." While I was explaining, I pulled a file folder out and started thumbing through a stack of sample photographs. "See here, this is actually a pretty shoddy job of changing a three to an eight. You can tell it used to be a three. At least I can tell. That's just one of the more obvious examples. Here look at these—this is a little easier. This is a photo of the original serial number stamped in a different place. Now, this photo shows you the changed numbers. Clearly, he changed the ones to fours. Pretty simple. Here's another of the more obvious—look at the eights."

"They look strange to me, but I'm not sure what they were originally," said Ed.

"They should be zeros. Here, now look at the original." I slid the photograph across the table. "It's very obvious when you can see what the original stamp looks like. However, some are a lot harder to see." I put two more photographs on the table to pass around. "Look at these two."

"These look like two sets of originals," Ed said.

"Exactly. This is the same vehicle with two different serial numbers. Can you tell which one is doctored? "

"Hell no," Ed exclaimed.

"That's because they changed the entire number. They ground off the original and then restamped it with a completely new number using a die stamp. The really good thieves use a die stamp that looks identical to the original, but there are lots of poorly made stamps that are obvious to the trained eye. Look-a-here. This is a Ford engine block with the serial numbers ground off and restamped. I can tell just by looking at it that those numbers are not original," I said.

"So if you bust the numbers guy, you've got 'em dead to rights for all of them because it's like leaving fingerprints at the crime scene of each theft?" said Ed.

"Bingo."

"So what else do you have?" asked Ersley.

"A lot. When I was in Baltimore, I met with the president of National Mutual Insurance, Bob Brooks. They hold the insurance policies for both Goldberg Motors and Neinstein's used-auto lot. He also introduced me to his son Joe. Long story short, the Brooks's agreed to help us out, and Joe gave me a list of stolen vehicles to cross-reference with the shipping manifest of the Clyde Line."

"These lists are really the critical evidence we needed to tie up some loose ends," Coonts said. "Thaye, we should have no problem getting the judge to give us a couple of warrants now."

"Julian, explain," Thaye said.

"The first list is from a Bureau agent in Baltimore named Ray Strong, and it has every auto shipped on a Clyde Steamer originating in Baltimore regardless of its destination. There are over a thousand vehicles on this list."

"How did Agent Strong come about this list?" asked Ersley.

"Let me back up a bit," I said. "I took a little impromptu ride on the Clyde, if you will, at Agent Strong's suggestion, from Baltimore to Savannah to check out a few suspicious automobiles. While on board, I got jumped by this goon that was working as the shipping clerk."

At that point everyone leaned in—especially Coonts.

"Anyway," I said, "Agent Strong has a guy down at the docks that was able to finger this guy as a member of the Coll gang. He's working for the shipping company that delivers the automobiles to Savannah. So Strong paid his manager a visit and came back with this list."

"Can I assume this *manager* provided the list without any undo coercion?" asked Ersley.

"Yes, you can assume that," I said. "Now, the second list is from the insurance company. Joe and his dad provided us with a list of almost two hundred automobiles stolen in and around Baltimore over the last twelve months."

"The challenge was finding the matches," added Coonts.

"How so?" asked Tomlinson.

I continued, "The stolen auto list uses the original vehicle registration numbers, which presumably have all been changed. We compared the two and there are no matches, which makes sense. So, I had to create a third list of suspicious vehicles that were known to be stolen and connected to the case. I have about ten of those. As it turns out, six of them are matches and a seventh is a partial match."

"Meaning what, exactly?" asked Ersley.

"Meaning, I traced six of the suspicious automobiles back to their original delivering dealers and corresponding original registration numbers, and all six original ID numbers are on Joe's list, and the fictitious or fake ID numbers are on the Strong list. Make sense?"

"Hot damn!" Jones said.

"Julian, give us the specifics on the six please, and explain what's different about the seventh?" asked Ersley as he turned the page on his legal pad and got ready to take more notes.

"The first auto was our Hupmobile. You already know the story on that one and the link to Al Neinstein. The next two were actually the first two reported—the two late-model Fords. They were the ones supposedly stolen off the lot in Savannah and ended up down here in Jacksonville at that used lot over on Union Street. They were registered in Georgia, but I was able to trace them back to Baltimore. The paperwork said Goldberg was the delivering dealer. It wasn't —it was a dealership in Maryland. Ben Bloomberg filed an insurance claim on behalf of Goldberg for those two vehicles."

Vernon interrupted, "That's straight-up insurance fraud, Julian."

"Right. And since I can prove that all six of these vehicles had the numbers changed by the same person, even if we don't find the guy that changed them, we shouldn't have a problem proving insurance fraud. That's what I meant earlier when I said we may not need any additional evidence on that."

"Go on, Julian," Ersley said. "I want to hear about the other four."

"So number four was Detective Byrnes's Chrysler Roadster."

"Who is Detective Byrne?" Ersley asked.

"He's part of Savannah PD."

"A dirty cop?"

"No. No. Nothing like that," I said. "He thought he was buying a straight automobile from Neinstein, and it ended up being hot. Rotten luck."

Ersley made some more notes and seemed satisfied with the explanation.

"The next one was the Ford I took out for a test drive in Savannah. I'll come back to that one in a minute because it's the only one with a partial match. Stolen auto number five was the Ford I found on the Clyde steamer. Vernon helped us impound it when it landed in Savannah so we could get a look at the confidential numbers, and I traced it back to another dealer in Baltimore. Its original identification number is right here on the Brooks's list, and the fake number I found on the block is right here on the Strong list."

I turned the list over so everyone could see. They were both circled in red ink.

"Number six was the Nash—also found on the Clyde. Fortunately, the confidential numbers were easy to locate, so we didn't need to impound it in Savannah. Here's the original number on Joe's list and the fake number on Ray's list. I made another copy of this with two columns, and I drew a line between the real numbers and the bullshit ones so it's easier to understand."

"This is really good work, Julian," Coonts said.

When he said it, I could almost feel his regret for putting me back on a desk. I looked at him and hesitated before continuing.

"Hang on, there's more. Let's go back to the Ford I test-drove. I didn't have an opportunity to identify the original numbers, so I can't match it to the Brooks's list, but I found the fake number that was on the block right here on Agent Strong's list. See here." It was also circled in red pen.

"Therefore, it was also put on the Clyde in Baltimore with fake papers and delivered to Goldberg as a new vehicle. I will bet money that when we get the confidential numbers off it, they will match one of these stolen autos on Joe Brook's list."

"And you're sure that the same person changed all of the numbers on the six automobiles?" asked Ersley.

"Yup. One hundred percent. They did a pretty decent job too. The paperwork is all nice and tidy. The forms are all correct and look original, and the notary seals are real. They knew what they were doing. This is the work of a pro."

"I don't think we'll have any problem nailing all of these guys," Coonts said. "But Julian, tell them about the Cloister and the beach incident, because this story gets even more interesting, and I know the Bureau has other interests beyond stolen autos and Goldberg."

"What happened on the beach, Julian?" asked Ersley.

"Neinstein showed up at the Sea Island casino. First, I'm pretty sure I saw him drop his uncle and Ben Bloomberg off at the front. I was a couple of cars ahead of them, so I was already standing near the door when they pulled up—in a '29 Cadillac Roadster, no less.

"Later, I saw him at the Casino. Well, technically not the casino. He jumped me in the dark—out on the beach. He had a message to deliver."

"And what was that?" asked Ersley.

"It was pretty simple. Stay away from Goldberg."

"Apparently, Julian didn't like the delivery," Vernon Chris said.

"How so?" asked Coonts, all of sudden a lot more interested in the story.

Vernon continued, "All I can say is, I saw this fella in the parking lot—face covered in blood. Looked like a broken nose. I didn't know who it was at first, but after we started investigating him, I realized it was Neinstein. A couple of employees at the Cloister said they saw 'Mr. Clark' approach Goldberg in the dining room and drop something in his glass—a switchblade." Everyone glanced at each other and then finally at Coonts—snickers included.

"Aren't we getting a little off track here?" I added. "The guy clearly knew we were on to something, which is all that really matters."

Coonts shot me a glance and was clearly not happy that he was learning about this from Vernon.

"So, Julian, did you ever see Al Neinstein inside the Cloister or at any time see him with Goldberg, other than when he dropped him off?" asked Ersley.

"No. That's actually the only time I've ever seen the two of them together."

"Julian, Gene says you met Jim Genna the same night," Ersley said. "Did you ever see Genna with Goldberg or any of Goldberg's associates?"

"No, I didn't."

"Did you actually *meet* Genna?" he asked.

"Actually, I did. A few minutes after my conversation with Mr. Walt Johnson here." I pointed at Vernon with a smile. "I guess you guys already know Vernon was there undercover. Well, not long after, Howard Coffin introduced me to Jim Genna. He was talking to Carl Fisher and a couple of other gentlemen when he asked what business I was in and then invited me and Frances down to Ybor City for dinner sometime. Seemed like a nice enough guy."

"Didn't Bill McCoy walk up and join the conversation with Genna while you were standing there?" Vernon said.

"He did, but it didn't appear to me that McCoy and Genna had ever met. I've known Bill a long time, and I do believe he's out of the bootlegging business, but I would be surprised if they didn't at least know each other's reputation."

Ed Lawrence leaned over the table on his forearms and said, "I would agree, Julian. According to our sources, McCoy has kept his nose pretty clean since he got out of jail. However, we can't say the same for Wilbur Moore, and his meeting with Jim Genna was indicative of something a lot more illegitimate."

"Ed, why don't you tell us about your investigation and what you were doing in Georgia?" Ersley said. Before Ed could start, Thaye looked over at me and said, "Thanks, Julian. Nice work. Go ahead, Ed."

"Okay," Ed responded. "As you are probably all aware, Palm Beach County continues to be a hotbed of rum-running activity on the east coast of Florida. One of the key players in the Palm Beach bootlegging business is a man named Red Overton. His son-in-law is also a well-known ruffian named Arthur Cadwell. He and Cadwell met in prison, of all places, doing time for auto theft and bootlegging. They became good friends, but when they got out, Cadwell married Red Overton's seventeen-year-old daughter, Hester, so now they are a lot more than just friends. We've arrested both Overton and Cadwell on multiple occasions, but they've always managed to get off."

Detective Tomlinson spoke up. "We're familiar with Red Overton, but what does he have to do with Wilbur Moore?"

"Moore is a runner for Overton. He's a pro known for bringing large amounts of red liquor up from Cuba or over from Bimini," said Agent Lawrence. "Actually, Overton helped him get established in the business. He and Cadwell were stealing automobiles when Overton introduced them to the liquor business, and he financed a couple of fast boats to make the run to the Bahamas and then helped him expand. Moore has become one of the biggest rumrunners in Florida. Lives in a big mansion on Lake Worth not far from the beach. Which brings me to the point of all of this. We've been keeping a close eye on Wilbur Moore for several months."

"Is this about the murder of that revenuer we heard about?" asked Detective Jones.

Agent Lawrence looked around the table before speaking again. "Wilbur Moore shot and killed a revenue agent on his front steps. The agent came to issue a warrant and Moore shot him. He said the agent entered his house without permission, and he felt threatened and claimed self-defense. He got a fancy high-dollar lawyer that used some sort of sundown law defense. The judge had to let him walk. We were watching Moore, hoping he'd slip up, when we got wind of the mob connection and heard he was leaving town, so I followed him."

"That's how you ended up in Brunswick?" asked Vernon.

"Right. I witnessed a meeting between Moore and Jim Genna in a warehouse at the port, although I didn't realize it at the time. I couldn't get close enough to hear what they were saying, but I saw enough to confirm the rumors about the mob."

"I don't understand how that confirms the connection to the mob," I said.

"Genna is part of the original Chicago Outfit. He and his brothers used to control the illegal liquor business on the west side of Chicago."

"So the rumors are all true. What the hell is he doing down here?" I asked.

Agent Lawrence said with a smile, "Retirement."

"Right," said Vernon. "And I've got some land to sell you out in the Everglades."

Thaye Ersley looked up from his notepad, "So Moore, who murdered a revenue agent in cold blood, is probably supplying Genna with liquor for his clubs in Tampa and Ybor City. Then, Genna shows up at Sea Island coincidently at the same time Goldberg and Neinstein are there—and oh by the way, so does your friend Bill McCoy," he added as he looked at me.

Coonts said, "Let's not complicate things. It's probably just that—a coincidence. There's no evidence, or even reason, to believe that Goldberg—or Neinstein, for that matter— is connected to Genna."

Vernon Chris said, "I agree, Gene. We can't just assume they are working together just because they were all at the same party. At the same time, we have to consider that it's not outside the realm of possibility."

My mind was spinning in so many directions, it was becoming hard to put the clues together. This was one of those times when I needed a long drive to sort out the pieces that didn't fit the puzzle and rearrange the ones that did. Later. Right now the thing that kept bugging me was the liquor business of Wilbur Moore and something Agent Lawrence said. Bimini. Then something clicked and I remembered a comment Harold Hunt made when we were out in the Hammock. *Do you have any idea how pissed off my brother was when you and that Detective Jones fella uncovered all that rum we brought up from Bimini in the back of those stolen vehicles?* Bingo.

"Hey, Bart, remember all the red liquor we found in those stolen Fords?" I asked.

"Uh, yeah. They were part of one of Truby Hunt's jobs, weren't they?" he said.

Coonts said, "What are you thinking, Julian? I've seen that look before."

"It may be nothing, but something Ed said reminded me of a comment Harold Hunt made when I busted him with that tobacco truck. He mentioned how mad his brother Alva was when Bart and I found all that rum they had brought up from Bimini. Bart, you even suggested that maybe the Hunt-Gant gang was involved in a lot more than just stolen automobiles."

"Maybe Hunt-Gant is working with Moore," suggested Tomlinson.

"Maybe Hunt-Gant is working with Genna?" Ed Lawrence said.

"Interesting connection, Julian," said Ersley as he jotted something in his notepad.

Tomlinson and Jones were having a side conversation when Coonts nudged Jones and said, "What?"

"We were just talking about the murder in Turtle Creek and that Ford we found nearby. Sheriff Karel over in Bronson made a positive ID of the body Julian uncovered. It was definitely the missing security guard that was watching the tobacco truck that got stolen and Julian recovered out in the Hammock," said Agent Jones.

"Yeah," said Tomlinson. "Julian traced that Autotruck back to Truby Hunt, and then we connected him to the stolen Ford near the disappearance of the guard."

Before I left Bronson, Sheriff Karel had that Autotruck tobacco truck towed out of the woods so we could get a better look at it. The numbers had been changed, and it was definitely a Hunt job—albeit a quick one. I'd seen enough of their work to know if they were involved. Truby Hunt was one of the best, but sometimes he got sloppy or just in a hurry. Clearly, he only had enough time to change a few numbers rather than do a completely new vehicle identification number, so it didn't take long to identify it.

After I returned to Jacksonville from Gulf Hammock, Tomlinson and Jones had the Turtle Creek Ford impounded in our garage, so I could take a look at it. The numbers had been filed off, but the interesting thing was, there weren't any new ones. It was clearly stolen—I found the confidential numbers and traced it back to a dealer in St. Augustine, but without any new numbers, I had no way to connect it to Truby Hunt, which I was sure was by design. Whoever stole it was planning to dump it anyway or come back and get it later.

Not until Tomlinson and Jones showed up at the garage later did we finger Truby Hunt for stealing that Ford. It turned out there was an eyewitness. As part of their investigation of the disappearance of the guard, Tomlinson and Jones checked out the surrounding neighborhood for witnesses. An old lady happened to be sitting on her front stoop when Truby Hunt pulled up and left his vehicle right in front of her place. She described a man fitting Hunt's likeness.

"There's something else. The trunk was full of rum—from the Bahamas," said Tomlinson.

"Interesting," said Ersley.

Coonts looked over at me. Maybe he was ready to forgive me for not telling him about busting Neinstein's nose on the beach, but I doubted it.

"So where does that leave us?" I asked.

Agent Ersley said, "First. Vernon—you, me, and Director Coonts will start working on the warrants for Asa Goldberg, Ben Bloomberg, and Al Neinstein. We've got enough evidence for automobile theft and insurance fraud in both Georgia and Florida, so we'll need to work this from both sides. We may get to court sooner in Florida with Goldberg and Neinstein than you can get to in Georgia with Bloomberg on the fraud charges. Either way, we'll keep up the pressure on both fronts, which will probably prove to be too much for them to defend simultaneously. Second. Ed—you and I will continue to pursue Wilbur Moore—with Agent Clark's help. I'm thinking we go after him for the stolen automobiles. We're likely to dig up a lot more in the process. Director Coonts, are you okay with that?"

Coonts replied, "If Moore's part of an auto theft ring, Julian's the man to find out and shut it down. However, he'll have to do it from his desk for at least a week."

Everyone looked at me and then quickly looked away as the awkwardness of the moment set in. Nobody dared ask what Coonts meant—they knew.

Coonts continued, "Julian, remember, this guy is a murderer. You don't go near him without backup."

"Got it," I said, already thinking several steps ahead about how best to bring him down.

Agent Ersley continued, "Ed, let's get that revenuer Grady Emory from U.S. Treasury involved if he isn't already. We need all the help we can get, and having already lost a revenue agent, they will be motivated. Last, the Hunt-Gant gang is running roughshod all over the state, and it appears that they are into a lot more than just auto theft. Julian, let us know if you uncover anything new on that front. Hoover's going to be in town in a few weeks, and I would love to tell him we've taken some of these folks off the streets."

Everyone agreed with the plans and how best to proceed. We all got up and shook hands and started heading for the doors.

* * *

By the time Gene and I headed back downstairs and out to the parking lot, Cohen's had been open for at least two hours. We walked out the front so we could go through the department store and see all the things they had for sale. It was one of the nicer department stores, but it was completely empty.

The Depression was already starting to take its toll. Empty department stores were a casualty of a much bigger impending collapse of the economy.

Coonts drove in silence on the way back to the office, but I could tell something was eating at him still.

"Sorry for not telling you everything about my encounter with Neinstein. I didn't think it was—"

"I know," he interrupted. "Just remember, I promised Frances I wouldn't let you get yourself killed. Don't make me break my promise."

"Yeah, but back there in the meeting, I should—"

"I know, Julian. Just don't embarrass me in front of the Bureau guys. Okay?"

"Deal."

We pulled into the parking lot, and I started to get out but noticed Coonts wasn't turning off his vehicle. "What are you doing?"

"Dropping you off. I've got some business to take care of."

* * *

I entered the building and snuck up behind Gwyneth. "Ms. Lovewell," I said as I leaned down close over her left shoulder like I was reading some of her papers. I reached out to flip through a few, and she slapped my hand away. I jerked it back.

"Julian Clark, where on earth have you been?" she asked. She turned her head back just enough so that our cheeks were practically touching. She smelled of lilac and daisy and something else I couldn't quite place.

"No need to get feisty."

"Don't encourage me, Julian."

I stood and walked over to hang my hat and coat on the rack across from her desk. "Always a pleasure to see you, Gwyn. Miss me?"

"Oh, Julian, you know a day doesn't go by without thinking about you."

"Flattery will get you nowhere."

"It never hurts to try," she said as I headed to my office. "I guess we will be spending a little more time together this week?"

"Don't get used to it," I said, walking away.

"There's a stack of messages on your desk. Please read them this time before you disappear again."

"Thanks, Gwyn." I ducked in my office and kicked the door closed with my foot. Sitting at my desk gave me time to reflect on what had happened earlier. I was going to be stuck here for at least a week. How the hell was I going to help with the investigation of Moore sitting behind this desk? A week without pay. Maybe I was lucky I still had a job, but I sure don't feel that way.

Chapter 9

It was early in the morning in Daytona. The sun just starting to peek up over the edge of the Atlantic as the waves gently lapped at the beach out front. The air was thick and salty without any breeze to stir it up yet. Katherine Hunt poured coffee for Riley and Hugh as they sat down at the big table. Katherine looked at her two brothers sitting next to each other. Men now. They did everything together—and here the three of them were living together—sort of. They kept their dad's house over in Webster and still spent most of their time on the west side of Orlando. She knew her brothers were into all sorts of questionable dealings—hell, she had even helped them steal a few automobiles back in the day. She had been a wild one when she first married their best friend, Alva Hunt.

The four of them used to hang out on Daytona Beach when they were teenagers. When they got tired of the sun and sand, they would wander up to the boardwalk for hot dogs. The strip had rides, skeeball, funnel cakes, cotton candy, arcade games, and plenty of other distractions to keep them out of trouble. But somehow trouble always found them.

Alva's daddy, H.D., always had fast cars, and he would let the four of them take one to Daytona for a weekend of fun. One of the few beaches in the country that allowed driving out on the sand, it was littered with automobiles all the time. There was always a lot of drinking and carrying on and racing cars and just hanging out by a bonfire by night. It was an interesting scene where the haves and have-nots mingled. Fights were common. Most weekends they just slept on the beach or on the back seat of one of Alva's cars. Waking up next to an extinct campfire and a strange boy or girl, wondering what the hell happened the night before, was a typical Saturday morning.

They were all tough, even Katherine, but nobody could fight like Harold. The beach was where he discovered his knack for boxing. It didn't hurt that he was a little crazy and fearless, but he was quick with his hands and feet and rarely took more than a few shots. Most of the time they tried to avoid a scrum, but not Harold. He wanted to fight and there were plenty of willing takers. They were just teenagers back then, but they all knew one day they wanted to live on Daytona Beach. Enough ill-gotten gains had made it possible.

"What's cookin', sis?" asked Riley

"Biscuits. Sausage and gravy too. I picked some really nice tomatoes yesterday that I'll slice up if you're interested."

"Where's Alva?" asked Hugh.

"Something going on I should know about?" she asked.

"None of your business, woman," Hugh replied with a smirk, but he knew Alva had probably already told her what they were up to. Alva told Katherine everything—almost. He made them swear on their lives they wouldn't say anything about the incident with that guard over in Turtle Creek. He couldn't bear the thought of her knowing they were responsible for something so reprehensible.

"He's still out there in the garage tinkering with that automobile. I'm not sure he ever came in last night. Something's been eating at him, but I'm not sure what. I'm sure part of it is about Harold, but maybe a little about that liquor business too," she added with a knowing look at her brothers.

"Hell, Katherine, you used to say we should have started bootlegging the day after they passed that stupid law. It's getting a lot harder to make a buck in the parts business, and the Depression is really wearing on us. You know that."

"Yeah, I know. I just worry about Alva."

"Don't worry about us. We'll be fine," said Riley.

"You know I'm kidding. I worry to death about you too. Every time you walk out that door, I never know if you are coming back. It's not the same without Harold around, and it just reminds me of your mortality."

Just then Everett Cooper walked in. He grabbed Katherine from behind and squeezed her and gave her a kiss on the cheek. "Don't go getting soft on us, Katherine. It doesn't fit you."

Katherine had gotten used to her brothers' friends staying at the house since the early days. The Hunt boys had friends all over Florida that knew they were always welcome. If you knew the Hunts or the Gants, you always had a bed and a hot meal in Daytona if you needed it. Katherine was a gracious host and fortunately loved cooking. She never knew who was going to show up, but it didn't matter. She loved having them around and listening to them carry on about their exploits and adventures. She only had one rule—no women.

When they first got the house, it was not uncommon for one of them to bring home a girl they met on the beach, but one night after Truby brought home this little trailer park girl, Katherine decided to put a stop to it. Truby snuck in late with her, both of them about half drunk, and he took her upstairs and started making out. One thing led to another and they got to banging like there was no tomorrow. That girl woke everyone else in the house up screaming, "Oh Truby, Oh Truby. Oh yes! Don't stop, Truby! Oh God, Truby, don't stop."

Katherine had finally had enough, and she went up there with a broom and started whacking this poor girl, who was ridin' Truby like a greased hog at the state fair. It was all she could do to hold on. She chased that poor girl all over the house with that broom.

"Get outta ma house, you little whore. You little, no-good, rotten whore." The poor thing finally found the door and took out without a stich of clothing. Ever since that night—no women.

"Everett, how's it going over there in Gainesville? I feel like I haven't seen you in a while," said Riley.

"It's all good, Riley. The last couple of times I was in Daytona, you must have been at home. I see Hugh all the time."

Alva walked in and sat down at the opposite end of the table from Riley. He was a few years younger than Riley, and although the two of them were basically the ringleaders of the bunch, everyone knew Riley was the boss. The two of them rarely disagreed on anything, but Riley had seniority and with it came the final decision on most things about their business dealings.

Katherine filled everyone's cups with fresh coffee and laid out the sausage biscuits and gravy. Hugh said, "Katherine, I'd love some of that tomato you were talking up." Her garden was legendary and they rarely bought vegetables.

"Lay it on us, Everett. What did you learn over in Bronson?" asked Alva.

"Well, it's a sordid, nasty tale—that's for sure. The story we heard about Harold bleeding to death is true. How he bled to death is one of the craziest things I've ever heard, though."

"What do you mean?" asked Alva.

"He was snake bit."

"What the hell do you mean, snake bit?" asked Hugh.

"Apparently, he was out there in the Hammock with none other than your pal Agent Clark. All our guy knew was that Agent Clark showed up that morning without barely any warning, asking Sheriff Karel for some help locating a stolen tobacco truck out in the Hammock. He and the sheriff are friends, and Clark's boss over in Jacksonville is a really old friend of the sheriff's. In spite of their history together, Sheriff Karel didn't have time to go out there with Clark, so he went alone. At some point, Harold spotted Clark traipsing around out there in the woods, they got into a fight, and Harold beat him unconscious."

"Well, that's certainly believable," added Hugh.

"Yeah, well, if it wasn't for a damn snake, he would have killed Clark and he'd still be alive," said Everett.

Alva said, "I still don't get it. How did he bleed to death if a snake bit him?"

Everett continued, "It sounds like the snake, a rattler, and it must have been a big one, bit him on the inside of his leg and punctured that big vein that runs down the inside of your thigh."

Katherine said, "It's an artery." Everyone turned and looked at her.

"Whatever. Doc said even if he had been there with Harold, there's not much he could have done to stop the blood loss. He said it depends on how bad the bleeding was, but it's likely that he grabbed the snake and pulled, which may have ripped it even worse than the initial bite."

"So that son of bitch Clark just sat there and watched?" said Riley.

"Harold had tied him up. Nothing he could do even if he hadn't been tied up. It took him over an hour to get free and find his way out, and by the time the sheriff found him, it wouldn't have mattered anyway. Harold had long since been dead. Oh, uh, sorry, Alva. I didn't mean nothing by it. I just meant ... never mind."

"Shit," sighed Alva. Katherine put her hands on his shoulders and tried to comfort him, although she knew there wasn't much she could do. "Would a rattlesnake bite have killed him anyway?"

"Not necessarily," said Everett.

Katherine interrupted, "They can be deadly, but most people get treated before it's too late. It takes a while for the venom to work, and it also depends on where you get bit and how much venom goes in you."

Everett said, "Had it not been for that 'artery,'" enunciating the word as he said it while looking over at Katherine, "he probably would have made it."

Everyone just sat there for a few minutes staring at his food. The realization that the whole thing was a stupid accident didn't make them feel any better. Harold was gone, and his death was still a direct result of them deciding to steal that truck.

Hugh broke the silence first. "What I want to know is how Agent Clark knew about that truck. How in the hell did he figure out to go looking for it in the Gulf Hammock?"

"The word is, he said he had a reliable source. He knew it was a tobacco truck, and he also mentioned several stolen automobiles full of red liquor they connected to the Hunts," Everett said, looking at Alva.

"I still think it's those damn wops running their mouths," said Hugh.

"Well, Harold was known to do the same from time to time. There's no way to know if he didn't accidentally say something to one of his lady friends. Loose lips could be our undoing, so we need to figure out who Clark's reliable source was and shut him, or her, up," said Alva.

"I think it's time we did something about that Agent Clark," said Everett.

Riley ignored Everett's comment. "Genna and his men are pros. Why would they say or do anything to jeopardize their own business? Besides, Genna wants to keep a low profile down here and stay out of trouble. It's not like the old days back in Chicago. Most people don't even know who he is."

"You can bet your ass the T-men know who he is and are probably keeping close tabs on him, so we need to be careful. I don't want any unnecessary attention," said Alva.

"I think we can all agree on that," said Riley. "Make sure Truby gets the message. Now we need to talk about tomorrow night. We've got a delivery to make and it's a big one—four thousand gallons."

"Jesus!" said Katherine. "How are you going to move four thousand gallons of whiskey?"

Alva and Riley both had huge grins on their faces.

Chapter 10

We are doing our best for you but cannot be expected to infringe on the prerogatives of our own people to help you enforce one of your fool laws.
—U.S. Counsel in Nassau

Wilbur Moore's latest deal with Vincenzo Genna had financed two very fast boats he affectionately named *Scylla* and *Charybdis*. They were long and sleek, at least forty feet in length, each powered by twin Liberty aircraft engines. They were capable of top speeds approaching fifty knots, and even the Coast Guard had trouble chasing them down. They were inconspicuous when moored with other boats of similar size, but when those motors were running, they became an entirely different animal—like a pair of wolves in sheep's clothing. Those Liberty engines had a distinctive sound, and as soon as they fired up, anyone could tell there was something different about those boats.

Moore's men had made the run from Bimini to Florida many times, and everyone knew the dangers. First they had to make it out of Bahamian waters without encountering any pirates. That alone made it a very risky business indeed. Speed was their friend until they made it to the Gulf Stream. The waters could be treacherous, occasionally reaching heights of fifty feet, and the distance alone made it a sort of endurance race as man and machine got beaten incessantly by the sea. The added risk of being stopped by the Coast Guard inside the international limit —sometimes with the shoreline in sight—added to the risk.

The new boats gave everyone a sense of invincibility against the usual dangers of long-distance rumrunning, but they still had to respect the seas, the weather, their rivals, and the radio. Even the fastest of boats couldn't outrun the simple click of a button on a marine radio to signal the next boat ahead of you.

Bimini was only about fifty miles due east of Miami, but rumrunners had to be prepared to travel just about anywhere along the coast of Florida to avoid the Coast Guard. Moore had assembled two crews of his best men for this inaugural run in his new boats. Not only was his investment in the hardware significant, each boat carried two thousand gallons of rum. He couldn't afford to take chances. In addition to the two crews leaving Bimini, he also had two more crews in U.S. waters on smaller boats ready to run interference for the runners. They could monitor radio traffic as well as intervene if a rival tried to get in the way. In this business he also had to consider the double-cross. His relationship with Genna was new, and although his reputation was solid, he never knew what to expect.

They timed their departure to arrive in Palm Beach County waters about 3:00 a.m. still under the cover of darkness. The usual drop points along the shores of Palm Beach were compromised, as the Coast Guard and revenue agents kept watch over most of them, so the regular runners rarely used the same drop twice. Tonight's drop would be farther north in Jupiter Inlet, about ninety-five miles from Alice Town, Bahamas. At forty knots, they could make it in a little over two hours, but they allowed themselves an extra hour to make time for slower speeds in the channels as well as idling around the inlet.

Scylla approached the waters off Palm Beach right on schedule and slowed to idle speed before turning north, allowing the *Charybdis*, which was about five minutes behind, to catch up. In spite of the calm seas, the men were fatigued from the long night of running. The boats had been stripped of most of the comforts of a typical seagoing vessel to reduce weight and make room for the massive fuel tanks, and sleep was hard to come by because of the constant thrum of the motors and the up and down motion of the sea. Not to mention the lack of adequate room to lie down on deck or anywhere below.

"Look alive, boys," yelled the skipper of *Scylla*. "We're getting close." The men began to rustle around and clear the cobwebs from their heads. A couple came up on deck to smoke while the youngest member of the crew went below to make coffee. It was his first run. He was the skipper's nephew, and he'd been begging to be included on one of the trips for months. His father had finally relented, and now here he was—practically straddling two thousand gallons of illegal whiskey.

* * *

Unbeknownst to the crew of *Scylla*, a boat anchored not far from where they slowed had noticed their approach. Three men were playing cards below deck when one of them heard the guttural sound of those Liberty motors approaching. He grabbed the boat glasses and headed above deck to get a better look. It was too dark to discern anything other than the single white light he saw on the stern and the green light on the port side of the bow. Based on the distance between the two, he estimated the length of the boat at between forty and fifty feet. After a few minutes watching it motor slowly north, he picked up the radio but held off making a call as he heard the approach of another boat that sounded just like the first.

The second boat slowed as it reached the marker and prepared to pull up to its twin on its starboard side. The skipper of the *Charybdis* signaled the other with a flash of his signal light. "What's the plan, skipper?" asked the lookout on the bow of *Charybdis*. "How much longer?"

The skipper replied, "Patience. Let me know when you see the Jupiter lighthouse. When we get in the Loxahatchee river, start looking for a creek on the south side of the Inlet. Once we enter the creek, it won't be far. Look for a signal."

"How will I know when—" he started to ask.

"You'll know."

* * *

Well inside the Jupiter harbor and safely hidden on the northern tip of Fullerton Island, three men kept watch. The squelch of a radio broke the stillness of the night. "Copy that, boss," the man whispered as he keyed the mike on his marine radio. Albert looked down at the two men sitting on the dock below him. They were anxiously waiting for him to tell them about the conversation he just had with the boat offshore. Most of the time these night watches were uneventful and boring as hell, so any chance of some action piqued their interest. "Two boats approaching from the south. Probably nothing, but the boss said to keep him posted in case they came in here. He said they sounded different. Fast. Something about them gave him a funny feeling."

"Roger that," one of them replied. Both men dropped their cigarettes in the water. The three men were heavily armed and ready for just about anything—almost.

* * *

Truby Hunt drove the big Chevrolet fuel truck down the road toward the water. He was to meet up with Hugh and Riley Gant, along with Everett Cooper and some muscle they brought along for the night. When he rounded the last bend, he came to a clearing with room for several vehicles. Two were already there, but he still had room to turn the big truck around and back it up to the narrow ramp that led down to the water. He noticed a couple of men resting on the bumper of one of the automobiles—one of them smoking a cigar. He could also make out three men still sitting in the other automobile—probably the Gant brothers and Everett. Not until he got out and approached the two men did he notice they were both holding rifles. When the Gants got out, they were both holding Thompson machine guns.

"You're late," said Riley.

"Are they here yet?" Truby asked.

"Not yet," said Hugh, "but they should be here any minute."

Truby replied, "Well then, I guess I'm right on time."

Riley was anxious to get this over with. He didn't like being exposed as they were, and he knew this was going to take longer than expected. So many things could go wrong, and he had considered all of them. This sure wasn't like stealing automobiles, and he still wasn't convinced they should be a part of it.

Hugh and Everett followed Truby down to the little dock at the end of the ramp. When they caught up, Truby asked, "What's got your brother wrapped around the axle?"

"Aw, don't mind him. He's just nervous somebody's going to spoil our little party. I'm going to leave one of the boys back there on the road in case someone approaches from the rear. I'll leave the other one with the truck, and the four of us will stand lookout down here by the water. Moore said he would have a couple of boats stationed out on the water, but we'll probably never see them. One is supposed to be sitting outside the inlet, and the other one will be stationed at the mouth of the river. As for us, there's some cover back in those trees with an elevated position above the dock and the water—just in case."

"Just in case of what?" Truby asked.

"Anything."

Everett pulled Truby aside and said, "Hey, buddy, I know how to find your man Clark."

"And how might you know that?" asked Truby.

"Don't worry about it. I'll take care of that little problem in due time."

Hugh approached them. "What's up?"

"Nothing. Let's be ready."

The sun wouldn't rise for another ninety minutes at least, but there wasn't a cloud in the sky and the stars provided some ambient light. It wouldn't be easy to see an approaching boat, but their elevated position was the best vantage point on the bank above the dock. Riley joined them down on the bank, carrying a signal lantern, as the three men decided to get into position.

* * *

146

Moore's men used the Jupiter lighthouse to navigate into the Loxahatchee River, and shortly after passing the lighthouse on their starboard side, they found the river entrance to their port. A small boat was tied to a dock just past the entrance to the river, and a red signal light flashed once as they made the turn. The skipper of the *Scylla* killed his navigation lights as his nephew climbed up on deck to smoke. "What was that?" he asked.

"It's one of ours," the skipper said.

The other men were relaxed, drinking coffee, but had rifles at the ready. Smith was sitting on the bowsprit of the *Charybdis*, scanning the banks, looking for trouble. Even at idle speed, the boats made a lot of noise, so it was hard to maintain stealth in these calm waters of the Loxahatchee.

Not far from their position, Albert Mobley and the two men hiding on Fullerton Island heard the rumble of a big motor coming toward them. The sound of a Liberty V-12 was unmistakable, and four of them made quite a commotion. Albert keyed the mike on his radio again, and whispered, "They're here." Without any running lights, they couldn't see much yet, but they were close enough to feel the disturbance in the air and the vibration of the props as the boats rounded the bend. One of Albert's men could see the glow of a cigarette in the dark.

* * *

Riley heard the motors first and grabbed the signal lantern. He flashed red one time and waited. A few seconds later, he saw the response across the water. "Show time," he said quietly to Truby and Hugh. "Let's get this over with. Help tie them up to the dock side by side and then get that pump running. I don't want to be here any longer than we have to."

Truby and Hugh jumped down on the dock to help the crew of *Scylla* tie her up. Once she was secure, the crew tied the *Charybdis* on the outside. Riley walked down on the dock and greeted the skipper. They exchanged a few words that nobody else heard before Riley turned and looked at Truby. "Let's get to work."

Truby ran up the ramp and grabbed the end of the hose that was mounted on the rear of the fuel truck. He started the generator before running back down the ramp, pulling the hose off the reel as he went. By the time he got to the water he could barely reach the outside boat, but the hose was just long enough to connect to the spigot on the base of the tank filled with rum. Truby ran back up the ramp and waited for the all-clear signal from one of the men below—then he engaged the pump. It sputtered and choked for a minute before priming itself and the splash of rum spilling down inside the tank could be heard. It would take about thirty minutes to unload one boat before they could start on the second.

* * *

Out on Fullerton Island, less than forty yards away on the other side of the river, Albert and his men watched.

"Son of a bitch," one of them whispered. "Bootleggers."

"You're a regular Sherlock Holmes aren't you?" the other replied.

Albert had turned the radio all the way down. He didn't dare take a chance that a call from the boss would blow their cover.

"What are we doing, boss?"

"Waiting."

"Are they pumping something into that truck?"

"Yeah. Whiskey, you dummy," said the other man.

"Damn. That's a lot of whiskey. Ashley ain't gonna like this one bit."

Albert looked down at him disparagingly.

"What? I'm just saying."

After thirty minutes they finished pumping the first boat dry and started on the second. In the predawn light Albert could make out three men standing on the dock, and he could see at least three on each boat. The silhouette of a man sitting on the bow with a rifle was unmistakable. He decided he couldn't wait any longer but needed to hike back around the other side of Fullerton Island to call the boss without being heard. There was no way those bootleggers could hear him use the radio through all those trees on the far side of the island. Before leaving the two men, he said, "Stay

148

here. Don't move a muscle and don't say a word. I'm going to call the boss. I'll be right back."

Albert got up slowly and headed around the east side of the island until he was far enough away he felt it was safe to use the radio. He keyed the mike and immediately he heard the boss say, "What the hell is going on over there? I've been calling you for thirty minutes."

Albert whispered, "They're right on top of us, and I couldn't use the radio without giving up our position." He explained the situation and waited for the boss to give him instructions.

"Are you sure?" asked Albert.

"Hell yes, I'm sure," came the reply. "Send whoever they're working for a message. Do you copy?"

"Copy that, boss."

* * *

The skipper on *Charybdis* heard the slap of a bullet hit flesh before he actually heard the report from the rifle. It slammed into the kid's head like a watermelon and covered them with red mist and pieces of brain matter. His lifeless body slumped over on the deck like a sack of rice. "God damn it," he yelled. "We got company." The men on the *Charybdis* returned fire briefly, but without a target they were shooting blind. Anticipating the next volley, fortunately they all took cover because just as soon as they did, a machine gun opened fire from across the river. The bullets riddled the side of the boat, sending bits of wood and splinters flying all around them. Smith took a round in his thigh, but it was only a flesh wound. The sound of bullets striking metal reminded the skipper they had reinforced the inside of the hull around those huge fuel tanks with steel plating. It was a good thing; a lucky shot could penetrate the fuel tank and blow them all back to Bimini.

Machine gun fire erupted from the nearest boat, and dirt popped in front of Albert and his two men. The three of them tried to stay low as bullets caromed off the trees around them.

Truby had just finished stowing the hose and was about to pull the truck back up into the clearing when he heard the rifle shot. "What the heck?" he said.

Riley and Hugh saw the flash of gunfire from the woods on Fullerton Island. Riley said, "Take cover. Someone's shooting as us from the other side of the river." Hugh's army training kicked in, and he and Riley both ducked behind the *Scylla*.

Riley looked at his brother and motioned to the bank up above them. Hugh gave him a nod, knowing exactly what he wanted him to do. Then Riley yelled over to Truby, "Get that truck out of here before they turn it into swiss cheese."

Meanwhile, the men on the two boats returned fire, keeping whoever was shooting at them pinned down—for the moment.

Hugh had found a perfect spot high up on the bank behind some trees. He waited for the next shot from the woods to lock onto their position and fired. His first shot hit one of Albert's men in the top of the head, taking the back of it clean off when it exited near the base of his skull. The men on the *Charybdis* strafed the bank with their Tommy guns, and the other man turned to run into the woods when a bullet hit him in the back of the leg and exited through his kneecap, shattering the bone. He went down hard but started crawling to get behind a tree.

Screaming profanities, Albert unloaded his machine gun, spraying bullets across both boats hoping to get lucky and hit somebody or something important. The other man regained his confidence with Albert's anger and propped himself up to rejoin the fight. What he didn't know is that Smith already had a bead on him. He was just waiting for the right opportunity.

There was a brief lull in the gunfire from across the water, so Riley leaned out from behind the boat and fired several shots, narrowly missing Albert before he could take cover behind a bigger tree. The skipper of the *Scylla* yelled, "Smith?" The only reply he heard was a single rifle shot. The bullet passed through a V formed by a fork in the trunk of the tree Albert's man was hiding behind. It hit the man in the throat and exploded out the back of his neck. They could hear the coughing and gurgling from the man as he

150

fell back and died. The skipper replied, "Thank you, Smith."

Outgunned and scared shitless, Albert decided to run. He made it to the boat on the backside of the island right as one of Moore's other boats came flying around the corner. They had heard the gunfire and came to see what it was all about. The skipper of the *Charybdis* motioned towards Fullerton Island. The other boat now had a Gatling gun mounted on the deck. The massive gun roared with a short burst of thirty-millimeter shells as they all watched it disappear behind the point of the island.

Albert couldn't hear the gun yet. It was drowned out by the sound of his own boat and the engine of the boat giving chase. As he got the stern line untied, he turned just in time to see bullet splashes tracking across the water toward him. In that split second he knew his only chance was in the water so he dove, but he was dead before he hit the water—flayed open by multiple rounds from the big gun. One of the shells hit him in the hip and cut him in half, and another took his arm completely off.

The gunmen focused his fire along the waterline of Albert's boat before working his way to the back and the fuel tanks. The huge bullets ripped the smaller boat to shreds before it burst into flames and started to sink. The destruction took less than a minute, and when it was over, and the whir of the big gun subsided, the peace and quiet of the early morning dawn was restored, save for the sound of their motor. They idled over to where Albert had hit the water, as if there was a chance he might still be alive. A big slick of blood rocked on the surface. When they found Albert's body, it was hardly recognizable as having been a person at all. A couple of small bull sharks were tugging at what was left. They watched them feed as a much bigger shark latched onto what was left of the torso and dragged it under.

"Damn," the gunman said.

Scylla and *Charybdis* were pockmarked with bullet holes and one had some broken glass, but other than that, they were still in good shape. The skipper of the *Scylla* surveyed the damage and checked on his men. There was blood everywhere, including on their faces and clothes as they began the gruesome task of cleaning up the deck and wiping themselves off. Two of the crew members wrapped his nephew's body in some croaker sacks they found below. He cranked the motors and started the bilge pumps just in case they were taking on water from any bullet holes below the waterline.

The *Charybdis* fired up its engines as the skipper checked on Smith. He had a nasty gash on his thigh, but it wasn't life threatening. Everyone was accounted for except for one. They searched all around the boats before finally locating the missing crew member floating face down in the water between the two boats. The men pulled his body from the water and got ready to pull out.

Riley and Hugh stood on the dock as the two skippers approached them. The men stood awkwardly before one of them said, "Hell of a shot from up there," looking at Hugh. "Thank you."

Hugh Gant replied, "Same goes to your man over there. Nice shooting. We're real sorry about your crew."

Riley said, "Come on, brother. We gotta go."

All that gunfire was bound to attract attention. Truby was standing behind them. Riley looked at him, expecting bad news, but Truby simply nodded and said, "We're ready to roll. The truck's in good shape minus a few scratches."

Everett led the way as Truby followed them down the road in the fuel truck, with Riley and Hugh bringing up the rear.

Chapter 11

I tried to stay busy for the four days I had been stuck in the office, but it was not easy. Moore had been on my mind all week. I decided it was time to take some action, so I headed down the hall.

"Is he in?" I said.

"Sure is," replied Gwyn.

I tapped on the door and leaned in. "Gene, I really need to go to the Motor Vehicle Department—in Tallahassee."

He looked up from what he was doing. "I agree," said Coonts finally.

I wanted to holler and pump my fist, but I just stood there stoically.

"Check all the out-of-state titles that ended up in the area," he added.

"Yes sir." I started to turn.

"And Julian ..." I stopped. "If you have time, check in with Sheriff Stodemeyer and Will England at NATB. And tell Gladys I said hello."

As I headed out, Gwyn looked up at me with a huge smile on her faced and winked.

* * *

The drive to Tallahassee was close to four hours, and it's not one of the most exciting drives you'll ever make. Fortunately, U.S. Highway 90 is paved and well maintained, but there's not much to see for most of the hundred eighty-mile drive. Even with stops in Lake City, Live Oak, and Madison, it's hard to pass the time. There is a ton of farmland and cattle and not much else.

This road ran through the county seat of fifteen different counties between the East Coast and the state line with Alabama, and it connected many of the courthouses in each county. I'd been to most of them, but Coonts had been to all of them so many times that everyone knew who he was when he passed through. Most of the NATB agents got to know every sheriff and police chief in their state, and the successful ones knew just about every prosecutor too.

Monroe Street was a welcome sight after all that driving, and I was looking forward to a good stretch before visiting the motor vehicle building. There was a filling station on the edge of town that I always stopped at because they had a soda fountain and air conditioning. It was a good spot to cool off, stretch your legs, and unwind after the long road trip.

Next stop—the motor vehicle department.

Gladys Huck was a librarian before she took over the department, and she organized the states record's like General Pershing himself had ordered it. She was tall with dark curly hair, and she always wore an ankle-length skirt with an arm-length white blouse that had ruffles around her neck and down the front. Her glasses were always perched on the tip of her nose, and when she spoke she tilted her head forward so she could look at you over the top of her rims. Her eyebrows arched up so as to tighten her face just enough so the glasses wouldn't slide off. Her lips bunched up into a tiny oval before she spoke.

The way she looked over those glasses always made me feel like she was looking down on me. Gladys was in charge of all the state's public records, including all automobile titles issued in the state. When she saw me coming, she immediately got up from her chair and came out from behind her desk to greet me.

"Agent Clark, how are you? It's good to see you again."

"Well, thank you, Gladys. It's always a pleasure seeing you too," I replied.

"Gwyneth sent word that you were on your way, but I wasn't expecting you until a little later. You made good time coming all the way from Jacksonville. The Bureau must be giving you gentlemen faster automobiles these days. Or maybe it's that lead foot of yours?"

"Probably more of the latter."

"Well, you better keep it under the speed limit while you're in Tallahassee, especially out there on Tennessee Street. They'll give you a ticket faster than you can say Tallahassee, Florida."

"Thanks for the warning, Gladys."

"So what brings you to town this time?"

"Gene and I are working on a couple of cases, and he sent me over here to look through some records. By the way, he told me to tell you hello."

"Lucky you, getting to drive all the way over here to do his dirty work," she said. "Follow me and we'll get you set up at a table and bring you the files. Speaking of Coonts's dirty work, we've been keeping a list of the 'general delivery' applications lately. We've got a half dozen or so worth taking a look at." She motioned to a young lady at another desk to follow us. "This is Alice. She can get you whatever you need."

"Nice to meet you, Mr. Clark," said Alice.

"It's *Agent* Clark, Alice," said Gladys.

"Please forgive me, *Agent* Clark," she said as we followed Gladys down the hall to the title room. I looked at Alice and gave her a wink, and she held back a giggle as Gladys looked back over her shoulder to see what was so funny. We both snapped to and tried to maintain a straight face.

"What counties are you interested in this time?" asked Gladys.

"Palm Beach mostly, but we should probably also look at Martin and Broward." On the drive over, I rewound as much of the conversations about the Palm Beach area as I could, and I remembered Tomlinson and Jones talking about Stuart and Jupiter when we were discussing the Hunt-Gant involvement. Stuart was in Martin County, and then I figured Broward since it was just south of Palm Beach. We could always expand our search if we needed to.

Alice headed off to find the files I requested, and Gladys went back to her desk. When Alice returned, she was carrying two boxes of Palm Beach County files and could barely see over the top. She set them down on the table and said, "The bottom one contains the dealer files, and this one on top contains the individual title requests. I'll be right back with Martin and

Broward. Martin doesn't even fill up a box, but Broward's pretty big."

"Are the indexes still in the front of each box?" I said.

Alice replied, "It sounds like you know what you are doing."

"I've spent a lot of time in here, Alice."

She returned a few minutes later with the Martin and Broward County files, and a separate folder that had "NATB" printed on the front and set them on the table. As she walked off, she said, "Let me know if you have any questions or if I can get you anything, Agent Clark."

"Yes, ma'am." I made myself comfortable and started arranging stacks of files on the table, and then I noticed Alice had hesitated before walking away.

"Agent Clark?" she said. "Would you mind showing me what you are doing? I would love to learn something new. It gets pretty boring in here."

"Uh. Yeah, sure. Why not? Basically, we are trying to catch a thief."

"Sounds exciting." She pulled up a chair and sat down next to me—a little too close.

"It can be. Unfortunately, this isn't the exciting part," I said.

"I don't care. I still want to learn. Will you teach me?" she asked.

"Okay. So what we're doing is looking for exceptions—outliers. Those little things that don't fit the normal course of things. The proof of ownership files are the best place to start looking for suspicious transactions. The most common is a quick transfer of title."

"But title transfers happen all the time. That's one of our most common routines."

"Right. However, we're looking for ones that don't fit the normal routine. We used to waste hours looking through title transfers until Gladys starting putting these indexes in the front of each county file with the date of the request. For example, let's say an automobile titled in New York showed up in Florida. Eventually, you're going to get the request to transfer that title down here."

"I process transfers like that all day," said Alice.

"On average, how long would you say that normally takes?" I asked.

"Months," she said.

"Bingo. So we're looking for transfer requests of less than ninety days. Ones filed after only a couple of weeks are super suspicious. Sometimes we focus on certain used-auto dealers that purchase a lot of out-of-state vehicles. A dishonest dealer can become a thief's best friend by providing a way to 'launder' a larger volume of stolen vehicles."

"So that's why Ms. Huck started having us include those indexes," she said.

"Thanks for that. You're saving NATB agents a lot of time."

"What else are you looking for?" Alice asked.

"Good question. So another suspicious activity is the use of general delivery mail."

"I always wondered about that," she said. "Why some people ask us to mail important documents like a title general delivery instead of to the person that owns the vehicle."

"You've got good instincts. Oftentimes we find a title in the name of John Doe, but then mailed general delivery to another name. Again, we're looking for exceptions. Anything that seems out of character with what we consider normal should get a closer look."

Of all the ways we uncovered stolen automobiles, this was certainly the most mundane. Especially since most of the suspicious paperwork we uncovered turned out to be completely legitimate. It was nice to have help, and Alice's interest in our work was refreshing.

"Okay, got it. Give me a county and I'll start digging. At least until Ms. Huck catches me." She laughed.

"Well, I don't want you to get in trouble."

"Don't worry about it. I wasn't that busy anyway, and I'd much rather be helping you. Just help me keep an eye out for her," she said.

"Okay. Let's do this," I said.

If I knew the name of the person that applied for the title, a search for that title was easy, so obviously as I searched through the files, I kept a lookout for specific names like Hunt, Gant, Overton, Moore, and a short list of others. I was not really expecting to find any of these names because, let's face it, most automobile thieves don't use their real names. Then a thought occurred to me.

"Alice. Stop what you're doing."

"What is it, Julian? What can I do?"

"I just had an idea that would make this go a lot faster." I pulled out a list of names that Coónts and I had been working on for some time. "This is a list of known aliases that a particular family has used for various criminal activity over the last couple of years. Do you think you could search for these names in the proof of ownership files to see if they applied for any titles in the last six months?"

"Yeah, sure. I'll get right on it. Let me see your list please," Alice said.

Hugh Gant and both Alva and Truby Hunt had an extensive list of aliases that we were aware of and no telling how many we weren't aware of. While Alice looked for several of Truby Hunt's and Hugh Gant's aliases, I planned to keep looking for suspicious transfers of title.

Two hours later, I was close to the end of the Martin County files and only had a few suspicious titles worth looking into. None of them sparked much interest and were probably legitimate. Alice hadn't found anything on any of the aliases I gave her either. I was about to give up when I accidentally knocked the single folder with "NATB" printed on the front off the table and onto the floor. It had gotten buried under my work and slowly made its way back to the surface as I put files back in their boxes.

When I opened the folder, I found only a dozen pieces of paper inside. Really just copies of titles and bill of sales, but in Gladys's telltale script inside the front cover were several names. She had also written the city next to each one.

I skimmed down the list and didn't recognize any of the names, but one of them was registered in Lake Worth. I thumbed through the pages until I found the Lake Worth title for a late-model Ford, bill of sale, and application. Randolph Mays. The name didn't ring any bells, but it was the only one in Palm Beach County. There was one in Deland not far from Palm registered to a Tommie Wallace. There was also one from Miami, which was close, but the others were from areas along the west coast of Florida and a few were from Orlando.

All the paperwork looked pretty clean, but it was easy enough to falsify. The crooks even had the notary seals to make it all look professional. The seller's name on the bill of sale was a man named Cadwell.

Cadwell. Cadwell. I repeated the name several times in my mind. I knew it sounded familiar, but I couldn't place it. Regardless, it was definitely worth checking out.

* * *

The hundred and eighty-mile drive back to Jacksonville was just as monotonous as the trip over—almost. I usually broke up the drive in the same places as the trip west. Madison. Live Oak. Lake City. On the stretch just east of Lee, I came up on an accident practically blocking the entire road. Five hundred yards away I could already tell there was a mess up ahead, and as I got closer I could make out a few people milling around and smoke. The closer I got, I could see the roadway was practically blocked by a damaged vehicle and something else I couldn't make out. The road was littered with small piles of—something.

I slowed down and pulled over on the shoulder behind what looked like had been a Lincoln. A couple of westbound vehicles had also pulled over to help. "Everyone all right?" I asked.

The man closest turned around and said, "Barely. Everyone but her." He pointed at a heap of hair, blood, and entrails lying in the back seat of his automobile. "And my automobile! How the heck am I going to get that out?"

The Lincoln Model L was easily one of the most beautiful automobiles on the road, and this one was no exception. Unfortunately, it was a Phaeton—or maybe fortunately.

"What happened?" I asked.

"I saw all those cows grazing, but they weren't moving and it didn't look like they were going to come out in the road. It just happened so fast. Next thing I know, she jumps off the little embankment right in front of me. I was on the brakes hard—and the horn, but there was nothing either one of us could do. I swerved as much as I could, trying to give her room, but there

159

was another vehicle coming toward us." He pointed to a Ford parked on the other side of the roadway.

While he was talking, I noticed his suit was covered with something dark and slick and his hair was all matted down with the same stuff. Blood. Or guts. Probably both. Then the smell hit me.

I walked around the Lincoln to survey the damage. The right front end was totally smashed almost to the windshield. It was remarkable they hadn't been killed or ejected. Somehow that cow managed to roll up and over the front and make it over both the driver and passenger's heads, tearing the roof off before landing in the back seat—sans head. Cow parts were spread all over the road like little land mines. The Lincoln was a beautiful red, so it was hard to tell where the paint stopped and the blood began.

The interior had wet, gooey bits of fur and cow all over the seats. I got closer to look at what was left of the cow in the back seat, and my right foot squished down on something soft. It made an oozing sound like if I had slowly stepped down on a giant slug. The head was missing, and a long strand of entrails was draped over the back seat onto the hood and almost touching the ground behind it. What a mess.

This was actually pretty common in Florida and even South Georgia. This was cattle country and the laws didn't require fences so it was basically all open range. Most of these cattle farmers leased the land from the state for next to nothing just for the right to let their cattle graze. Cows wandered out into the highway all of the time.

"Lots of people get killed this way," I said. "You gentlemen are lucky. I've never seen one end up like that, though. Hit one myself between Savannah and Jacksonville. Made a mess out of my automobile, but fortunately, I could still drive it. Cow wasn't so lucky."

About that time I noticed a man coming across the field on horseback from the direction where all the cows were grazing. I motioned toward him and said, "That's probably going to be the man that owns this herd. He's going want to be compensated for killing one of his cows."

"You can't be serious!" the driver of the Lincoln exclaimed. "That damn thing almost killed us!"

The driver of the Ford yelled across the roadway, "Hey! We found the head." He was pointing at something on the front of his vehicle. Somehow that cow's head had gotten wedged between the spare and the engine cowling—another first for me.

"I'll stop in Live Oak and send a tow truck this way if you like. I know the sheriff there too. I'll let him know what happened. A lot of us have been trying to get the open range laws changed so we can get some fencing out here."

"How are we going to get the cow out of my backseat?"

"You'll probably have to tow it to Live Oak and get some extra help. The shop there might be able to lift it out with an engine hoist. I don't know—they'll think of something. Maybe just cut it up and do it piece by piece."

The passenger of the Lincoln was already pale and queasy, but the thought of having to cut up the cow was too much for his stomach. He turned around and vomited on the the side of the road. Can't really blame him—the smell was really starting to get to me too.

"Thanks for the help, mister."

I got back in my Chevrolet and slowly pulled around the Lincoln while trying to dodge some of the larger cow parts. That stuff gets up under your vehicle and really gets to stinking once it gets hot, and I don't want to smell burnt hair and flesh all the way back to Jacksonville. It was like driving through a minefield.

Cows got hit all the time out on the highway, and the farmers usually had no way to find the driver. People just left them out there to rot. I imagined it could be pretty costly to be losing cows like that. I'd heard plenty of stories about farmers dragging cows from the road to a nearby railroad track, then claiming the train hit them so they could get compensated by the railroad for killing their cattle. That poor fella back there was going to have to fix that Lincoln *and* pay for the cow.

* * *

I spent an extra hour in Live Oak telling Sheriff Choate what happened and getting a tow truck to head west and help out. Fortunately, nobody got hurt, so we had a good laugh about the whole thing. I warned the tow truck driver about the mess and that he should probably take some help.

It was good catching up with Choate—he and Coonts had known each other for a long time. He had a couple of cases that we needed to look into, so I asked him to send us what he had.

It was almost dinnertime by the time I got home, and Frances was already fixing to put out the meal. She gave me a big hug at the door like we hadn't seen each other in forever. I could smell peanuts roasting in the kitchen.

"Harry's coming over for dinner."

"Oh, really," I said.

"I'm pretty sure he wants to talk to you about something."

"Well, I'm pretty sure he uses his little talks as an excuse to come see you."

"He's harmless, Julian, but you're probably right. You better watch out, though. Lately, I feel like I talk to Harry more than I get to talk to you. How was Tallahassee?"

"Exactly what I needed."

"Have you got your head on straight now?"

"Almost, but I think my trip to Palm Beach might finally do the trick."

I looked back at Frances from the living room and caught her glancing back at me with that sly look she liked to give me. "Baby, do I have time to get cleaned up?"

"We'll wait for you."

Harry Mega had become a good friend since we moved to Jacksonville. Tomlinson and Jones had known him ever since he moved down here from New York, and they introduced me and Frances to him first. It was obvious he took a liking to Frances early on, but I think he genuinely wanted us to love Jacksonville like he did, and he wanted to help us fit in and meet people.

Everybody in town knew Harry. He was one of biggest used-auto dealers in the state and had at least five locations that I knew of. Only two were in Jacksonville, though. Harry's dad emigrated from Greece to the United States back around 1880 and settled in New York. Harry's real name was

Haris Megara, but he changed it to Harry Mega when he moved to Florida.

He wasn't trying to hide anything, at least not that I was aware of, but the way he told it is, he wanted to be the biggest used-automobile dealer in the country, and he needed a way to market himself. What better way to do it than call his first lot Mega's? He built a hugely successful business around the name, and so of course it made perfect sense now.

Harry was a born salesman—and a handsome devil too, which certainly didn't hurt if you were trying to sell automobiles. He had a very Mediterranean look with a dark, olive complexion. His hair was jet black and thick and so was his brow. He also had large eyes and a perfectly straight nose. He was loud and gregarious, but small in stature—barely over five feet. Harry could talk to anyone and never met a stranger. He was an interesting, worldly type of man who was always good for a story, but once you got to know him, you realized that everything he did was about making a buck.

On occasion, Harry would call my house with a tip. He always called the house, not the office. Mostly because I think he wanted to talk to Frances, but he always said it was because he didn't want the word to get around he was helping us out. Anyway, he would tell Frances to let me know we needed to talk when I had time. During our little "talks," he would offer up some information about a suspicious auto from up north being offered for sale. He always turned these vehicles down because he was afraid they were stolen, and then he'd have someone follow these suspicious cars and see where they ended up. We recovered numerous stolen autos on his information.

Harry was an opportunist so I knew there was some quid pro quo going on. The funny thing was, I wasn't sure what something he was getting from me. Dad had a saying when it came to cards, business, and women—if you don't know who the sucker is, it's you. I had a feeling about Harry, and I was usually a pretty good judge of character. There was more to him than most of us were willing to admit, but the truth is, we all liked Harry, and he had helped us a lot. Dad had another saying—sometimes a known devil was better than an unknown angel. I'd rather keep Harry close, especially being in the used-auto business. So far it was a relationship that was still paying dividends.

Harry showed up fifteen minutes after I got home, just as I finished getting cleaned up. I could hear him and Frances carrying on in the kitchen.

"Harry! Good to see you, old man."

"You better watch yourself," he said. "This old man can still whip you."

"Make yourself useful, Julian, and set the table, please," said Frances.

"Anything for you, dear."

Harry chuckled and was about to say something when Frances handed him a bowl of cornbread and pushed him toward the table. "You too."

"Well, now we know who can whip us both."

Once everything was on the table, I blessed the food and we sat down to eat. We made small talk for a while and covered most of the usual subjects. The weather, the beaches, and the next hurricane season were some of the standards. Frances wanted to know about certain people or goings-on she had seen in the neighborhood or about someone she met in the garden club. It was hard to avoid the subject of the growing depression and what it was doing to people and businesses.

"How are you two making out?" asked Harry.

"Fortunately, we are both employed," said Frances. "Bell is actually still hiring in some towns. With the popularity of the telephone, it's hard to imagine this company not continuing to grow, but who really knows how bad things could get? Julian and I talk about it all the time, though. We are saving as much as we can to be prepared. There's talk about limiting households to one job."

"That would be a shame if I had to stay home while you went to work every day, Frances."

Frances said, "Such a gentleman."

"I don't know what's going to happen, but fortunately, J. Edgar Hoover has our backs in Washington. Of course, they could cut our budget or do away with the NATB altogether, but the insurance lobby is pretty powerful, and I don't think they will let that happen. As long as people keep stealing automobiles, it's business as usual, but changes are coming—that's for sure. What do you think, Harry?"

"This whole idea of volunteerism Herbert Hoover is touting isn't going to work. You can't tell a business they can't cut wages or lay people off if they aren't selling anything. As much as we would all love to keep paying our employees, it's simply not realistic."

"How's your business doing?" I asked.

"For now, we seem to be the beneficiary of the downturn at the big dealers. People are buying more used cars because they either can't afford a new one or don't want to spend the money. I think they are just being cautious, which is smart. I wish I could say it's going to last, but something tells me this is going a lot deeper and even the used-auto business is going to take a big hit. I'll probably cut my inventory in half over the next six months and try to ride it out."

"What about this Smoot-Hawley thing?" I asked.

"Another terrible idea hatched by the government. What makes Washington think our overseas competitors won't raise tariffs too? Seems like a trade war nobody is going to win, but what do I know? I'm just a small businessman trying to scratch out a living."

Frances added, "We have some friends in Atlanta that were doing real well. He was a stockbroker and she didn't even have to work. Now he's out of a job, and we heard they had to move out of their house."

"So what else is on your mind, Harry? I know you well enough to know something is eating at you. Let's hear it."

"I suppose you're right, Julian. Listen, I really am sorry about what happened out there in Gulf Hammock. I never in a million years would have suggested you go out there looking for that truck if I had known how dangerous it would turn out. Besides, you were supposed to take Sheriff Karel with you."

"Don't sweat it, Harry. It all worked out. I never should have gone out there alone anyway. Coonts was pretty hot about the whole thing, but I was already there, and Sheriff Karel was busy. We never would have suspected anyone would stay out there in those woods. Rotten luck it turned out to be Harold Hunt."

"I was pretty hot about it too, in case you forgot." Frances shot me a look that could have killed. "He walked out of here that morning and told me to expect him home for dinner! You believe that? Next thing I know, Sheriff Karel is calling to let me know that not only is he not coming home for dinner, he's not coming home for another day or so and not to worry."

"Frances, can you ever forgive me?" asked Harry.

"Oh sure, Harry. It's going to take a little longer to forgive him, though."

"Well, don't wait too long. He's too good a man."

"Thanks, Harry," I said. "You got any other leads for me?"

"Don't even think about it, Julian," Frances said, standing up to start clearing the table.

We both helped clear the table and then helped Frances clean the dishes and the kitchen. After Frances and Harry said their goodbyes, I said, "Come on, Harry, I'll show you out." We walked out on the front porch and I closed the door behind me. "So what's really on your mind, Harry? I know there's something more you wanted to say in there."

"You didn't hear this from me."

"I never do."

"Stop in Deland on your way to Palm Beach. There's a good chance you'll find a Hunt or a Gant there. Talk to the sheriff first. This time I mean it. Don't go doing anything stupid, Julian. I know you can take care of yourself, but Frances will skin us both if you get in trouble again, and if she thinks I had anything to do with it."

"Not to mention Coonts," I said.

The front door opened and we both looked back to see Frances glaring at us.

"Thanks again for dinner, Frances. Take care of yourself, Julian. Don't do anything I wouldn't do down there in Palm Beach."

"Thanks, Harry."

I turned to go back inside, but Frances was blocking the door. "What?"

"What were you two talking about out here?"

"Not much." Frances had that look. "He was just warning me about the Hunt-Gant gang after my little brush-up with Harold and seeing as I was the last person to see him alive."

"Is that all?"

I couldn't lie to her—she knew me too well.

"Just guy talk, Frances. That's all."

She wrapped her arms around my neck and pulled herself in close. "Please try to be more careful, Julian. I don't know what I would do without you."

"Frances, you know me better than that. I won't take any unnecessary chances, but my job has its risks."

"I know, Julian, but promise me you'll come back in one piece. No black eyes this time?"

"Harry did have some . . . information." I was hesitant to call it a tip because those always turned out to be dangerous.

"Of course he did." She pulled her head off my chest to look me in the eye.

"He suggested I go see the sheriff in Deland on my way to Palm Beach. It's no big deal."

"No black eyes?"

"I'll do my best, baby. Now can we go inside?"

"Promise?"

"I promise."

"Juney—thanks for telling me."

"I love you, baby."

* * *

The next morning I decided to stop by the office and see Coonts before heading south to Palm Beach. I needed to talk to him about going to Deland too. Maybe we could get the sheriff on the phone before heading down there.

"Julian, I'm glad you're here. What's your schedule?"

"I'm on my way to Palm Beach."

He hesitated as if to consider whether he was going to let me go.

"Good. Well, sort of—just not yet. Can you give us an hour?"

"Us?"

"Tomlinson and Jones."

"I've got thirty minutes tops. Also, do you know the sheriff in Deland?"

"Sure. Sheriff Hutchins. Why?"

"Harry suggested I might find one of the Hunts there —with a stolen Ford." Director Coonts looked at me with his usual sideways glance. "I know what you're thinking, but has he ever steered us wrong?" I could tell Coonts was on the fence this time, but I knew he would come around.

"Come in my office. Let's see if we can get him on the phone." He started to walk away and then turned back. "First, go tell Tomlinson and Jones to come up here in ten minutes, and let them know you don't have much time before you leave."

Coonts was hanging up the phone with the sheriff down in Deland when I walked in his office. "Sheriff Hutchins is expecting you. He'll fill you in when you get there, but he says they do have a man fitting Truby Hunt's description holed up at a little motel outside of town."

"Well, I'll be," I said.

"Exactly. Be careful and do not go over there alone. Do you understand me?"

"Yes sir," I said.

"Are we clear?" he added.

"Crystal."

Tomlinson and Jones came in and we had a brief conversation about warrants for Goldberg and the dismantling of their theft ring, but I really needed to get going. It was just over a hundred miles to Deland and would probably take me at least two hours, so I told everyone I had to leave.

Chapter 12

Just after lunch I got to the sheriff's office in Deland.

"Julian. Glad to meet you. Coonts said you were on the way, but damn, you made good time," Sheriff Hutchins said.

"I'm actually on my way down to Palm Beach," I said.

"Palm Beach?"

"We're investigating several leads down there. Really just trying to help the Bureau and Treasury solve a crime that happens to involve some stolen autos."

"Okay, sounds good. Let us know if we can help."

"You may already be helping. Coonts said you were keeping an eye on someone fitting Truby Hunt's description," I said.

"That's right. This man showed up four or five days ago and has just been hanging around out at this tin-can tourist court on the edge of town. One of my deputies was out there looking into a domestic dispute, and something didn't sit right with him about this fella. Got him a girl out there too. Young. We've been keeping an eye on him."

"What's he driving?" I asked.

"Brand-new Chevrolet. That's what tweaked my guy's suspicion first. We're familiar with the Hunts and the Gants," the sheriff said.

"How do you want to handle it?" I asked.

The sheriff leaned over toward the open door and yelled down the hall. "Clifton. Come in here, please."

The man that walked in had to be at least six feet tall. He looked down at me and nodded.

169

"Yes sir?" he said.

"This is Agent Clark from NATB in Jacksonville. Julian, this is George Clifton," the sheriff said.

We shook hands as the sheriff continued

"Julian's investigating some stolen autos and got a tip about one of them possibly being out at Gundek's. Why don't you take him over there and find out what our guy is up to?"

"Let's go," Deputy Clifton said.

"What's Gundek's?" I asked.

"Henry Gundek owns the place. He gets some pretty unsavory types out there. Doesn't ask questions—if you know what I mean," said the sheriff.

"Got it," I said.

Deputy Clifton said, "Julian, are you able to determine if the vehicle is straight or not?"

"Yep. No problem."

"By the way, Julian—who's Harry Mega?" the sheriff asked as we headed out the door.

"Just a friend," I said. "In the business." The sheriff looked at me inquisitively.

We decided to take my Chevrolet instead of George's vehicle so we didn't spook the couple by showing up in a sheriff's cruiser. We were still just acting on a tip, so it could turn out to be nothing.

When we got there, we went to the office first to talk to the gentleman that owned the place. The office was just inside the gate and sat up on a hill. The rooms, which were more like cabins, were all situated down the hill behind the office, so after someone checked in, they had to drive around back and find their cabin. Each one had two parking spaces out front.

Tourist courts were pretty cheap places—cheaper than a motel—and this one was no exception. The property wasn't maintained at all, and every structure needed a coat of paint. The pool beside the office had about two feet of black water in it along with what looked like twisted sheet metal from a roof that might have provided shade before being knocked down by a storm. The rusted support posts were still standing on one side. There

170

were weeds growing in the parking lot.

We walked inside the office, which smelled musty, damp, and a little like the old blue tick hound that was lying in the corner. He lifted his head slightly and sniffed the air before going back to his nap. There was a dead roach on the carpet near the door. I rang the bell on the counter, and we waited for the owner to come out.

"Can I help you?" we heard a voice come from the office in back.

George said, "Henry. It's Deputy Clifton, and I've got Agent Clark with me from the NATB. Sheriff Hutchins sent us over."

"Oh. You again. Be right with you."

The man who operated the tourist court came out from his office wearing dirty overalls, and he had an unlit cigarette hanging from the corner of his mouth. He directed us to the cabin where this suspicious couple was staying and said, "Try not to damage anything."

I thought to myself—how would he know? George looked at me like he was probably thinking the same thing.

We drove around back and went down the hill until we saw the new Chevrolet out front of this one-room cabin where they were staying. A young lady was standing on the threshold —a real looker in her twenties. The owner told us they were registered under the name Wallace. Well, coincidentally, one of the records Gladys had given me in Tallahassee was a registration in the name of Wallace. I still had it in my briefcase. The title had been mailed out general delivery to a little town near Deland. My gut was telling me the Chevrolet we were looking at was stolen. It certainly fit the description.

When we pulled up, the young lady in the doorway didn't act concerned at all. Confident was the way she looked. We got out and walked up to the cabin—still no movement out of the woman at the door. She was leaning against the doorframe, smoking a cigarette and had what looked like a highball in her hand.

Deputy Clifton tipped his hat to her and said, "Ma'am." No sooner had the word left his mouth than we heard someone inside bark, "Well, who the hell is it Marie?"

Deputy Clifton said, "Is there a Tommie Wallace here?"

She gestured over her shoulder with a slight nod of her head.

As we walked up to the door, she moved inside to let us in. I was still impressed with her cool demeanor. Inside the room was this man lying on the right side of a bed, propped up against the headboard with some pillows behind him, wearing nothing but a pair of khaki pants and a fedora. He was using his left arm to prop his head up, and his right was stretched across the bed but underneath the pillows. It was none other than Truby Hunt.

I said, "Hello, Truby."

"My name's not Truby."

"I know you, and your name is Truby Hunt."

"You're mistaken, mister. My name's Wallace."

Might as well play along. "Well, in that case you must be just the Wallace I'm looking for. I've got a title in the name of Wallace for a stolen automobile, and I'm willing to bet it's that Chevrolet sitting right out front."

"And who are you?"

"I didn't say." It had been at least a year since the first time I arrested Truby, but I knew it was him as soon as I saw him. Fortunately, he hadn't recognized me. I guess we could add another alias to the long list used by the Hunt family.

He realized he was about to get pinched. Deputy Clifton saw it too, and his hand made an almost imperceptible move toward his pistol. "Almost" is the key word, because Hunt, or Wallace, noticed it too and already had his hand on a rifle under the pillow next to him. Before Deputy Clifton could move, this man pulled a rifle from behind the pillows and had it drawn right on me. I've never seen someone pull a rifle out as fast as he did.

He jumped up off the bed and came across the room at me. "Don't even think about it, deputy, or he gets it," he said, motioning at me. Then he yelled at his girl, "Marie, go get my shirt out of that automobile!"

Just as she turned to go past me, her body briefly shielded me from the barrel of that gun, and blocked Truby from seeing George draw his weapon. As his gun came out in his right hand, he was moving towards Truby with his left hand out. As soon as Marie cleared the barrel his hand was already pushing it upwards as he swung his pistol at the side of Truby's head. I don't know how George got it out that fast, but wielding a rifle in close quarters is not easy to do, which gave George the upper hand. His pistol sight must have hit Truby above his brow because blood started squirting out just like he stuck a pig, but he wasn't giving up.

With the barrel of his rifle now pointed at the ceiling, he tried to use the butt of the stock as a weapon by pulling his left hand towards him while thrusting the butt up and around towards Deputy Clifton's jaw. The gun fired with a deafening crack, but the bullet went up into the ceiling, and the stock missed the Deputy's jaw by a fraction. Clifton had seen it coming and was making his next move as well. He had gotten his left foot slightly behind Truby's right heel. Truby's weight was already on his back foot so all the Deputy had to do was keep pushing with his left hand, which still had a hold of the barrel of that rifle, and send Truby to the floor on his back with a thud. He had blood all over his face, and it was clear he didn't have any fight left in him.

Deputy Clifton flipped him over and cuffed him. Marie made a run for the vehicle out front, and I ran out after her. She got in the Chevy and was trying to start it when I reached in through the window and grabbed her hand and squeezed it hard enough for her to turn loose the keys. When she did, she slapped me just as hard as she could.

"Young lady, we can do this the easy way, or we can do this the hard way." She just stared forward and didn't say a word. I tried again. "Why are you hanging out with a lowlife like Truby Hunt?" Still nothing. Not even a glance. So with my face stinging like the dickens, I opened the door and waited for her to get out and walk back up to the cabin. George had Truby up on his feet and was holding a bandage on his head to try to contain the bleeding.

Truby looked at me and said, "I know you. You're that damned Agent Clark. You killed my brother Harold."

"I didn't kill your brother," I said. Marie wound up and tried to hit me again, but I was ready this time. I caught her arm mid-swing, "Don't do that again, or I'll cuff you just like him." George put Hunt in the back of the

173

stolen Chevrolet, and I gestured for Marie to get in the front seat.

"Keep an eye on them, please. I'm going up to the office to call the sheriff and have him send a squad car to transport these two to jail."

While we waited for the sheriff to send a deputy over to pick up Truby and his girl, I decided to take a closer look at that Chevrolet.

"What are you doing up there, Clark?" I heard Truby ask from the back seat.

"Oh, just collecting evidence to put you in jail," I said from under the hood.

"Evidence? You don't know shit, Clark," he said.

The numbers had definitely been changed, and they matched the numbers on the title and bill of sale I had in my briefcase. It didn't take long to locate the confidential numbers on the frame, so it wouldn't be hard to trace it back to the original owner.

I let the hood drop with a bang and walked around to Truby's open window. "It's got your fingerprints all over it, Truby."

Marie said, "Fingerprints? I thought you said—"

"Shut up, Marie," Truby said.

"You see, Marie," I offered. "You investigate enough stolen autos and you start to recognize patterns."

A sheriff's deputy pulled up and Deputy Clifton opened Truby's door. "Let's go."

"We need to take him to see a doc and get that cut stitched up before we book him on auto theft charges," Clifton said to the other deputy.

"What about her?" the deputy asked.

"Put her in back with Hunt."

Once they were safely locked up in the back of the deputy's vehicle, George came around to talk to me. "I think we should let Ms. Skinner walk."

"Fine by me. Thanks for the help. That was some mighty fine work. That could I have gotten ugly."

"Anytime, Julian. You want to follow us back in that?" He nodded toward the stolen Chevrolet.

"Yep."

Another tip from Harry Mega had paid off. The real question was; how

174

did he know where Truby was going to be?

There wasn't enough time to drive to Palm Beach, so I decided to spend a night in Cocoa. As I left the sheriff's station, I wondered if Marie Skinner would stop hanging out with the likes of Truby Hunt. Doubtful. She was only twenty years old.

Chapter 13

The drive to Palm Beach from Cocoa is about one hundred thirty-four miles or a little over two hours.

I left early the next morning and made my way south from Cocoa Beach just as the sun was coming up. I loved the drive south down Highway One. The road hugged the Indian River for about seventy-two miles before turning inland between Ft. Pierce and Stuart. Then it worked its way back toward the water and the Intracoastal Waterway for the rest of the drive to Palm Beach. I loved the water and the drive was absolutely beautiful.

All that time on the road gave me time to think about the Hunt-Gant business as well as Wilbur Moore and his connections. Ed Lawrence made it pretty clear that Moore was dangerous and into some big league criminal activity. But what, if anything, did it have to do with Jim Genna? More important, what did it have to do with Hunt-Gant and stolen vehicles? Maybe nothing, but we'd been investigating Alva Hunt and Hugh Gant long enough to know it wouldn't be easy to pin anything on either one of them. They obviously thought I had something to do with the death of Harold, so a run-in with anyone from either family was likely to get dicey. Especially now that we just arrested Truby Hunt. Tomlinson and Jones had warned me about those guys coming after me.

As I bumped along A1A, about to cross the St. Lucie River into Stuart, something else clicked. Cigarettes. That was the connection I kept searching for in my mind, but I simply hadn't connected the dots yet. Were the Hunts working for Jim Genna? Why else would they have stolen that tobacco truck? I was reminded of my conversation with Vernon Chris at the Cloister about

Jim Genna being there, and he also mentioned cigarettes.

At the time, I had no idea why any of these folks would be connected, but now it was starting to make sense. The Hunts had to be working for Genna, so they stole that truck and sold him all those cigarettes. That's also why we started finding bootleg liquor in some of those stolen autos. It was for Genna—or Moore. Maybe Moore brought it in and Hunt-Gant moved it. Either way—it didn't really matter. Genna needed liquor and lots of it for his clubs, same with cigarettes. He could have bought those legally, but if your runners showed up with a truckload offering them up for pennies on the dollar; why not?

On the way down to Palm Beach, I thought about going straight to Wilbur Moore's house and checking it out, but I promised Coonts to play this his way, so my better judgment took over. I was at least an hour early, but I decided to go ahead to Ed Lawrence's office and see if he could shed any light on the evidence I picked up in Tallahassee. Ed was pretty excited when I got there and suggested we go over to the courthouse and find Grady Emory and Sheriff George Baker. Grady was a revenue agent working for the U.S. Treasury, and if anybody wanted Wilbur Moore locked up or dead, it was those guys.

"Hey, Grady," said Ed as we walked into his office. "This is Agent Clark with the NATB in Jacksonville. He's helping us out on a couple of cases, one of which may implicate Wilbur Moore."

Grady scoffed, "Man, I would love to nail that son of a bitch with something. Nice to meet you, Clark."

Ed continued, "Julian's been in Tallahassee doing a little research before coming down here. Remember I told you about our meeting in Jacksonville with Thaye Ersley? We were hoping we might get lucky and catch Moore with a stolen automobile or maybe find some reason for a warrant to search his place."

"Well, let's see what you found, Julian," said Grady.

"Unfortunately, it wasn't much, but on the way down here I came up with my own theory about how we might connect him to some serious bootlegging. First, let me show you what I dug up in Tallahassee." I put my briefcase on the table and snapped the latches open. Ed practically had his head inside it before I could get it opened. I pulled out a file and laid it on the table. "Ever hear of a fella named Tommie Wallace?" They both looked at me with blank faces. "What about Gordon Fletcher?"

Nothing.

"What about a fella named Randolph Mays?"

"Seriously? Julian, Randolph Mays is Arthur Cadwell's brother-in-law. Why?"

I knew Cadwell sounded familiar.

"Red Overton's son-in-law," reminded Ed.

"Right. Right. Well, Coonts and I had one of the clerks in Tallahassee keeping a lookout for certain suspicious transactions, and this was one of them." I handed him a copy of the title and the bill of sale. After a few seconds he looked up at me with a grin.

He asked, "Arthur Cadwell sold this Ford to Randolph Mays?"

"Yup! Three weeks ago. And the title was mailed general delivery. Get me an opportunity to take a look under the hood of that Ford, and I'll bet you anything it's stolen."

"But it's still possible it's straight, right?" asked Grady.

"Sure," I said.

"Anything's possible with that crowd," said Ed. "But this is what Cadwell does—steal automobiles."

"And, we've busted plenty of auto thieves with straight cars." Grady was giving me a funny look. "I know it sounds strange, but sometimes just having a warrant and harassing one of these characters will get them to say or do something stupid. Or sometimes the automobile we are looking for is straight but there may be others that aren't. Just get me a look at it and let's see where it leads. Sometime you have to shake a few trees and see what falls out."

"Okay. Now about that theory of yours," said Ed.

"On the way down here, something kept niggling at me, but I couldn't figure out what it was. Finally, it clicked—those cigarettes."

"Cigarettes. What cigarettes?" ask Grady.

I proceeded to tell Grady about the tobacco truck I tracked out in Gulf Hammock and my run-in with Harold Hunt. I also told him about the other stolen autos we traced back to Hunt-Gant and the red liquor we found in them. "So I figure they're either working for Genna, or more likely—Moore. Ed, you witnessed Moore and Genna together in Brunswick. Moore probably needed somebody to move all that booze around. Make deliveries for Genna—or *to* Genna."

"Makes sense," said Ed.

"By the way, I arrested Truby Hunt yesterday in Deland on my way down here," I said.

"Nice work!" said Ed. "You didn't waste any time, did you?"

"Well, it was a stroke of luck," I said.

"So what's the plan?" asked Grady.

"I'll get us a warrant to search Cadwell's, but first we'll go shake down the Mays kid. We'll need Sheriff Baker too, so Grady, why don't you find him and let him know what's going on. Depending on what we find, maybe we end up at Moore's."

"Sounds good."

"Let me know if anything comes up. Meanwhile, I'll be at the hotel," I said.

On my way to the hotel, I started thinking about Moore. He and Cadwell must be pretty close. Ed said that Cadwell supplied vehicles to several of the local gangsters. And, Cadwell was married to Red Overton's daughter. Red was one of the biggest rumrunners around. He and Moore met in prison, of all places.

I knew where Moore lived. I saw the address on one of Ed's files. One of the things I'd gotten good at in this line of work was reading upside down. I knew the area pretty well too. In retrospect, I always knew I was going to Moore's house. It just took time for my mind to sort it out and then eventually justify it.

What's he going to do—shoot me? He doesn't even know me. A drive-by couldn't hurt, and at least I could see what we might be dealing with later. I promised Coonts to play this by the book, but I really didn't have anything else to do. Really, my going over there was just a convenient detour. I practically had to drive right by it to get to the hotel anyway.

Moore's house was on the northeast part of Lake Worth. Lots of swells lived over there. I wondered how many of them knew what a dangerous scumbag lived right next door. He probably donated to the garden club and the rotary and no telling what else, and everyone thought he was something special.

When I crossed the Royal Park Bridge, I could see the backs of the houses to my left along the bay, and I knew his was about halfway between the bridge and the Flagler Hotel somewhere up South Lake Trail. I slowed down to get a better look. Most of the houses were substantial and they had large docks along the lake—many of them sporting large yachts. The view was incredible, and seeing all of those boats made me think of Captain McCoy. I wondered if he built any of them or if he knew their names.

The gate was open and I could see a couple of automobiles out front. One of them was the same make and model as the vehicle Randolph Mays supposedly bought from Cadwell. That was my probable cause. I turned in the drive and left my Chevrolet blocking the gate so there was no way out.

"Who is it?" asked a young lady wearing a maid's uniform. The door was mostly glass, so she could see me standing on the front stoop. I removed my hat and with my most innocent smile replied, "Oh, uh, hi, ma'am. I'm Julian Clark here to see Mr. Moore."

"Just a minute, please."

I could only imagine what he was thinking. "Clark? Who the hell is Clark? Did you ask?"

A moment later a large man in a too big white linen suit approached the door. His sleeves practically covered his hands, which looked like sausage stuffed in a casing that wasn't big enough. He had beads of sweat on his forehead.

He opened the door. My mind was racing. Was this how it happened before? The last time an agent visited him? The one he shot. "What can I do for you, Mr. Clark?"

Today I was going with the direct approach. "Actually it's Agent Clark. NATB."

180

His defenses came up immediately and his whole demeanor changed. I could almost feel the adrenaline surge. I felt my own for sure. Watch the eyes—they always give them away.

"NATB?"

"National Auto Theft Bureau?"

Relief crossed his face but only slightly. His posture relaxed somewhat, but he was still on high alert.

"Hasn't the government harassed me enough already?"

"I'm not sure what you are referring to, Mr. Moore. I was in the area. Really just passing through. Our office is in Jacksonville."

"Long way from Jacksonville, Mr. Clark." He was bringing it back down. Still searching for reasons why I was standing on his front stoop, but not overly alarmed anymore. It was just an auto theft guy.

"*Agent* Clark."

"Whatever. Is there something I can do for you?"

"No need to be rude. Like I said, I was just in the area. I'm looking for an automobile—same make, model, and color as that one out front. The gate was open."

"Maybe so, but this is private property."

"Is that your Ford out there?"

"What if it is?"

"It looks like the one I'm looking for."

"It's not."

"But it could be. People buy stolen automobiles all the time and have no idea. Nothing wrong with that."

"There are lots of them just like it all over town. Besides, I think I would know if I bought a stolen auto."

"Would you?"

"Yes."

"Mind if I take a look."

"Yes." His pressure was rising. We were inching back up towards seven or eight. "Tell you what, Clark. Wait right here." He shut the door in my face. Again, I was wondering if this was how it went down the last time. Did the

Treasury man ever actually cross the threshold? How long do I wait? What's he doing? Getting a gun? Not likely, he already had one on him—no need for another one. Talking to someone inside or calling somebody?

A few minutes passed, but it seemed like a lot longer.

"I called my lawyer. Do you have a warrant? You're on private property."

"The gate was open. I saw something suspicious and decided to check it out."

"Well, my lawyer says not to let you look at that vehicle, and if I don't do what he says, there's not much reason in having one, now is there?"

"So you're not going to let me look at it?"

"No. It's not my automobile anyway. Besides, I'm leaving. Headed to Miami for the prize fights. Sorry I can't help you, Mr. Clark." He backed up and shut the door in my face—again.

I considered ringing again but decided against it. He wasn't going to budge, so I might as well leave. I drove around the block and pulled into a vacant lot on Palm Way. I had a view of A1A to the east and the bridge to the west. If he left for Miami, he had to pass by me on one side or another. I sat there wondering how long I was willing to wait before I gave up and headed to the hotel. Before long I saw that Ford coming around the corner. He came down A1A and then turned west on Palm and drove right by me. It was definitely Moore.

I gave him a comfortable lead and then pulled out and followed him down Palm. When it was clear that he really was headed south, I turned around and headed back to the courthouse to find Ed or Grady to tell them about my change of plans.

* * *

"You did what?" asked Ed. "What the hell were you thinking, Julian? You're lucky he didn't shoot your ass."

"Actually, we had a nice little exchange there on the front stoop. Well, I was on the front stoop. But listen, this automobile we're looking for was sitting right there in the front yard. He wouldn't let me near it. He actually went inside and called his lawyer for advice on what to do about me."

"You are one crazy son of bitch. You know that, right?"

"I'm going to Miami."

"What's in Miami?"

"The prize fights."

"What?"

"Moore said he was going to the prize fights. You've never been to a fight. They hold them over at the American Legion."

"What are you going to do when you get there?"

"I haven't figured that out yet, but I have an idea. Get Captain Mitchell on the phone." Ed sat there staring at me with this ridiculous look on his face like I was nuts.

"Please," I added.

Coonts had already authorized my assistance regarding Moore, so if he was headed to Miami in a stolen automobile, I needed to follow him. I might as well leave today rather than wait another day. Ed got Captain Mitchell on the phone, and the captain told me to come on down. He would have a plan by the time I got there.

Before I left, Ed and Grady suggested we go ahead and find Randolph Mays just like we planned and see what we could find out about Cadwell and Moore. I agreed but made them promise not to say anything to Coonts about my visit to Moore's house alone.

* * *

Grady Emory, Ed Lawrence and I headed over to the Dixie Court Hotel to find Randolph Mays. He was a bellhop there, which was pretty rare. We hardly ever saw a white bell hop anywhere. The manager said he would find him and tell him a few fellas wanted to talk to him in the lounge. We had a couple of deputies outside watching the doors in case he tried to run.

Randolph was this skinny, wiry kid with bad acne all over his face. I couldn't imagine him stealing anything, but definitely not automobiles. He must have been on a break because it took him ten minutes before he showed up in the lounge.

"Have a seat, Randolph." I'm Special Agent Lawrence with the Bureau of Investigation, and this is Grady Emory with the Department of Treasury, and that's Julian Clark with NATB."

The look on his face turned to panic. "What, what can I do for you gentleman?" he said.

"Do you know a man named Arthur Cadwell?" asked Lawrence. He sat there like he was really searching deep. He was probably trying to figure out if he could make a run for it but must have decided against it.

"No. I can't say I do. No, that name is not familiar to me."

Agent Lawrence pulled out the bill of sale I had given him. "Are you sure about that, Randolph? Maybe you forgot. Think really hard—maybe you bought a vehicle from him recently and just don't remember."

"Oh, that Cadwell. Now I remember, sort of. What about him?"

Agent Lawrence slid the bill of sale across the table. "It says here on this bill of sale that you bought a late-model Ford from him not too long ago and applied for a tag."

Beads of sweat had started appearing on the kid's forehead, and he was fidgeting nervously, looking all around.

"Look at me, young man. Do you know this fella Cadwell?"

He didn't say anything, but the look on his face told us all we needed to know. "Listen, kid, this isn't about you, it's about Cadwell. So, this will go a lot easier if you just tell us what you know about him."

"If he finds out I said anything . . ." he started.

"If that's what you're worried about, we won't say anything we had this little conversation," said Emory.

"I didn't know it was stolen," Randolph said.

"Where can we find him?" asked Ed.

"It's probably too late. He—he took the Royal Palm back to Cincinnati. Always does. You can't tell him I told you that."

Grady got up and went outside to talk to the deputies watching the front of the hotel.

Agent Lawrence said, "Tell you what, Randolph. We'll keep this conversation to ourselves. But if we find out you're lying to us, well, that would change things. You understand what I'm telling you?"

"Uh, yes sir. I'm telling you the truth. The Royal Palm—that's where he is. The train station. He lives in Ohio."

Ed Lawrence and I got up and went outside to find Grady Emory and the four deputies. Grady said, "The Palm leaves in thirty minutes, so we may still have time. What do you think?"

"Well, if we hadn't convinced Mays to go pigeon, we wouldn't have a shot. Let's go. This guy's got a reputation as a real character, so we should expect a confrontation."

"Yup."

* * *

The platform to board the train was so long and so crowded with people, we were afraid we'd miss him amid all the confusion. Fortunately, luck was on our side because not long after we arrived, one of those deputies noticed a vehicle pull up and recognized Red Overton driving it. The man with him was Cadwell. Just as soon as Cadwell jumped out and started running up the platform to catch the train, two deputies closed in on him and tried to grab him. But as soon as one of the deputies had a hold of his elbow, Cadwell bolted. He pushed several people out of his way as he headed down the platform.

The crowd was so thick, it was hard for them to keep up and keep an eye on him. Cadwell headed toward the back of the train, and the deputies kept following, hoping to push him toward Lawrence and Emory, who were supposed to be coming from the rear of the train forward. At some point they were planning to corral him in the middle.

Grady jumped up on a bench to see over everyone's heads, but the sea of people made it nearly impossible to pick Cadwell out. As his eyes scanned the crowd, he finally noticed the two deputies coming toward him. One of them waved and pointed towards the thick group of people trying to board one of the cars about halfway between us, which gave me an idea.

"Hey, Ed, you and Grady keep working your way up the platform. If they chase him down this way, be ready."

"Where are you going?"

"I'm getting on the train in case he boards with all those people. I'll get on here and work my way forward."

Ed and Grady both gave me a thumbs up, so I pushed my way through the river of people and jumped up on the steps leading up to the train-car door. Fortunately, the passenger cars weren't nearly as crowded, and when the door closed behind me and cut off all the noise, it was like entering a vacuum that was practically silent.

I started making my way forward, checking each row and especially the holding areas between cars, which were the only good places a man could hide. I looked out the windows and could see Ed Lawrence making his way up the side of the train. He looked like a fish trying to swim upstream. Grady was making better progress by staying between the people and the terminal building.

I had searched two cars and entered the third when I noticed a commotion at the far end. I looked out the window and saw a lot of pushing and shoving near the doors. Then I noticed the two deputies trying to get into the scrum. I moved forward slowly, pretending to be a passenger looking for his seat. Hat down, eyes down—there was no way Cadwell would identify me as anything other than another passenger. I took another look to my right and saw Agent Lawrence almost parallel with me outside. Lawrence gave me a signal—using two fingers he first pointed at his own eyes, then pointed toward the door where all the commotion was; indicating he had eyes on Cadwell.

What I didn't see was Cadwell, who was already in the entrance to the train car, looking out the window as well. He happened to notice the signal from Ed and followed Ed's eyes back to me as I was coming toward him up the aisle of the passenger car. It must have been obvious we were working together.

As my focus turned back to the interior of the car, I heard a commotion and a lady yell, "Hey, watch out, mister." The man with her gently pushed her out of the way to confront another man who had just shoved his wife from behind. Cadwell. He was reaching into his coat to draw his weapon from his shoulder holster. The woman screamed when she saw the gun coming out. I was already moving towards them, but I had to cover at least half the length of the passenger car to reach them. The woman's husband started to back up when Cadwell pistol-whipped him, sending him stumbling backward into the laps of two people already seated.

I had cut the distance in half, but now Cadwell was turning toward me. It was going to be close—too close. I considered diving into an empty row when the man Cadwell had already pistol-whipped tried to kick him. It was just enough to throw him off balance and gave me the extra second I needed. I was only a step away when Cadwell regained his balance and started to lower the gun barrel toward my head. I kept my center of gravity low as I barrelled up the aisle. At the last second, I lunged releasing all of the energy I had coiled in my calves and thighs. The collision with Cadwell knocked the wind out of him and forced the gun toward the ceiling just as he pulled the trigger. The sound of the gunshot was deafening inside the railcar, which triggered a panic both inside and outside. People started screaming and scrambling to take cover, not knowing where the shot came from.

My weight and momentum drove Cadwell to the floor and using our combined motion, I brought my knee up into Cadwell's groin. As the air rushed out of his lungs from the impact, I gave him a right cross with my elbow making solid contact with the man's jaw. His head slapped the floor nearly knocking him unconscious, so I pressed my forearm across the man's throat to choke him. Cadwell was in a world of hurt, not to mention now he couldn't get a breath, all he could do was submit. The gun fell to the floor and he went limp. I grabbed the weapon, got up, and shoved it in the back of my waistband while keeping my foot on Cadwell's chest so he couldn't move. By that time, the two deputies had boarded and were making their way down the aisle.

"He's all yours, boys," I said as I turned to the man who tried to kick Cadwell and offered him a hand to help him up. Blood was running down his check from a gash in his temple, but he was going to be fine. "Thank you," he said.

As I walked down the steps of the car back to the platform, Ed Lawrence approached. "You are one lucky S.O.B. I saw the whole thing play out from the curb. There wasn't really anything I could do except watch."

"Get Grady and let's get out of here," I said as I pulled Cadwell's pistol from my waistband and handed it to Ed.

Chapter 14

When I got to the Miami police station the clerk sent me back to Captain Mitchell's office. He was kicked back in his chair with his feet up on the desk. "Julian Clark, damn glad to see you, young man. How's Coonts?"

"He's doing well, but he doesn't know I'm here yet, so he's going to be surprised when he finds out."

"Let's call him together." He picked up the phone. "By the way, how's Frances? Has she taken to Jacksonville living?"

"She's great. She's still working for the phone company, so watch out. She might be listening in on your calls!"

"Coonts! It's Captain Mitchell."

I couldn't hear what Coonts was saying.

"I'm with Agent Clark," the captain said. "I'm not in Palm Beach—I'm in Miami."

I could hear his reply. "What the hell is Clark doing in Miami?"

"He followed this fella Wilbur Moore down here in a *maybe* stolen Ford," Mitchell said. He gave me a look when he said "maybe." "Don't worry, we'll take care of him. I've already got it worked out how we're going to get him a closer look at that Ford."

Captain Mitchell was smiling and listening to Coonts. He said, "Sure thing. He's right here." He reached across the desk to hand me the phone. "He wants to talk to you."

I took the phone and put it to my ear. "Hey, boss." He wasn't angry; he just wanted to remind me not to get near Moore and to follow the captain's

189

lead. "Yes sir, boss. I'll be careful. Perkins? Yes sir. Okay, thanks."

"Everything okay?" Captain Mitchell asked.

"Yup. Thanks to you," I said. "Coonts is calling Agent Perkins. So, what should we do about Wilbur Moore? I'm pretty sure he's driving a stolen Ford, but I need to get a closer look at it. Got any ideas how we can do that?"

"Sure do. We're going to fight night down at the Legion. It shouldn't be too hard to find your Ford."

"Let's do it."

The Legion was located down on the waterfront. It looked out over Biscayne Bay and was really a beautiful spot. Every month they hosted prize fights, and some pretty famous boxers had fought there. The Legion only held about fifteen hundred people, but the crowd looked a lot bigger when we approached it in my Chevrolet. The lot was full, as were several lots around the block, and there were cars parked all up and down Biscayne Boulevard.

"Must be a big fight tonight," I said. "Any idea who's in town?"

"Primo Carnero," said Mitchell. "The big Italian. He's over six and a half feet tall. A real brawler—weighs in at something like two-fifty. This guy Carnero is a bruiser, I tell you. No idea who he's fighting, but I feel sorry for him already. It's going to be a big crowd tonight. Too bad we can't see it."

"So what are we doing down here, Frank?" I asked.

"This fight has been sold out for weeks, Julian. Besides, we're working. Just drive down Biscayne slowly until we see your Ford. You have the tag, right?"

"Right here," I said, handing Frank a piece of paper with the description on it.

It didn't take long to identify the Ford we were looking for. It was parked on Biscayne not far from the Legion.

"Pull over up ahead, Julian," said Mitchell. A few minutes later, a patrol unit pulled up next to us with the window down. Frank rolled his window down to talk to the deputy driving it.

"That's it over there. That yellow Model A. Not the breezer, the business coupe," Mitchell explained to the deputy. I couldn't hear what the deputy

190

said back, but Frank rolled up his window and said, "Okay, we're in business. Let's head back to the station."

As I pulled out and turned around to head back to the office, I looked over at Frank and asked, "What happens next?"

"We've got a tow truck around the corner. Charlie's going have it towed back to the station so you can take a look at it," he said with a huge grin on his face.

"And then what?"

"When Moore comes outta that fight, he's going start looking for his vehicle. I'll give him about ten minutes before he ends up at the station."

"And why would he end up there?"

"Because he's going to think somebody stole it. And what do you do when somebody steals your vehicle?" Again the big grin on his face.

"You go to the police and file a report," I said, slapping my leg.

"Charlie will be down there on patrol. My bet is, he flags him down and gets a ride," said Mitchell, both of us chuckling.

"Man, I would love to see the look on Moore's face when he comes out of that fight and can't find his automobile," I said, still laughing.

We arrived at the station a few minutes later and went back to Frank's office.

"By the way, Julian, does Ed Lawrence or Grady Emory want me to arrest him if we determine that vehicle is stolen?"

"No. Just let him go back to Palm Beach. It will make it a lot easier to get a warrant from the judge if we can prove he's driving a stolen automobile."

"Okay." Frank kicked back in his chair, put his feet up on his desk, and said, "Now, we wait.

It didn't take long. Charlie stuck his head in Captain Mitchell's office and gave us the thumbs-up signal. We could hear somebody out front cussing about his automobile being stolen. There was somebody else with him. We sat there for a while listening to the two of them bitch and moan about what happened.

"I can't believe this shit. We drove all the way down here from Palm Beach for the fights. Now I got no way to get home," we overheard Moore say to no one in particular.

The clerk asked them, "Are you sure you didn't park illegally? If you parked illegally, they'll tow it."

The other man said, "We didn't park illegally! We parked just like everybody else. What kind of business are you running down here anyway?"

The clerk replied, "I'm just saying. Lots of people get towed around the Legion. It's gets pretty crowded down there on fight night. Lots of illegally parked cars."

"I said we parked in a goddamned parking spot!" Moore said, raising his voice again.

Frank and I were trying to keep from laughing out loud before Frank said, "Maybe I should go out there and talk to them."

I said, "No, he might get suspicious if he sees you. I wouldn't risk it."

"He doesn't know me from Adam. Let's just see what happens." Frank got up and walked out front. "Can I help you gentlemen? I'm Captain Mitchell."

"You sure as shit can. Somebody stole my automobile down at the Legion during the fight. We drove down here from Palm Beach and now I got no way to get back."

"Well sir, if you'll file a report—"

The other gentleman interrupted, "We're not filing a report. We need you to get out there and find our damn vehicle."

"And who might you be?" Captain Mitchell asked.

"I'm his lawyer."

I didn't dare peek my head out of Frank's office, but the temptation was pretty good just to see those two arguing with the captain. Moore was not dumb. He might recognize me and connect my visit to his house with the disappearance of that Ford.

"Well sir, I don't really care much for lawyers," I heard him say. I don't know how he kept a straight face throughout the whole thing.

"Listen here, Mitchell," said Moore. "You need to find our vehicle or get us a ride to Palm Beach."

"Gentlemen, I can't spare a deputy to be driving all the way to Palm Beach. Why don't you finish filing your report and we'll contact you when we find it?"

"This is bullshit and you know it. I don't know what the fuck is going on around here, but you can sure as shit count on hearing from us again."

"I look forward to it. Now, if you'll excuse me." Frank came back to the office, still trying to hold back from laughing out loud. We overheard Moore ask to use a phone so he could call his wife, which really got us tickled. We could overhear him yelling at her to come and get him and his lawyer. She must have really been hot because the last thing we heard was Moore say, "I don't care if you are in the bed. I need you to come and get us," and then slammed the phone down.

* * *

The next morning the hotel clerk handed me a couple of telegrams when I came down to have coffee. "Good morning, Agent Clark. The *Herald* isn't here just yet—they must be running a little late this morning—but I'll bring it to the lounge just as soon as they deliver it."

"Thank you, Patty. I'll be in there having coffee. Oh, by the way, Agent Perkins and I are having breakfast together, so if you see him, will you please let him know where I am?"

"Certainly."

The Patricia Hotel in downtown Miami had a fantastic view of Biscayne Bay from the upper floors as well as the Miami River across the street. It was one of the smaller hotels in the city, but the service was excellent and who could beat the location? The owner, Gillis McCrary, was also the safety commissioner for Miami-Dade County and had helped the NATB on several occasions.

We used the hotel quite frequently and Mr. McCrary charged us a fair price. He was a true patriot and his hotel had one of the biggest American flags I had ever seen on the roof. The flagpole must have been another two stories above the eighth floor, and I had heard many a boat captain say he used it as a marker when coming across the bay. The hotel was right on Brickell Point. George's daughter Patty managed the hotel—that was her at the front desk. He named the hotel after her.

While I waited for Perkins, I couldn't help but think about what a piece of work that Moore was with his lawyer last night. I'm not sure what was funnier, those two reporting a stolen automobile or Moore having to call his wife to come pick him up. Captain Mitchell was planning to call him later and let him know we found his automobile. Surely, he wasn't dumb enough to come back to Miami and get it.

Patty came hurrying into the lounge with a copy of the *Miami Herald* under her arm, "Here you go, Agent Clark. Sorry about the wait."

"Don't worry about it, Patty. I've just been sitting here admiring the view. How's your dad?"

"Oh, he's fine. You'll probably see him around shortly. Excuse me, but I have to get back to the front and check out a guest," she said as she hurried back to the lobby.

Five minutes later, Agent Perkins walked in. He looked like most Bureau agents, wearing a dark suit and dark tie, except that Perkins had a beard. Very few agents that I knew of had beards. Actually, I couldn't think of anyone else. He was also a real card—Emmett Perkins. Kind of a goofy fellow, he was pigeon toed as all get out, which gave him a funny sort of lope when he walked, and he was a bit of a klutz. He loved to have a good time when he wasn't on duty. He was a good agent, but it wasn't uncommon for him to arrange a card game or throw some dice.

"Emmett, how are you?"

Agent Perkins said, "Doing well, Julian. It's great to see you. I've been wondering when you were going to get down here. I guess you've got it pretty good up there in Jacksonville too, but it's hard to beat Miami."

"So why is it every time I'm down here, it's to chase some gangster or thug?"

"We get a lot of interesting folks down here in Miami because there is so much going on."

"Is that so? Like what?"

"Oh, you know—the prize fights, horses, nightclubs, the numbers, prostitution, water, weather, women, wine —should I go on?"

"I think you covered it. It's a good thing you don't work for the department of tourism."

"Maybe that was my true calling. We've got it all. That's for sure."

"Sounds like Miami has just the right stuff to keep a lawman busy."

"Oh, we attract only the best. Torrio. Nitti. Capone. Prignano. Genna. Hell, Capone's got a house over on Palm Island. Seems like every wop this side of the Mississippi has been down here lately—keeping us all busy, I'll say that. Probably shouldn't complain, though—it's sure nice to have a job."

"That it is." I couldn't keep a straight face any longer. Not while Perkins was shoveling all that bullshit.

"You know the boss man will be here tonight?" said Perkins.

"Hoover?"

"Nah, Coonts. Yes, Hoover."

"Oh, good. I need to talk him about his man in Miami."

"You're funny, Julian."

"You guys going to hit the town? Let me guess—the Roney Casino?"

"I wish. I'm sure I'll end up chauffeuring him around. But on a serious note, Thaye Ersley gave me the background on your investigation. What brought you down here, and how can I help?"

I told Agent Perkins about Moore and my impromptu visit to his house and how that led to Miami. I also told him about the bellhop and Cadwell's apprehension at the train station, trying to get on the Royal Palm. We had a good laugh about Moore and his lawyer actually filing a report about that stolen Ford. That was a first for both of us.

"Say, I've gotta go back over to the impound lot and identify that Ford. If you don't have any plans, why don't you go with me?"

"Nah, I've gotta go over to the office for a while, and I've got some business out in the Glades too," he said with a wink.

* * *

When I got to the impound lot, Captain Mitchell was waiting for me inside the fence with someone else I didn't recognize. I parked my Chevrolet near the front and grabbed my investigator's bag off the back seat and headed over to the Ford we needed to ID. The captain had brought one of the newer deputies with him so we could teach him how to identify a numbers job. The kit in my bag had everything we needed.

"Julian, this is Deputy Stuart. He's a rookie, so I figured he could use a lesson in identifying a stolen automobile. Stuart, this is Julian Clark with the Auto Theft Bureau. He's probably the best at this in the Southeast so pay attention."

"Deputy," I said. "Model A's are pretty easy to investigate. There's plenty of room under the engine cowl to work, and the serial numbers are usually stamped on the block in an obvious place and easy to find. Some of the other models are a lot less conspicuous and require some tools or sometimes you have to get up underneath to see them. You investigate enough automobiles, you learn what to look for and where based on its year, make, and model because they are all different. This one shouldn't be too difficult. First thing we want to do is find the original stamping. See here?"

I had him lean in for a look while I shined the little flashlight I always carried on the spot where the numbers were located on the left side of the engine above the water intake.

"Okay. I see the numbers. How do you know if something's wrong with them?" asked Stuart. "They look okay to me."

"It depends on how sophisticated the operation is. Usually they start by grinding off the original numbers with a grinding wheel. Once the numbers have been filed off, they use a different type of wheel to smooth it out to cover up the marks. They might use a torch or file or some other implement to create a smooth surface like they were never there, and they also need a smooth surface to stamp the new numbers into. The thing is, the original stamping at the factory is deep. What I mean is, the die leaves an impression in the metal that's deep enough so even if you file down the surface until it's smooth, you can still read the original numbers if you know what you're doing."

"So these numbers are fake?" he asked.

"Yup. But this one is a little different. Rather than file off the originals, they simply changed the numbers that were originally stamped on the block. It doesn't take as long and it's a lot easier to do. In a minute, I'll show you how to find the original numbers."

I went back over to my bag and pulled out the papers I brought from Tallahassee. "Look here. This is the title and bill of sale I got from the proof of ownership file in Tallahassee. The number on that block should match the number on the papers they filed for the new title. Captain, read me those numbers off the block, will you?"

As Captain Mitchell read off the numbers, Stuart and I verified they did indeed match the paperwork. "After a cursory look, most automobile dealers would conclude this was a clean vehicle. Actually, most of them wouldn't even check unless there was something suspicious. And certainly no buyer would ever think to check any of this. So now this young man, Randolph Mays, has what looks like a clean automobile that he bought from this other guy—Arthur Cadwell. If Mays ever wants to sell the vehicle, which is likely what was getting ready to happen when I showed up at Arthur Moore's house up on Lake Worth, he's got matching paperwork to this vehicle and nobody is the wiser."

"Sounds pretty easy."

"Unfortunately—a little too easy. Cadwell steals the vehicles in Ohio, where he lives most of the time. He drives them down to Florida, has the numbers changed, and sells them. Then he takes the train back to Ohio to do it all over again. This is just a side hustle, though. They probably only steal a half dozen automobiles a year, so these guys aren't on anyone's radar for auto theft. If they weren't working for some of the bigger players in Florida, we wouldn't even be talking about them."

Captain Mitchell interrupted, "I heard you guys nabbed Cadwell at the train station yesterday. Ed Lawrence called and told me how it went down. Nice work."

"Thanks."

"Agent Clark," Stuart said. "I still don't understand how you know this Ford was stolen,"

"So rather than change the entire serial number, they chose to only change

197

a few numbers. It's easier and faster."

"Okay, but how do you know that?"

"Because I've seen thousands of them and I know what to look for. I think there are three numbers on this that aren't original. The "8" used to be a 3. The "4" used to be a 1. And the letter "P" was probably an I."

"You *think?*"

"Well, I'm pretty sure. But now we're going to confirm it. Go grab that creeper over there."

While Deputy Stuart went to get a creeper, I leaned down inside the engine compartment and felt under the block with my hand. I gently rubbed my fingers back and forth on the underside of the block until I found where it was smooth and then felt a brief rough patch before it became smooth again. Bingo. A blind man probably could have read me the numbers without me having to get underneath.

When Stuart came back, I lined up the creeper in the right spot next to vehicle and then had him lie down on his back while I pushed him underneath. "Can you see the underside of the motor okay?"

"Yep. What am I looking for?"

"Hang on." I leaned back down inside the engine compartment and felt in the location where I knew the numbers would be. "Look right here," I said as I fingered the stamp.

"Hand me that flashlight of yours."

I passed the light down inside to Stuart underneath. "See anything."

"Yes. It looks like another serial number, but it's different from the one on top."

I smiled at Captain Mitchell. They hadn't bothered to change the one on the bottom. They probably didn't even know it was there. "Tell me what that first letter is."

"*I.* Well, I'll be," he added.

"What about the second number? Is it a 3?"

"Yep."

"And the last one?"

"1. You nailed it, Agent Clark."

"Come on out." While he pulled himself from underneath the automobile, I grabbed my Ford casting number guide and looked it up. According to the number and letter convention guide, the original number would definitely have belonged to this year, make, and model—a 1930 Ford Business Coupe.

I handed the little guide to the deputy. "It all checks out. Stolen. Probably a dealer in Ohio, but that's easy enough to trace."

"Thanks, Julian," said Captain Mitchell. "Nice work. I can't wait to call that lawyer up in Palm Beach and let him know they were driving a stolen automobile." He was cracking up as he said it.

* * *

Later that afternoon when I got back to the hotel, I stopped at the front desk to check for messages. The only message was from Agent Perkins. The note said, "Julian, Room 750, I've got something for you."

I needed to drop some stuff off in my own room on the eighth floor, and then go down to his and see what he wanted to show me. I wondered if it had anything to do with Hoover's visit.

When I knocked on Perkins's door, I heard some commotion inside before he asked, "Julian, that you?"

"Yep," I said.

I heard another commotion and then Emmett fumbling with the latch before he finally opened the door. "Come on in. I got something for you."

Sitting on the table by the window was a gallon jug of corn whiskey and a couple of glasses he'd gotten from downstairs. One of them was already being used. Oh boy, I thought. I could smell it across the room—or maybe that was Perkins. Clearly, he had started without me.

"It's really good corn liquor. You have to try this stuff. Put some hair on your chest, Clark."

I took a drink and told him I thought it was pretty good corn liquor. The burn was reminiscent of my time with Captain McCarthy in Savannah, but it was pretty good stuff.

"Where'd you get it?"

"The Glades."

I must have had a quizzical look on my face because he followed that up with, "It's need to know."

I added a little more to my cup.

"What's the head honcho in town for? Anything special?" I asked.

"Horse races. He loves to gamble and 'tis the season," replied Perkins. "He'll probably take in a fight too. So tell me what happened today. You get a look at that Ford?"

"Sure did—pretty good job but not very thorough. Too easy to tell it was stolen. Paperwork was legitimate enough. Looks like it was stolen in Ohio and brought down to Palm Beach."

We were getting pretty loose and enjoying ourselves.

Agent Perkins said, "The boss will be in here tonight, so I've got to hide this stuff. How 'bout you take it upstairs since you have your own room? I can't afford to keep it down here because Mr. Hoover might smell it."

"My room? What if he wants to come up there for some reason?" I said.

"Julian, he's not going to go up there," replied Perkins.

"Fine, but I can't promise you there will be any left when he leaves."

Perkins looked back over his shoulder at me to see if I was kidding, and when he turned back to grab the jug he knocked it off the table. When it hit the floor it broke and went all over the rug.

"God almighty!" Perkins said.

"What the hell happened?"

"Quick, Julian! Throw me one of those towels," he replied.

I grabbed a towel off the rack and threw it to Perkins, but the whiskey had already soaked into the rug. The fumes were overpowering.

"Shit! This is never going to work. How are we going to get that smell out?" he asked.

"Open the window." I said. "Damn, that's strong."

I could hardly stay in the room, the odor was so strong It made me dizzy just to breathe the fumes. We tried to clean it up, but then we had to get out. I could tell Perkins didn't know what in the world to do, and he was getting concerned about it. Hoover would be here soon and there's no way

200

he wouldn't pick up on the odor in that room.

"Listen here, Emmett. Let's go find Patty and ask her to swap out the room with another one."

"It's worth a shot," he said. We took out of that room and headed to the lobby.

The clerk downstairs told us Patty had already left for the day and the hotel was full. When she asked what the problem was, we just looked at each other blankly.

Finally, Agent Perkins said, "Uh, we had a little mishap in the room and spilled something."

The look she gave us was like a teacher looking at a couple of third graders who had just spilled paint all over the floor. She didn't have to ask what it was—she knew. She could probably smell it on us.

I said, "We need to find a room for J. Edgar Hoover. What if we swap out my room with Agent Perkins?"

She tried not to laugh and said, "Excuse me for just a second." As she stuck her head around the corner of the office behind her, I overheard her tell someone to find Mr. McCrary and something about a maid. She returned to the counter and said, "Let's see what we can do." She flipped a few pages, scanning the reservation list, before saying, "Agent Clark, you know your room isn't nearly as nice as the one we had reserved for Mr. Hoover."

"I figured as much," I said.

Hoover; after all, was the head of the Bureau of Investigation. Perkins and Hoover had adjoining suites, and Hoover had suggested they room close so they could meet.

A maid approached the counter and waited for the clerk to acknowledge her before asking what room she was going to. She was holding a mop and several fresh towels.

"Room 750," said the Clerk.

As I turned to look at Perkins, I noticed some movement behind me at the door. It was none other than J. Edgar Hoover himself. The look of panic on Emmett Perkins's face was evident.

I said, "Emmett, go distract him. Tell him to have a seat in the lounge while you get him checked in and you'll bring him his key."

"Right. Good. That's good. I'll be right back," he said.

Just then McCrary walked up.

"Gentlemen. How can I help you?"

"Don't go anywhere. I'll be right back," said Perkins. He hurried toward Hoover to head him off.

It was clear to McCrary we were in a lurch, so I explained the situation as quickly and discreetly as I could so as not to let Hoover catch on. Meanwhile, Perkins came back after sending Hoover to the lounge.

"Thank God you're here," he said to McCrary. "Please tell me you can help."

"No problem, Emmett, we'll figure it out," he said reaching for the guest list.

Fortunately, Perkins knew McCrary pretty well too. After some switching around to make sure they had a nice enough room for Mr. Hoover, we finally got it all worked out. And, I didn't have to hide Perkins's contraband while the head of the Bureau was staying there. I can only imagine trying to explain that one to Coonts if I got caught.

* * *

That night after dinner, Perkins and I were standing on the curb in front of the Patricia Hotel while he smoked a cigarette. It was a quiet night with hardly any breeze coming off the bay. We were standing under the little yellow and white striped awning on the front of the hotel, and Perkins had his back to the water.

"You wouldn't believe this guy we arrested in Homestead, Julian. Guy had to be crazy. He started shooting as soon as we got out of the vehicle," Perkins said.

As I stood there listening to Emmett's story, I noticed a slow-moving automobile over Perkins's right shoulder. Normally, I wouldn't have thought twice about it, but it seemed to have a purpose about it the way it made the turn onto Second Street.

As it got closer, Agent Perkins must have noticed my eyes were looking past him, because he stopped talking. "What are you looking at, Julian?" He started to turn his head.

"It's probably nothing." As soon as I said it, I noticed the barrel of a gun come up slowly and stick out the rear window.

My Chevrolet was parked directly in front of the hotel, but the angle was wrong since it was a full length to our right. If they started shooting now, we were totally exposed. I only needed to say one word to Perkins for him to start moving in my direction. "Gun."

It was as if we were standing in molasses while trying to move toward cover. The automobile was rolling a little faster now that they realized we had made them and started to take cover. The first bullet shattered the plate glass next to the door directly behind where we were just standing. A volley of bullets followed it and tracked our path as we dove for cover, leaving pockmarks in the stucco on the front of the hotel.

We both instinctively dove behind my vehicle, the only cover for twenty-five yards in any direction. I hit the pavement with a grunt and took the skin off both my elbows as I slid behind the Chevrolet. Several bullets traced our path along the sidewalk, nearly hitting Perkins's feet before he ended up next to me on the ground.

The sound of the Thompson gun was deafening, but it wasn't hard to distinguish the sound of glass breaking or bullets striking metal as they strafed the side of my automobile on the way by. A few of the bullets made it through and whizzed over our heads as they struck the planters in front of the hotel. The window behind us exploded from a bullet that had ricocheted off the pavement. Glass fell down on us like rain as we covered our heads.

As we lay there looking at each other, wondering what to do next, we could hear the vehicle idling on the other side of mine. They were just sitting there. I looked under my Chevrolet to see if I could see anyone getting out—the ringing in my ears masking all other sounds like doors opening or closing. I turned back toward Perkins and noticed he was holding his gun ready—cigarette still hanging from his lips. We expected them to get out and finish the job, but a couple of seconds later we heard the engine rev as they started to pull away.

I jumped up and headed around the other side of my Chevy as Perkins got in the passenger seat. I checked the damage first, making sure the tires hadn't been hit before getting in and firing it up. I looked at Perkins, who was yelling, "Let's go, Julian!" He flicked his cigarette out the window.

I hit the gas and we took off down Second Street as the men that just tried to kill us fishtailed around the corner, headed north on Second Avenue. By the time I made the turn, they were a couple a blocks away. When we passed the Olympia Theatre we were hauling ass and the Ford we were chasing had turned east on Flagler. I reached the corner in seconds, and we skidded around the turn toward the bay. I could see up ahead they were carrying too much speed into the turn on Biscayne and they slammed into the side of a parked auto, allowing us to make up some of the distance, but by the time I made the turn on Biscayne they had straightened out and were a couple of blocks away, headed north fast.

Apparently, the left rear tire had been hit because I could feel the sluggishness in the rear as I tried to accelerate. It must have been a slow leak, because it looked okay when I first checked. The chase was over. As I made a U-turn on Biscayne to head back to the Patricia, we could see their taillights disappear. We limped back to the hotel, lucky to be alive.

"Did you get a good look at them before they started shooting?" asked Perkins.

"Not really. All I saw was the barrel of that Thompson."

We barely made it back to the hotel. People were standing out front, surveying the damage—including Mr. McCrary, who did not look happy. Glass was strewn all over the sidewalk and a few shell casings littered the street.

"You boys okay?" McCrary asked.

"I think so," I said.

"Good. Then you won't have any trouble explaining to me what the hell is going on out here and why my hotel just got strafed with bullets," said McCrary.

"Sorry about the mess, but we have no idea. At least I don't," said Perkins.

"What about inside?" I asked. "Anyone hurt?"

"Fortunately, nobody got hit," he said.

We all went inside to see how bad it was. There was glass all over the floor inside the front door, and several bullet holes marked the wall on the other side of the lobby. The front desk clerk looked like she was in shock. I could hear sirens in the distance. I walked back to look out the big window that was now gone.

Perkins came up behind me. "That was close."

Apparently not close enough. I could hear the sound of a motor revving at high rpms and the skidding of tires coming around the corner, and it wasn't the police.

"Everyone, get down!" I yelled.

The vehicle didn't slow down as it passed the hotel, but I could hear the sound of something break just before the whomp of a fire starting. Perkins looked up at me as we both recognized the sound of a Molotov cocktail breaking and setting fire. The automobile sped off as I jumped up to see my Chevy engulfed in flames.

"Son of a bitch! They actually came back!" said Perkins.

The sirens we heard were out front now, and McCrary yelled at the clerk to call the fire department.

"Dad gum," I said to no one in particular.

"Perkins and Clark!" we heard a voice yell from across the lobby. "What in the hell is going on down here?" It was Hoover. I guess he heard the commotion downstairs.

I looked at Perkins. "Uh-oh. I'll let you take this."

* * *

After the fire department put out the fire, I inspected the hulk of molten rubber and steel that had once been my Chevrolet—or I should say, the NATB's Chevrolet. Still, I loved that vehicle like it was my own, not to mention I had sunk some of my own money into it. This was personal.

I could almost hear Coonts all the way from Jacksonville ripping me up and down for this incident. It was not my fault, but he'd say it's no coincidence I always find trouble. Might as well sleep on it and worry about it in the morning. I needed transportation, but that would have to wait too. Mr. Hoover suggested I go over to Russell Garnet's tomorrow and get me a new ride, but I had a better idea.

* * *

"Mr. Moore, so good to see you again. Please, have a seat," said Vincenzo Genna. He was sitting at his favorite table in the corner of the bar room. The staff of the Columbia Restaurant all catered to him as if he owned the place. Actually, everyone in Ybor City knew him. He ran two successful nightclubs and a molasses business—among other things—and he was their most famous resident as of late. As Wilbur Moore pulled out a chair to sit down, a waiter brought two cups of Cuban coffee.

"Thank you, Che." The waiter nodded and disappeared as quickly as he had appeared. "This place has the best coffee in town."

"After the drive up from Palm Beach I could sure use it," replied Moore.

"Hopefully, you can stay the night and enjoy more of what Ybor City has to offer. I would be happy to host you tonight at the club. You won't forget it."

"I'm sure, but I really must get back to Palm Beach tonight. Business is booming, as you know."

"Well, I'm sorry to hear that you can't stay—maybe next time. But I'm glad to hear business is doing so well. I must confess I was skeptical at first. I mean, I trusted you to pull it off, but there were so many things that could go wrong."

"You don't know the half of it. That first delivery almost ended up in the river."

A gentleman in a tuxedo approached the table and waited politely for us to acknowledge him.

"Ah, Casimiro," Genna said.

"Are you ready to order, Mr. Genna?" Casimiro asked.

206

"*Dos sopa de garbanzo*, a tossed salad for two and two *mixtos, por favor.*"

"Yes sir," he replied. "Will you be having some sangria this afternoon? Or maybe a pitcher of mojitos?" he asked.

Genna looked at Moore.

"Not for me, but thank you," said Moore.

Genna said, "Not today, Casimiro."

Moore had no idea what Genna had ordered, but he assumed the man knew what he was doing. However, Genna could sense his apprehension.

"This place is known for the bean soup and Cubano sandwiches. The tossed salad is incredible too. If you don't like it, we'll get you something else—how about that?"

"No problem. It all sounds great."

"So back to that first delivery—I heard it got a little dicey," said Genna.

Moore looked around like he was worried somebody was listening.

"I can assure you that we are quite safe to speak freely here. Casimiro and his family are discreet. You have nothing to worry about."

Moore was still self conscious about discussing their business in public, but he decided it was as good a place as any.

"I learned early on in this business you have to plan for contingencies, and you can never have enough backup. That first delivery could have gone south if we had not done both. My men made the crossing without incident, but by the time they got to the drop point, they had been made. We're still trying to figure out how. The Ashley brothers had some men staked out nearby, and they started shooting. We lost two men in addition to a few other minor casualties. The boats needed some repairs, but all in all, it could have been a lot worse."

"What happened to the other side?" asked Genna.

"Taken care of. As I mentioned before, we were prepared for contingencies. I think Ashley and his boys will think twice before trying to hijack us again," explained Moore. "I can't blame them, though. If somebody was moving in on our territory, I would have done the same thing."

"What about the onshore part of the delivery?"

"No worries there. Alva Hunt and Riley Gant are about as reliable as you'll find. Actually, if it wasn't for Riley and Hugh Gant, we probably would have lost that first shipment. The last two deliveries went off without a hitch, so I think we've got the kinks worked out."

"Twelve thousand gallons of rum without spilling a drop. Congratulations and thank you," said Genna, raising his cup. "So far this little operation has been a huge success."

As Genna spoke, Moore couldn't help but think about Red Overton. He wondered if Genna even knew about him. Regardless, if Red found out Moore was up here meeting with Genna, Moore was as good as dead.

"What about Agent Ed Lawrence?" asked Genna.

"What about him?"

"It's my understanding that the Bureau has taken quite an interest in the local bootlegging business around Palm Beach County. Agent Lawrence is the lead agent down there, isn't he? He's got resources too. The revenue office down there is one of the largest in the state."

"Let me worry about the revenuers," replied Moore.

"I'm sure you are quite capable of taking care of business, but I can't stress to you how important our arrangement is to the success of my business, so keep that in mind, and let me know if I can help."

Moore looked on with his usual smug demeanor. He didn't appreciate Genna's intrusion in his affairs, and he surely wasn't planning on asking Genna for help. That would be tantamount to admitting he was weak. He might own Ybor, but he didn't know shit about Palm Beach County. Moore considered it the big leagues.

"I'll keep that in mind, Jim."

"You said yourself you weren't sure how you got made on that first delivery. Maybe you are being followed or maybe someone in your camp is dirty."

"Clearly, it wasn't the Bureau, as evidenced by the Ashley involvement, and I can guarantee you it wasn't one of my men." Moore's ire was starting to get up.

Sensing he had overstepped his bounds, Genna added, "I'm confident you will take care of your end. I was just trying to help."

Fortunately, their soup arrived.

Chapter 15

The Rod & Gun Club was situated in Everglades City, located on the southwestern tip of Florida. It was pretty remote—hidden deep in the Ten Thousand Islands on Chokoloskee Bay, but for the outdoorsman, it was one of the best-kept secrets in the state. The club itself was situated on the Barron River just inland from the bay and was protected from hurricanes and harsh weather. It was a magnificent old Florida hunting and fishing lodge built some sixty-six years ago, but recently purchased by Barron Collier as his personal playground. Collier turned it into a private club whose members were a who's who of the rich and famous, and even a couple of presidents had stayed there.

Big Bill McCoy was delivering a sailing yacht to a client in Naples and planned to spend a couple of days at the Rod & Gun on his way back to Jacksonville. His mate followed him in Bill's forty-five-foot Chris Craft, 3 Mile Limit, while Bill captained the client's boat.

I pulled into the little parking area of crushed shells and gravel behind the club and parked between a brand-new Cadillac Roadster and a Rolls-Royce Phantom. The inconspicuous entrance in back belied what lay within. A small hallway led to a beautiful foyer of dark hardwood floors and Victorian furniture.

There were mounts of all the local fish species—tarpon, snook, redfish, trout and grouper. Deer, waterfowl, otters, and turkeys adorned the walls in addition to a full-size mount of a Florida panther, black bear, bobcat, and an alligator.

There was a billiard table in front of a huge brick fireplace with a giant tin hood, pistols, rifles and a variety of fishing rods hanging from the walls or in cases around the room. The smell of the wood mixed with the saltiness of the air, and whatever was cooking back in the kitchen was intoxicating. I paused in the middle of the room to take it all in.

"Sir? Sir? May I help you?"

I must have been daydreaming because I hardly noticed someone was talking to me. I turned around to find a young lady behind the check-in counter. "Sir, may I help you?"

I removed my hat and stared up at the staircase that wrapped around the counter and led up to the second floor behind the young lady. "Actually, yes, you can. I'm looking for Bill McCoy."

"You must be Agent Clark. Captain McCoy is waiting for you out on the porch."

"Thank you." I passed through the screen door to a huge porch that wrapped around the back of the lodge and looked out over the Barron River. Several yachts were moored behind the club, and a variety of fishing boats were tied up to the dock. McCoy saw me approaching and immediately stood up and said, "Julian! You made it." Several other people occupied the porch, spread around three or four tables, and that big booming voice of Bill's made them stop and look in my direction. I walked over to Bill's table and pulled out a chair.

"This is great," I said.

"You can say that again," Bill said. "A real sportsman's paradise."

"Are you going to join?"

"I swore to myself on the way over from Sarasota I wouldn't, but now that I'm here—I don't know. Collier knew damn well I wouldn't be able to resist if he could just get me here."

"Is he here?"

"Nah. Hardly anyone's here right now. Barron will be here tomorrow. They are throwing a party for some of the new members while trying to attract a few more. We're supposed to fish tomorrow morning and then go hunting in the afternoon with a big dinner banquet tomorrow night. You know, you should stay. I can talk to Collier and set it up."

"That's tempting, Bill, but Frances is expecting me home tomorrow night."

"Just tell her you're with me."

"That will only get us both in trouble."

"Just think about it. I gotta go use the head."

Bill left me sitting there, staring out over the water, thinking about how to work this out. Man, I would love to go fishing while I was already down here. This place was truly a fisherman's paradise. I noticed a boat out back that had just pulled up to the dock. A man got off the boat and walked around the side of the lodge until I couldn't see him anymore. A few seconds later, he came around the porch with a couple of young laborers following him. Just as Bill came back out, the two laborers helped the man haul two big barrels out from the hold of that boat up onto the dock, and then proceeded to roll them around the side of lodge from where they came.

Bill noticed me staring and said, "Want some mangrove moonshine? They make it right out there in those islands."

"When in Rome ..."

"Hey, Julian, by the way, where's your Chevrolet? I didn't see it out front." Bill stood up from the table. "Let's go inside to the bar. I'm sure there's a story behind this."

We were the only two people at the bar at the Rod & Gun Club, which was just as fantastic as the rest of the place. Huge tarpon on the walls—largemouth bass, whitetail deer, and one of the biggest snook I had ever seen. Lots of nautical-themed antiques and trinkets littered the place. The bartender fixed a rum drink and set it in front of me. "What about him?" I asked.

"You know I don't drink, Julian," Bill said with a grin.

Just then someone else walked in, and we both turned to see who it was. It was none other than Joe Brooks.

"Joe?" I said. "Are you kidding me?"

"Hello, Julian. Bill. Y'all must be here for the cast and blast."

"Yes sir!" said Bill. "I'm just trying to talk Julian into staying, and you're just in time to hear all of his excuses as to why he can't."

"Julian, I heard y'all were close to wrapping up the Goldberg case. I hope that information we provided helped."

"You have no idea, Joe. Thanks again. When I left Jacksonville, Coonts and Thaye Ersley with the Bureau were going to work on the warrants. It was tricky tracing all those stolen automobiles you gave us, but we ended with half a dozen matches or so. Tell your dad how much we appreciate his help. Once it's all wrapped up, we'll let you know. We may even need you to testify."

"Whatever you need, Julian. Actually, that sounds like a good excuse for me to go back to Savannah. Maybe we can turn that into another fishing trip?"

"I like the way you think."

The bartender came back and Joe asked him for whatever I was having. I raised my nearly empty glass to him for a refill. Joe sat down at the bar, and I told them about the last couple of days in Miami, starting with Captain Mitchell and Wilbur Moore's Ford and then J. Edgar Hoover's visit. By the time I got to the to chase and subsequent firebombing of my Chevrolet, they were practically in tears laughing.

"I'm glad my almost dying is so entertaining."

Bill said, "Julian, you can't make this stuff up. I have never met anyone that manages to find trouble as much as you do. What in the hell did Frances think about all that?"

"She doesn't know—yet. And neither does Coonts, for that matter. Well, he knows about my automobile, but I left out some of the details."

"So how did you get here, Julian?" asked Joe.

"That's the best part. I took that stolen Ford out of the impound. The one we towed from the Legion."

Hearing that, they both about fell off their stools laughing. I thought Big Bill McCoy was going to bust a gut. "That is too rich, Julian!" Bill finally caught his breath and wiped a few tears from his eyes. "You actually have people so plugged, they want to kill you. How do you even sleep at night? I may have to change my mind about you staying here. We might get mixed up in one of your shootouts and catch a bullet meant for you."

"Oh, I doubt that."

"Do you have any idea who tried to kill you outside the Patricia Hotel?" asked Joe.

"I have a pretty good idea, but how do you know they weren't trying to kill Emmett Perkins?"

"Call it a hunch, but the cast of characters you have plugged pretty much tells me it was you they were after."

"Is that so?" I said. "Why don't you enlighten me then, detective McCoy?"

After he regained his composure, he started, "When I got out of the whiskey business a few years ago . . ."

I looked over at Joe and winked. The way Bill said it made it sound like he just decided to get out of a legitimate business one day and start building boats. No mention of jail or practically getting blown to pieces by the Coast Guard.

"My departure created a void in the market that wasn't empty for long. Wilbur Moore took the opportunity to fill it along with a few others. But Moore is just a runner. He needs buyers and Red Overton is one of the biggest bootleggers in Florida.

You see, Julian, there's a supply chain you have to consider when it comes to illegal whiskey and beer. Somebody has to make it—illegally, I might add—unless it's coming from offshore. Then somebody has to broker it and maybe store it, and then move it around, and then sell it to somebody else to eventually be consumed. There could be three or four different middlemen involved between manufacture and consumption. Are you with me now?"

"Go on."

"Everyone has their strengths or niche. Guys like Red Overton are good at the buying and selling part. They have connections and they know how to use those connections to stay out of trouble. He's got cover. For example, you're not going to catch Overton stealing autos to transport his booze, but somehow he's got to move it. He's got a guy for that."

"And who might that be?"

"His brother-in-law. Cadwell. But he probably has three Cadwells, so you're never going to get all of them—especially when half the cops and politicians in PBC are getting kickbacks to look the other way. Some of the really big players control their entire supply chain, but not Overton. When it comes to legal whiskey made offshore, Wilbur Moore is the man. Overton didn't want any part of the rumrunning, so he and Cadwell helped Moore get established."

"And how does this involve me?"

"Patience, young man. I'm getting to that part. So Moore has become one of the biggest rumrunners on the East Coast. His reputation attracts other big players."

"Like Jim Genna." Now it was all starting to fall into place.

"Genna isn't a player like he was back in Chicago, but he's got a pretty good business around Tampa, Clearwater, and St. Pete. He gets most of his supply from the west coast, but somehow he hooked up with Moore."

"Hold on. So now Moore is supplying Overton *and* Genna?"

"That's right. And just like Overton needs a guy to transport his product, so does Genna."

"Enter the Hunt-Gant gang," I said. Bill just sat there with a big smile on his face. Joe was listening to the whole thing, just as interested as I was. As I reflected on what Bill was saying, I realized I had only been half right. I wrongly assumed that Hunt-Gant was working for Moore and delivering to Genna. They were actually both working for Genna.

"Are you with me now?" he said.

"I'm with you," I said.

"Okay, good. So all the big players like Overton and Genna have plenty of people on their payrolls that can transport a truck full of illegal whiskey anywhere they want. But these guys don't want to get their hands dirty with stolen automobiles. It's beneath them. That's where guys like Cadwell and your pal Truby Hunt come in. I know it sounds crazy, but Prohibition has created a nation of scofflaws. People are going to get their booze, and law enforcement is only going to feign interest in stopping it. The reality is, guys like Genna and Overton will probably never be prosecuted for selling whiskey. However, stealing automobiles will put them behind bars faster than getting spooled by a big tarpon."

"Overton is probably not very happy with Moore's decision to start supplying Genna," I added.

"That's an understatement, but only because Overton is the one who helped him get established. So what you have is a good old-fashioned feud going on between two bootleggers. Simple as that. And you, my friend, are right smack in the middle of it."

Joe said, "Congratulations, Julian."

Bill added, "It's hard to say who is actually trying to kill you. But if you're messing with their delivery system—my guess is Hunt-Gant."

This was a lot to sort out, but it made sense. There was more to it than even Bill knew. They blamed me for Harold Hunt's death.

"Julian, you barely touched that drink."

"You know, I'm not much of a drinker, Bill. But at this late hour, I might as well stay the night."

Joe said, "You might as well go snook fishing with us in the morning too."

"I suppose I will."

Bill slapped me on the back. "That's great, Julian! You won't regret it. I've got Ren Stanley picking us up at the dock at sunup. He's one of the best around. Knows these islands like the back of his hand, and he's a fellow boat builder."

"I can't wait."

* * *

I had Captain Stanley drop me off at the dock behind the Rod & Gun club at lunchtime so I could pack my things and head back to the east coast. We had a ball fishing that morning. We caught several nice reds and a half dozen big snook. Joe jumped a tarpon on one of his fly rods, but there was no stopping that tarpon on such light tackle. She was greyhounding across the bay until Joe got spooled. Bill and I were still ridin' him about that fish when we got back to the dock.

Fishing in the Glades was like nothing I'd ever done before, and I had no idea how Captain Stanley kept from getting lost. The Glades were basically thousands of islands formed by myriad rivers, cypress swamps, estuarine mangrove forests, marsh grass, and backwater bays that all looked identical. I guessed, growing up on the water he learned to recognize the subtle differences of each little inlet, waterway, hardwood hammock and bay enough to find his way home, but it was no wonder the moonshiners used those islands to make illegal whiskey.

It was one of the most serene places I'd visited. The Glades were teaming with wildlife, most notably the manatee, American crocodile, and Florida panther. The waters were home to three of the most exciting game fish known to man—tarpon, snook, and redfish. There were lots of other species, but those were the most sought after.

After I got my stuff together, I was headed down the main staircase to that magnificent lobby when I heard a familiar voice.

"Hello, Janice," he said, entering the lobby.

Startled, the desk clerk, who had been reading a book behind the counter, stood from the stool she was half sitting on and said, "Oh, hi, Mr. Collier. We weren't expecting you until later this afternoon."

"I got a head start. Plus, I wanted to be sure everything was in order for our guests this weekend."

They both noticed me coming down the stairs and looked up. Collier said, "Julian Clark? I didn't expect to see you here this weekend. What a pleasant surprise."

"Mr. Collier, you have a magnificent place here. I wasn't really expecting to be here myself. I was just passing through, but Bill McCoy and Joe Brooks talked me into to staying a night and fishing with them this morning."

"Call me Barron. My dad was Mr. Collier. I'm so glad you liked the place and you got to fish. How did you all fare?"

"Oh, the fishing was great. We landed some redfish, several snook, and Joe even hooked a tarpon, but she got away."

"It must have been a big one—they always get away, it seems like."

"We also saw a pod of manatee and several big crocs. We even saw a panther not far from Chokoloski. It's really a beautiful place. I'm just sorry I have to leave. I need to get back to Palm Beach and wrap up some business."

"Oh, that reminds me, Agent Clark," said the young lady behind the counter. "You received a telegram while you were out fishing."

"*Agent* Clark," said Barron Collier. "I knew there was more to you than Jones was letting on." He was looking at me suspiciously and probably wondering if he was under some sort of investigation.

"The auto theft bureau—not the other bureau."

"Thank goodness. No telling how many laws have been broken here just since the sun came up."

All three of us laughed, but I could tell Collier wasn't totally kidding. "Well, I apologize, but I really must be getting on. Thank you for your hospitality. You really do have a magnificent place here."

Collier said, "Well, don't tell anyone about it, please." He winked at me when he said it and added, "Julian, you are welcome here as my guest anytime you want."

"Thank you, Barron. I just may take you up on that offer sometime."

"I sincerely hope you will. Safe travels."

"Thank you Janice," I said, grabbing my telegram off the counter.

When I got to the Ford, I decided I better read the telegram before heading out in case there was something important that required a response or something that might change my destination. It was from Ed Lawrence.

JULIAN, STOP BY OFFICE ON YOUR WAY BACK TO JACKSONVILLE. WE NEED TO TALK ABOUT MOORE. ED

Chapter 16

When I got to Palm Beach, it had been a long day already, but I stopped in to see Ed Lawrence to find out if he had anything new to share and to tell him about what happened in Miami.

"So what happened in Miami?" asked Ed. "We heard you and Perkins got into a little scrape down there."

I couldn't help but chuckle. "Captain Mitchell is a real piece of work." I told him the story about Moore and his lawyer reporting that Ford stolen. We both had a good laugh before I recounted the chase involving me and Perkins and the subsequent firebombing of my Chevrolet.

"You really got somebody worked up. Do you think it was Moore?"

"He couldn't possibly have figured out I had anything to do with the disappearance of his ride back to Palm Beach. Even if he had, there's no way he could have orchestrated the attempt to kill us. No, I suspect it's connected to one of the other auto theft rings I've been investigating. Who knows?"

"You better watch yourself, Julian."

"Thanks. I've been hearing that a lot lately. What's the latest on Moore?"

"We've been keeping a close eye on him ever since he returned from Miami the other day—from a house down the street as well as a boat out back. The judge has already agreed to issue a search warrant based on your finding that stolen Ford in his driveway, but we don't want to jump the gun. We need to make sure we find something, so we're waiting for the right opportunity. Let's go talk to Grady Emory and Sheriff Baker and find out if they have anything new."

CHAPTER 16

* * *

We headed out to the parking lot to leave.

"I'll drive."

"Wait, you're driving Moore's vehicle?" asked Ed.

"It's not his."

"He thinks it is."

"So what? Just because he reported it stolen in Miami doesn't make it his," I added as we headed north on the county road.

We pulled up to the next intersection, which was at Royal Palm, and I stopped at the crosswalk to let some people by. As they cleared out of the way, I noticed a vehicle to our left that was coming to a stop at the same intersection. There were two men in it and something familiar about both of them. I eased forward, since it was our turn and Ed noticed me staring, so he leaned forward to get a look out the window at whatever had caught my eye.

"I'll be," I said.

"Son of a gun," was all Ed could get out before the man in the passenger seat started pointing at us and yelling something at the driver.

"That's my goddamn Ford!" yelled Moore. "That's the son of a bitch that showed up at my house! The auto theft agent—Clark or something! He's driving my automobile. How did he ...? Son of a bitch! Go! Follow him."

"It's Moore," I said. It really shouldn't have been that big a surprise. After all, he lived right around the corner. It didn't occur to me that he might recognize us in that Ford. There must be a dozen just like it within two miles.

"And that bellhop—Randolph Mays. Step on it, Julian!" Ed said.

Halfway through the intersection I jammed the gas to the floor and got ready to shift. I wish I still had my Chevrolet right about now. A couple of people were still crossing the road on the other side of the intersection, so I laid on the horn and they started hustling to get out of our way. Meanwhile, the other vehicle took out after us and nearly rammed the side of a delivery truck that was making a left turn. As we headed toward the Flagler Bridge,

I looked in the mirror to see them fishtail through the left turn behind us.

"What are the chances we would run into those two while driving their vehicle?"

"Apparently, they are pretty good." And stop saying that!" I yelled.

We were tearing north, approaching Poinciana. Decision time.

"Go left!" yelled Agent Lawrence.

"I know, I know." We were going way too fast to make the left turn toward the bridge so I braked just enough to drift around the corner. I lost sight of them briefly before they careened around the same turn and started gaining speed.

"Get ready to duck!" Before Ed could ask why, the sound of a Thompson gun told him all he needed to know. Bullets rattled the back of the Ford, shredded the spare mounted on the rear, and ricocheted off the rumble seat lid.

"They're shooting at us, dammit!" Ed yelled over the noise of the gunfire and sound of the engine revving and tires squealing.

"Thanks!" I said.

I kept that Ford headed west toward Dixie Highway as fast as I could, but the four-cylinder engine just couldn't outpace the bigger V8 in that Marmon. They closed the distance easily, so I took to swerving to make us a harder target. We took the left turn on Dixie practically on two wheels before I got it straight again.

There were lots of vehicles parked on the sides of the road and the occasional pedestrian, but my bigger concern was traffic. We approached a slower-moving southbound vehicle, and as I was about to swerve left and pass them in the northbound lane, the rear window exploded as a bullet came through it and fortunately lodged in the back of Ed's seat. Just as I swerved to avoid the slower vehicle, Moore let loose a burst of gunfire. It throttled the back of the other vehicle and caused them to swerve right into a parked Ford along the curb. The jolt of the collision pushed the parked Ford forward a good ten feet, and the other vehicle was rocked up on its two front wheels before slamming back down on the street. Ed looked back and was relieved to see movement inside the crashed auto.

"I think she's okay, but we can't keep this up. Innocent people are going to die. It's time to go on offense." Ed pulled out his revolver and turned around to fire out the rear window. I almost rear-ended another slower vehicle and swerved left into oncoming traffic to avoid them. The violent change in direction made Ed drop his weapon on the floorboard. We narrowly hit another vehicle head-on before I jerked the wheel right and cut back into our lane. The abrupt lane change gave me an opportunity to get off Dixie Highway, so I stayed on course and hung a right on Okeechobee.

The kid was good. He made the turn smoothly and accelerated through it to gain some ground on us. By then Ed had his gun ready. "Slow down some, Julian."

"What?"

"I need them to get closer," he said.

Ed Lawrence carried one of the new Smith & Wesson heavy-duty revolvers, which fired a .38 caliber load, and was capable of penetrating the metal hood or front end of that Marmon. A few rounds through the grille or a tire could end this chase. Not to mention a well-placed shot through the windshield. I made sure there weren't any other vehicles coming toward us, or pedestrians on the sidewalk. The Mays kid was closing the distance. The occasional burst from the Tommy gun fortunately hadn't done much more than riddle the back of that Ford with dents and holes. Then I eased up just enough to let Mays get close.

"I hope you know what you're doing," I said.

Ed had turned himself around so he was facing the rear. The rear windshield was already gone, so he didn't have to worry about that. I noticed the barrel of Moore's gun coming back out the passenger window.

"Look out," I yelled.

Ed took aim and fired once. The bullet went through the windshield, leaving a huge hole right in the center and continued between the two men until it hit the rear glass, which shattered on impact. It was enough to scare Moore back inside. Ed fired two more shots into the front of the big Marmon, and smoke started coming out of the radiator. In spite of the damage, Mays wasn't losing ground on us yet, but at least they were being more cautious.

I made a hard left at the next street, and Ed took that as his opportunity to get a shot at them broadside. He was ready when the powerful V8 barreled around the corner. He fired two more times—the second bullet punching a hole in the door just behind Mays. It still didn't slow them down, and we could see Moore starting to lean out the window for another round.

He now had half his body out the window, holding the Tommy gun in both hands. As he got ready to fire, Ed raised his weapon with its long six and a half inch barrel and fired first. The hot round took out the right front tire and actually fractured the wheel, causing the automobile to jerk hard to the right. It took Mays by surprise, and he wasn't ready for the abrupt change in direction. I was watching in the mirror, but didn't have a full view of what happened next. It didn't matter; I knew it was bad.

"Shit," Ed said.

The right front corner of the Marmon hit the rear quarter panel of a parked automobile. They were still going so fast that the contact with the other vehicle caused the rear end of the Marmon to whip around to the left. Moore was flung from the vehicle like a ragdoll and hit the pavement and rolled. Meanwhile, the violent spin of the collision sent their vehicle into a roll down the middle of Okeechobee Boulevard. That Marmon must have rolled three or four times—each one throwing parts, a wheel and the spare, the rumble seat—before coming to rest on the driver side. I slammed on the brakes and stopped in the middle of the road.

We both looked back at the smoldering remains of the Marmon lying on its side in the middle of the road. There were auto body parts strewn all over the street, and we could see Moore lying motionless about a block back in the roadway.

I said, "Let's go check on the kid. Maybe he got lucky. I can't say the same for Moore. I don't think he could have survived that."

When we got to the mangled Marmon and looked inside, it was clear Randolph Mays was indeed not lucky. During the roll, half his body had been thrown out the window and the vehicle had rolled over him. He was clearly crushed from the waist down so badly I had to look away until I heard something. I turned back to look at Mays—his eyes blinked and he coughed and gurgled as blood ran out of the corner of his mouth. He tried to say something, but it sounded like he was drowning. Then he was gone.

"Poor kid," said Ed. "Too bad he got mixed up with this crowd. I'll check on Moore." We could hear sirens in the distance.

* * *

Back at the police station, Ed Lawrence and I had just finished debriefing the captain when one of his deputies came in. "You won't believe what I just heard. Your man Cadwell is dead."

"What? How?" I asked.

"Apparently, he drank some kind of chemical—an insecticide or cleaning fluid. They found him this morning in his cell."

Ed looked at me. "Suicide?"

Chapter 17

It was good to be back in Jacksonville, although it would have been a lot better had I been driving my Chevrolet. A lot had happened since the last time I was in the office and I knew I was going to have to answer a lot of questions, but that Ford, with all its bullet holes and broken glass, raised a lot more.

"Good morning, Gwyneth," I said as I hung my hat on the rack.

"Julian Clark!" She jumped out of her chair and gave me a big hug.

"Well, if I'd known I would get that kind of a greeting, I'd stay gone more often."

"Oh, Julian. I've been so worried about you."

"Gwyn, you know me better than that."

"That's what worries me."

"Outside of nearly being stabbed on the beach, crushed under the hood of a Nash, brained to death with a giant wrench, shot by Truby Hunt, killed in a drive-by shooting, torched in my automobile, chased by gangsters, shot at, and nearly fired by J. Edgar Hoover himself—I'm fine."

"Oh, Julian, do be more careful in the future. This job would be such a bore without you around."

"So I'm just here for your entertainment?"

"I wish. Speaking of Torch."

"Were we?"

"He came by yesterday. Says he's got something for you when you get time and to go see him at the garage."

"I can't wait. That Ford I've been driving looks like it was involved in war.

Is the boss in?"

"He is. He can't wait to see you too."

"I'll bet."

"Julian."

I looked up to see Coonts glowering. His hulking body took up his entire doorway. He crooked his finger and I followed him into his office.

"I guess you're probably wondering what happened in Miami," I said.

"And Palm Beach," he replied. "What the hell happened at the Patricia Hotel?"

"Did Mr. McCrary call you?" I asked.

"I wish. No, Julian, J. Edgar Hoover called first. Then Captain Mitchell."

"Geez. I had no idea. I'm sorry."

After I finished explaining the drive-by shooting at the Patricia Hotel and the chase that killed Wilbur Moore and Randolph Mays, Coonts gave me a tongue lashing the likes of which I wouldn't forget for a long time.

"Make damn sure I don't hear about stuff like this from anyone but you next time! Got it?"

"Yes sir," I said.

"One more thing. Go see Torch. He's got something for you."

* * *

I couldn't wait to get over to Torch's garage. We had been friends most of our lives, attending grade school and high school together in Georgia. He had moved to Jacksonville first, and it was sheer coincidence that we both ended up down here. He was a real character, and he could work wonders with an engine. Torch had been bald since we left high school. Probably because he wore a wool black watch cap every day of his life. Even in Florida. He claimed it kept his head warm.

When I entered the garage, he had his head inside an Auburn. I could hear a ratchet clicking away as he tinkered with something inside. A giant Rottweiler with a head twice the size of Torch's was lying on the floor next to the automobile. He heard me enter and his ears went up. He bolted upright in defense mode until he recognized me. I got down on one knee and called him. "Come here, boy. Come here, Zeus." He ran across the shop and practically knocked me backward as I grabbed his huge shoulders to maintain my balance. I cupped the sides of his head and scratched the back of his ears. He bowed his head in submission before pushing his huge muzzle against my cheek. "Good boy, Zeus."

I could still hear that ratchet cranking away. I noticed another automobile next to the Auburn, but it had a cover over it.

"What happened to my Chevy?" More ratchet and then some clanking like he was hammering on something.

"That was a Bureau Chevrolet," I said. "It got torched."

He finally stopped whatever he was doing and looked up. I tried to keep a straight face, but just couldn't do it and so he started laughing. "Very funny, Juney."

He gave me a giant bear hug and lifted me off the floor. Zeus stood on his hind legs pawing at me like he wanted a piece of the action. "You son of bitch! You torched my Chevy. Do you know how much time I put into that vehicle?"

"Well, maybe if you had made it a little faster, the guys that torched it wouldn't have gotten away."

"You wish. It was probably your sorry driving."

"Or maybe all the gunfire had me distracted."

"Excuses. You get to have to have all the fun."

"How 'bout a break?"

We spent the next hour talking about what each other had been doing over the last several weeks, since we hadn't seen each other. I told him all about the Goldberg case, the fight with Al Neinstein on the beach, and my trip to Baltimore. The scrape I got into on the Clyde. Moore and his stolen Ford and then getting shot at, and of course the car chase around Palm Beach. I could tell he was envious. Torch and I used to get into a lot of scrapes together as kids. He was one of the nicest people I'd ever met, but get on his bad side and he would whip your butt. Torch wasn't afraid of anything or anyone.

"So why did Coonts make sure I came over here today? What's up?"

Torch didn't say anything, but just grabbed a corner of the tarp I noticed when I first came in and gave it a good yank.

"Is that what I think it is?"

"If you think it's a Model B, then yes, it's what you think it is," he replied.

"Sweet Jesus. This can't be. Where did you get it?"

"Coonts."

"Seriously?"

"It's been out back for almost five years. It was a recovery, but I guess they couldn't find the original owner or maybe the insurance company had already paid out on it. I don't know, but it was in really bad shape—found in some barn and didn't run. The motor seized up without any oil, so it just sat. It had some minor damage—a few cosmetic issues, couple of wheels were busted up, and a headlight was gone. Coonts had it towed over here, but I never got around to doing much with it. I took the original motor out and used it for parts. I may have used the rest for a few parts over the years too," he added, laughing.

"A Chrysler Model B," I said. "Hydraulic brakes, right?"

"Yep. I had to find a new hand valve, which wasn't easy. I think I used the original on another rebuild. Anyway, it works now."

"Twenty-four?"

"Actually, it's a five."

"You said the motor seized. What's under the hood?"

"That's the best part. A couple of years ago I bought an Imperial off a man that had wrecked his Model B. The motor was about the only thing left, but that's all I needed. It's a great motor. High compression. Seven bearing crank. Aluminum pistons. Pressure lubed. This automobile was way ahead of its time when it first came out. It was a hell of a lot lighter than the Buick—and faster. When this baby came off the assembly line, it was already getting ninety-two horses."

"What about now?" If I knew Torch, it had been hopped up.

"It's easily pushing a hundred. The original Imperial would do eighty miles per hour, so this ride should have plenty of speed. I pity the next gangster that attempts a drive-by on you, Juney."

The Chrysler Model B-70 was one of the fastest cars built in the mid-twenties, which was why those hydraulic brakes were so important. The "70" in the name stood for a top-speed of seventy miles per hour. The Model B could hold its own against most of the eight-cylinder automobiles manufactured around the same time, and it used technology that the competition wouldn't embrace for several more years. It was light with a smooth ride due to the hydraulic shock absorbers and soft springs. It was also durable, torquey, and had a three-speed shifter on the floor.

As I walked around the front, dragging my hand along the engine cowling I stopped at the hood ornament, which doubled as a radiator cap. I gently caressed the wings of Mercury—a distinctive design feature Chrysler used because of the Model B's speed.

Torch noticed my attention to it and said, "That radiator cap was the hardest part to replace. I sold the original years ago. Apparently, kids like to steal them because they're cool. Chrysler put a temp gauge in the instrument cluster, so you don't need one of those little Moto-Meter cap gauges. Did you know that Viking look was designed by Oliver Clark. Clark!" He reiterated. "Is that neat or what?"

I was already speechless. It was such a cool automobile. I was still having a hard time believing it was mine. As much as I missed my Chevrolet, this was too much.

"I had to ditch the original wood-spoke wheels for these because it only had two that were still usable. Hey, come check out the inside."

Torch opened the door for me and let me slide into the driver's seat. It had rich, overstuffed cushions—I wondered if they could be original. As I sat there taking it all in, he said, "Don't crank it yet. Give me a second." He hustled over to the little office inside the garage and came running back out a few seconds later.

"Okay, fire it up."

I slowly pushed my foot down on the clutch, pulled the choke out, and took a deep breath when I noticed my heart was racing. A couple more breaths slowed it down a little until I turned the key.

The straight six caught with a subtle rumble. There was nothing like the sound of a finely tuned automobile with a powerful motor and modified exhaust. The little Model B wasn't boasting its prowess. It was an understated rumble that belied its true nature, but I could sense there was more to it. That was part of Torch's genius. Not too soft and yet not to loud. It was just right. A sleeper.

The Model B wasn't pretentious anyway, but this one was so ordinary, it wouldn't deserve a second look. It was actually the perfect ride for an agent.

Torch grabbed my elbow, shaking me half to death. "That's music to the ears, isn't it, Juney!" practically yelling at me even though we were sitting shoulder to shoulder. That was just Torch's way. His enthusiasm for everything was contagious. I realized I had a huge grin on my face just listening to that Chrysler idle. "Check that out, Juney!" pointing at the gauges. The instrument cluster glowed with life. "How cool is that? The first time I cranked her up, I couldn't believe the little lamp still worked," he said.

A backlit instrument cluster was rare in 1925, and most of the competition had just started using them today.

"I still don't understand. How did you and Coonts pull this off?"

"He's the boss—ask him. But like I said, this was a Bureau vehicle anyway. When Gene told me about your little fire, I told him to hold off getting another Chevrolet because I might have something a little more"—he paused—"practical," he added with a big smile. "By the way, I saved you guys a lot of money because all your agency has to pay for is the engine and the labor I had already put into getting it running."

"I still can't believe it."

"You know Frances is going to hate it," said Torch.

"Probably."

"Let's go for a spin, Juney! Why are we still sitting here?"

Torch got out and opened the big sliding double doors, and waited for me to back out. He closed the doors and jumped back in. "Let's ride."

I eased the clutch out, and we exited the little parking lot in front of the shop. I let the rpm's wind up pretty good before shifting into second. It still had plenty of torque and didn't take long to get to forty, but the shift to third was anything but smooth. The synchronizers were probably worn out.

We were on a nice straightaway section of country road, so I put the pedal down to see what it would do. As we passed sixty miles per hour it was still humming along smoothly and felt stable. There was a lot of engine noise, which was a good thing, but also a lot of road noise. At seventy-five it felt really light and at eighty-five I noticed a wobble in the steering that went away at ninety. She felt like she still had room to stretch, but I was running out of road, so I let my foot off the gas.

"What are you doing, Juney?" Torch yelled. "Don't you want to know where she tops out?"

I looked over to make sure he had his hand on the door handle and then in the rearview mirror to make sure nobody was behind us, and then I stood on the brake pedal. All four wheels locked up and we skidded to a stop as a huge cloud of dust and smoke overtook us. Those hydraulic brakes had great balance, and we stopped in our lane without pulling to either side. I looked at Torch with a big grin on my face. "What did you do to the engine?"

"Oh, not much. A tweak here and there is about it."

"Come on, Torch."

"You know I can't share all my secrets."

"You haven't shared any."

He just stared forward.

I revved the engine and popped the clutch, and we barely moved as she just spun her tires and threw gravel and dust up. When she finally regained traction, I was already shifting into second. When we got back to the garage, I pulled up to the big doors and turned it off.

Turning to Torch, I said, "I'll take it."

"Not so fast. I got something else for you." He dug into his pocket and pulled out a key ring with a round piece of metal attached to it. On the face were Mercury's wings and engraved underneath were the initials J.H.C.—Julian Harbour Clark.

"Did you make this?" I asked.

"Sure did, buddy. Be careful out there—and try not to destroy another one of my babies."

"Thanks, Torch. This really means a lot."

Chapter 18

"Alva, it's Riley. I guess you heard about Truby?"

"That goddamned Agent Clark just won't give up. I still can't figure out how that guy seems to stay one step ahead us. Hell, I'm surprised he didn't show up at the river the other night in Jupiter."

"Careful. This is a party line—no names. And by the way it's because he's not a revenuer. He's with NATB. If we had been moving automobiles, you can bet your ass he probably would have found out."

"Let's get together and figure out how to handle this. We need to get Truby out too. Meet me at the house tonight. I'll let Katherine know to expect us for dinner."

"See you tonight," said Riley and hung up.

* * *

The house in Daytona was the most logical place to meet. It was close to Deland, and the Hunt and Gant families had a lawyer in Ormond that had done some work for them in the past. Alva had already contacted him about getting Truby out of jail. Both families had a pretty long list of aliases they had used over the years, so it was unlikely that Truby would ever see the inside of a courtroom, much less a cell. They had been playing this game for years and seldom spent any meaningful time in jail.

Riley was getting more and more concerned that their luck was going to change because they had seriously ratcheted up their list of crimes to now include murder. He never intended it to go this far, but then who does?

Bootlegging was a natural progression from stealing automobiles. The money was good and the Depression was starting to take a toll on everyone. It was no wonder so many turned to crime to stay afloat.

"Hey, Katherine," Riley said as he gave his sister a kiss on the cheek. He had taken his hat and coat off to hang in the closet by the front door when she asked, "How's Dad?"

"Getting old, but hanging in there. I think he's finally resigned to letting us run the business and retire. We'll see, but he's doing good."

"I didn't expect you back so soon," Katherine said.

"It's good to be back. I haven't had a decent meal since the last time I was here."

"I've got dinner on, but in the meantime, Alva's out in the garage. He said to come on out when you got here. I'll let you boys know when it's time to eat."

"Thanks, sis," said Riley as he headed out the kitchen door to the garage.

When Riley walked in, Alva was underneath another project. This time it was a 1916 Packard Twin Six open-wheel racer.

Alva heard the door open and grunted from under the auto, "Who's there?"

"Who do you think?" Riley said.

Alva reached out from under the automobile, grabbed the side, and gave himself a quick pull. The creeper he was lying on came shooting out from under the Packard.

"Easy! You almost took my toes off with that thing." Alva just rolled his eyes at Riley and put his hand out for Riley to help him up.

"Dinner ready?" Alva asked.

"Not yet. Katherine said she would call us."

"So, what do you think?" Alva asked, nodding toward the hulk of rusted metal sitting on blocks.

"Is it bent?" asked Riley

"Hell no. I bought it from Bible's."

Lee Bible was a garage operator and racecar driver. He had been killed attempting to break a land speed record last year.

"You paid for this?"

"Very funny. Do you know how many races this automobile has won?"

"In this decade?"

"You'll see. When I get this baby running, you're going to be jealous. You know it."

"If I had a nickel for every time you said that about one of your projects, I wouldn't be in the bootlegging business."

Alva looked hurt. "This time is different. They still have an open class for collectors. We could make some money racing this baby."

Riley had heard all of this before. Alva had wanted to race on the beach since they were teenagers. He always ended up selling his unfinished project autos before they ever saw the track. Mostly just to get them out of the way to make room for the next "diamond in the rough" he would come across. Or sometimes because Katherine told him to get rid of it and clean up the garage. "Hey, let's talk business before Katherine calls us. This is a conversation I don't want her listening in on."

"Fine by me," replied Alva.

"Did you reach Griesedieck?" asked Riley.

"Finally. That lowlife makes me feel like I need a shower every time I'm near him."

Dewey Griesedieck was the only lawyer they could afford, but he was effective, and he knew how to grease the right palms—pun intended. His last name was pronounced like it looked, which didn't help his overall persona. He wore cheap gaberdine suits and used too much Brylcreem to keep his too long hair greased back. Shaking his hand was like shaking a hunk of slimy dough, and it gave you the urge to wash your own as quickly as possible. Having a law degree was irrelevant, since he rarely followed the law to get something done. He was basically a con man, but he had successfully kept all of the Hunts and Gants from doing any serious time behind bars. He made problems go away, and they had plenty of those to go around.

"What did he say? Did he get Truby out?"

"Yeah, he got him out. Fortunately, he was using an alias when he stole that Chevrolet."

"What about prints?" asked Riley.

"Greisedieck has a guy on the inside. He made them disappear. Nobody can figure out what happened to them, so basically the case is going nowhere because they don't know it was Truby. Dewey told him if he stays the hell away from Deland, there's a good chance he never hears about it again."

"What about Agent Clark?"

"Truby said he recognized the NATB man as soon as he stepped in the door. Clark did too, but Truby stuck to his story until they had him nailed, and then he started blabbing about Harold. Clark knows it was Truby, but there's not much he can do about it now. Truby's long gone and the judge will probably dismiss the case once they figure out there's nobody named Tommie Wallace anywhere near Deland. Plus, he's got bigger fish to fry than my brother for stealing that Chevy."

"Were there any other witnesses?" asked Riley.

"Only that trollop Marie Skinner he was running around with, but she won't say nothin'."

* * *

Just then the door burst open and in walked Hugh Gant. "Who called this meeting and why wasn't I invited?" he said.

Riley and Alva just stood there and gaped for what seemed like an eternity before Hugh finally burst out laughing. "I wish you could see the look on your faces right now." They both relaxed and started laughing with him.

"You scared the shit out of me, Hugh—bursting in here like that," said Alva. "Don't pull that shit again."

"What are you two hooligans up to anyway?"

"Where did you come from?" asked Riley.

"Don't act so happy to see your little brother," Hugh said. "Witnesses to what?"

"Truby got busted. Again." The way Alva said it was like there shouldn't be any reason for a seasoned automobile thief like Truby to ever get busted.

"Yup. Heard about that. I also heard he was already out," said Hugh. "Griesedieck?"

"Yea. Fortunately, he was using an alias," said Riley. "We were talking about witnesses to his arrest. Marie Skinner was there."

"Well, she won't say nothin'," added Hugh.

"What about that NATB man—Agent Clark?" asked Alva.

"What does he have to do with anything?" said Hugh.

"He's the one that made the arrest," said Riley.

Hugh's demeanor changed in an instant. It was like somebody flicked a switch and he became somebody altogether different. They could sense the rage inside him building like water pressure in a boiler that had no escape valve. They could see the anger in his eyes and his complexion turned red. His fingers curled up into fists that were like balls of granite.

Alva remembered back to a previous explosion. It had been a typical day on Daytona Beach—hanging out, drinking beer, playing grab ass with the girls, and having fun. Alva had had his eye on a certain girl for weeks, but she was already with another boy that considered Alva a rival. His name was Kyle O'Neil and her name was Cindy. Alva always had one of his daddy's automobiles, and Kyle was relentless with his challenges to drag race. Alva's daddy had one stipulation for letting him take his ride to the beach – no racing.

Alva did his best to ignore the teasing and jabs from Kyle and his buddies about being scared and a momma's boy. They called him names and bullied him every chance they got. It was obvious Alva was sweet on Cindy, and she didn't help the situation because she was always throwing him looks. Clearly, Kyle was jealous of Alva because of the rides he showed up in. Harold was itching to teach him a lesson and kick his ass, but Alva always talked him out of it. He wasn't worth the bloody knuckle, he would tell Harold.

One night Cindy wandered over to their fire and started talking to Alva. Riley and Hugh wondered what was up. Harold wasn't with them that night. Before long Kyle stormed into our camp, looking for blood. It happened so fast nobody saw him coming, but he cold-cocked Alva from behind. That's when Hugh jumped in.

The rage inside him exploded and he beat Kyle to within an inch of his life. It took three of them to pull him off Kyle. The boy's face was a bloody mess. He spent a week in the hospital with broken ribs and multiple skull fractures. They didn't think he would make it. They never saw Kyle or Cindy on the beach again. It was that day they realized Hugh had a dark side deep down.

"How the hell does that sorry bastard keep turning up in our business? I don't even care anymore. Maybe it is just luck or maybe somebody is clueing him in, but it ends now. It's high time we solved this problem—permanently." He practically spat the words out. "Maybe these run-ins have all been coincidences, but if I find out somebody has been feeding him information—I will kill that son of bitch too!"

"Let's not get carried away, Hugh," said Riley.

"Carried away?" yelled Hugh.

"He's right, Riley," said Alva. "Harold's dead and that son of a bitch was there, and Truby just got arrested again by none other than Agent Clark—for the second time! I'm with Hugh on this one. Something needs to be done about this guy!" Alva turned to Hugh, whose face was still red with rage. "What happened in Miami?"

Hugh just stood there staring at Alva, almost willing him to take back the question. When it was clear he wasn't going to say anything, Riley grabbed Hugh's elbow to get his attention and said, "What's he talking about, Hugh?"

Hugh snapped around and pushed Riley's hand away. He started to say something and stopped. Riley waited a beat and turned to Alva, "Somebody had better start talking. What the hell have you two been up to?"

Alva looked at Hugh and said, "You might as well tell him."

Riley interrupted, "What the hell happened in Miami?"

"Everett and I tried to take care of Agent Clark in Miami. We rounded up a couple of friends and tried taking him out in front of his hotel. We burned his Chevrolet too, but he got away. We figured we at least scared him enough to stay out of our way."

"That's like expecting Ness to stop chasing Capone, you idiot. How did he know it was you?" asked Riley.

Alva and Hugh just looked at each other blankly. The tables had certainly turned. Riley was used to Alva being the voice of reason.

Hugh said, "he didn't."

"So what makes you think he learned a lesson? It could have been anyone. How many auto thieves do you think want his head on a pike?" No answer. "So now what?" asked Riley.

Hugh said, "We get it right. We take care of business and move on."

Alva said, "Well, this time take care of the problem yourself. Everett could screw up a wet dream."

"It wasn't Everett's—" Hugh started to say before Alva interrupted.

"I don't care. Just deal with it. Do what you have to do."

The three of them just stood there staring at nothing in particular. Alva leaned up against the old Packard and crossed his arms. Hugh finally turned and headed for the door, but just as he was about to open it, the door swung open and Katherine was standing there.

"Dinner's ready." Perfect timing.

"I'm not staying," Hugh said as he leaned in and kissed his sister on the cheek. "Thanks anyway." Then he brushed past her and left.

"What's eating him?" she asked.

Alva and Riley glanced at each other before Riley said, "You know Hugh. It's always something with him. Come on—let's eat."

The three of them left the garage and headed back inside.

* * *

Ybor City was the epicenter of the cigar industry in the United States. Founded by Cuban immigrant Vicente Martinez-Ybor only forty-five years prior, it was located on what had previously been forty acres of scrub on the northeast side of Tampa. The location was near the port of Tampa and Henry Plant's new railroad, but it also had the humid climate necessary for storing tobacco, making it the ideal place Vicente Martinez-Ybor had been searching for since setting up shop in Key West. He had been forced to flee Cuba during the Ten Years' War as Cuba fought for its independence from Spanish rule.

As business boomed, Ybor hired thousands of Cuban, Spanish, and Italian workers. He built hundreds of affordable houses for the immigrants who were paid well to work in the factories. Before long his competition moved in and took advantage of what he had built and the incentives he created to attract employees. Ybor City was unique in that it was one of the few towns in the United States almost entirely populated and owned by immigrants.

Only a short year ago, a half billion cigars came out of Ybor's cigar factories each year, but the Depression was taking a toll. Layoffs were rampant and the local immigrant community was starting to bear the brunt of the economic downturn. As was the case with most luxuries, people were turning to cheaper alternatives. Cigarettes were a lot less expensive than cigars—especially good ones that had been hand-rolled. New rolling machines had already started to supplant workers, but the Depression compounded the problem. Without a booming cigar trade, the demographics of Ybor City changed.

The Cubans and Spanish were at the top of the local pecking order because their fathers, grandfathers, and great-grandfathers had all been tobacco farmers and cigar makers. Not the Italians—they had no heritage in the business and so they got the crap jobs. That is until Vincenzo Genna came along. Most of the Italian immigrants had come from Sicily—just like Genna—and he was quick to hire them away from the foundering cigar companies to work for him. The business of illegal whiskey was booming, and it helped prop up his nightclubs and speakeasies.

Jim Genna owned several warehouses in Ybor City including one that previously housed one of the largest cigar-rolling factories in the country. He employed over two hundred fifty men, all Italians who didn't know the first thing about rolling a cigar.

The cavernous brick building had the sweet smell of tobacco permanently infused into its very existence. Millions of pounds of highly sought-after Cuban tobacco leaves had been stored under a canopy of oak beams and columns and then later rolled into some of the finest cigars money could buy. Before Genna, a thousand Cubans sat at rows of rolling tables for hours on end, expertly rolling cigars that stoked the nation's demand. Smoking was not only permitted, it was encouraged.

Now the tables were gone—so were the workers—at least the Cuban ones were. Replaced by Italians who were loyal to Genna. Large stainless tanks had replaced the rolling tables, and the loading docks that once saw countless deliveries of tobacco now supported the delivery of a different kind of staple. Molasses—or so it seemed. Genna had come up with an ingenious way of storing the crop of his real business—booze. His tanks all had a partition that allowed for two different liquids to be kept inside. The smaller compartment in the bottom of the tank held molasses. The larger one held liquor. If someone were to check the contents, the spigot would release a viscous torrent of dark molasses and they would be none the wiser. A hidden spigot on the back of each tank revealed its true contents.

Genna had even found a few of Martinez-Ybor's original tanks from his brewery in the back of one of the warehouses he purchased. He used them up front and they contained nothing but molasses—just in case a revenuer decided to drop in.

In the rear of the warehouse were several offices, one of which was Mr. Genna's. Riley Gant had been there before and declined an escort from the young lady answering the phone in the lobby. He didn't like being here, but it was necessary.

"Hello, Riley. It's good to see you again, although I didn't expect you back so soon."

"That makes two of us, Jim."

"I appreciate you coming in person. Business is good, but some things—or should I say, some people—are creating unnecessary risks that neither one of us can afford."

"I couldn't agree more. I guess you heard, Wilbur Moore's dead."

"What happened?"

"Well, as the story goes, he was being chased by the Bureau and he died in an automobile crash. Pretty violently, I heard. He had plenty of enemies, especially at the Bureau. They've been bird-dogging him for months. Lots of accusations but nothing ever stuck. Ed Lawrence in the Palm Beach County Bureau office and a revenuer named Grady Emory have been trying to bust him for killing one of their own. His luck was bound to run out sooner or later."

As Riley spoke, Genna reflected on his mention of Agent Lawrence. The Bureau man had become a thorn in his side, and he wasn't going to go away quietly.

"How do you know all of this?" asked Genna.

"We got a guy inside Palm Beach PD," replied Riley.

Genna sat there in silence, thinking about what Riley had told him. "This Agent Lawrence—it's not the first time we've crossed paths, so to speak. One of my men spotted him snooping around one of my warehouses in Brunswick. I was meeting with Moore at the same time. I warned Moore about him, but the cocky bastard wouldn't listen."

"That's Moore for you."

"Now I have a supply problem I hadn't counted on. I didn't like Wilbur Moore, but at least he was reliable."

"I'm sure the Ashleys would be happy to step in," said Riley. "There are a few others."

"Yeah, I'm working on a couple of options already. What about you?"

Riley didn't see that coming, but carefully considered what Genna was asking him before he responded. "Not our business." He could tell Genna wasn't used to being turned down, but he and his brothers didn't know the first thing about boats or crossing the Atlantic. Riley got seasick the only time he went out on open water. The memory came back and reminded him of the nausea that had paralyzed him for hours. The Hunts weren't any more capable seafarers than he was. Replacing Moore was definitely not an option.

"Think about it. In the meantime, I'll make other arrangements."

"Well, make sure they are permanent because I've already thought about it, and it's not going to happen. But thanks for the consideration."

Genna was disappointed, but he respected Riley for knowing his limitations. This situation was just a hiccup, but still a nuisance to deal with. However, he had dealt with much worse. Eventually, he would have to deal with Agent Lawrence too.

"I need to get moving. Let me know what you figure out and we'll be ready."

"Thanks, Riley. I'll be in touch."

Riley Gant walked out of the office and back into the warehouse. As he made the long walk back to the front, he considered all that had happened recently. Harold was dead. They were already responsible for the murder of an innocent man, and Hugh was likely about to commit another. It wasn't too late to stop the violence. He feared losing someone close was inevitable, and the feeling was suffocating. Alva had been skeptical about their foray into the liquor business and for good reason. It was easy to blame their decisions on the growing economic situation, but it was hard to deny that working with Genna was a decision they never would have turned down even in the best of times.

* * *

Not long after Riley Gant had left, there was a knock at the door. It was Big Sal, Genna's right-hand man and lieutenant. Genna had been staring out the window, lost in thought about how to fill his tanks.

"Hey, boss. Sorry for bothering you."

"It's no problem Sal. What's up?"

"That Cadwell thing we talked about. It's done."

"How?"

"He drank something—by accident. A chemical of some sort."

"Thanks," was all Genna said. Sal turned and walked out.

Chapter 19

Coonts was in an especially good mood when I got to the office, but it shouldn't have been a surprise. We had spent months on the Goldberg case, and we had finally reached the climax of all that work. The case took us in lots of directions and across multiple jurisdictions, but the coordinated efforts of the NATB, Bureau of Investigation, multiple police and sheriff's departments as well as Bob and Joe Brooks at National Mutual Insurance ultimately led to our success. A lot of good detective work had brought down one of the biggest auto-theft rings in the Southeast.

Sheriff Barnhart from Savannah helped us serve warrants to Goldberg and Bloomberg. Captain McCarthy was hesitant to make any arrests at first because of Goldberg's reputation around town, but eventually he had to get on board. The evidence was overwhelmingly against the auto dealers and they had to go down. The Brooks family was instrumental in helping solve the cases too. Without the list of vehicles stolen in the Baltimore area as well as every vehicle put on the Clyde up there, we would have spent several months trying to figure out how they were getting to Jacksonville.

Neinstein disappeared. Somehow he got wind of his pending arrest, and when the sheriff showed up at his house, all he found was that crazy Irish woman who wouldn't say a word. Neinstein's Cadillac was still out back. He couldn't stay on the lam forever. Eventually, someone would see or say something and give him up. In the meantime, we had to settle for putting Goldberg and Bloomberg behind bars.

Detective Byrne was also a huge help because he really wanted to take down the men responsible for screwing him out of so much money. He definitely had skin in the game and it showed. Fortunately, it had a happy ending for him. The insurance company had already paid the claim of the original owner of his Chrysler, and he had already bought another one. The guy didn't have any interest in having his old one returned, so Byrne got to keep his ride.

When he heard Neinstein got away, he was plugged to no end. Detective Byrne knew he was a scumbag, but for him it was personal. His sister had gotten mixed up with Neinstein, and he roughed her up a couple of times. Thomas had a score to settle, but he was patient. I pitied the man that crossed Thomas Byrne.

* * *

Accolades from the NATB in Atlanta, as well as from J. Edgar Hoover himself, had really put our office on the map. Hoover suggested that our success was a perfect example of the vision he had for the NATB when he helped write its charter. Shutting down a large theft ring was one of our primary responsibilities, and these guys were guilty of stealing hundreds of automobiles. There was a good chance it would probably lead to the takedown of the Coll gang in Baltimore too, which was a very big deal. Hoover wanted to personally thank us, which is why everyone was in the office today.

Gwyneth had taken the liberty of decorating the office with garlands and some balloons. She also made one of her famous pound cakes while several of the other ladies made cookies or desserts. Everyone was excited about Hoover's visit, but Gwyneth was especially giddy and making a big fuss about the whole thing. Her excitement was contagious, and every time she passed me, she gave me a look. That woman really knew how to make a man's heart skip a beat.

Hoover pulled me aside at one point to congratulate me. "Nice work, Julian."

"Thank you, sir," I replied.

"That was quite a mess you and Perkins stirred up down there in Miami,"

Hoover said.

"Yes sir," I replied.

"Ever figure out who was behind it?"

"We have a good idea, sir."

"Let me know if we can help," he added.

"Yes sir. Thanks for the offer."

He started to walk away and then turned back and said, "One more thing. You boys enjoy that 'shine down at the Patricia?

My jaw dropped. "Uh, yes sir."

He winked at me and walked away.

By the end of the day, almost everyone had gone home. Coonts was still in his office, no doubt doing some menial paperwork he refused to leave until tomorrow. He had basked in the glory of the commendations straight from director of the Bureau of Investigation himself.

On my way out, I stopped in the lobby to gaze at the plaque Hoover had dedicated to us and read the letter accompanying it. Gwyneth had already framed it and created a special place for it on our "wall of fame." No one could enter the building without seeing both. The embossed seal of the Bureau immediately conveyed its prominence to any onlookers, and standing there reading his letter, I realized we had done some really important work.

All of a sudden I felt a hand on my shoulder. I knew who it was without taking my eyes off the plaque. Her scent was unmistakable, and the way she touched me was altogether sensual.

"You know, Julian, everyone in this office knows there's only one man truly responsible for earning that award." Her hand stroked my back as she said it, and she leaned in closer.

I started to deny it when she put her finger to my lips. "Congratulations, Julian," she whispered. She lingered for a second before turning and heading out the door to go home.

Chapter 20

F rances and I had just finished dinner when there was a knock at the door. She looked at me curiously, since neither of us was expecting anyone. Darkness had fallen, and we hadn't noticed any lights approach or come into the drive. I got up to go see who it was. Before asking who was there, I tried to get a glimpse of the front porch from the small window next to the door. Whoever was out there was standing close enough to the door and over to the side enough so that I couldn't see who it was—only that it was a very large individual—definitely a man. The shadow he cast across the porch and onto the lawn was huge.

Another knock—this time a lot more forcefully. Frances looked around the corner from the kitchen where she had been cleaning up, and I could tell she was alarmed. As I grabbed the handle and leaned closer to ask who was there, another knock sounded like it would take the door down. "Julian! Are you in there?" The voice was immediately familiar.

"Bill?" I responded.

"Yes, it's me. Are you going to open the door?"

Frances and I both relaxed as I turned the handle. When I opened the door, big Bill McCoy was standing there with a grin on his face. "I hope I'm not interrupting anything."

Frances disappeared around the corner, no doubt to fix her hair. "Hey, Bill," she said. "I'll be out in a minute."

His shrugged his shoulders at me as if to question what was up.

"It's fine. Come on in, Captain. We just finished dinner," I said.

Bill looked around me to make sure Frances wasn't looking and then leaned down and picked something up from the porch floor. When he stood up, he was holding a brown paper sack that clearly had a bottle in it.

I looked back to see if Frances had come back and then whispered, "You can't bring that in here. Just leave it out on the porch. I'll get it later."

"Fine," he whispered back.

"Thanks, buddy. Come on in, Bill. What brings you by this time of night?"

"I figured you'd still be celebrating. Congratulations, Julian!"

"For what?" I said as Frances came back in the room. I did a double-take because she had changed and was wearing makeup.

"Is he always this humble, Frances?" he said as he gave her a huge hug and lifted her off the floor. Bill had to be twenty inches taller than Frances.

"You know how he is, Bill," she said. "It's so good to see you. Thanks for stopping by."

"I was just using Julian as an excuse to see you."

"Should I leave you two alone?" I said. Bill was still holding my wife.

"Aw, don't be so jealous, Juney," said Frances.

"Jealous of this big lug? Get serious, baby."

"Julian, do you really think you can compete with this?" Bill replied, gesturing to himself.

"Okay, you two. Are you going to start comparing biceps next?

We both started rolling up our sleeves when Frances rolled her eyes and headed to the kitchen. "Bill, can I get you anything? Tea or coffee?"

"No, thanks," he said.

"I'm fine too, Frances," I added.

"All kidding aside, Julian—congratulations. I heard Hoover came down personally to thank you for your service."

"Not exactly, but thanks, Bill. I really appreciate it. It was a team effort, though—"

"Sure it was," he interrupted.

Frances returned with a cup of tea and suggested we all sit down. All of the recent attention had been really nice since we busted Goldberg, but I was not an attention seeker, and it was uncomfortable being lauded as such an accomplished detective when I knew how many other people aided in my success. I had received several congratulatory letters from our Atlanta, Baltimore, and Palm Beach offices as well as a few phone calls. The best of which had been from Aubrey Warren. Obviously meeting J. Edgar Hoover was special, but Aubrey was my mentor and one of the best detectives in the South.

"I never got a chance to thank you for getting Juney that invitation to the Cloister for dinner. It sounds like you boys had quite an evening," said Frances.

"You don't know the half of it, Frances, but you're welcome."

I cut my eyes at Bill and Frances said, "Oh, I'm quite sure I do." She raised her eyebrows at me after she said it.

We spent an hour carrying on before Bill finally said he had to get going. Frances would have let him stay all night and even offered to let him stay in the guest room since it was so late, but he was adamant about getting back to the marina. In spite of a few indiscretions in his past, Bill was a salt-of-the-earth kind of guy and a true gentleman. I was lucky to have him as a friend.

* * *

After Bill left, Frances went back to the bedroom to get ready for bed while I went to the kitchen to tidy up. No sooner had I turned on the water and gotten my hands wet than I heard another knock at the door. Drying my hands, I started trying to think of what Bill possibly could have left when Frances hollered, "I'll get it, Julian."

I couldn't think of any reason for Bill to be back. As a matter of fact, Bill was pretty serious about getting back to the marina. Just as the thought occurred—I turned and yelled at Frances, "Don't open that—"

It was too late. Frances turned the handle and the door flew open, knocking her back. There was a loud scream as she regained her balance only to be pushed backward onto the sofa. The intruder kicked the door shut behind him.

"Frances!"

"Julian!"

"Shut up, woman," the man said, slapping her across the face.

I rounded the corner at full speed with no idea what or who I was going to encounter, but as soon as I entered the room I was staring down the barrel of a very large pistol.

"Stop right there, Clark!" he yelled at me.

It was all I could do to put the brakes on before I ran into the man. He was wearing a long trench coat, and his face was narrow and gaunt and pockmarked with scars. He smelled like cigarettes.

"What do you want?" I said.

Frances was on the sofa holding her cheek, and she began to sob. She was clearly terrified.

"Don't do this, Neinstein. We can work this out."

"Shut up, Clark. I've had enough of you. We had a good thing going until you came along and screwed it up."

"What's he talking about, Julian," asked Frances.

He looked at her and sneered. "I told you to be quiet. Don't make me shut you up again."

"Stay the hell away from her, Albert. This doesn't involve her."

"You're not in much of a position to be making demands, Clark. I should put a bullet in you and leave you for dead and take the missus here with me."

Frances started sobbing again. My pistol was in the bedroom, so there was no way I could get to it. Somehow I needed to get closer to Neinstein and figure out how to disarm him. I can't believe this scumbag was standing in my living room. How the hell did he know where I lived?

"What do you want?"

He reached in the pocket of his coat and pulled out a coil of rope and tossed it on the floor in front of me. "What I want is for you to tie up your wife in that chair over there. Then you and I are going for a little ride."

I didn't move, so he raised his hand and pointed his weapon right at my face. "Do it, Clark, and don't make me ask you again."

I slowly bent over and picked up the rope. "It's okay, baby."

Neinstein motioned with the gun for her to get up and sit in the chair, which she did slowly. As she walked toward me, her eyes conveyed the terror she was feeling. Her cheek was red and starting to swell, and a bruise was forming near the corner of her eye. When I got the chance, I would kill the man responsible, with my bare hands if necessary. I could barely contain the rage building inside me.

Frances sat down in the chair and I made a couple of wraps around her torso and the back of the chair. "Make sure it's tight and get her hands in there. I'm going to check it, so don't screw around."

As I leaned down to make another wrap, I took the opportunity to whisper in her ear, "It's going to be okay, baby."

"Now get her feet too. Tie them to the chair and make a good knot in the back."

When I finished, he reached into his pocket again and pulled out a gag. He tossed it in Frances's lap. She was wheezing, but trying not to cry. I put the gag in her mouth slowly and then tied it as loosely as I could behind her head. She started crying again and Neinstein approached like he was going to strike her. I stepped around the chair and got between him and her and said stop. I put my hands up. "Please."

He poked the gun in my chest and motioned for me to get away. He walked around the back of her and checked the rope and my knots. "Not bad, Clark. Now let's go."

I slowly started moving toward the door. "Where are we going?"

"Oh, I didn't tell you? That's because it's not important. Now get moving and shut the fuck up." Neinstein gave me a hard shove from behind, pushing me into the front door. Then he pistol-whipped me from behind. Frances tried to scream from behind the gag, and I went down hard. I could feel the blood running down my scalp until it reached the back of my neck and then started dripping on the floor. My eyes met Frances's and I realized I probably wasn't going to see her again. I needed to get outside and away from the house so he would leave her be.

"Get up."

I was dizzy from the blow to my head, but managed to get up—slowly. I turned my back to him and opened the door. I noticed an unfamiliar shadow on the porch, but I couldn't focus and assumed it was my vision blurring and playing tricks on me. I slowly moved forward out the door, trying to maintain my balance. Neinstein followed—his pistol aimed at the center of my back.

As soon as he started to cross the threshold, I detected movement to my right. I glanced over my shoulder just in time to see big Bill McCoy swinging an axe handle upward towards the hand holding the gun. He made solid contact with Neinstein's wrist, forcing his arm, and the gun, up. Neinstein pulled the trigger, but the bullet went into the ceiling. Before he could bring it down again, McCoy gave him a quick jab to the throat with his left fist. The gun fell out of his hand, and he used both of his hands to grab his throat. I was sure Bill had crushed his larynx. Bill had a hundred pounds on the smaller man, and a shot like that would have been devastating.

Regardless, Bill moved in close with the axe handle again, and whacked Neinstein across the side of his head. It sounded like the handle cracked—or maybe that was Neinstein's skull. It was a sickening sound. He dropped to the floor. Still holding his throat with one hand, he tried to get something out of his pocket. He finally found what he was looking for. The click of the switchblade made Bill take a step back. Neinstein began flailing with the knife, trying to get Bill's leg or foot. He tried to use the doorjamb to get to his feet, but Bill took the opportunity to stomp down violently on the man's knee. The joint folded like a piece of balsa. The man tried to scream, but not much came out because his throat was crushed.

I tried jumping on him with the intent to choke out whatever life was left in the man, but Bill sensed the rage in me and grabbed my arm, pulling me back.

"Let me go, Bill! He deserves to die! Look what he did to Frances!" I've never felt so much anger for another human being. Bill pulled me back and held me off him.

"Julian!" I kept thrashing and trying to get free of his bear-like grip. "Julian! He's not worth it. Let it go. Just let it go."

I wanted him dead. I wanted to feel the life leave his worthless body. It was all I wanted after the look of fear and terror I had seen in Frances's eyes.

To make someone so beautiful and innocent feel that fear—I couldn't push it out of my mind. I couldn't unsee it. Somehow, I forced the urge to kill him back down into the primitive place that existed in all of us. I felt the urge to be sick, but I kept it down with the rage. Once I was sure I could stand, I headed inside to Frances.

Tears were streaming down her face as I untied the gag and then the rope. She let out a series of gut-wrenching sobs before turning to me. The blood from my head had soaked my shirt and was dripping all over the floor. She hugged me like she would never have the chance to hug me again and cried.

Bill let us be. He grabbed Neinstein's ankle and dragged him back out across the threshold onto the porch. We heard a siren approaching. I wondered how they knew.

Bill came back inside and waited for us to calm down before asking us if we were okay.

Frances gave Captain McCoy a huge hug. "Thank you, Bill. I felt sure he was going to kill Julian. Maybe me too. Thank you for saving our lives." She started crying again.

"What are you even doing here, Bill?" I asked. "I thought you had left. I'm glad you didn't, but what happened out there?"

"When I was leaving the neighborhood, I saw an automobile parked down the street that wasn't there when I first arrived. As I drove by, I realized someone was sitting in it and there was something about the whole situation that didn't seem right. So I drove around the neighborhood and circled back just in time to see him get out and start walking toward your house. I parked around the corner and followed him back here. I saw him push his way inside, but I couldn't get to the door fast enough, so I had wait on the porch. I'm sorry, Frances, but I had to wait for the right time. I heard him say he was going to take Julian for a drive, so I figured that was going to be my best opportunity to catch him off guard."

"I can't thank you enough, Bill," I said.

"I'm just sorry Frances got roughed up. Are you okay?"

The side of her face was swollen and red, and she was developing a pretty good black eye too.

252

"I'll be okay. I'm just glad you came back. I really think he was going to kill Julian." She had a hard time keeping it together. "Julian, who is he?"

"He's Goldberg's nephew—the one with the used automobile dealership. He's the one Sheriff Barnhart went to arrest but had disappeared."

"Is he the one that you got into the fight with on the beach at Sea Island?" Frances asked.

McCoy looked at me.

"That's the one."

Chapter 21

The Columbia was mostly empty except for a few stragglers that showed up for a late lunch—or maybe it was an early dinner. Regardless, it was still bustling with activity. The kitchen was almost always open, and even though the dining areas were not, the local immigrant community knew they could show up at the kitchen door and get a Cuban sandwich any time of day.

Referred to as the "Mixto," it included fine Spanish ham, Genoa salami from Sicily, and Mojo marinated roast pork from Cuba. The local Spanish, Italian, and Cuban immigrants contributed to the mix of flavors.

Saturdays were special, so the restaurant was a lot busier than normal. The waiters folded linen napkins, filled the hutches with crystal, set out china, and made ready all the tables. The chef, along with several other cooks, was busy getting ready for a large dinner crowd. Pots and pans clanked as the bases for several of their main dishes were prepared. The exquisite aromas wafting from the kitchen ran the gamut from the land to the sea.

The Columbia served gallons upon gallons of two local favorites—sangria and mojito—both made tableside by the pitcher. Both were supposedly served virgin—after all alcohol was prohibited. The local law enforcement was well aware of what was going on, but they were well paid to look the other way. A few of them might even show up for a drink later.

Ed Lawrence arrived early to be sure he got a table. He wanted to be in the La Fonda dining room for the best views of the action, and because he had been told it's where Genna always ate dinner on Saturday night. Within an hour of his arrival, every table was occupied and there was already a lengthy wait.

Ed had always loved the food, but this visit was more business than pleasure. He and Thaye Ersley had been following Wilbur Moore's trail for months, assuming it would lead to Genna at some point. Now that Moore was dead, the two had decided it might be time to rattle Genna's cage. Showing up on his home turf might create a break. The local NATB man, Agent Tom Chevis, was aware of Riley Gant's recent trip to Ybor City and told Director Coonts and me in Jacksonville. The link between Genna, Moore, and Hunt-Gant was undeniable, so Director Coonts suggested I go to Tampa while Ed Lawrence was in town.

Yet tonight something wasn't right. Maybe it was intuition trying to tell him something, but Genna should have been seated at his usual table by now. His table was occupied by two couples clearly enjoying the night out based on the amount of laughter. The noise in the restaurant had steadily grown as the place filled up, and people were practically yelling at each other just to be heard.

When I arrived with Tom Chevis, the hostess asked us to follow her. The place was somewhat of a maze, so getting around could be a challenge. Although Tom was from Tampa, this was his first visit to the Columbia. As we followed our hostess to the table to meet Ed Lawrence, I noticed a sign for the rest rooms, so I told Tom to go ahead.

"Julian? Julian Clark?" asked a familiar voice from down the hallway. I looked to my right to see Jim Genna approaching from what looked like a private area of the restaurant.

"Oh. Hey. Mr. Genna. What a surprise," I said.

"Well, I could say the same. And call me Jim. I hope you didn't decide to take me up on my offer of dinner without telling me," he said with a grin.

"Oh, no. I'm here on business. Well, not exactly, but I'm here with some friends for dinner." I realized I sounded like an idiot and I might as well have waved a red flag when I said I was there on business.

"Working on a Saturday, huh?"

"Yesterday—we got here yesterday and decided to spend an extra night," I added.

"Well, don't work too hard," he said with a wink.

Trying to change the subject, I said, "Are you staying for dinner?"

"Actually, I have some business of my own to take care of. I came early to talk to the owner about something and had a quick bite, but I must go now. Don't stay too late without Frances being around, Julian. This place can get pretty crazy, if you know what I mean."

"Thanks for the warning. I'll keep that in mind."

Genna looked like he was in a hurry as he headed off toward the front. Odd. I went ahead to the men's room and as I exited, I bumped into a man headed toward the same private door I had seen Genna come out of. He grunted and said, "You shouldn't be here." There was something familiar about him and his voice, but I couldn't place him. The lighting wasn't very good at the end of the hall, and he brushed by me and continued on and disappeared.

As I wandered the halls, looking for my table, I passed another hostess, and I asked her to point me toward the Café Dining room. "Follow me, sir." On the way, all I could think about was how disappointed Ed was going to be when I told him I just ran into Jim Genna—on his way out.

She took me through the La Fonda room to reach the Café room. They were separated by a large bar that ran down the center of the room. Both rooms were full of people either dining or standing by the bar, waiting for a table. The noise was excessive, and it was clear that everyone was drinking.

I saw my party in the back right corner of the Café dining room. Ed Lawrence saw me a second later and waved me over.

Ed was seated in the corner with his back to the wall and a clear view to the exits as well as the large opening near the bar that lead to the La Fonda room. Tom Chevis was seated to Ed's left, so I took the chair on Ed's right, which also gave me a good view of the room.

As soon as I had hit the chair, a teen busboy was filling our glasses with water. A waiter followed, but as he introduced himself, a finely dressed gentleman approached the table and said, "Excuse me for interrupting, Ronaldo. I am Casimiro Hernandez Junior, and I would like to welcome you to my restaurant. Mr. Clark," he said, looking down at me, "Mr. Genna felt bad that he couldn't stay and has offered to take care of you and your friends." Casimiro was practically yelling at us to be heard.

"Oh no, we couldn't possibly—" I started to say.

Casimiro interrupted, "Any friend of Mr. Genna's is my special guest. I insist. I hope you have a wonderful evening, and if you need anything, please don't hesitate to ask."

I looked across at Tom, who shrugged his shoulders in confusion. I glanced at Ed, whose chin had dropped and his mouth was wide open. "That's quite generous of Mr. Genna. I'll be sure and thank him later," I said.

"Ronaldo will take good care of you this evening." He turned to the waiter and made several comments in Spanish and then disappeared.

"Gentlemen, would you care for something to drink other than water. Perhaps some sangria?"

Ed quickly said, "I think we'll pass."

"Very well. Manuel will be back with your soup and salad."

A drink sounded pretty good to me right now.

As Ronaldo headed toward the kitchen, the three of us stared at each other for several seconds before anyone could say anything. Ed finally asked, "What the hell was that all about? I don't get it—where's Genna?"

"Gone," I said. "I actually ran into him back at the men's room."

Tom said, "I didn't realize you and Jim Genna were pals?"

"I didn't either. I mean—we're not. It's a long story, but I had been in Savannah, working on the Goldberg case." I explained how we met that night, and reminded Ed that it was the night Vernon Chris had been there undercover.

"That's pretty much it. I haven't seen him since. He invited me to Ybor with Frances to have dinner sometime."

"How did he know you were going to be here, Julian?" asked Tom.

"He didn't. I just ran into him when I left you going to the men's room. I asked him if he was staying for dinner. He said he had already eaten and had some business to take care of. He was clearly in a hurry and left."

"Well, if that doesn't beat all," said Ed. "Does he know who we are?"

"All I said was, I was having dinner with friends. How could he?"

"Son of a bitch is probably laughing his ass off wherever he is. And then he buys us dinner. We look like idiots."

"Speak for yourself, Ed," I said, grinning at Tom. I know how Ed felt, but I couldn't help ribbing him. I didn't know how Genna could possibly know who I was with or even who Ed Lawrence was, and Tom Chevis was just another auto theft guy.

Tom had been an insurance salesman in Tampa before joining the NATB. Thaye Ersley introduced him to Director Coonts because he also had a law degree from the University of Florida. Tom was smart, but his gregarious nature and likeability made him a natural salesman. By the time Coonts met him, he had made a lot of money in the insurance business and was ready for a new challenge. He was short and stocky with a distinctive paunch, but strong as a bull and still quick on his feet.

We ate that incredible Spanish bean soup pretty much in silence while watching all the people carrying on around the bar. When Ronaldo returned, we watched him toss a huge salad as another waiter brought us a *tapeo* sampler—compliments of Genna and recommended by Hernandez. It had three tapas including croqueta de jaiba, the roasted pork ribs, and grilled chorizo. It was delicious.

While we waited for the main course, making small talk and people watching, I thought about the man I ran into coming out of the men's room. Something was bugging me about his comment—"You shouldn't be here." What did he mean? Was it because he was headed toward a private area or did he mean it literally—that I shouldn't be at the Columbia? I knew there was something familiar about him, but I still couldn't place it.

As if it wasn't loud enough, the band started playing flamenco music, and several dancers came out from the kitchen and started dancing around the dining rooms. The crowd was singing along with the music, and the dancers grabbed random men from the bar and started dancing with them. The bartenders were throwing wads of napkins in the air, letting them rain down on the crowd. Everyone was feeling the music, senses dulled by the alcohol. Just when we thought the volume level had reached its zenith, the band ratcheted it up another notch.

We would be lying if we said we weren't enjoying ourselves as much as the revelers around us. So much so that Tom broke down and ordered us each a whiskey. Everyone's attention had shifted to a pair of beautiful flamenco dancers in front of the band. They wore long red dresses that exposed their backs and flared when they spun or kicked their feet up, revealing perfect legs in impossibly high heels. The suggestive nature of the costume left little to the imagination, and the bright color made it hard not to notice them.

Two lithe bodies moving to the beat and so much skin glistening with every movement. I could see the strength in their arms, legs, and back. Their shimmering dresses exposing every curve. Flawless skin the color of coffee and long, shiny brunette hair pulled back so tightly it seemed like it was pulling the skin around their made-up faces into a suggestive grin. The rhythm of the music and their movements could only be described as altogether sexual. Every eye was upon them—even the women were caught in their magnetism. The men were undressing them with their eyes, and the entire room had an air of primal lust about it.

The allure of the dancers was mesmerizing, but something broke my focus, and my attention shifted to a man making his way through the sea of people around the dancers. His movements were different from everyone else's, which is what drew my eyes away from the women because he was moving against the flow. He was dressed in black with a long trench coat that nearly reached the floor. His fedora was pulled down low. His right han d appeared to be in his pocket, but it was also holding the front of his coat close against his body. His left hand hanging freely. His gait was steady. Methodical. There was a purpose in the way he strode.

By the time the words crossed my mind again, it was too late. *You shouldn't be here.* The entire movement of the room had shifted to slow motion, and I felt like I was listening to a conch shell, but at an impossibly loud volume. *You shouldn't be here.* The words reached out to me like the smoky fingers of a spirit that only had to whisper to be heard in spite of the cacophony around me.

Ed's eyes were also distracted by the movement of the man, but now he was only ten feet from our table. The Thompson machine gun was already coming out from under his coat. Tom Chevis and I started pushing our chairs back from the table, and with the realization of what was about to happen, Ed tried to flip the table up as a shield. As the song reached its crescendo, the gunman opened fire.

The first bullet struck the floor, ricocheted up through the wood of the upturned table, and glanced off to the right. It hit Tom in the calf, but the velocity had slowed it such that it didn't pass through. As the gunman brought the barrel up firing on full auto, a burst of bullets flew out like angry hornets and traced their way up the center of the table until they cleared the top edge where Ed was still trying to get down. He was too late. The last couple of rounds found his mass before he hit the floor. His legs had been cut to ribbons. The bullets tearing flesh and shattering bone, but the ones that found his torso did vital damage to his lungs and heart. He never had a chance.

I went over backward as my chair flipped from the force of pushing myself away from the table. My head slapped the floor hard enough to blur my vision momentarily. It was so loud in the restaurant, most of the crowd hadn't even realized the popping sounds they heard were gunfire. By the time the realization of what was taking place reached the tables nearest ours, the gunman had already started walking away.

The screams coming from the ladies made it apparent that something had gone horribly wrong. Realizing the danger had passed, I rolled over on my left side to look for Ed, who was clearly the target. His eyes were open, but the life was gone from them. A pool of blood was growing around him and a trickle of blood ran from the corner of his mouth. Tom was holding his calf, writhing in pain. People started to scramble for the doors, creating chaos, when I noticed something wet on my back. I tried to get up, but only made it to my knees before realizing it was soup and not my own blood.

Chapter 22

Frances still hadn't fully recovered from the invasion of our home by Al Neinstein, but knowing he would be behind bars for a long time helped. However, Ed Lawrence's murder in Ybor City cast a shadow over my work that would be tough to undo. I had to admit, I was shaken up pretty bad by the events at the Columbia. The drive back to Jacksonville gave me plenty of time to second-guess every decision I had made leading up to it—including my decision to work for the NATB.

I also had to be honest with myself. I loved my work, and I was good at it. People had put their trust in me by giving me this opportunity, and Frances and I knew the risks associated with this move to Jacksonville. I didn't know how to do anything else.

The Goldberg case was a career booster in spite of almost getting me killed. That was an exception, not the rule. And Al Neinstein was an outlier—wasn't he? Director Coonts and I had discussed it, and he couldn't think of more than a couple of occasions when he encountered life-threatening circumstances on the job.

The situation with Ed Lawrence wasn't targeting me. I was simply in the wrong place at the wrong time. It could have happened to anyone. At least that was what I told myself. The Hammock was also an unlucky coincidence. It really wasn't my fault Harold was dead, but it set into motion a series of events that had become deadly. Hunt-Gant clearly wanted me out of the way. Whatever they had gotten involved in had progressed far beyond stealing automobiles. That didn't excuse it, and it was not going to go away until I put them away.

I knew I was in denial, but it was easy to rationalize my actions and their subsequent consequences as merely part of the job or even a series of unfortunate coincidences. The reality I was struggling with was whether or not a pattern could explain all of this or if I was taking unnecessary risks.

* * *

"Julian, why can't you see how dangerous this job has become? I agreed to move to Jacksonville for you—for us—but I never agreed to have gangsters breaking into our home or assassins shooting our friends in plain sight. This is crazy."

"Baby, I know it seems like things have gotten out of control, but they aren't a normal part of the job. You heard Coonts say it yourself. Besides, I'm fine. We're fine."

"You may be fine, but I'm not."

"Baby, you know what I mean. We are going to be okay."

"You don't know that, Julian."

"Frances, all I can say is that these events are exceptions. Let's try to put them behind us." As the words left my lips, I wondered if I was still trying to convince myself. "It was a series of unfortunate coincidences. You know I'm capable of taking care of myself—and you. I will never let anything happen to you."

Does my promise sound empty? If Captain McCoy hadn't shown up, would either of us be sitting here today? My subconscious voice is casting doubt on everything, but I know these things aren't normal. This internal struggle is putting a strain on my psyche.

"I'm scared, Julian. I'm scared for you—for us. You have no idea what it's like not knowing if you are going to come home each day." I was reminded of my conversation with Vernon Chris in Savannah.

"I know, baby. I know. Let me at least tie up some loose ends. Not just for me and the job but for Ed too."

"What do you mean?"

"We're close to nailing Hunt-Gant, and they are a big part of the problem.

262

If we can take them off the street, we'll all be a lot better off."

"I don't know, Julian."

"Baby, this depression is only getting deeper too. I don't know what else I would do, and right now government jobs are still paying well. All the men at the office don't think our pay will get interrupted."

"Is it worth losing your life over? The other night in Ybor City—that could have been you. There are so many things out of your control."

I took hold of Frances's hands and looked into her eyes.

"I know it's hard for you, but I need to finish this. I'll be more careful. I'll check in every night I'm out of town unless there's no way too. I'll take Director Coonts with me when I can. Or Tomlinson and Jones. We always work with local law enforcement anyway—I'll make sure I at least have a deputy with me when I'm working a case, if not the sheriff. Let me finish this and then we'll talk about it some more." I looked at her with pleading eyes and hoped she understood.

A tear rolled down her cheek. I gave her my handkerchief. She slowly wiped her eyes and looked back into mine.

"You know how much I love you, Julian. Please don't let anything happen to you. I know how much you need to do this. Do what you need to do."

She left me there sitting on the sofa alone with my thoughts. I wasn't completely sure what I needed to do, but I knew that Hunt-Gant was part of it. My thoughts swirled around the events of the past several months. Faces and names randomly popped into mind and then as quickly as they appeared, they were gone. Harold Hunt. Asa Goldberg. Benjamin Bloomberg. Al Neinstein. Moe Stevens and his boys. Wilbur Moore. Arthur Cadwell. Jim Genna. Alva and Truby Hunt. Riley and Hugh Gant. The last four faces lingered.

* * *

Thaye Ersley was the last to arrive. I had asked Tomlinson and Jones to meet Director Coonts and me at the diner for coffee. We figured Agent Ersley could help shed some light on what happened to Ed Lawrence, so we invited Thaye to join us too. He looked tousled as usual, but something was different. He looked tired—older. I'm sure the recent death of his coworker and friend had taken its toll.

I had already debriefed him and Coonts on the night at the Columbia along with several other agents, including a couple Hoover sent down from DC. I knew they would leave no stone unturned, but they still had little to go on other than my description of the gunman. Tom Chevis remembered less than I did and never really saw the man's face. They had gone to Ybor City and questioned everyone that worked at the restaurant, including Casimiro Hernandez. Nobody knew anything.

Bart Jones said, "Thaye, all of us at the Jacksonville PD will do whatever we can to help. We're really sorry about Agent Lawrence. Anything we can do to get the son of a bitch that did this, just let us know."

"Thanks, guys—we really appreciate your help. I'm sure we'll be in touch."

"What's the latest?" I asked Agent Ersley.

"Still nothing. Nobody's talking and we can't find anyone that knows the gunman—or at least anyone that will admit it. We're offering a reward for information leading to his arrest, but I doubt anything will come of it. That's a tight-knit community of immigrants used to looking out for their own."

"I'm sorry, Thaye." It wasn't the first time I had said it. We all liked Ed, and I feel guilty for not being able to help more. I was right there beside him when he died. "Any ideas about it?"

"I think Genna was behind it, but I can't prove it. I can't prove anything, but somehow all of this is connected."

Coonts asked, "All of what?"

"Genna. Moore. Probably Cadwell."

"Cadwell?" I asked.

"He wasn't poisoned in jail. The coroner found a needle mark. Somebody injected him with an insecticide they use on the property—made it look like he drank something. We have reason to believe the Sicilians were behind it."

"How so?"

"We have sources on the inside just like they do. Word is, Genna had him offed because he works for the competition."

"The competition?" asked Coonts.

"Red Overton. Cadwell worked for him, and don't forget, Overton's daughter is married to him."

My mind raced back to the conversation I had with Captain McCoy at the Rod & Gun Club about the feud between Genna and Overton. By killing Cadwell, Genna was sending Overton a message. A pretty nasty one at that.

"Also, Hester Overton—actually Hester Cadwell—showed up at the jail demanding answers about her husband's death. Apparently, she went nuts and starting spouting off about Italian gangsters. She really lost it when they couldn't tell her anything. She bit a guard bad enough to send him to the infirmary to get stitched up. She pulled a big wad of hair out of another guard before they got her subdued. She's crazy anyway, but Cadwell's death in jail sent her over the edge."

All of this was looking less like a series of coincidences. And just like McCoy said—I was right in the middle of it.

"Guys, I need your help. This whole mess has Frances scared to death about me, and you all know better than anyone how that can impact your job."

"I never should have let you get involved in all of this," said Director Coonts.

"That goes for me too," said Agent Ersley.

"It's easy to say that now, but don't beat yourself up. It made sense at the time—and at least Arthur Moore is out of the picture."

"What do you have in mind?" asked Jones.

"Somehow we need to get Hunt-Gant off the street. I arrested Truby Hunt last month, but he was out in a matter of hours. Alva manages to keep his hands clean, but he's as dirty as his brother. They both think I killed Harold. Riley and Hugh Gant are just as angry and dangerous, and all four of them are working for Genna—at least we think they are."

Tomlinson said, "We could arrest Truby for the Turtle Creek Ford. It shouldn't be too hard to hold him on that. We've got an eyewitness that saw him park it front of her house. And Julian, since you arrested him over in

Deland, you can identify him as the same man using that alias he was using. What was it?"

"Wallace."

"We can include that Autotruck you caught Harold with out there in the Hammock. The evidence is thin—certainly not enough to get a conviction, but with the other two, it demonstrates a pattern," said Coonts.

"More like a career," said Tomlinson.

Jones jumped in, "Let's go to Daytona and surprise 'em. Judge Carlisle will give us a warrant for Truby's arrest no problem. Maybe a search of the place will turn up something on the others. They've been using their old man's dealership in Bushnell to move stolen autos. Isn't it about time you shut that operation down?"

"Hugh Gant is still running the fencing operation out of Webster too," said Tomlinson.

"I have another idea," said Ersley. "Let's pin that murder on them too. Maybe one of them starts talking? Either way, it will get them off the street for a while."

"What's our evidence? We have plenty against the Hunts, but what about the Gants?" asked Ersley.

"Harold basically admitted to the whole thing. He wasn't planning on me making it out of there alive. He flat out said Riley Gant was there for the whole thing, which means Hugh was too," I said.

"Well, what are we waiting for? Let's do this," said Ersley.

Chapter 23

Taking down the Hunt-Gant gang would take time. The Bureau of Investigation had men watching the house in Daytona, since we knew it was a gathering place for all of them. They also had agents in Bushnell watching the dealership, as well as several confidential informants who provided information on their whereabouts. At some point they would all end up in Daytona. We just had to wait them out.

In the meantime, we had to obtain warrants, which proved to be harder than we thought. Ultimately, Judge Carlisle gave in after hearing evidence from the Bureau, the NATB, the local police department, and the sheriff's department. The prosecutor was a good friend of both Coonts and Ersley, so that didn't hurt. We obtained arrest warrants for Alva and Truby Hunt as well as Riley and Hugh Gant. We also had a search warrant for the Daytona Beach property.

We spent several days planning the arrest so we would be ready when the time came. I should say *they* spent time planning it. I was *part* of the plan, but not directly. My role was to identify any stolen automobiles that might be in their possession after they were taken into custody.

The plan was pretty simple—surround the house with heavily armed men while the Hunts and Gants were inside and then send the sheriff to the door to serve them. Once they opened the door, we would overwhelm them with force and flood the place with law enforcement. Every plan has its risks and this one had many. We had no idea how heavily armed the men inside would be. However, it was assumed they would have plenty of guns and be willing to use them. The element of surprise was about all we had going for us.

It was widely debated how best to enter the property or to even attempt entering at all. The local police wanted to wait until they were leaving before taking them into custody. The argument to make routine traffic stops after they left seemed logical, but the risk that a chase might ensue, endangering innocent people, was too high. The case for containment within the property won out.

I spent the next couple of weeks waiting for the word to go to Daytona. Coonts and I stayed busy with a few smaller auto-theft cases, but the anticipation of the Hunt-Gant operation kept us on edge. Frances knew most of the details, and was relieved to hear that I was only peripherally involved. She also knew that taking them off the street would make it safer for all of us, so in spite of her anxiety around the coming operation, she was reluctantly on board.

Tomlinson and I finally got to do some fishing like we had been talking about for weeks, which was a nice distraction. He was a lot like me, needing the solace of the water to recharge and clear his mind. We talked about everything other than work, spending most of the time just enjoying each other's company in silence. And we caught a lot of fish.

The waiting game was part of the job, but fortunately, we didn't have to wait long. Only three weeks had passed since that morning in the coffee shop when the Bureau's informants got wind of a get-together that weekend in Daytona.

During the course of the investigation into Ed Lawrence's murder, they had also uncovered additional evidence, albeit circumstantial, of Hunt-Gant's involvement with the Sicilians. A revenuer saw Truby Hunt and Hugh Gant driving a tank truck in Tampa. He followed them to Ybor City, but had to give up the tail once they pulled into a warehouse or risk getting made. It was later determined that the warehouse wasn't owned by Genna, but the company that did own it was in the sugar business and owned by Tampa Bay Molasses, which *was* owned by Jim Genna.

It was time, and everyone was ready. I packed an overnight bag, said goodbye to Frances, and headed to Daytona Beach. The plan was to rendezvous Friday night in Daytona at the Hotel Clarendon with Thaye Ersley, Tomlinson, Jones, Sheriff Westbrook, and the chief of police to go over the plan one last time.

* * *

I had been sitting in my Chrysler for at least an hour. I'm not sure which was worse, the wait or not knowing what was happening. I was worried for all of the men risking their lives over at the house, but I was also excited to put Truby Hunt back in jail and hopefully the others. I was parked on the side of the road five hundred yards away from the house where the raid was to take place. They were to send a deputy to get me once the place had been secured. I was tired of waiting. Surely, they had already gotten things under control by now. I hadn't heard a thing, so it must have gone down without any trouble. I decided to go take a look. I fired up my Model B-70 and let her idle for a minute while I contemplated my next move. I really should wait, but it had been over an hour. As I let out the clutch and eased out into the lane, I heard what sounded like tires skidding. A couple of seconds later, an old beater Packard open -wheeled racer came flying around the corner right at me. As the other vehicle passed, I noticed it was being driven by none other than Riley Gant, so I hit the gas and spun around going off the other side of the road into the dirt before I got her straightened out again and back on the pavement.

Gant was running pretty good when he passed me, so it took several minutes to even get another glimpse of the rear of that Packard. Basically, I followed the wake of dust he was kicking up until I closed the gap enough to see him take a turn practically on two wheels. We were both doing about sixty miles per hour when the road we were on changed to a combination of gravel and sand before it turned completely to sand. I knew my way around Daytona pretty well, but I wasn't familiar with plenty of the roads. I had a pretty good sense of direction and knew we were headed north parallel to the beach and probably only about a quarter mile from it. This road was probably used by a lot of the racecar drivers.

Fortunately, it was relatively straight with only a few subtle curves, but at the speed we were driving, it could still be deadly. The Model B was keeping pace, and she still had plenty of go left in her.

I finally got close enough to Riley to make out the automobile he was driving. It was a twin six open-wheeled racer—twelve cylinders of raw racing power that was built for exactly what we were doing. It had rusty patches all over in addition to splotches of primer that needed sanding. I made a mental note to thank Torch the next time I saw him for building me this Chrysler. He would be proud to know his baby was keeping time with a racecar that probably had more than a hundred horses under the hood.

Gant started pulling away as he got more comfortable pushing the Packard through the turns. He was clearly learning its limitations as well as when he could kick it and accelerate on the straights. I was doing my best, but it occurred to me all I could really do was try to keep up and hope he dumped it in a ditch. A couple of times I thought I heard sirens, but couldn't be sure over the noise of the engine. Maybe help was on the way.

The next turn turned out to be a big meandering right back toward the beach before we came to an even tighter turn south. Gant wasn't ready for it and the light Packard had a wicked under-steer, which took him by surprise. He almost lost total control in the turn, but somehow got it straight, narrowly missing a stand of palmettos on the side of the road. I made it through the turn, but not without a heavy brake, and then jumped on the accelerator as I came out of it. I could just make out pavement through the dust up ahead, and I noticed the transition must be pretty rough by the way that Packard jumped.

This was not going to be good, and it was too late to slow down. Just as I was about to hit pavement I held my breath and clenched my teeth, expecting the worst. My knuckles were white, I was holding on so tight, and as I hit the transition I knew I was in trouble. My butt completely left the seat, and the Chrysler shuddered and bucked like I had hit a curb. There was a loud bang as something broke underneath.

It didn't take long to figure out what happened because as soon as the front tires returned to the ground, my right front wheel snapped back at a ninety-degree angle. As I wrestled with the steering wheel to keep it on the road, I downshifted to let the engine slow it down before jamming on the brakes. Somehow I kept it out of the ditch on the right-hand side of the road before coming to a stop.

A cloud of smoke, dust, and rubber swirled past me and filled the inside of the automobile so that I could barely take a breath. Riley Gant was long gone, and all I could do was sit there with my hands on the wheel and thank God I hadn't gone in that ditch.

After what seemed like five minutes, but was probably more like sixty seconds, I heard something up ahead. As I looked up, I saw what looked like that Packard Racer coming back down the road. The vehicle approached me cautiously, and then eased up next to my Chrysler and stopped. I could hear sirens in the distance, but it was hard to tell from what direction they were coming. A lot of dust was still swirling in the air, and when Gant stopped I could smell oil and rubber, and I could feel the heat coming off those twelve cylinders.

He just stared at me for a few seconds before his hand came up with a gun in it. He slowly pointed it right at my face.

"What is it with you Clark?"

A million things were going through my mind, but all I could think to say was, "I didn't kill Harold," I said.

Riley just stared at me—his finger on the trigger.

"I didn't know he was out there in those woods. I was out there looking for a tobacco truck. "

"Who sent you?"

I just stared at him, confused. What was he talking about?

He yelled it again: "Who sent you?"

"I don't know what you mean." But I *did* know, only there's no way I was giving up my source. "I got a lead that someone had seen it out there."

"You're a liar, Clark."

He stared at me for a few seconds, probably trying to decide if pulling the trigger would only make things worse. I prayed that was the conclusion he came to. I decided to wait him out. Then he put the gun down, revved the motor, and peeled out, spraying dirt and gravel until his tires got traction.

* * *

The drive back up Highway One to Jacksonville gave me time to think about the events of the last several days. I kept the specifics of my encounter with Riley Gant to myself, and while having a gun pointed at my face was scary, I never figured he would actually pull the trigger. I didn't want Frances to find out, and it wasn't relevant to catching him anyway. I also didn't need anyone thinking I was being reckless.

The sirens kept getting closer until eventually they found me sitting on the side of that desolate two-lane road. They hadn't seen the Packard—Gant was probably long gone. I got a ride back to the house in Daytona and made arrangements to have my Chrysler towed over to Lee Bible's to get fixed. Coonts, Ersley, and the rest of the men back at the house wanted to hear all about the chase and that Packard Riley was driving.

Truby, Alva, and Katherine had all been arrested without incident and were already on their way to jail. Hugh was a no-show. According to Ersley, the arrests went down relatively smoothly until Riley took off in that Packard. When the sheriff knocked on the door, Katherine Hunt answered it and they flooded the house with law enforcement. Alva and Truby were sitting in the living room right behind Katherine and never had a chance to even stand up. Nobody resisted and they weren't carrying. A search of the house later turned up several shotguns and a couple of pistols, but nothing like the cache they expected to find.

Once Ersley and his men had secured the house, they started questioning the Hunt brothers about the Gants' whereabouts. They never said a word. The sheriff's men only made a cursory search of the garage because not long after they started questioning Alva and Truby, everyone heard an engine crank out in the garage. Riley took off in that Packard Twin Six before anyone realized what had happened. He must have been hiding somewhere in the garage.

It didn't take me long to determine the automobile that Truby was driving was stolen. We charged him with stealing three other vehicles, including the Turtle Creek Ford, the Autotruck I found in the Hammock, and the Deland Chevrolet. Ersley also charged him and Alva with bootlegging and for conspiracy to commit murder. They arrested Katherine as an accomplice and for harboring a fugitive.

Fortunately, they didn't know anything about my involvement, but that wouldn't last long. With Riley on the run, word would eventually get around that I had been the one that chased him from the house. It didn't matter because I would have to testify in court on the stolen automobile cases. Without the Gants, the murder charges were too flimsy to stick on the Hunts, and we knew eventually the charges against Katherine would be dropped. It was a good day, though. Two dangerous men were off the street, and one of the biggest auto theft rings had been busted. Coonts and I had done our part.

Later that afternoon they found that Packard abandoned on the side of the road. No sign of Riley. The automobile was actually straight, much to our surprise. When I went to pick up my Chrysler this morning, I asked about the Packard. Jared Doggett, who had worked for Lee Bible and now ran his shop, knew about the racecar. It had been one of Lee's and he used to race it on the beach. It was built in 1916 but had long since been retired. Wrecked several times and missing its transmission—among other things—Alva Hunt bought it to fix up with plans to race it again.

The mechanics at Bible's were surprised he got it running as well as he did, and they were pretty excited to hear about my chasing it in that Model B. They had to find a part for my vehicle in order to repair it and said it would probably take a couple of days, so I told them where they could reach me and headed back to the hotel. We had reports to write and paperwork to file regarding our bust, so I could use the extra time anyway.

* * *

When I got home a few days later, Frances was so glad to see me she couldn't stop hugging me. "Oh, Juney—thank God you made it home safely. I was so

273

worried about you until Gwyneth called and told me the whole story and that everyone was safe."

"Baby, I told you not to worry."

"I know, Juney but you know how much I worry about you—especially lately. Thanks for keeping your word. Now, I want to hear all about it."

Just then the phone started ringing. "Don't answer it, Frances," I said, squeezing her tight.

Pulling herself away, she said, "Well, it might be important." She hurried into the kitchen, and I heard her say, "Hello?"

After a brief pause she stuck her head in and said, "It's for you. It's Mr. Coonts."

"Mr. Coonts? I wonder what he wants?"

I walked into the kitchen and took the phone from Frances. "Yes sir, Gene. It's good to be back home. Are you still coming over for dinner?"

"Oh, I'll be there, all right. Especially since Frances is cooking."

"Good. Good. So what is it that couldn't wait until then?" I asked.

"Well, I thought you would want to know something I just found out. It's big news."

"Do tell."

"Riley Gant is dead."

"What?" I said incredulously. Frances was now standing right in my face with a concerned look on hers while trying to get me to tell her what's going on.

"You heard me. He's dead," repeated Coonts.

"What happened? How?"

"Apparently, he and Hugh were involved in a robbery of some sort down in Palatka. A security guard caught them in a warehouse full of red liquor. I don't have all the facts yet, but it sounds like somebody saw something suspicious, so they called the police. Before they arrived, they heard shots being fired. The guard said they were both armed and they fired first. He took out Riley Gant with a shotgun blast to the chest. They think the other man was Hugh, but he got away."

"You don't say."

274

"Julian! What is it?" asked Frances.

"Riley Gant is dead."

"Oh, my word! Really?"

"Thanks, Gene. We can talk more later."

"I can't believe it," said Frances, taking the phone from my hand and placing it back on the cradle. "That's good, right?"

"Yeah baby, it's good. I mean—now we don't have to worry about him anymore."

"Why do you look like you're in shock, then?"

"Because I am in shock. I just saw Riley a few days ago and now he's dead. It just doesn't seem real."

Chapter 24

That night Frances and I had dinner with Coonts at our house. It was a fitting end to another closed case. Coonts was excited to talk to Frances about our recent successes with the Goldberg case and the recent arrests of Alva and Truby Hunt. He also knew how important it was for Frances to hear from him that everything was going to be okay and that taking these guys off the streets made us all a lot safer. But first I could tell he had something on his mind that he needed to tell us.

Mr. Coonts and Mr. Patterson, the NATB director in Atlanta, had had a hard enough time convincing us to move to Jacksonville, and Coonts knew how important it was for my career to have Frances support me. He was great like that, and I knew I could count on him to help give her the reassurance she needed.

"Mr. Coonts, thank you for watching out for Julian. He's all I've got, and I really would like for him to keep coming home in one piece," Frances said half in jest.

"Don't you worry, Frances. Julian is perfectly capable of taking care of himself, and please stop calling me Mr. Coonts. It's Gene from now on. And just so you know, we have some strict rules about traveling with another agent and using local law enforcement anytime we are conducting an investigation. Before long Julian will know every sheriff, police chief, and prosecutor in the state of Florida."

"Well, I appreciate that, Gene. Now if we could only make him follow the rules a little better," she said, glancing at me.

"You let me worry about that. You know, in spite of the few scrapes he got into over the last few months, we couldn't be happier with Julian's performance. He's becoming exactly the kind of agent Patterson and I expected. The Goldberg case was a mighty big feather in his cap. Not to mention the Hunt gang."

I could feel my cheeks flush, listening to Gene brag about me. I sure hoped Frances felt as proud as I did. This move to Jacksonville was such a big risk for us, but I certainly didn't have any regrets. Hopefully, she didn't either.

We said our goodbyes and watched Coonts pull out of the drive from our front porch. I turned to Frances and pulled her close. Looking down in her eyes, I said, "Penny for your thoughts."

She replied, "Maybe it's time we start working on the baby you keep promising me."

* * *

When the phone rang it startled Everett Cooper. He had been deep in thought about the news of Riley's death. He let it ring several times before answering.

"Hello?"

"Everett, I need your help."

"Hugh?"

"It's time to take care of that problem."

"Clark?" he asked.

"Meet me at the beach."

References

1 Brooks, Joe. *Joe Brooks On Fishing*. Edited by Don Sedgwick. Foreword by Lefty Kreh. The Lyons Press. 2004.

2 Martin, Harold H.. *This Happy Isle: The Story of Sea Island and the Cloister*. Sea Island Company. 1978.

Parish, Samuel. *Central Florida's Most Notorious Gangsters: Alva Hunt and Hugh Gant*. The History Press. 2008.

Heitmann, John A. & Morales, Rebecca H.. *Stealing Cars: Technology & Society from the Model T to the Gran Torino*. Johns Hopkins University Press. 2014.

How It All Came Together

In 1989 my grandfather, Julian H. Clark, picked up a cassette recorder and started dictating. It would be two years later before he put it down.

Julian, the consummate storyteller, mostly unbeknownst to his grandchildren, lived a life of excitement and intrigue. Not only did he want to share his experiences on life in the first part of the 20th century, he also wanted to share the many stories of his life on the road chasing car thieves, bootleggers, and bank robbers. It was fun, and it was dangerous. His stories span three decades with many ups and downs for him personally and for the country, but they also span some of the most interesting times in American history.

I grew up hearing "Papa's" stories all the time and as a native Georgian like him, I loved learning about our state's remarkable history and culture through his tales. I also spent a lot of time in Florida in college, and many of his best stories take place in Florida. We used to talk about the places he lived and worked when I was home on breaks. Unfortunately, it wasn't until around 2013 before I popped the first of his tapes into the cassette player of my father's old GMC pickup and started to listen. Hearing his voice amidst the hiss and crackle of a twenty-four-year-old recording in an old truck five years after his death was like being transported back in time. I was hooked. At the end of each tape, I couldn't wait to listen to the next one. It took me several months to listen to them all because the only tape deck we had was in dad's truck. Having died out about the same time Julian did, cassette players are hard to come by these days. It wasn't long before I started finding excuses just to drive that old pickup.

Julian led an interesting life to say the least, but his stories about chasing car thieves around the southeast were just too good not to do something with. When I embarked on this "little" project, I had no idea what I was getting into. It was *much more difficult than I imagined, but it quickly became a labor of love. It started with the purchase of an old Panasonic Dictaphone Transcriber with a foot pedal for about fifty dollars on eBay. It's a tech dinosaur for sure, but it really was the best way to listen to him talk about his life while typing at the same time.*

It took me over two years to transcribe all of his tapes. They degraded over time, and I found myself having to borrow my sibling's and mother's copies to listen to several versions before I captured everything. Julian had one of the coolest jobs around, and it all happened against the backdrop of Prohibition and The Great Depression. While this book is a work of fiction, it is based on the true stories of Julian's exploits.

* * *

Enjoy this book? You can make a big difference.

Reviews are the most powerful way for independent writers like me to get attention for their books. As much as I'd like to, I don't have the influence of a big New York publisher. I can't advertise in the New York times or plaster my name on billboards all over the country. I don't have the "stroke" the big-name publishing houses have. (At least not yet!)

But something I can do is build a following of committed and loyal readers. Honest reviews of my book will help bring it to the attention of other readers.

If you've enjoyed this book, I would be grateful if you could spend just five minutes leaving a review (it can be as short as you like) on the book's Amazon page. You can jump right to the page by clicking below...

https://www.amazon.com/dp/B08TVXHY8L

Thank you very much.

* * *

GET A FREE AUDIO CLIP FROM THE REAL AGENT CLARK - MY GRANDFATHER JULIAN H. CLARK

Help me develop a relationship with my readers. Occasionally I'll send updates on new releases and bits of news related to Agent Clark.

And if you sign up for the mailing list, I'll send you a short audio clip of one of my grandfather's (the real Agent Clark) stories, and a true short story about J. Edgar Hoover.

You can get one of Agent Clark's hilarious stories, as told by Julian H. Clark himself now if you sign up for the mailing list at https://www.subscribepage.com/agentclark.

About the Author

Hadley Benton was born in Atlanta, Georgia in 1970. With the exception of a four year stint in Tallahassee, Florida, he has called Atlanta home for over 50 years. He is an avid reader, writer, fly fisherman, hunter, pickleballer, and sometimes golfer. When he's not spending time with his girls or on any of the aforementioned hobbies, he's busy working for the largest publicly traded fleet leasing and management company in the world as SVP of Sales. Hadley is the author of the new *Agent Clark* series. He makes his online home at www.hadleybenton.com. You can connect with him on Facebook or Twitter below or you can send him an email at info@hadleybenton.com.

You can connect with me on:
- https://www.hadleybenton.com
- https://www.facebook.com/hadley.benton.3

Subscribe to my newsletter:
- https://www.subscribepage.com/agentclark

Made in the USA
Monee, IL
02 October 2021

79252631R00173